THE BRUTAL HEART

THE BRUTAL HEART

A JOANNE KILBOURN MYSTERY

GAIL BOWEN

McCLELLAND & STEWART

Library and Archives Canada Cataloguing in Publication

Bowen, Gail, 1942-
    The brutal heart / Gail Bowen.

ISBN 978-0-7710-1687-5

    I. Title.

PS8553.08995B78 2008   c813'.54   C2008-900777-8

 We acknowledge the financial support of the Government of Canada through the Book Publishing Industry Development Program and that of the Government of Ontario through the Ontario Media Development Corporation's Ontario Book Initiative. We further acknowledge the support of the Canada Council for the Arts and the Ontario Arts Council for our publishing program.

Typeset in Trump Mediaeval by M&S, Toronto
Printed and bound in Canada

This book is printed on acid-free paper that is 100% recycled, ancient-forest friendly (100% post-consumer recycled).

ANCIENT FOREST
FRIENDLY

McClelland & Stewart Ltd.
75 Sherbourne Street
Toronto, Ontario
M5A 2P9
www.mcclelland.com

I   2   3   4   5   12   11   10   09   08

For Suzanne North and Don Buckle
with thanks
for the gift of Anglin Lake

CHAPTER

1

My husband's birthday is May 1, the day when Mother Nature officially declares the garden of earthly delights open for the season. It's a good fit for a man with a lusty heart and the greatest passion for life of anyone I've ever known. When we began to plan the barbecue we were hosting to celebrate Zack's fiftieth, I reminded him that the rule for the number of guests at children's parties was the child's age plus two. Undeterred, Zack kept adding names, and we mailed out seventy-five invitations. It promised to be a lively crowd: our family, Zack's law partners and associates, friends of mine from the university and politics, people we simply wanted to get to know better. On the afternoon of the party, Zack came home early and together we made a last pass through the house, making sure everything was where it should be. As we checked out the rented crystal in the kitchen, Zack was impatient. "Come on," he said. "If there aren't enough glasses, people can drink out of the bottles. There's something I want to show you outside."

"I'm all yours," I said.

He grinned. "And I'm all yours. Now come with me." He steered his wheelchair across the deck onto the ramp that led to the side of the house. Before we turned the corner, he reached up and took my hand. "Prepare to be dazzled," he said. And I was dazzled. Sometime during the day, our forsythia had burst into full golden bloom. It was the first splash of colour from the summer palette, and for a moment we stood, hand in hand, simply letting the brilliance wash over us.

"My God, that's a beautiful sight," Zack said. "I love that bush. I love this house. I love our life, and I love you – not in that order, of course."

"Of course not." I leaned down and kissed him. "It's good to have you back," I said. "Since Ned died, you've been pretty unreachable."

"I know, and I'm sorry. There was something I had to take care of, and I was trying to keep you out of it."

"Zack, I don't want to be kept out."

He met my eyes, and I could see the pain of the last two weeks etched on his face. "Who was it who said that it's the loose ends of our lives that hang us?"

"Do you want to talk about what's been going on?"

"Nope, because the problem's gone. I've taken care of it – at least I hope I have." He took out his pocket knife, cut a twig of blossoms from the bush, and handed it to me. "For you," he said. "The dark days are over. Let's get back to having the time of our lives."

I stuck the forsythia in the buttonhole of his jacket. "I'll drink to that," I said. "In fact, why don't you mix up a couple of Ned's Bombay Sapphire specials and we'll christen those snazzy new martini glasses I gave you."

Zack made the drinks, and we took them to the deck and waited for our guests to arrive. It was a five-star afternoon – filled with birdsong and blooming. Signs of new life were everywhere. The trees along the creek banks fuzzed green, the Japanese lilacs against our fence were in tight bud, and the first bright shoots were pushing through the perennial beds. As I sipped my martini and turned my face to the sun, I could feel myself unknot. When our guests began arriving, it seemed that they, too, were shrugging off the heaviness of winter. Free at last of the burden of boots and jackets, our granddaughters raced around the fishpond, thrilled by the possibility that a careless step could send them into the shining waters where they could splash with the koi until responsible hands plucked them out. The adults were equally light-hearted. Shoes were kicked off and sweaters abandoned. The bar was well stocked, the appetizers were piquant, and the arrival of a surprise political guest set the freshets of rumour and innu-endo rolling.

Our country was in the midst of a federal election that was too close to call, and one of the tightest, dirtiest bat-tles was being waged in our riding. The incumbent, Ginny Monaghan, had stopped by to wish Zack many happy returns, and no matter their political stripe, our guests were riveted by her presence.

Six months earlier, I had interviewed Ginny for a tele-vision project I was working on about women in politics. We met at her Regina constituency office at the end of what must have been an exhausting day for her. She'd flown from Ottawa that morning and been in meetings all day, but as she swept the remains of someone else's fast-food chicken dinner into a wastebasket, put her feet up on the newly cleared desk, and discussed her future, Ginny exhibited the same energy and unshakeable confidence she'd shown twenty years earlier when she'd been the ponytailed captain of the Canadian women's basketball team. The night of the interview, it seemed that nothing could alter the smooth tra-jectory of her plan to become Canada's next prime minister.

From the moment Ginny's team medalled at the Olympics, she hadn't taken a false step. She had hired a sports agent, who negotiated the endorsement deals that turned her bronze medal into gold. Then, without breaking a sweat, she finished her degree in marketing; signed on as the public face of an investment conglomerate; married Jason Brodnitz, the handsome and ambitious vice-president of a rival conglomerate; produced engaging twin daughters; and ran successfully for the Conservatives, the party currently in power. Grudgingly accepting the fact that he had a rising star in his caucus, the prime minister appointed Ginny minister of Canadian heritage and the status of women, and she was on her way. It had been a flawless performance, but then Ginny and Jason's marriage had imploded, and the personal became political.

For months, Ginny's supporters had been gleeful at the prospect of an election that would allow her to display her intelligence, showcase her appealing family, and position herself for the leadership race ahead. But when the writ was dropped, Ginny was not shaking hands and burnishing her profile, she was closeted with her lawyer preparing for a court battle for custody of her fourteen-year-old twins. Any confirmation in court of her rumoured sexual rapacity and her seeming indifference to her children might cost her not just custody of her daughters but her political future. Sean Barton, a young associate at Zack's law firm, was representing Ginny. He was good, but his case was not. Ginny had been careless. Like many people on whom the sun has steadily shone, she believed she was invincible. Jason Brodnitz had been smarter. He was a player, but he was a player who appeared to know how to cover his tracks. He also knew how to hire a private investigator. Ginny was in big trouble.

As she picked up a drink and began to circulate, there were whispers; there was also the subtle shifting away that pack animals exhibit when a member is wounded. I was relieved when Sean Barton joined Ginny and the two found privacy in the shelter of the lilacs.

My daughter Mieka and I were bringing out appetizers, and she nudged me as Sean and Ginny leaned towards each other and began what appeared to be an earnest conversation.

"I'd give a shiny new penny to know what those two are talking about," Mieka said.

"I'll take your penny," I said. "Ginny's preparing to do a meet and greet, and Sean's filling her in on who's worth approaching."

As Ginny strode across the lawn towards Zack and my younger son, Mieka chortled. "Bad start. Zack's worth the attention, but unless the Honourable Ms. Monaghan wants to hear how law school has opened new neural pathways for Angus, she's going to be bored spitless. Plus, Angus doesn't even vote in this riding."

"But he is part of this family," I said. "Ginny's presence here is strategic. Falconer Shreve Wainberg and Hynd is showing our little corner of the world that the firm is behind Ginny Monaghan all the way."

After the obligatory few minutes with Zack and Angus, Ginny moved towards my elder son, Peter, who'd taken charge of the barbecue. Peter would rather have been pecked to death by a duck than make small talk with strangers, but he beamed as Ginny chatted and peered with interest at the boneless prime rib roast turning on the spit. Clearly, she hadn't lost her touch.

She hadn't lost her sense of timing either. Peter was only the stepson of a senior partner in the law firm representing her, so she didn't tarry. She did, however, take her leave with the charming reluctance I'd seen in other skilled politicians who knew how to make voters feel they would have stayed forever had pressing commitments not called them elsewhere.

As it turned out, Mieka and I were Ginny's pressing commit-
ment, and as she made her way across the lawn towards us,
Mieka braced herself theatrically. "Batten down the hatches,"
she whispered. "It's our turn to be seduced by power."

Ginny was not a beauty, but at a shade over six feet with
a body blessed by good genes and constant training, her powerful physicality had made her equally appealing to both
genders. When I held out my hand to her, she took it with
the firm, dry grasp of a politician at the top of her game.

"It's good to see you again." I said. "I don't know if you
remember me, but I'm Joanne Kilbourn. I interviewed you for
a TV project I was working on."

"Of course," she said. "*Political Women and the Media.*
We talked about whether the landscape had shifted and the
media had begun treating female politicians the same way
they treat men."

"And the answer is . . . ?" I asked.

There was an edge to her laugh. "Only in our dreams," she
said. "But given my widely rumoured political demise, it
might be time to revisit your topic."

"You're prepared to do another interview?"

"Why not?" she said. "I may be finished, but my old coach
always told us you can learn as much from a loss as you can
from a win. Now, let's talk about something that matters."
She turned to Mieka. "Sean tells me that basil dip you're
holding is amazing."

Mieka held out the tray. "Decide for yourself."

Ginny spooned the appetizer onto a cracker and took a
bite. "God, that *is* good," she said. She popped the rest of the
cracker into her mouth and fixed herself another. "Do me a
favour, Mieka. Keep the dip close."

"I have a few dozen other things I should be attending to,"
Mieka said, offering the tray. "What happens to the dip from
now on is between you and it."

"In that case," Ginny said, "I'm going to pour myself another drink and sneak into the bushes with this. I'm tired of introducing myself to people who've just finished telling a joke where I'm the punchline."

I slipped my arm through hers. "Stick with me," I said. "I've never been able to remember the punchline to a single joke."

That afternoon, people I'd known for years surprised me with their reaction to Ginny. A month earlier, they would have been falling over themselves for the chance to chat up the woman who might become the next prime minister; now they were coolly courteous, making only the briefest eye contact and moving on after a perfunctory greeting. Ginny was stoic, but I empathized. My late husband had been a politician, and I knew how it felt to realize you were going to lose an election.

When Ed Mariani came across the lawn towards us, my spirits rose. Ed was the head of the school of journalism, but despite a lifetime of teaching students how to deal with people determined to reveal the best and conceal the worst, he was optimistic about his fellow beings. There was something else. By a coincidence that proved, once again, that the gods are puckish, Ed and Ginny were wearing silk garments in the same shade of buttercup. Ginny's dress was designed to reveal an athlete's toned limbs, and Ed's shirt had been custom-made to hide his considerable girth. As I introduced them, Ed beamed.

"Clearly, we're cut from the same bolt of cloth, Ms. Monaghan. I'm Ed Mariani, and I've wanted to talk to you for ages. Is your dance card filled?"

Ginny's voice was husky and mocking. "It's your lucky night, Mr. Mariani. Not a soul at this party wants to dance with me."

"In that case, let's find ourselves a table for two and get acquainted," Ed said, and when he offered his arm, she took it. Ginny Monaghan had never been a woman who needed rescuing, but as I watched her being led to safety by her portly knight, I was relieved that chivalry was not dead.

When we sat down to dinner, I invited Ginny and Ed to sit with Sean and our family and one of Zack's partners, Kevin Hynd. Like all the partners in Falconer Shreve, Kevin and Zack had been friends since their first year of law school, but five years earlier, obeying an instinct that told him the law was not enough, Kevin had walked away. His trek had taken him through Bhutan, India, Nepal, Tibet, Mongolia, China, Vietnam, and Thailand. I hadn't known Kevin before his journeys, but Zack said he had returned a changed man: purged of ambition, focused on using the law to attain a greater good. Angus, who at twenty-two believed the law *was* the greater good, thought Kevin was a flake. So, I'm certain, did Sean, who made no secret of his ambition. Mieka, however, who was twelve years older than her brother, knew about quests. Hers had led her to leave her marriage to search for answers at the very point when Zack and I, after years alone, decided the answers we sought could best be found together. Add Ginny Monaghan, who had been so confident of her ability to climb to the top that she hadn't checked her footing, and Ed Mariani, who had found true contentment with his partner, Barry, for a quarter-century, and the conversational possibilities were wide-ranging. Given that we were celebrating a birthday, it wasn't surprising that we soon settled on the topic that mattered to us all: happiness.

It was good talk: spirited and inclusive, but by the time the last scrap of prime rib was eaten, a topic even more pressing than happiness presented itself. The temperature had begun to drop; the stillness that comes before a storm settled over us, and the family dogs skulked towards the basement – a sure sign that falling weather was on its way. Mieka had handled more than a few outdoor parties, and as we headed in to get the dessert, she eyed the low dark clouds rolling in. "Time to move inside?" she asked.

I glanced back at our table. Another of Zack's partners, Blake Falconer, had joined the group. Angus was telling a story. When he steered clear of the legal information sluicing down the new neural pathways from his brain, my younger son was a funny guy, and everyone, including Blake, who had seemed preoccupied all evening, was enjoying him. After Angus finished his story, Zack clapped him on the shoulder and gave one of his deep, full-body laughs.

"Let's take a chance and stay outside," I said. "Zack's having a great time."

"I thought he always had a great time," Mieka said.

"The last couple of weeks have been difficult."

"Because Sean's case hasn't been going well," Mieka said, and her face was troubled.

"It has nothing to do with Sean," I said. "Zack's been a lawyer for twenty-five years. He knows that no one wins every case."

"Then what is it?"

"Zack's having a hard time dealing with Ned Osler's death."

"That's the old lawyer who shot himself," Mieka said. "Sean told me about it."

I raised an eyebrow. "Second mention of Sean in ten seconds," I said.

"Don't get your hopes up," Mieka said. "He came over to the house with some papers for me to sign about the divorce, and we talked a little. Actually, we talked about Zack. Sean was worried about him too. I guess suicides are always hard."

"Ned Osler's death was particularly sad," I said. "His wife died last year. Apparently theirs was a great romance, and Ned didn't want to face his last years without her."

"So he chose his own time," Mieka said thoughtfully. "Sean said he didn't have a family."

I gave my daughter an appraising glance. "Third mention of Sean – not that I'm counting." In the distance, thunder rumbled. "Time to get the cake," I said.

Mieka frowned. "Are you sure about this?"

"No, but everybody's having fun. I don't want to spoil the mood. Let's take a chance."

"Hey, you take a chance the day you're born. Why stop now?" Sean Barton's voice was decisive. "I have now officially contributed my two cents' worth. I'm here on a champagne run – a mission of mercy for the dry and needy."

As soon as she heard his voice, the colour spread from Mieka's neck to her cheeks. I understood. Sean was an extraordinarily good-looking man – tall, blond, fine-featured. Only his crooked grin saved him from male model perfection.

"Plenty of champagne in the fridge," I said. "Birthdays come but once a year."

Sean nodded. "Right," he said. "Joanne, I haven't had a chance to thank you for making Ginny welcome. There's been so much hostility towards her lately, I thought she could use some friendly vibes."

"My pleasure," I said. "Ginny's good company. I just wish some of our other guests had been more open to her. She has a tough battle ahead."

"Then she's lucky she chose a good lawyer," Mieka said.

Sean lowered his gaze. "Maybe I should get you to write a letter of reference."

"Anytime," Mieka said. She picked up the tray with the dessert plates, cutlery, and napkins. "Grab the cake, Mum. The window of opportunity is about to slam shut."

As we started down the lawn, I gave the sky one last

anxious glance. It was lowering. No doubt about it, we were in for a gully-washer, but as I placed the cake in front of Zack and our guests gathered to sing "Happy Birthday," I was glad we'd taken the chance. The warmth towards Zack was palpable and there was no rain. Our luck was holding. I leaned over and lit the candles.

When they blazed, a smile of pure delight spread across Zack's face. He took my hand. "Want to know what I wished for?" he asked.

"No," I said. "Because if you tell before you blow out the candles, your wish won't come true."

"Then I'd better get to work," Zack said. He bent towards the blazing cake and blew. The candles guttered a little in the wind but remained stubbornly alight. Our twelve-year-old daughter, Taylor, and her two best friends, Isobel and Gracie, had crowded in beside Zack for the big moment. Bright as tulips in their spring dresses, the girls pressed their hands to their mouths, stifling laughter as Zack tried again to blow out his candles. Successful trial lawyers have a sixth sense about hidden motives, and as Gracie Falconer, her face as innocent as a pan of milk, urged Zack to give the candles another try, he smelled a rat. He leaned back in his chair and eyed the girls. "I'm exhausted," he said. "Why don't you young women take over?"

The girls exchanged furtive glances. "They're trick candles," Taylor said finally. "The only way to put them out is to drop them in water."

"I grew up with brothers," Mieka said. "I've dealt with these candles before." She reached for the cake and began plucking out candles and extinguishing them. "Zack, if you're interested in revenge, give me a call," she said. "I know some really cool tricks with whipped cream."

"Make a list," Zack said. "If I remember correctly, Isobel has a birthday coming up."

"My pleasure," Mieka said. "But let's deal with this cake first. You slice the first piece, and I'll do the rest." She glanced at the guests who, champagne glasses in hand, had gathered round for the celebratory moment. "Would it be okay if I propose the toast?"

Zack was clearly surprised. "Is it going to be like the trick candles?"

Mieka had made no secret of her opposition to our marriage the year before, but Zack had obeyed his first rule of dealing with opposition: stay in your opponent's face. You'll either win them over or they'll walk away. Mieka hadn't walked away.

"No trick candles," Mieka said. "Also no whoopee cushions or dribble glasses, but don't expect eloquence. Public speaking is number one on my personal fear factor list." She tapped her glass and called for attention. As all eyes focused on her, she fiddled with the neck of her sweater, but when she raised her glass, her voice was clear. "To Zack – everyone here is glad that you're part of their life."

There was a murmur: "To Zack." At that moment, a thunderclap split the evening quiet, and the skies opened. Laughing, gulping champagne as they ran, our guests sprinted towards the house. Mieka picked up the cake, and Zack began wheeling his chair up the ramp that led to the deck and the safety of the kitchen.

I ran over to him. "Are you doing okay?" I asked.

"Couldn't be better," he said, navigating the turn on the ramp. "I'm interpreting that thunderclap as a cosmic sign of approval," he said.

I shook my head. "You are one confident guy."

The party continued. The kids cajoled our bouvier and our mastiff into slinking back upstairs, and when Zack pushed the piano bench out of the way and moved his wheelchair into place, Willie and Pantera lumbered over and collapsed on the floor beside him. In the year and a half Zack and I had been married, the dogs had developed an insatiable appetite for show tunes. Zack has never had a piano lesson, but he has a good ear, and as he played, Taylor and her friends danced with the little kids and then, thrillingly, with some boys their own age who, according to the girls, had just happened by. In the hall, Angus and his girlfriend, Leah, alternated between slow dancing and smooching. Ginny and Ed were more public. It turned out that they were both passionate tango dancers, and as they glided by in their matching buttercup silk, Ed dipped towards me. "How do we look?"

"Like the finalists in a ballroom dance contest," I said. Clearly the celebration was moving in a good direction.

Mieka and I had just started taking the coffee around when Sean stepped in and took my tray. "Mieka and I can handle this, Joanne," he said. "Why don't you kick back and spend some time with the birthday boy?"

"Good plan," I said. "Thanks." I went over to the table where the bar had been set out, poured two small cognacs, went over to Zack, placed his snifter on the piano, and whispered, "I'm plying you with liquor."

He gave me a sidelong glance. "I don't need to be plied. When it comes to you, I'm ever ready." He let his fingers drop from the piano keys to caress my leg.

"Better hold off on that," I said under my breath. "We have a houseful of guests."

"Send them home," Zack said. "Tell them your husband can't keep his hands off you."

I brushed an imaginary crumb from his shirt and let my fingers linger. "That works both ways, you know."

"Whoa. Everybody out of the pool." Zack thumped a chord that brought the loin-throbbing rhythms of *Jalousie* to a halt, picked up his brandy snifter, and swivelled his chair to face me. "I'm at your service."

At that moment, his cellphone rang. "I thought you turned that off," I said.

Zack shrugged. "I forgot. Want me to let it ring?"

"No," I said. "Probably just somebody wanting to wish you a happy birthday."

Zack flipped open his cell and answered. One look at his face and I knew the call was serious. He listened without comment. Finally he said. "I'll be there in ten minutes. And, Debbie, thanks for the heads-up."

"Problems?" I said.

"There's a situation," Zack said evenly. "And it's something you and I should talk about."

"Can it wait?"

"No," Zack said. "It can't. Let's go to our room."

I'd left the sliding doors to the deck outside our bedroom open to catch the fresh breeze, but now the storm was lashing and the hardwood in front of the doors was wet. I picked up a towel from my bathroom and skated it across the hardwood until the floor was dry. Zack watched as I pitched the towel in the hamper. "You are admirably unflappable."

"Comes in handy since I met you." I sat on the bed. "So what's up?"

"That was the cop shop. Inspector Debbie Haczkewicz says they need me to come down."

I groaned. "Come on, Zack, a client – *tonight*?"

"There's no client," Zack said. "I'm the one they want to talk to."

"About what?"

"It's complicated," Zack said. "But it starts with the reason Ned Osler committed suicide."

"He didn't want to live after his wife died," I said. "I thought that was common knowledge."

"He was also being blackmailed by a prostitute," Zack said. "She'd filmed their sexual encounters and she was going to put them on the Internet unless Ned paid her off. That isn't common knowledge and I hope to God it doesn't get to be."

A finger of lightning arced from sky to earth, throwing the trees along the creek into sharp relief. "I can't believe this," I said. "Ned was such a gentleman. When the three of us had dinner at his apartment, it was like stepping back in time. He was so gracious, helping me off with my coat, holding my chair before I sat down at the table. And the next day, there was always a hand-delivered note thanking me for the pleasure of my company and mentioning some detail of the evening that had brought him delight."

Zack nodded. "Ned was a gentleman of the old school. That was the problem. Most of the guys I know would have told a lady threatening blackmail to go for it, put the tapes on the Internet, show the world Super-Stud in action, but Ned was a principled man. When this woman said she was going to make his private life public, he found the prospect insupportable."

"Did he pay her off?"

"No. He refused to capitulate to behaviour that, in his view, was as unacceptable as his own."

"Did he consider going to the police?"

"Believe it or not," Zack said, "I suggested that. But Ned said the acts he'd indulged in were unspeakable, an insult to the life he and his wife, Evvie, had together. He said he'd rather die than stain his wife's memory. I asked him to give me the name of the woman who'd threatened him, and I'd take care of it, but he said he'd made up his mind: he was going to exit honourably. That was it. Ned poured us each a serious slug of single-malt Scotch, and when we'd finished our drinks, he thanked me for my friendship and said goodbye. Three hours later, he shot himself."

I took his hand. "I wish you'd told me."

"I couldn't. I'd given Ned my word, Jo. The only reason I'm telling you now is because of that phone call from Debbie."

"Something's happened."

Zack sighed. "Boy, has it ever. I'll give you the broad strokes. At Ned's funeral, I watched his partners march up the aisle and I knew that before the sod on Ned's grave had taken root, the woman who'd tried to blackmail Ned would be knocking on the doors of Osler Meinhart and Loftus. Anyway, I hired a private detective to track her down to see if I could head her off."

"Did you find her?"

"Actually, she found me. Her name is Cristal Avilia. She called this morning and said she needed to talk to me about Ned."

"So you saw her."

"Yeah, I did." He stroked my hand. "Christ, I'd give anything not to be having this conversation with you. Yes, I saw her, and as it turned out, it wasn't the first time we'd met. I'd used her services myself, Jo."

My heart squeezed. "Since we were together?"

Zack leaned towards me. "Oh God, no. Jo, you're all I've ever wanted and then some. But as you know, the mechanics of sex don't always work for me. With us, it doesn't matter, we just fool around till we're both happy, but it was different for me before. I could be dynamite in the courtroom all day, but if I couldn't get it up at night, it drove me nuts.

"So you went to a prostitute," I said.

"It seemed like a good idea at the time," Zack said dryly. "Most of the women I could have had sex with were other lawyers. It's an adversarial relationship, and you don't want your adversaries to know you're a dud in the sack. So I kept searching for the magic bullet. Cristal was just the last of many. I'm not proud of it, but there it is."

"So was Cristal the magic bullet?" I asked.

His nod was almost imperceptible. "She was very skilful. Then I met you, and you know the rest of the story. I never saw Cristal again until today."

There was a tap at the door, and Mieka opened it and peeked in. "The girls and I are taking off. They wanted to say goodnight, but if we're interrupting . . ."

Zack's face softened. "Couldn't ask for a more welcome interruption."

Sleepy but still coasting on a sugar high, Madeleine and Lena raced in and crawled up on Zack's lap.

"Did you like our present?" Madeleine asked.

"A man can never have too many flashlights," Zack said.

"It's for flashlight tag," Madeleine said. "We can play it next time we come over."

"Somebody's going to have to teach me the rules," Zack said.

"I will," Madeleine said. "Lena doesn't care about rules. But she's a really good runner."

"I'm not much of a runner," Zack said. "So what can I do?"

Lena rubbed at a grass stain on her knee of her jeans. "You can be *It*," she said thoughtfully.

Her sister frowned. "Nobody can always be *It*."

"Zack can," Lena said. Then she aimed a kiss at Zack's cheek, slid off his knee, and both girls ran to their mother. Zack wheeled his chair after them. "Mieka, I didn't have a chance to thank you for the toast."

Mieka met his gaze. "I didn't exactly have them rolling in the aisles, but I meant what I said. I'm really glad you're around, Zack."

I closed the door after them and Zack turned to me. "Do you think she'll still be glad to have me around when she finds about Cristal Avilia?"

"Is there a reason why she needs to know?"

There was a crack of thunder and Willie, who'd followed Mieka and the girls to the bedroom, whined. I rubbed his head. "It's just thunder," I said. "You're okay. I'm okay. We're all okay." I turned to Zack. "We are okay, aren't we?"

"No," he said. "We're not." He splayed his hands on his knees and stared down at them. "Cristal's dead, Jo."

"Oh God. What happened to her?"

"She was murdered. At some point between the time I left her around two this afternoon and six tonight, when the lawn service went out to fix the underground sprinklers, Cristal fell, jumped, or was pushed over the railing of her balcony. The police are leaning towards the third possibility."

"How do they know it wasn't an accident or suicide?"

"They don't know," Zack said. "Cristal's condo was on the fourth floor. She could have fallen or jumped, but her body had been pulled towards the side of the building so the other tenants wouldn't discover it when they came home from work."

I felt my nerves twang. "Zack, the police don't think that you – "

His laugh was short and humourless. "There aren't a lot of advantages to being a paraplegic, but I think even the cops would see that a guy in a wheelchair would have trouble pushing a healthy thirty-four-year-old woman over a balcony railing, then zipping down to the place where she fell so he could pull her body out of sight."

I walked over and pressed my forehead against the cool glass of the patio doors. The rain was falling hard now, and the trees at the bottom of our yard were thrashing in the wind. "Thirty-four," I said. "Mieka's age."

"Too young to die," Zack said. "Also too young to have lived the life she lived." He moved his chair to the place beside me, and for a moment, we were silent, looking out together at the night.

Finally, I said. "How did they connect you with this?"

"Through one of my more egregious fuck-ups. I thought I was handling the blackmail threat exactly right. I played hardball. I told Cristal I knew she'd been taping her clients, and I wasn't going to deal until the camera was turned off. It was in a smoke detector on her bedroom ceiling, angled to pick up the bed and a special chair she reserved for what she called *boutique requests.* Of course, while she was *boutiquing,* her camera was able to get a nice clear shot of her client."

"Including you?" I said.

Zack shrugged. "Honestly, I don't know. Logic would suggest that I'd be worth taping – I have money and people know my name – but she never approached me."

"But the police called *you.* They must have found something."

"They did indeed. They found the camera that I so shrewdly insisted she turn off. She must have forgotten to turn it back on."

"So as far as the police know, you were the last one to see her alive."

"Right," Zack said, "but looking on the bright side, they didn't hear me offer her $10,000 for the Osler DVDs."

"So they don't know about Ned's involvement with Cristal."

"No, and I'd like to keep it that way."

"Had she agreed to take the money?"

"I thought she had. She brought out the DVDs. I put one in the machine to make certain I wasn't paying $10,000 for *Bambi.* I watched long enough to see what I was buying, then I took out the envelope with the cash. That's when it got weird."

"Weird how?"

"Cristal wouldn't take the money. She said she never dreamed that Ned would commit suicide. In her words, his death was just 'tragic collateral damage.'"

"That sounds as if she had a larger agenda."

Zack sighed. "No flies on you, my love. I should have picked up on that myself, but at that point, Cristal started to cry. She said she knew she'd made a mistake. She'd deleted the files from the camera, but she wanted me to know she was trying to rectify what she'd done. Giving me the DVDs was the first step."

"Why did she care about what you thought?"

"She'd been at Ned's funeral. I didn't notice her, but there were hundreds of people there. I probably wouldn't have rec- ognized her anyway. She's changed her hair – it's lighter or something. I don't know – she just looked different. Anyway, she told me she couldn't stop thinking about that poem I used in the eulogy. Remember? It was the one Ned e-mailed to me after 9/11."

"'September 1, 1939,'" I said. "Auden really made the rounds after the World Trade Center was attacked."

"I don't exactly travel in literary circles, but I must have received six copies of that poem," Zack said. "Anyway, Cristal latched on to what I said about how Ned never let the darkness engulf him and how he believed it was our duty as human beings to show 'an affirming flame.' Then she announced she was going to change." Zack pounded his palm with his fist. "It really pissed me off."

"Why would that piss you off?"

"Christ, Jo. If you knew how many times I've had to listen to people bleat on about how sorry they are for what they've done, and how they're going to reform. Usually, I just watch the clock and let them pile on the billable hours, but Cristal had driven a decent man to suicide. It was a little late for tears."

"Did you tell her that?"

"Nope. I didn't say anything. I tried to leave, but Cristal stepped in front of me and blocked the way. She asked me if I believed in evil. I said I wasn't a theologian; I was a lawyer. She said that the people who thought she was evil were wrong – that all she did was let people live out their fantasies."

"Had she ever said anything like that before?"

"Not to me. Of course, she and I didn't talk much. And today, I just wanted to get the hell out of there, so I told her I didn't think she was evil. I thought she was like me, someone who provided a necessary service."

"And that satisfied her?"

"I guess so. She let me leave, and I had the DVDs in my possession. Thank God for that. I wouldn't want the boys and girls at the cop shop to be sitting around watching those right now."

"Were they that bad?"

"Objectively, no. As sexual acts go, what Cristal did to Ned was pretty tame. In the romantic language of the courtroom, she fellated him."

"Why would Ned kill himself over that?"

"Because all the time Cristal was fellating him, Ned called her 'Evvie.'"

"His dead wife's name."

"Right, and when he was finished, he closed his eyes, stroked Cristal's hair, and thanked her for taking him into her mouth and letting him be part of her private world."

Except for the sound of rain splashing through the eavestroughs and hitting the ground, the room was silent. "That breaks my heart," I said.

Zack stroked my arm. "You're a gentle soul. Ned was a realist. He knew that most people would just see the tape as sordid – an old man getting a blow job and fantasizing."

"So you made sure his private life was kept private."

"It was the least I could do," Zack said. "Ned has always been on my side. The legal community here is tight. Everybody knows how everybody else operates, and everybody knows that the Law Society has rapped my knuckles on more than one occasion. A lot of people would be delighted if I really stepped on my joint and got disbarred, but Ned was a friend. If he heard that I was getting too close to the line, he'd invite me for a drink and, in the most gentlemanly of ways, remind me that discretion is the better part of valour."

I touched his cheek. "I'm glad you got the DVDs."

"I am too," Zack said. "When I was trying to talk Ned out of committing suicide, I told him he had many, many reasons to live."

"But he didn't see it that way."

Zack shook his head. "No. He said that in the end everybody loses everything – the only choice we have is deciding the order in which we lose the things that matter to us."

"And Ned decided he'd rather lose his life than his reputation."

"It wasn't his reputation Ned was concerned about; it was Evvie's. He didn't want people to know the man whom Evvie had loved for all those years was incapable of remaining faithful to her memory. He said that satisfying himself with a prostitute cheapened everything he and his wife had been to each other."

"So he shot himself?"

"As you said, Ned was a gentleman of the old school."

I straightened the sprig of forsythia in Zack's buttonhole. "I love you very much."

Zack sighed. "Hold that thought, Ms. Shreve, because I have a feeling that we're in for a rocky ride." He tousled my hair. "But what the hell, as long as we're together, there's nothing we can't handle, is there?"

A bone-rattling clap of thunder shook the heavens, and I shuddered. Zack was sanguine. "Listen to that," he said. "The gods are definitely on our side."

CHAPTER

2

Sean Barton drove Zack to the police station. Zack had had very little to drink – a martini in the afternoon and a glass of wine with dinner. The cognac I'd poured for him had remained untouched, but given the prickly relationship between defence lawyers and cops, he was always cautious about sliding behind the wheel. After the two men left, the party began the slow dissolve to finish. The clouds in the west were still threatening, but the rain had stopped, and Peter, Angus, and Leah took advantage of the lull to give the dogs a run. The guests, too, decided it was time to head out. Ed Mariani was going to the airport to pick up his partner, Barry. During their time together Ed and Barry had never missed an airport reunion, and as Ed brushed my cheek with a kiss, he had the glow that comes when you know that the person you love will soon be in your arms. Even those who weren't on their way to welcome their beloved had reason to move along. The next day was a working day, and their agendas were full.

Within an hour, Ginny Monaghan was the only guest left, and I was trying to conjure up the diplomatic words to speed her on her way. I'd had enough. Zack's news had shaken me, and I needed time alone. Ginny, however, showed no signs of moving along. As the caterers began carrying out the rented glasses and dishes, I tried the last ploy of the weary host. "Can I get you anything, Ginny?" I asked. "A drink or a cup of tea?"

Ginny's smile was mischievous. "Directions on how I can exit through the front door?"

I laughed. "Subtlety has never been my strong suit."

"You're doing fine. I'm playing the obtuse guest because I need to talk to Sean about what's going to happen in court tomorrow."

I glanced at my watch. "They shouldn't be much longer."

One of the caterer's helpers came in and began collapsing chairs. The clatter reverberated through the silent room, and the young man looked at me questioningly.

"We'll get out of your way," I said. I turned to Ginny. "How would you like to see my second favourite room in this house?"

When we fell in love, Zack set himself the task of finding the perfect house for our family. His quest had not proven easy, but he'd been resolute, and, like all knights errant, in the end he triumphed. The house we decided on had been built in the 1960s, and it was solid enough to accommodate the retrofittings we needed and filled with enough space and light to please us all. The fact that our house had an indoor pool had sealed the deal. Taylor and I were committed swimmers, and after spending eighteen hours a day in a wheelchair, Zack needed exercise to give his cardiovascular system a workout, help control the spasms that harassed him, and just have fun. But the pool had been installed for therapeutic reasons and the area surrounding it was antiseptic, soulless, and depressing. It was a space in desperate need of transformation, and Taylor had thrown herself into the task.

Taylor's birth mother had been my friend Sally Love, a painter whose work now routinely sold in the high six figures. Sally died when Taylor was only four, but from the moment I adopted her, I knew she had inherited her mother's gift. Confronted with a space that was bare and ugly, Taylor made beauty: a mural depicting an underwater scene of swimmers – human, finned, and crustacean – that filled three walls and pulsed with colour and movement. The ceiling and the fourth wall were glass. Ed Mariani supplied a small forest of tropical plants; Taylor and I painted the wicker furniture that came with the house a shade of dusty rose the paint chart described as "azalea," and we had a room that was a potent antidote to the grey months – just the ticket for a man whose frustration at navigating the snow and ice of a northern winter from a wheelchair spiked his blood pressure. Thirty minutes of laps unknotted Zack's muscles, and twenty minutes with a chilled martini completed the job. Taylor's mural and the moist gardenia-scented air were powerful restoratives, and that night they restored Ginny.

As soon as she came into the room, she collapsed on one of the wicker lounge chairs, kicked off her sandals, and flexed her feet. "It is so good to be away from all those eyes," she said.

I lay back in the lounge chair next to hers. "You're handling it well," I said.

"Training," she said. She raised the leg closest to me and began to rotate it from the hip. As she moved, the silk of her skirt fell back. She was wearing a string thong, but she was a woman at ease with her body and it was clear she took pleasure in experiencing its subtleties. "Athletes learn that personal victory means personal mastery," she said. "You have to block out everything that gets in your way."

"That can't be easy," I said.

"It isn't," she said. "But it can be done." She switched legs; then, as the rain drummed on the glass above us, Canada's latest infamous MP did hip rotations and talked about sports psychology.

"You have to clear your mind," she said, and the measured cadences of her public voice disappeared. She sounded younger – both open and fervent. The words might have come from a training manual, but Ginny was a true believer. "You have to train yourself not to hear the noise or see the fans or feel the exhaustion or listen to that inner voice that tells you you're going to fail." For a beat she was silent. When she spoke, her tone was self-mocking. "Maybe instead of tuning out that inner voice, I should have listened to it. I really believed I'd become prime minister, Joanne. Looks like the only thing I'll be remembered for now is being a dependable free-throw shooter."

"There are worse things to be remembered for," I said. "Drawing a foul is one of life's most satisfying manifestations of justice. The other team gets punished, and you have a chance to rub salt in the wound by scoring free points."

Ginny shot me a look of surprise. "You played basketball," she said.

"Enthusiastically, but not well," I said. "Mieka was really good, especially at sinking free shots."

"Nothing feeds the ego like sinking a free shot," she said. She dropped her leg and closed her eyes. "You stand on the line. The referee approaches. He bounces the ball to you. You line the seams up." As she recreated the moment, her fingers splayed. Her hands were large and powerful, the nails unpainted and cut short. "Fingers spread over the ball. Focus. Bounce once, then twice. Breathe in slowly. Raise the ball up to your forehead, feel the balance of perfect form, elbow in line with the basket. Look at the top knot of the mesh and relax your chest. Breathe out slowly; your lungs are almost empty. The shot releases itself; your body knows what to do. Your legs and arms are in sync. The shot swishes dead centre and snaps the cord. Nobody can describe what a perfect shot sounds like, but when you're a shooter it's all you can hear." Ginny's voice was dreamy, but she was quick to shake off the memory and bring herself back to reality. "I'd give a lot to hear that sound right now." She examined her hands with interest. "I'm going to lose, you know."

I'd seen the campaign photograph of Ginny with her daughters. They were close to Taylor's age: coltish girls with their mother's long limbs, shoulder-length dark blonde hair, and the unfinished look some girls have on the cusp of adolescence. In an ideal world, Ginny and her daughters would be battling over whether the girls could get tattoos or pitch their sleeping bags outside the Centre of the Arts overnight to be first in line for tickets to hear a hot new band. There would be tears and a reconciliation made poignant by the awareness on both sides that, as C.P. Snow said, the love between a parent and a child is the only love that must grow towards separation. But Ginny's custody battle had removed her from the ideal world, and as I glanced at her worn face, I knew the prospect of being legally severed from her daughters was taking its toll.

She hugged her legs to herself. "I could have made a difference," she said.

"You still can," I said. "Even if your ex-husband gets custody, you'll have rights. Your daughters are growing up. There's a lot you'll be able to give them."

Ginny levelled her gaze at me. She looked perplexed. "Em and Chloe don't need anything from me. They're smart and strong. Contrary to what you've undoubtedly heard, I've been a good parent. They'll be fine if they end up with Jason."

I was astounded. "If you don't care about the custody, why are you going to court?"

Ginny's slate-blue eyes were cool. "Because I have – or did have – political aspirations, and it would have been political suicide not to put up a fight for the girls." She read my face. "Now, I've shocked you. Tell me something, Joanne. If I were a man, would you be shocked at what I just said?"

I stared at the tranquil water of our pool. "I wouldn't give it a second thought," I said. "I apologize."

Ginny seemed amused. "My old coach used to say, 'Don't apologize. Do something.'"

"All right," I said. "I'll do something. How would you feel about me helping you get your case in front of the public?"

She stiffened. "'The Rise and Fall of Ginny Monaghan'? I don't think so. There are enough people lining up to throw a handful of dirt on my political grave."

"This wouldn't be a sensational piece. Did you see that NationTV special on the religious right and the values war in Canadian politics?"

"One of my advisers made me watch it, but I'm glad I did. It was good. Fair, balanced, and I actually learned a few things."

"That's what I was hoping for," I said. "I wrote it. And I've talked to the producer about doing some more specials along that line. She says we should pitch the shows as Issues for Dummies."

"Never overestimate the intelligence of the voting public," Ginny said.

"I'm hoping if we give viewers small nibbles at big questions, they might want to learn more."

Ginny cocked her head. "And you think my story might give them a taste for more?"

"I've taught a graduate class in Women and Party Politics for the past five years. I have the research, but I could use a human face."

"Or, even better, a human sacrifice," Ginny said. "Well, why not? Nineteen days till E-Day. Follow me around, and you'll be able to give the public some dynamite insights into the best prime minister Canada never had." She smoothed her skirt, swung her legs off the lounge, and leaned towards me. "Consider me officially in, but no cameras, no tape recorders – just you and your notebook."

Outside a car door slammed. Ginny stood up and stretched. "The men return," she said. "Impeccable timing."

When Sean came in with Zack, I didn't encourage a visit. It was clear we'd all had enough. I told Ginny I'd see her the next day in court, then we said goodnight. After I closed the door, Zack shot me a quizzical look. "So what was that all about?"

"Ginny and I have struck a mutual assistance pact. I'm going to be inside her campaign for the next couple of weeks, and in return, I'll use Ginny as my focus in that politics and women program I'm working on for NationTV."

"So a good evening," Zack said.

"No, but one good outcome. How about you?"

"Lousy evening. Lousy outcome." Zack turned his chair towards the hall. "But I am soaked to the skivvies, so you're going to have to wait for the blow by blow till after I have a shower."

"I'll give you a rubdown when you're ready," I said.

Zack looked at me hard. "You do realize that most women would be ready to kill me right now."

"The possibility crossed my mind," I said. "But we took an oath to stay together for better or worse, and as you reminded me at the altar, a deal's a deal."

He took my hand. "Thank God for legal training."

Casual physical intimacy was difficult for Zack and me. We couldn't walk hand in hand along the beach at our cottage, grope each other in the kitchen when we were drying the dishes, or make out at the movies. But we were deeply in love, so we had built some small rituals into our day that gave us both pleasure. The mutual nightly massage was one of them. Sometimes as we kneaded each other's muscles, we talked about our day; sometimes we were silent, content just to feel the comfort of deep touch. As I worked the knotted muscles of my husband's shoulders, he groaned.

"Better?" I murmured.

"Getting there," he said.

"Do you want to talk about it?"

"No, but we have to."

"Let's have it, then," I said.

"Boy, where to start? Debbie Haczkewicz is leading the investigation, which isn't exactly a break for me."

"I thought you liked Debbie."

"I do. And that makes it harder."

I followed his thinking. "Harder to lie?"

"Uh-uh. Unless you're a cop, lying gets you in serious trouble. But there are ways of telling the truth that leave the facts open to interpretation."

"And that's what you did with Debbie."

"Bingo. I told her that I went to Cristal's condo to pay her off so she wouldn't show a DVD that was personally embarrassing on the Internet."

I poured more massage oil into my palm. "And Debbie

naturally assumed that the person who would be embarrassed was you."

"Yes."

"Didn't she ask to see the DVDs?"

"Yep, but I said they'd been destroyed, and that was the truth. As soon as I left Cristal's condo, I went back to the office. We deal with a lot of stuff that's too hot to toss without shredding. Cops have been known to go through trash. Anyway, I asked Norine to shred the discs, and she did."

"No questions asked?"

"Norine's been my assistant for fifteen years. She knows not to know what she shouldn't know."

"And Debbie accepted your word that the discs had been destroyed?"

"Debbie's a smart cop. She probably had her guys picking through the firm's garbage while she was interviewing me, but she was gracious. She knows I'm married. Of course, she's still a cop, so we had a little go round about destroying evidence, but I pointed out that when I was dealing with those DVDs they weren't evidence because Cristal Avilia was still alive."

"So you're home free."

"No one's ever home free, Jo. That's why the cops keep burrowing in. Tonight after Debbie was finished making nice, her buddies showed me their crime scene photos."

"Why would they do that?"

"Just in a sharing mood, I guess. Truthfully, I imagine they wanted to watch my reaction to seeing Cristal."

"I hope you kept Sean with you."

"I did. Over the years, I've probably instructed at least two thousand clients not to say anything to the cops, but there's something about staring at pictures of a dead body that loosens the tongue. Anyway, I didn't screw up, but there were some shots of Cristal that are going to stay with me for a while." Zack's body tensed and I dug my fingers more deeply into the spaces along his spine. "She was young and she's dead," he said. "That's bad enough, but there was one thing that really got me. Whoever killed Cristal went to the trouble of placing a book on her chest. It was that novel you and Ned talked about the last time we had dinner."

"*Portrait of a Lady*," I said.

"Right," Zack said. "Debbie's tough, but even she was taken aback at the cruelty of that gesture."

My heart lurched. "The night we had dinner, Ned told me he'd given a copy of the book to a young friend who was determined to make something of her life. He said his friend was like the character Isabel Archer – too good for her world."

I squeezed some more oil into my hand and began to rub the scarred area at the base of Zack's spine. His upper body was powerful, but his lower spine was criss-crossed with scarring from botched surgeries that failed to fix what a drunk's car had done to him forty-three years ago when he was coming home from baseball practice.

I smoothed oil on the raised tissue of his scars. "What was Cristal like?"

"To be honest," he said. "I don't know. When I saw the tape of her with Ned, I was really surprised. Not at the sex, but at the way she was with him: affectionate, attentive, the kind of young wife he must have remembered. With me, there was none of that."

"What was she like with you?"

"She was exactly what I wanted. All business," he said wryly. "Your turn now." Zack pushed himself to a sitting position, then used his arms to inch himself back so the pillows piled against the headboard supported him. It was an awkward process, and once at the beginning of our marriage, I'd offered to help. He'd been curt, and I hadn't offered again.

When Zack was settled, he took a deep breath. "I'm ready.

Move on in." He picked up the massage oil I'd given him for his birthday. "Okay if I use this stuff or do you want some-thing else?"

I sniffed my fingers. "Rosemary, jasmine, and a hint of wood and ocean breeze. At least that's what the website promised. Can't ask for more than that." I removed my pyjama top. Zack kissed my shoulder. "Wood and ocean breezes aren't as sexy as the perfume you're wearing."

"I'm not wearing perfume," I said.

Zack kissed the hollow of my neck. "I hope you know I feel like shit about that relationship with Cristal."

I reached over and turned out the light. "It was another time," I said. "Everything's different now." I kissed him and slid down in the bed.

Zack moved beside me and caressed my breast. "You're going to miss out on your massage."

I slid my hand over his nipples. "A massage is only a massage," I said. "But a good cigar is a smoke."

Our lovemaking that night was urgent, as if we thought the heat of physical passion could burn away the ugliness of the last two hours. Usually, when the sex was that good, we both fell asleep afterwards, but that night, sleep did not come easily to me. I lay watching Zack's chest rise and fall and thought about our life together. We had both embarked on middle age when we met, but perhaps because it had been the right time for us both, we had negotiated the tricky labours of day-to-day life together with surprising ease. My first husband had been a politician, whose star was still rising when he was killed on a snowy Saskatchewan highway. We had a young family, and before his death, I was the woman behind the man. Suddenly, there was no man for me to stand behind. Initially, I was devastated, then I was terrified, but ultimately, I'd learned to stand alone. Zack had always been a lone wolf. Abandoned by his father, dismissed by his mother, until we met, his emotional life began and ended with his work and with the legal partners he'd known since their first year together at the College of Law. No one had been more surprised than we were when we fell in love.

Six months after we met, we were standing in front of the altar at St. Paul's Cathedral exchanging vows and wedding bands. As the dean pronounced us husband and wife, the old wives' warning crossed my mind: "Marry in haste, repent at leisure." For once, the old wives had been wrong. Until we met, Zack had travelled through life unencumbered, and I feared he would chafe at family life, but he gulped up domesticity like a starving man. Having kids, owning dogs, learning how to run a household were new adventures for Zack, but he wanted to be part of everything. Grateful for the sweetness of our new existence, we were careful never to let everyday contentment slip through our grasp. But that night, it wasn't the sweetness of the day that I remembered, it was Zack's bleak statement that we are hanged by the loose threads of our life. It was a truth I had seen played out too often, and despite the afterglow of lovemaking, I felt a thrill of existential terror. I moved closer to my husband, put my head on his chest, and listened to the rhythm of his heart until I, too, fell asleep.

The next morning when the dogs and I got back from our run, the newspaper was in the mailbox. I picked it up and headed for the back lawn so Willie and Pantera could rub some of the mud off their feet. While they chased each other around the yard, I scanned the *Leader-Post*. As they would for more days than anyone could have anticipated, Ginny Monaghan and Cristal Avilia dominated the front page.

The story about Ginny focused not surprisingly on her daughters. The paper had printed side-by-side photos of the

girls with each of their warring parents. The picture of
Ginny and her daughters had come from her campaign literature. The twins were immaculately groomed, but their
smiles were tight, and I remembered the misery of getting
our kids to pose for the requisite family campaign portrait.
The photo of the girls with Jason Brodnitz was a candid shot
of the three of them skiing, ruddy with cold and pleasure. In
the battle of the photo op, Ginny had lost round one.

There was no picture of Cristal Avilia, and the story was
sketchy on details – a thirty-four-year-old woman had
become the city's sixth homicide victim of the year. Cristal
Eden Avilia had been found dead outside her condo in the
warehouse district shortly after 6:00 p.m. Wednesday. The
police were not releasing the cause of death. Anyone with
information about her death was asked to call police.

I dropped the newspaper on the picnic table. No use starting the day with a reminder of the complexities of the outside
world. I called the dogs. "Come on, you two, let's go inside
and say good morning to our big sparkly top banana."

When I walked into the kitchen, it seemed the universe
was unfolding as it should. The coffee was brewed; the
juice was poured; the porridge was made; and Zack was
sitting at the breakfast table thumbing his BlackBerry,
wholly absorbed. I never tired of my husband's face. He was
a handsome man: balding, thick-browed, and dark-eyed,
with a generous, sensuous mouth and a vertical fold, like
a bloodhound, in his right cheek. In court he could freeze
an opponent with his barracuda smile, but at home his
mouth softened and his smile was melting. The dogs loped
over to him, and I kissed the top of his head. He flicked his
BlackBerry off. "Breakfast is ready, our daughter is safe in
her bed, and you and the dogs are here. Life is good."

"You bet," I said. I filled the dog bowls.

Zack watched with awe as Willie and Pantera inhaled their food. "Imagine loving any food as much as they love that stuff," he said.

"And it's the same thing, day in, day out." I read the label on the sack. "Ground yellow corn, poultry by-product meal, animal fat preserved with mixed-tochopherols, animal digest . . ."

Zack frowned. "What the hell is animal digest?"

"I don't know, and I don't want to know." I brought our coffee over to the table and began ladling out the porridge. "Mmm," I said. "Cashews – my lucky day. So what's with all the messages? It's only a little after seven."

Zack sipped his coffee. "It seems that Cristal had many clients. Judging from my messages, a lot of them are lawyers."

"If they're lawyers, why don't they talk to someone from their own firms?"

"Because the lawyers in their own firms are respectable, and they've done something they're ashamed of. Sometimes only the Prince of Darkness will do."

"Is that why Ned sought you out at the end?"

Zack sipped his coffee. "I guess, and isn't that a hell of a note? He'd been partners with Doug Meinhart and Gerry Loftus for fifty years, but when he decided to end his life he couldn't go to them because he'd indulged in a common sex act and some desperate fantasy." Zack drained his juice. "Not nice stuff, according to the rigorous standards of Osler Meinhart and Loftus. Do you know that every Friday for fifty years the partners and staff there have gathered in their boardroom to have a glass of pale amontillado sherry. Ned told me once they look forward to it all week. Jesus, what a bunch of bloodless sticks." Zack dug his spoon into his porridge. "Anyway, that explains why Ned came to me."

"Does it ever bother you that you're not Atticus Finch?"

Zack's spoon stopped in mid-air. "No, because I don't know who he is."

"The lawyer in *To Kill a Mockingbird*. Gregory Peck played him in the movie."

"Whoa, Gregory Peck." Zack's tone was sardonic. "So I'm guessing that Atticus Finch was noble, and that he won his case."

"No, he lost his case, but he lost nobly."

Zack swallowed his porridge. "Maybe if he'd been willing to get his hands dirty, he would have won."

I didn't respond, and Zack looked at me hard. "So does it bother you that I'm not Atticus Finch?"

I met his gaze. "I'm getting used to living on the edge," I said. "Want some toast?"

"No time. I have to be in court this morning. And I haven't quite figured out what I'm going to do."

"Is it a big case?"

Zack shook his head. "Nope. Simple assault. Remember that woman who punched the mayor in the nose? It was in the news a couple of months ago."

"The homeless woman," I said. "She was protesting the gentrification project in the warehouse district."

"Right," Zack said. "Well, that's my client. Her name is Francesca Pope, and she's schizophrenic. The day of the incident, she was off her meds. She is quite literally not guilty by reason of insanity. She really didn't understand what she was doing when she assaulted that officious prick."

"So you can get her off?"

"Without breaking a sweat, but therein lies the problem. If I argue she's unfit to stand trial, the Crown will go along with me, and she'll be committed to the hospital in North Battleford."

"Wouldn't that be the best thing for her? She'd be cared for, and she'd get treatment."

"And she'd be locked up, which is exactly what Francesca doesn't want because she's afraid they'll take her bears away."

"Her bears?"

"She has a backpack full of stuffed bears. She tells me they're called Care Bears."

"Mieka used to collect those when she was little."

"I hope they were in better shape than these. The smell of them just about knocks me out. But gross as they are, they are Francesca's treasure. Really, Jo, those Care Bears are like her kids. Try to think of it in those terms, and you can understand why she's so frightened of being locked up."

"But, Zack, if she's a danger . . ."

"She isn't. She's no more a danger than you are, but the mayor was annoyed because the bears were ruining his picture, so he kicked them out of the way."

"So you're going to try to get her off?"

"That's what she wants. The Crown will want to send her to North Battleford for treatment, but there aren't many spaces. She'll have to wait, and in the meantime she'll go to Pine Grove and be thrown in with the general population. She'll be housed and fed and her meds will be administered, but there'll be no treatment. Pine Grove is a tense place, Jo, full of people who are quick to judge and quick to take advantage – just about the worst possible atmosphere you could imagine for a schizophrenic."

"And the alternative is the street."

"Right, where there's no one to take care of her or make sure she has her medication, but where she will have her bears." Zack swept a hand across his eyes. "So which door would you choose, Ms. Shreve?

"I don't know," I said.

"Well, luckily it's not your problem," he said. "Anything going on tonight?"

"We have that meeting about the Farewell at Taylor's school."

"Jeez, I almost forgot. But I'm prepared. Taylor told me exactly how to vote."

I smiled. "Did she now? So, are you going to fill me in?"

"Let's see." Zack squeezed his eyes shut in concentration. "No on semi-formal dress because last year the boys kept pretending to hang themselves with their ties. No on a PowerPoint presentation of baby pictures, and no on having the principal read lame poems about the future. Yes on ham, yes on Nanaimo bars, and yes on getting the class picture taken at Waterfall Park."

"You're amazing," I said.

"Especially since when I was in Grade Eight, there weren't any ceremonies when we made it to high school. The teachers just booted us out the door."

"And look how well you turned out," I said.

"Any complaints?"

"Just the same old lament. I wish you didn't work so hard."

"I'm cutting back. I've turned down a couple of big cases lately."

"Alleluia," I said. "So are you finally going to start handing off some of your files to Sean?"

Zack shook his head. "No, not to Sean. I have somebody else in mind, but we haven't had a chance to talk, so nothing's official."

"That's a surprise," I said. "Have you told Sean?"

"Yeah. I told him last night when we were driving back from the cop shop."

"How did he take it?"

"Not great. He didn't throw me out of the car or anything, but he was disappointed."

"Understandably," I said. "I'm sure he thought he was the heir apparent. He's been working with you for a long time."

"True, and while he was working with me, I was able to get a pretty good idea of his capabilities."

"Good enough for an associate but not for a partner?"

"Yup. Sean is competent, but he's not partner material."

"That's sad," I said. "He's devoted to you."

"I'm not having him euthanized, Jo. As I reminded Sean last night, he has options. He can go to another firm or he can stay on as a senior associate at Falconer Shreve and eat what he kills."

"What does that mean?"

"Right now, Sean gets a percentage of his billables and if his billables are high, he gets a bonus. As a senior associate, he'd get to keep pretty much everything he brought in." Zack raised his hands, palms up. "He eats what he kills."

I shuddered. "That terminology's a little brutal, isn't it?"

Zack pushed his chair back from the table. "Life is brutal. Madeleine could tell you that. On the five occasions she and I watched *March of the Penguins*, she alerted me to the line, 'Not all penguins survive.'"

After we'd cleared away our breakfast things, Zack went to shower and dress and I went to Taylor's room to get her moving. She was a girl who loved creature comforts, and her bedroom caught the morning sun. Nested in her sheets with the sunshine warm on her face and her cats, Bruce and Benny, at her feet, Taylor had many reasons for staying in bed, but even more reasons for getting up. I kissed her hair. "Time to get up," I said.

She threw back her sheets and bolted upright. The hormones were kicking in. "Tonight's the meeting about the Farewell. I am soooooo excited."

"I guess we should start thinking about what you're going to wear," I said.

"I know what I'm not going to wear," Taylor said.

"That's a start," I said. "So what are you not going to wear?"

"The same thing everybody else is wearing: sparkly T-shirt, short ruffly skirt, and sandals with plastic flowers."

I sat on the bed beside her. "You sound like your mum. When we were in high school, we were both invited to the Battalion Ball at Upper Canada College. Your mother knew that all the girls would be wearing little pearl earrings, pearl necklaces, strapless pastel dresses with tulle skirts, and shoes with illusion heels so they wouldn't be taller than their dates.

Taylor moved closer. "So what did she wear?"

"A slinky black silk dress with a high neck and long sleeves. She also wore spike-heeled shoes that made her about six inches taller than the boy she was with. He didn't care. Every time he looked at her, he just about fainted because he couldn't believe he was with such a knockout."

It had been a long time since Taylor curled up on my knee, but that morning she put her arms around my neck and moved in close. "I guess you don't have a picture of her at that dance."

"No, Taylor, I don't. I've kept a lot of other pictures of your mum. Whenever you're ready to look at them, you let me know."

Taylor nodded. "I've always just liked looking at the art she made." She drew closer. "That's been enough."

For once, Taylor and I didn't hurry our time together. We each had our own thoughts, and we both realized moments like this had become finite. Taylor was the one who broke our reverie. "I'd better get ready for school," she said. "At the Farewell, I'm actually getting some dorky prize for attendance."

She started to leave, then stopped. "What did you wear to the dance?"

"Little pearl earrings, a pearl necklace, a strapless pastel dress with a tulle skirt, and illusion heels so I wouldn't be taller than my date."

Taylor's smile reflected both love and pity. I felt a pang. It was the smile her mother had given me a thousand times in the years when we were best friends.

When I came out of the shower, Taylor was in my bedroom dressed, munching a piece of toast with peanut butter, and looking critically at the outfit I'd planned to wear to court: a champagne blouse and slacks outfit that I'd loved for fifteen years.

"How come you're getting all dressed up today?" she asked.

"I'm going to court with Ginny Monaghan.

Taylor rolled her eyes. "Boy, you should hear the jokes the kids tell about her. They say she's a cougar."

"Nice," I said.

Taylor chewed thoughtfully. "It is kind of mean, isn't it? And you know, last night, she really did seem nice. None of the boys would dance with Gracie because she's so tall, and Ms. Monaghan told Gracie that it was great being tall – you could see more." Taylor turned her attention back to my clothes. "Is this what you're wearing?"

"I like it," I said.

"I like it too," Taylor said. "Except you wear it everywhere." She cocked her head. "That scarf Zack gave me for Christmas would make it look a little less . . ."

"Boring?"

Taylor raised an eyebrow. "I was going to say 'beige.'" She flashed off the bed and came back with her scarf: a Paul Klee print that was neither boring nor beige. She held it against the blouse. "Okay?"

"More than okay," I said. "Thanks. Now you'd better scoot. You don't want to forfeit your dorky prize."

I'd just opened my laptop to check out the press coverage of Ginny's case when the phone rang. It was Ed Mariani, sounding buoyant. "I know it's never too early to call you," he said. "You're like Barry – an early bird. After all that travelling yesterday, Barry was up at the crack of dawn, fresh as a daisy, doing his sit-ups. He still has a twenty-eight-inch waist. I tell him that, after the age of forty, no man but a drag queen has a twenty-eight-inch waist, but he just pats the place beside him on the mat and invites me to join him in a few stretches." Ed sighed. "As if I could. These days, even bending to tie a shoelace is a hero's journey for me. But I didn't call to whine. Your Martha Washington geraniums are ready to be hardened, and when Martha's ready, she's ready. Can I drop them by some time this morning?"

"Sure, but can you make it in the next hour? I promised Ginny Monaghan I'd be in court with her this morning."

"How come?"

"Quid pro quo. I'm going to stay with her campaign until E-Day, then use Ginny's experience for that script about women in politics I showed you."

"Shrewd move," Ed said. "What you wrote is thoughtful and well researched, but it's a little . . ."

"Beige?" I said.

Ed laughed. "Well, the exploits of a sexual swashbuckler would add colour."

"And make a point," I said. "Ginny seems to feel the rules for female swashbucklers are different from the rules for men."

"She's right, of course."

"I know she is," I said. "And because of her politics, she doesn't have a lot of natural allies."

"Including me," Ed said. "To be honest, Jo, when I saw her at the party, I was prepared to leave her a wide berth, but she was your guest, and you looked a little desperate. I thought I'd take her off your hands for a while, but I really liked her. Anyway, if you want some company today, I'd be happy to come. Take one for the team."

"Ginny's not on your team, Ed."

"Ah, Jo, you have no idea how large and varied our team is. The walking wounded cover the earth. The least we can do is offer one another a little support when the terrain is unfriendly."

CHAPTER

3

Half an hour later, I'd finished reviewing the media stories on Ginny Monaghan, and I was dressed and trying to find a lipstick that wasn't a stub. Taylor came back, ready for school, to give me a final inspection. "Cool," she said. "And that lipstick I gave you for Christmas would be perfect with that scarf."

"The lipstick in the gift with purchase?"

"It was full size," Taylor said. "Anyway, since you weren't using it, I kind of borrowed it back. Want me to get it?"

I held up the stub in my hand. "Anything's better than this," I said.

Taylor went to her room and came back triumphant. "Here," she said, handing me the lipstick. "It's called Tiger Eye – great colour, eh? And Mr. Mariani's outside with a ton of plants for you."

I took the lipstick. It was muted but managed to pick up the deep red in the scarf. "Perfect," I said. "Taylor, how do you know these things?"

Taylor scrunched her face in dismissal. "Everybody knows that stuff."

I filled in my lips and threw the lipstick into my handbag. "I owe you," I said "Now, let's go help Ed unload."

He was standing in the driveway with the trunk of his Buick popped and a tray of Martha Washingtons in his arms. The blossoms were dark red rimmed with silver. "Halos," I said. "My favourites."

"Wait till you see what I have for you out back."

Taylor picked up her backpack. "Can I look after school? I'm already late." She kissed Ed on the cheek, and he beamed.

"Aren't you and I about due for another evening of Barry's paella and some serious art talk?" he said.

"Definitely," Taylor said. "Except not this Saturday because it's Marissa's birthday party and not Friday because Isobel and Gracie are coming over to watch scary movies, but any other time is good."

"I'll look forward to it," Ed said. We watched her bounce off. "She's growing up," Ed said.

"High school next year."

"It all goes so quickly." Ed's smile was rueful. "Gather your Marthas while ye may."

"That's exactly what I'm doing," I said. I buried my nose in the foliage and inhaled the pungent scent of new growth and potting soil. "I love the smell of spring."

Ed's moon face split with a smile. "My grandmother called this the unlocking season: the ice cracks; the water begins to run; the sap flows; the ground warms; people throw open their windows and set out the porch furniture, and we're part of our neighbours' lives again."

"Whether they want us to be or not," I said.

Ed laughed. "True enough. "

Ed and I didn't dally over the Marthas. Courtroom C was small, so we knew that if we wanted a seat we'd have to be there early. As we entered the courthouse foyer, I glanced up at the Florentine glass mosaic that greeted everyone who came into the building.

Ed followed my gaze. "The God of Laws with his hand-maidens, Truth and Justice," he said.

"Let's hope they're on the job today," Zack said.

His voice caught me by surprise. "Where did you come from?" I said.

"This new chair of mine is called the stealth model," Zack said. He was wearing his barrister's robes and he was with his client.

It wasn't in Norine MacDonald's job description, but when it came to transforming bikers, slackers, punks, and hookers for their court appearance, Zack's executive assistant was a whiz. Zack said admiringly that Norine could make Darth Vader look like a guy who deserved a second chance, but Francesca Pope had clearly proven to be a challenge.

Francesca's clothes had been chosen to make her look respectable and responsible: a navy pantsuit, a crisp white blouse, and black walking shoes with a hard shine, but although it was a warm day, Francesca wore winter gloves and her thick grey hair was erratically hacked, as if someone had attacked it with dull scissors. She was calm, but her lips were moving silently in an internal monologue that seemed to absorb her. Zack introduced us matter-of-factly. "Francesca, this is my wife, Joanne, and the gentleman with her is our friend, Ed Mariani."

Francesca regarded us without interest. When Ed said hello, she nodded, but when I started to extend my hand, she shook her head violently. "I don't shake hands," she said. Her voice was surprisingly rich and assured, a singer's voice.

I withdrew my hand. "Well, good luck this morning," I said.

She nodded. "Thank you."

Zack touched her arm and smiled encouragement. "Time for us to go in," he said.

Francesca started to follow, then her face became animated. "Look over there," she said, pointing towards the door. The three of us turned and saw Ginny Monaghan coming in with Sean Barton. A couple of media people were pursuing them with cameras. Francesca stared at the group. Then she said, very loudly, "I know who you are."

"That's Ginny Monaghan," Zack said. "Her picture's been in the paper a lot lately." He touched Francesca's elbow again and steered her towards the courtroom. Francesca moved in the appropriate direction, but her head was still turned towards Ginny, and her face was dark with anger.

Ed nudged me. "What do you suppose that's all about?"

"I don't know," I said. "But I don't think Ginny's going to get Francesca's vote."

Court wasn't scheduled to start for fifteen minutes, but the room was already crowded. "Full house," Ed said sardonically. "Never underestimate the public's appetite for prurience."

I raised a mocking eyebrow. "Of course, our interest isn't prurient."

"But we're professionals. These other are . . ." He peered at the public benches. "Good grief. Who do you suppose all these people are?"

"Well, I recognize some of them," I said. "They're lawyers, and like my husband, they're courtroom junkies. If Zack doesn't have a case, he drifts in to watch somebody else's." I pointed to the front row. "There's space up there. Shall we give it a shot?"

We made our way up and discovered that, in true Canadian fashion, the spectators had presumed the empty front row was reserved. We took our places, and within seconds, Ginny Monaghan joined us. Her closely tailored pantsuit was the colour of dark honey and her creamy leather handbag matched her silk blouse. She was the epitome of assured success. She was also incredibly alone.

She brightened when she saw us. "Right on time," she said. "I'd planned to save you a place, Joanne, but it seems you beat me to it. And you brought Ed."

"To support you in any way I can," Ed said with a little bow. He lowered himself onto the bench and breathed with the pleasure of a big man who is finally off his feet. "As long as I can render my support from a seated position," he added.

I gestured to the lawyers' tables, where Sean was riffling through the papers he'd shaken from his briefcase. "I thought you'd be sitting up there with Sean," I said.

Ginny shook her head. "In this court, we don't sit with our lawyers. In fact, unless they're testifying, the parents don't even have to show up. Sean says a lot of lawyers are happier if their clients stay home. It seems parents have a tendency to micromanage their cases. I've promised to be a model client: legs crossed demurely at the ankle, hands folded in my lap, mouth zipped."

Sean's table was close, and when he heard Ginny's voice, he turned, winked at her, and gave Ed and me the thumbs-up sign. Obviously, he wasn't bearing a grudge about being passed over for partner, and I had my own reasons for being relieved.

Jason Brodnitz's lawyer, Margot Wright, was sitting at the table across from Sean. Even in her barrister's robes, Margot was a man-magnet. She was a true blonde, with shoulder-length, softly curling hair, creamy skin, and a dust of freckles across a nose that a romance novelist would describe as saucy. She had made flame-red lipstick and nails her trade-mark, and that morning, she was, as always, riveting, but it gave me no pleasure to acknowledge her charms.

One night at a banquet for a retiring judge, Margot and I had had an encounter in the ladies room. She had been drunk. After she'd told me more than I cared to know about Zack's romantic adventures before we met, she assured me that like every woman before me, I would be dumped.

Later, when she defended an old friend of mine, I came to respect Margot as a lawyer, but in my personal pantheon, she was still a question mark. Contemplating her history with my husband was not pleasant, so I turned back to Ginny.

"So what happens?" I said. "I don't know much about custody trials."

"Jason and I testify. Then it's on to the girls' teachers, whom I've never met; the principal of their school, whom I've also never met; the girls' basketball coach, with whom I showered after a fundraiser for their school gym. Then the experts Jason and I hired to produce favourable assessments of our parenting skills testify. Then the court-appointed social worker reports on her talk with the girls. After hearing all that, the judge makes her decision."

"Your daughters don't have to testify," Ed said, and his relief was palpable.

"No," Ginny said. "We at least spared them that." Her shoulders slumped, and for a beat, her mask of invulnerability slipped. Then the court clerk entered.

"All rise. Court is now in session. Madam Justice Susan Gorges presiding." Madam Justice Gorges, a petite woman wearing the black and red robe of a Queen's Bench judge, strode into the court.

"Do you know her?" Ginny whispered.

"No," I said. "But Zack says she runs a tight ship."

"Good," Ginny said. "Because nobody wants this to drag on."

Ginny was the first to testify. Not surprisingly, for a woman whose moves had been scrutinized since she was a seventeen-year-old bounding across the basketball court, she was a good witness. Head high, spine straight, she delivered her testimony clearly and factually. Sean phrased his questions about her work schedule in a way that allowed her to talk about the projects involving women and children that had been among her initiatives as minister of Canadian heritage and the status of women. She confronted the fact that the girls lived with their father head-on, explaining that she had given the twins the option of moving to Ottawa, but that they'd decided to stay in Regina and start high school with their friends. They had chosen a private school with an excellent reputation for academics and sports. Ginny had attended the school herself, so she had agreed. She said she came back to Regina as many weekends as she could manage, but cabinet business often kept her in Ottawa. Then she pointed out that Jason had become a stay-at-home father through necessity rather than choice. Business reverses had forced him to close his office and work from home. "Like many couples," Ginny said, "our child-care decision was dictated by finances. I didn't choose to stay away from my girls any more than Jason chose to stay home with them. It just worked out that way."

Sean finished by asking Ginny how she would characterize her relationship with her daughters. Surprisingly, Ginny seemed taken aback at the question. "I'm not a milk-and-cookies mother, if that's what you mean. But Em and Chloe are strong, independent girls. They can get their own milk and cookies."

When Margo approached the witness box, she and Ginny eyed each other warily, taking each other's measure. Successful and assured, they were, in every essential way, alike, but that didn't keep Margot from going for the jugular.

"Ms. Monaghan, you say you're not a milk-and-cookies mother. No one would dispute the fact that the work you do is important or that it's time-consuming. That said, women in our generation are fortunate. We have options. We can be

prime minister; we can be milk-and-cookie mothers."
Margot glanced at Madam Justice Gorges. "We can even be
Queen's Bench judges." After Susan Gorges favoured her
with what might have passed for a smile, Margot continued.
"Ms. Monaghan, no one questions your right to be politically active, but you're here today seeking custody of your
daughters, so the court has a right to know how involved
you are in your daughters' lives."

"They're fourteen years old," Ginny said. "They have
lives of their own."

Margot permitted herself a small smile. "Still, fourteen-
year-olds aren't allowed to live on their own." She paused. "Of
course, they don't live alone, do they? They live with their
father. My client has made a home for Emma and Chloe."

"A home that I subsidize." Ginny shifted her gaze to Jason
Brodnitz. "My ex-husband has suffered some serious business reverses. I also pay for the girls' school."

Ed leaned towards me. "Did you know that?"

"No," I whispered. "And judging from the fire in Margot's
eye, she didn't know it either."

Margot might have been taken aback, but she recovered
quickly. "You wouldn't dispute the fact that my client is the
parental presence in the home."

"Because he has the time," Ginny said coldly. "And, Ms.
Wright, I am present in my daughters' lives: I talk to them
every night."

"From four thousand kilometres away."

"If the need arises, I can be in Regina in five hours."

"Did you come home when Em broke her arm?"

"No. It was a clean break."

"And you were in Puerto Vallarta with a male friend."

"Yes."

"Did you come home last year when Chloe had her appen-
dix out?"

"Yes."

"On a direct flight from Ottawa?"

"No. I stopped in Toronto overnight."

"Were you alone?"

"No. I spent the night with a friend."

"A male friend?"

"No. Female."

Margot shook her head. "Girls' night out, huh? How about when you're in Regina? Are your daughters with you then?"

"Yes. They stay in the apartment with me."

"And you're there with them all night."

"As a rule, yes."

"I understand there was an incident when Em awoke in the middle of the night vomiting and you weren't there."

"Chloe called me on my cell, and I was home in twenty minutes."

"Were you with a lover?"

Years in politics had taught Ginny how to sidestep land-mines. "As I said, I was home in twenty minutes."

Jason Brodnitz fared better in the witness box than his ex-wife had. Slender, physically graceful, grey hair cut very short, he bore an uncanny resemblance to the actor Richard Gere. Jason might have suffered business reverses, but the lightweight, single-breasted suit he was wearing hadn't come off the rack, and he moved to the witness box with the assurance of a man who expected to do well.

I wasn't an expert, but it seemed to me Margot had done a better job of preparing her client than Sean had. She made no attempt to present Jason as anything other than what he was. She dealt with the question of his financial difficulties head-on, and he was matter of fact in explaining that while his client base had diminished after he'd made some bad investments, he was turning the situation around. Like his ex-wife, Jason had missed his share of large events in the lives of his daughters, but Margot offset that by encouraging him to talk about the events he had attended: the vacations he'd shared with the twins, and the daily routine of life in the Brodnitz house. The life he described wasn't *Father Knows Best*, but it wasn't neglect. The only tense moment came when Margot asked him about his own romantic life. Before answering, Jason shot his wife a glance that seemed pleading. Then he said that he and his ex-wife had been living separately for several years and that he had the normal instincts of a healthy man his age. Sean's cross-examination was perfunctory, but Ginny didn't seem troubled by the lack of rigour. When Jason returned to his seat, Ginny seemed to relax. "Well, it could have been worse," she said.

When Madam Justice Susan Gorges declared a recess for lunch, Margot and her client exchanged smiles. He helped her off with her barrister's robe; she flung it over the back of her chair, revealing a smart red suit that showed off her terrific legs; and she and Jason headed for the exit.

Ed touched Ginny's arm. "Would you like to join us for lunch?" he asked.

"I'll have to take a rain check," Ginny said. "Sean wants to talk to me about what's happening this afternoon."

Ed smiled "Well, a Mariani rain check is redeemable any time."

"I'll remember that," Ginny said, and she seemed surprisingly touched.

We ate at Java Deposit, a coffee place that had once been a bank on the main floor of an office tower near the courthouse. The building was full of lawyers, including my husband's firm, and whenever court was recessed for lunch, Java Deposit was packed.

As Ed and I came through the door, a server with a sneer pushed his way towards us. There was, he said, a small table vacant inside the vault, but if we wanted it, we'd have to move quickly.

We moved. After we'd elbowed our way to our table, explored the menu, squirmed to make ourselves comfortable on our dainty wrought-iron ice-cream chairs, and settled in to wait for the reappearance of our server, we looked at each other.

"Why did we come here?" Ed asked.

"Because Falconer Shreve's new offices are upstairs and they have some art you ought to see."

"Reason enough," Ed said. "I never thought these words would pass my lips, but let's eat fast." He sighed. "So why did Falconer Shreve move? Their offices in those two old houses were charming."

"I agree, but the firm has plans to expand, and the old place just wasn't big enough for extra people."

"So is Zack pleased with the move?"

I shrugged. "It doesn't affect him much. When he's not in court, he works at home most of the time now."

"And you work at home too."

"As much as I can manage," I said. "Zack and I like being together. So everybody's happy, especially Pantera, because it turns out he's afraid of elevators."

Ed's eyes widened. "Am I missing something here?"

"Pantera goes nuts if he can't be with Zack, so he always went to the old office. The day Falconer Shreve moved here, Pantera trotted off happily with Zack. For some reason, the elevators spooked him. Zack brought in a dog trainer, but nothing helped, so Pantera retired."

"I take it Zack isn't planning to follow suit."

"He keeps promising he'll cut down," I said. "At the Bar Association Christmas party, someone told me that the average time between a trial lawyer's first case and his first heart attack is twenty years. Zack's already had five years grace, and his paraplegia doesn't increase the odds in his favour."

"Still, he took on Francesca Pope's case, and I would have expected a kid from Legal Aid to handle that one."

Our server came, and Ed and I ordered the special. As the server began pushing his way towards the kitchen, Ed was lugubrious. "I don't hold out much hope for the Italian wedding soup. That takes a knowing hand."

"Well, nobody can screw up bruschetta," I said.

Ed sniffed. "That remains to be seen."

"What do you know about the Francesca Pope case?" I said.

"Not much," Ed said. "One of the students in my Documentary Theory and Production class started to do a piece on it, but he hadn't finished when he decided to drop out, move to Alberta, and make his fortune in the oil fields. All I know is that the mayor and a clutch of civic leaders were in the warehouse district congratulating one another for their gentrification project when a scuffle broke out and Francesca Pope broke His Honour's nose."

"And, of course, with Francesca's invariable bad luck, the cameras were rolling," I said.

"I saw the footage," Ed said. "Zack's client looked pretty disturbed."

"She was disturbed. She was off her medication. The mayor and his cronies were in her neighbourhood, or what used to be her neighbourhood, and the mayor had kicked her backpack out of the way because it would have looked unsightly in the pictures."

"If the mayor thought a backpack was unsightly, I wonder how he feels about a murder in one of his shining condos," Ed said. "The dead woman's fellow condo owners certainly aren't happy."

My pulse quickened. "Do you know someone who lives in the Pendryn?"

"Yes, our friend David Schaub. Barry and I were at a party there not too long ago. It's quite an experience. There's all that drama about entering through the freight elevator, then the doors open and you step into a dream. The whole place is open-concept, twenty-four-foot vaulted ceilings and skylights, a huge stretch of the original brick in the living room, and two very large, very private balconies. The view of the city from the bedroom just about stopped my heart. As, of course, it should for $629,000."

"That's pricey for Regina," I said.

"The building caters to a very special clientele."

"What do you mean?"

"People buy into that particular building because of the privacy. Most of the other warehouses that have been converted are close to Albert Street, but the Pendryn is the only building in a three-block area that's been restored. There's a courtyard with a pool and an exquisite little Japanese garden, but it's cut off from the rest of the neighbourhood by security fences topped with razor wire."

I made a face. "Not very neighbourly."

"The people who live in there aren't eager to see the welcome wagon. They're willing to pay for the privilege of doing what they want to do – no questions asked."

"By other tenants?"

"By anybody. I have a nagging suspicion that there's more to Francesca Pope's case than meets the eye."

"Based on what?"

"Based on the fact that your husband is representing Francesca. Zack's the most expensive trial lawyer in the province. And you know the old journalists' axiom: follow the money. It would be interesting to know who's paying the tab."

I glanced at my watch. "If we ever get served, you can ask Zack yourself. He usually stops by his office over the lunch recess, and we're going up to Falconer Shreve to look at the art anyway."

Ed squirmed on his chair. "No food. No service. And chairs that seem to be intended for dolls. Let's cross this place off our list, shall we?"

"Consider it done," I said.

Falconer Shreve's offices were on the fifteenth floor. The elevator was mirrored, and as Ed caught sight of himself reflected repeatedly from every angle, he sighed. "I understand Pantera's misery about being in this elevator. These Andy Warhol repetitions of my bulk make me want to howl too."

"We're the only ones in the elevator," I said. "Go for it."

The elevators opened directly into the firm's reception area, where hard-polished floors gleamed and walls painted the gentle shade of old silver perfectly complemented two large, eye-catching works: a shimmering metallic drape by Miranda Jones and an intricately painted Ted Godwin tartan.

At her low glass desk in front of the tartan, Denise Kaiswatum was simultaneously signing for a package, taking a telephone call, and smiling reassuringly at a frightened and unhappy-looking woman. When the courier left, Denise hung up the phone, directed the unhappy woman to the client waiting room, and gave Ed and me an apologetic smile.

"You just missed Zack," she said. "He came in to check his messages, then he and his client went back to court."

"Is it all right if I give Ed the art tour?"

Blake Falconer came out of his office. When he spotted us, he came over. At Zack's party, Blake had looked careworn, but he seemed restored this morning. He was past fifty, and his reddish gold hair was greying, but he kept it scrub-brush short and his skin was ruddily freckled and youthful. He extended his hand to Ed. "Good to see you again," he said.

"I was hoping we'd get a chance to talk last night, but Ginny Monaghan seemed to be enjoying your company, and we try to keep our clients happy."

"Very wise," Ed said. "And luckily, I have no need of a lawyer. I'm just here to see the Falconer Shreve collection."

"I can take you around," Blake said. "I know nothing about art, but I've been with land developers all morning, I could use a break."

Blake hadn't exaggerated when he said he didn't know anything about art, but as he filled us in on Falconer Shreve's future plans and pointed out the new pieces, he was thorough if not inspired. That changed when he led us into the boardroom to see the Joe Fafard ceramic group portrait of the founding members of Falconer Shreve. "I must have seen this a hundred times since it arrived, but it gets me every time," he said and his eyes were moist. "Anyway, that's us – the way we were the year we graduated from the College of Law."

I turned to Ed. "They called themselves the Winners' Circle."

"Because we were perfect in every way," Blake said. "Or so we thought."

"Zack told me that when he was invited to join the Winners' Circle, he was like a drunk discovering Jesus," I said. "Dazzled. Born again."

Ed leaned in to look more closely at the witty figures of the founding five. Fafard had worked from a photograph taken on the day they'd graduated. They were wearing their academic robes: it had been windy and the robes swirled. "My God, Fafard's good," Ed said. "You can feel the wind at their backs." He looked more closely at the young faces. "You can see the hope."

Ed gazed at the expensively appointed boardroom. "It appears the Winners' Circle realized its promise."

Blake shrugged. "Appearance is not reality," he said. "Let's go look at the big man's office."

"Saving the best till last," Blake said, but when he tried the door, it was locked. "Shit," he said. "I should have remembered that Zack has a client who refuses to leave the office until she knows her possessions are safe. I'll get the key from Norine."

Francesca's backpack with her bears was on one of the client chairs. Everything in Zack's office had the high sheen of money and attention; Francesca's bears were refugees from a sadder, crueller world. For a time when she was little, Mieka had collected Care Bears. With their cotton-candy-coloured furry bodies and the cartoon portraits proclaiming their identity and their special caring mission on their tummies, these emissaries from the cloud-land of Care-a-Lot had always struck me as too cute by a half. There was nothing cute about Francesca's bears. Their fur was mildewed, patchy, and filthy; their faces and feet had been eaten away by rot or rats; and most of them were missing eyes or noses.

As he gazed at them, Ed's face was suffused with pity. "What's the story there?"

"That's her treasure," Blake said thoughtfully. "Zack says when the mayor kicked Francesca's backpack, she felt as if he was kicking her children."

"So she was trying to protect them," Ed said.

"We all do terrible things for love," Blake said. "At least Francesca still has her bears."

"Blake, how did Zack end up with her case?" I said. "It's not the kind of thing he usually handles – it's not high profile, and I'm guessing it's not big money."

Blake's answer was a beat too quick. "Just doing a favour for a friend," he said. He took Ed's arm and led him to the Ernest Lindner watercolour of a moss-covered stump behind Zack's desk. "Give this one a closer look," he said. "I didn't see much here at first, but Joanne got me interested." He turned to me. "This is called high realism, right?"

"Right," I said.

"Lindner was fascinated by the process of decay and regeneration in the natural world," Blake said. "At least that's what Joanne told me." His smile was bashful, the schoolboy found out showing off, but I wasn't deflected.

"So who was the friend who got Zack to take on Francesca Pope's case?" I asked. "One of your developers with a heart of gold?"

Blake averted his eyes. "No. The friend was me." He glanced at his watch. "God, look at the time. I've got a meeting. Have fun." He kissed my cheek and pressed the key into my hand.

As Blake passed Ed, he patted his shoulder. Then, except for the lingering woody scent of his aftershave, Blake was gone.

"There's a man living a lie," Ed said.

"What do you mean?" I asked. I was surprised. Ed was careful with language and careful with assessments. "Blake's had his problems, like all of us, but I would say he's a lucky man."

Ed's face was troubled. "Maybe once upon a time," he said. "Not any more." Ed pointed to the intricate whorl at the heart of the fallen tree in Lindner's watercolour. "Look at that," he said. "Even with trees, destiny unfolds from the heart."

Unlike Zack, I tend to drift off during trials. As a citizen I'm grateful that the wheels of justice grind exceedingly fine, but as a spectator, I'm aware only that at times they grind exceedingly slow. I knew that the outcome of the Monaghan-Brodnitz custody deliberations would alter the lives of Ginny, Jason, and their daughters, but that afternoon with the sun slanting through the courtroom windows, the air warming, and the lawyers wrangling about procedure and reading the law into the record, I found my eyes growing heavy. The parade of witnesses who marched up to be sworn in did nothing to stir my blood. In their civilian lives, these good people might have been witty and incisive, but the demands of testifying stripped them of individuality and muffled their voices in a thick fog of clichés and buzzwords. As an earnest young social worker who didn't look old enough to flip burgers explained in jargon-riddled detail the difference between being an enabling parent and an empowering parent, Madam Justice Gorges's sigh of impatience was audible. I wasn't surprised when at a little after four, she declared that court was recessed.

The scene that greeted me after Ed dropped me off at home was a familiar one. Taylor and Gracie Falconer were sitting at the kitchen table, deep in conversation, with a carton of Ben and Jerry's Cherry Garcia between them. I liked all of Taylor's friends, but Gracie was a favourite. Bouncy with mischief and energy, her skin ruddy and sprayed with freckles, Gracie's sunny exuberance lit up a room. She was fun to have around.

"So what are you two up to?" I said.

Gracie held out her spoon. "Pounding calories," she said. "I refuse to read what the carton says about the percentage of fat in this, but after basketball, I am so hungry."

"How's your team doing?" I asked.

"Great. Of course, we have the miraculous Brodnitz twins to save us from disaster and show us how the game is played. At least that's what Coach tells us four hundred times a practice." Gracie dug her spoon viciously into the ice cream and raised her voice. "'Young women, if you're serious about the game, watch Em and Chloe. They know how to win.

They always respond to the challenge. They never give an inch until the final buzzer sounds. They're fearless. They pay the price without whimpering. They always give 110 per cent because they know no one ever drowned in sweat. And they know how to focus.'"

Gracie had a talent for mimicry, and as she ripped through the hoary sports clichés, Taylor chortled. I laughed too. Encouraged, Gracie carried on barking in high coach mode. "'Em and Chloe don't look to me to tell them what to do. They've assumed responsibility for their own games. That's maturity. That's what makes a winning athlete.'" Gracie pulled her spoon out of the ice cream and licked the fudge meditatively. "The coach totally *worships* those girls, but they're not human. Even when they get hurt or they get a bad call or the crowd yells at them, they remember to focus, focus, focus. I think they're robots."

"Maybe they just hold everything inside," Taylor said.

Gracie nodded. "That's exactly what they do. A couple of weeks ago, I forgot my watch after practice. When I went back to the change room to look for it, Chloe was sitting on the bench crying. She'd taken this really punishing fall during the game, and I asked if I could help. She just about took my head off! She said she was fine, she didn't need anybody. Then she jumped up and hobbled off."

When I came out of the shower that night, Zack was already in bed, working on his laptop.

He patted the spot beside him on the bed. "Take a look at this," he said.

I got into bed and slid over. The Care Bear website was on the screen. There were postage-stamp-sized pictures of each bear and, at the bottom, a note. I read it aloud. "Wherever the Care Bears go, and whatever the Care Bears do, in their soft, fuzzy, and funny way, they share their special gift of caring with everyone they meet." I shuddered. "That makes my teeth ache."

"Mine too," Zack said. "But my job is to be Francesca's advocate and her adviser. I'm supposed to understand what she wants and what she needs, and I haven't got a clue." He turned off his laptop and moved it to his night table. "I've been able to figure out ways to make justice serve the needs of psychos, sickos, and run-of-the-mill sons of bitches, but Francesca has me stymied."

"What's going to happen to her?"

"Well, I'm pretty sure I can convince the judge that locking Francesca up is not in her best interests or in the best interests of the community, but my client is going to have to control herself."

"Has that been a problem?"

"Not in the courtroom – at least not yet – but there was another incident in the courthouse when we came back for the afternoon session."

"What happened?"

"I'm still trying to figure that out. After I took Francesca back to the office to show her that her bears were safe, we had to deal with lunch – not a simple matter as it turned out. Francesca can't eat indoors because the artificial light makes her head buzz, so Norine ordered some sandwiches for us to take to the park. Anyway, Francesca and I had a nice time, listening to the traffic and the birds. She was relaxed, and she was lucid. I thought she was in great shape to prove to the judge that she could live safely in the community."

I hugged my knees to my chest. "So what went wrong?"

"I honestly don't know," Zack said. "When we were coming back into the courthouse, we ran into Ginny and Sean, and Francesca went nuts. She started screaming."

"What was she saying?"

"Two things, over and over. 'I know who you are,' and 'I know what you did.' Sean tried to hustle Ginny away, but Francesca clawed at him. The security guy was on his way over. I didn't want that, so I told Sean to get Ginny out of there. Once they were gone, Francesca calmed down."

"Did you ask her why she's so angry at Ginny?"

"No, because I didn't want another outburst. But I did tell her that she was going to have to control herself if she wanted to keep living on her own on the street with her bears."

"How *does* she live, Zack?"

"Handouts. Her new neighbours give her money – guilt, I guess. The gentrification of the neighbourhood has pushed people like Francesca out of their little warrens."

"So she gets by."

"Yes," Zack said. "She gets by."

"And you're acting for her pro bono."

Zack met my gaze. "No, the file is being billed at the usual rate."

"So who's picking up the tab?"

Zack's smile was wry. "I've been waiting for that question. If you'd asked me yesterday, I could have told you I didn't know, and that would have been the truth."

"But now you do know," I said.

"Yes, Blake called just before you got home. He said you'd been by the office, and that you might bring up the subject of billing. Blake thought you should know that the person who was paying for Francesca's defence was Cristal Avilia." Zack shifted his body so we were face to face. "I know it's hard to believe, but I honestly wasn't aware of this till this afternoon."

"How could you not know?" I said.

Zack shrugged. "Law firms have people who take care of billing. That's their job. My job is to get the best possible outcome for my clients. Period."

"And nobody ever told you that a woman you'd been intimate with was paying the shot for a case you were handling?"

"Blake was the only person who knew there was a connection between Cristal and me. As long as the money was handled according to Hoyle, it didn't matter. Money laundering is a huge issue for law firms and for the Law Society, so we're careful. If a client wants to pay cash, both the client and a representative from the firm have to sign the receipt. If a client pays by a cheque, a credit card, or debit card, the account number can be traced. And it's not just the Law Society who has an interest in this. It's us, the partners. The money for legal services has to be accounted for. If it isn't, we breach our partnership agreement." He looked at me hard. "Too much information?"

"No," I said. "Not enough information. Blake brought the case to you, but you were the one who knew Cristal. Why didn't she get in touch with you herself?"

"Because I'd stopped seeing her, and Blake hadn't."

"Blake was seeing Cristal too?"

"Yes." Zack reached down and rubbed my foot. "Aren't you going to say anything?"

"I don't know what to say. Gracie was here this afternoon. The idea of her father spending time with a high-priced escort is pretty repellent."

"You know what Blake's marriage to Lily was like," Zack said. "He had this aching love for her, and half the time he didn't know where she was or who she was with."

"So he found solace with Cristal."

"Apparently."

"And he was still finding solace with Cristal when she died."

"Yes."

"I don't get it," I said. "Lily's been dead for almost two

years. Blake's alone. He's good-looking; he's successful; he's charming. Without even trying, I can name a dozen women who'd be delighted to be with him. Why would he still be paying for sex?"

"I don't know. I don't know if he even had sex with Cristal."

"Then what was he paying for?"

Zack dropped his eyes. "Intimacy? Blake's relationship with Lily just about killed him. If he hadn't had Gracie, I suspect he would have just checked out." Zack ran his hand across his head. "Jo, I'm not a shrink. Blake and I are probably as close as two guys can be, but even when I could see that Lily's infidelity was destroying him, I never brought up the subject."

"So he carried all that inside him," I said.

"Apparently not," Zack said. "He told me this afternoon that he talked to Cristal about it. I guess he talked to Cristal about a lot of things. Go figure. Blake's surrounded by people who love him, and he still has to pay for a friend."

"Zack, did Blake say why Cristal paid for Francesca Pope's defence?"

Zack's face relaxed. "Actually, that's a question I can answer. According to Blake, Cristal wanted to help Francesca because Francesca was being dicked around by men. Cristal said she knew what that was like."

"So she was just being a good Samaritan?"

Zack shook his head. "No. Francesca wasn't a stranger to her. There's a little shed at the back of the warehouse next to Cristal's condo. It's one of Francesca's favourite haunts. It's abandoned, so nobody cares that she's there."

"Francesca and Cristal were neighbours."

"Oh, I think it went beyond that," Zack said. "According to Blake, Cristal gave him a very large retainer and told him she'd pay whatever it took to keep Francesca free."

CHAPTER

4

Saskatchewan is one of the few places in North America that does not spring forward for daylight saving time. In May, the time difference between Toronto and Regina is two hours. When she'd lived in Saskatchewan, Jill Oziowy and I ran together at five-thirty in the morning. She knew my schedule and, after she moved to Toronto, she often called while I was tying my running shoes.

As always, Jill wasted no time on preamble. "What do you know about the murder of that escort in the warehouse district?"

Jill and I had been friends for thirty years, but I wasn't ready to spill the beans on this one. "The escort's name was Cristal Avilia. Her condo cost close to three-quarters of a million dollars, and her clients paid $500 an hour, more for 'special requests.'"

Jill groaned. "If I'd wanted a précis, I'd have called our newsroom. I want deep background, scurrilous details, unsubstantiated rumours, blood, gore – the works."

"I've told you everything I can."

"Zack's firm is involved in the case?"

"Jill . . ."

"Okay, I'll back off. But for the record, we had more fun before you were married to a lawyer."

"I didn't have more fun."

"All right. But if you learn anything that's going to become public knowledge anyway, I get first dibs."

"Jill, why is the network so interested in this case? Prostitution is a dangerous business. The death of a single sex-trade worker doesn't usually attract national attention."

"You're not going to like the answer. It's money. Cristal Avilia wasn't a strung-out fifteen-year-old in the core turning tricks to pay for drugs. From what we hear, Cristal was the crown jewel of your local escort scene, and her contact list contained some fascinating clients."

"Come on, Jill. This is Regina."

"Take a look around you. There's crude oil in them thar hills – also uranium, potash, diamonds, and gold. Plus B-moviemakers who love those big prairie skies and govern-ment tax breaks. These days the hotel rooms in Saskatchewan are filled with guys with fat wallets who've already checked out the options on pay-per-view."

"So they hire a call girl?"

"They hire, and I'm quoting from an escort ad in your city, 'an escort who can give them a moment that they will cherish forever.' That means a woman who will slide her legs around theirs on the elevator, be the perfect companion at the corporate cocktail party, then go back to their hotel room and fake an orgasm that will make them believe they haven't lost their manly powers."

"That's a pretty tall order."

"Read the ads. Better yet, talk to somebody who knows the world. Escort services are the universal panacea. Anyway, my spidey sense is tingling about this Cristal Avilia case. I think it's going to be big. We've got some eager young thing looking into it, but you have some useful connections, and you might as well earn some brownie points if we're going to pitch your Issues for Dummies series."

"A trade-off," I said.

"Life's full of them," Jill said cheerfully. "Get on it."

Zack had already left for a breakfast meeting when I got back from my run. I was relieved. I didn't want to keep Jill's call secret, but I also didn't want start my day with Zack talking about Cristal Avilia. Ed Mariani was a different matter. I was picking him up, so we'd just take one car downtown, and as soon as he settled in the passenger seat and snapped his seat belt, I pounced.

"Jill called this morning. She thinks the Cristal Avilia murder is going to be big news."

"Jill's right," Ed said. "If I were more ambitious, I'd be out there knocking on doors and making phone calls."

"Where would you start?"

"With her client list."

"That's exactly what Jill said, but I don't imagine the police are handing out copies."

"No, but other people might know who her regulars were."

"Other people, meaning other escorts?"

"Yes."

"Can you suggest anybody I could talk to?"

"Why this sudden interest in the Cristal Avilia murder?"

"I honestly don't know. Jill says that if I come up with something, NationTV will be more inclined to green-light my issues series. But it's not just that. When Jill and I were talking, it occurred to me that I know nothing about the lives of those women, and I should."

"I'm not sure I agree," Ed said. "Slapping a genteel title on the job doesn't change the fact that escorts work in the sex trade. It's not a pretty world, Jo. People get hurt. Look at what happened to Cristal Avilia."

"I'm just going to ask some questions, Ed."

Ed was silent until we drew near the courthouse. "All right," he said finally. "I'll arrange for you to meet someone." He smiled. "Her name is Vera Wang."

"As in Vera Wang, the designer of bridal gowns?"

"No, as in Vera Wang, the woman who, until she retired, ran a discreet escort service that served two generations of our most prominent citizens."

"And she chose Vera Wang as her *nom de guerre*?"

"No, it's her birth name. Vera's my neighbour, and she's quick to point out that Vera Wang the designer was born on June 27, 1949, and that she herself was born on March 4, 1940. She had the name first. Want me to call her?"

"Please," I said. "She sounds intriguing."

"Oh she's that and a bag of chips," Ed said.

By the time I found a parking spot, Ed had arranged for me to meet Vera Wang later in the week. When he clicked off his cellphone, Ed's expression was theatrically lugubrious. "The deed is done," he intoned. "There is no turning back."

When we walked into court, Ginny Monaghan was sitting next to her ex-husband, with her arm resting on the bench behind him and her lips close to his ear. Even from a distance, it was clear their conversation was intense. Ed and I took our place in the front row and waited. Ginny was quick to join us. Her smile as she greeted us was edgy.

"Guess where I spent the night?" She waved her hand in dismissal. "No, don't guess. I was in the emergency ward with Chloe. She cut herself – deliberately."

Ed's face drooped with concern. "Is she all right?"

"She's fine," Ginny said tightly. "The doctor I spoke to was most reassuring. Luckily for me, Dr. Dolcetti is a supporter, so he won't feel compelled to blab to the media."

"No doctor would do that," I said.

Ginny rolled her eyes. "You live in an innocent world, Joanne. There's always a way to get damaging news to the public. Anyway, Chloe's fine. Dr. Dolcetti talked to her, then he talked to me. He says the cutting wasn't a suicide attempt, just a way of relieving pressure."

Ed frowned. "What did she use?"

"A box cutter that she took from her father's house. Anyway, the wounds weren't deep, and according to the good doctor, Chloe's cuts didn't indicate that she meant business."

"So this was just a warning."

"The doctor seemed to think so. He was puzzled because typically adolescents make cuts on their arms, and Chloe's cuts were on her stomach. When I explained that Chloe was a basketball player with a charity game coming up this week, he seemed reassured."

"Did she talk to you about why she did it?" I asked.

Ginny's eyes tracked away. "She said it was a mistake, and it wouldn't happen again."

"That's a good sign," I said.

"It would be if I believed her." Ginny raked her fingers through her hair. "It's not that I think she's lying. It's just that I didn't see this coming. She and Em have always handled everything so well. Maybe we expect too much of them."

I remembered Gracie's poignant sketch of the lives of the miraculous Brodnitz twins. "I'm not minimizing this," I said, "but at least Chloe has let you know she is in trouble."

Ginny nodded. "That's pretty much what Dr. Dolcetti said. He also pointed out that cutting is a fairly common phenomenon for girls her age. Apparently, it offers them some way of coping with the pressures of their lives."

"But you're still worried," Ed said.

"Wouldn't you be?"

"Of course," Ed said. "Did Dr. Dolcetti suggest anything?"

"He's getting us a referral to a psychologist who specializes in adolescents. Of course, it'll be six months before Chloe gets in. Till then, I guess we just have to muddle through." Her eyes travelled away again. "Today's the day the court-appointed social worker delivers her 'Voices of the Children' report. I guess Chloe was overwhelmed by the prospect of knowing that what she said about her father and me would be read out in court."

"Does it have to be read publicly?" Ed said.

"It's a public document," Ginny said. "In my opinion, it's not worth the paper it's printed on. Do you know how long the social worker talked to our girls? Three hours. Three hours to ferret out the truth about Jason's and my lifestyles, assess the stability of the environments we offer the girls, evaluate the emotional ties the girls have to each of us, and form an opinion about whether Jason and I are capable of fostering a healthy relationship between our daughters and the parent who doesn't get custody." Ginny's half-smile was withering. "Three hours to analyze their lives and decide their future – Jason says we shouldn't be surprised that Chloe panicked. He says she didn't have enough time to say what she needed to say and the cutting was her way of making us hear her voice loud and clear."

"So he knows," I said.

"I told him," Ginny said. "Against the advice of my lawyer."

"Sean has to consider all the possibilities," I said. "Jason could use this against you."

"He could," Ginny said. "But he wouldn't."

Ed moved closer to her. "You sound very certain."

Ginny met his gaze. "There are things people who've been together for a long time know . . ."

"And would never tell?" Ed's question was gentle.

"Marriages fall apart," Ginny said. "That doesn't mean you don't have loyalties." She glanced towards Jason; he had been watching her, and the look that passed between them when they locked eyes was more eloquent than words.

The name of the court-appointed social worker was Rebecca Sen. She was sixtyish and trim, with a shock of white hair, a brilliant turquoise sari, and a firm and maternal manner. She was a woman who put a premium on clarity, and her report was mercifully devoid of jargon. Much of it was excerpted from the transcript of her interviews with the girls, and as she read their responses to her questions, it was possible truly to hear the voices of the children.

To judge by their words, the Brodnitz twins were thoughtful, articulate, and assured. But within the past twelve hours, Chloe Brodnitz had deliberately and repeatedly cut herself, so I listened to her words with special care. Chloe fielded Rebecca Sen's questions about the time she and her sister spent alone expertly, explaining that they had both taken babysitting classes and knew how to handle emergency situations. She said she felt both parents would do their best to foster a healthy relationship with the noncustodial parent. When asked which parent she would choose to live with, her reply was revealing. "Both of them, of course," she said. "That's what anybody would want."

After Ms. Sen read Chloe's answer, she looked up from her notes. "At this point, Chloe broke down. When she regained her composure, she stated that as long as she and her sister were together, she didn't care where they lived."

There were murmurs in the courtroom. Madam Justice

Gorges didn't need a gavel to quash the chatter. Her glance was glacial, and when silence was restored, Ms. Sen continued her testimony. "The other answer that I regard as significant came when I asked Chloe her feelings about basketball. She said that the only time she was in control of what happened next was when she was on the basketball court, and that was important to her."

Ed swallowed hard, but Ginny was stoic. When Rebecca Sen stepped down from the witness box it was eleven-thirty. Madam Justice Gorges recessed the court for lunch and said counsel for the parents could make closing statements when court resumed.

We all rose as Susan Gorges left the courtroom. As the crowd started to disperse, Ginny picked up her bag. "I'm going to the girls' school to check on Chloe," Ginny said, getting to her feet. "I thought she should stay home this morning, but Em said the sooner her sister got back to normal the better, so after a night in the emergency ward, Chloe dragged herself off to class." Ginny's eyes took us both in. "Will you be here this afternoon?"

"Of course," I said.

"Good. So I'll see you then," Ginny said, and she began pushing her way through the crowd towards the door.

Ed pointed to the courtroom's side door. "Looks like less action over there," he said.

"Fine with me," I said. "We're in no rush."

On our way towards the lobby, we passed a men's room. Ed pointed to the door. "I'm going to make a stop."

"As our old premier used to say, 'Never miss a chance.'"

As it turned out, Ed wasn't the only one who didn't miss a chance that day. Jason Brodnitz and his lawyer, Margot Wright, had followed us out the side door, and Sean Barton was right behind them. When Jason took a detour into the men's room, Sean was on his heels, and Margot wasn't far behind. She hit the brakes just as the door swung shut in her face.

It was a cartoon moment, and I had to suppress a smile. "Are you okay?" I asked.

She turned on her heel furiously. "No," she said. "I am not okay. I don't want Sean Barton in there with my client."

"How much trouble can two men get into in a public washroom?"

Margot curled her scarlet lips. "Come on," she growled. "You're not that naive."

I met her gaze. "No," I said. "I'm not. It was a joke."

"Thank God," she said. "I'd hate to think Zack had saddled himself with a dunce. Anyway, I'm glad I ran into you. I forgot about Zack's birthday party. I could make up an excuse, but the truth is I was working on a file and I forgot all about it."

"The one excuse Zack understands," I said. "But we missed you. It was a lot of fun."

"So I heard," Margot said. "I really do wish I'd been there. Zack's a lot easier to take these days. You've curbed that mammoth ego of his. He's almost bearable."

"I'll pass along your compliment."

"Don't. He might have a relapse." Margot stared at the door to the men's room, her brow creased with annoyance. "What's taking them so long?"

"My guess is that apart from the obvious, they're talking," I said. "Some of the most intriguing conversations I've ever had have been in the powder room."

Margot narrowed her eyes. "Holy Crudmore. I met you in the bathroom at the Hotel Saskatchewan, didn't I?"

"You bet. All those mirrors – I had multiple images of you warning me off Zack."

With her artful cleavage, her closely fitted, expensive black suit, her chunky gold bracelet, and her spike-heeled pumps, Margot was the image of burnished sophistication, but her grin was as open as the main street of her hometown, Wadena, Saskatchewan. "Don't rub it in," she said. "I never wanted anything permanent with Zack. He's way too aware of how good he is. He gets under my skin. Once he made me so mad I threw a box of tacks on the floor of his office, so he'd puncture the tires of his wheelchair."

It was hard not to smile. "Somehow, I can't imagine Zack letting that one get away."

"He didn't. He enrolled me in a course on anger management and sent me a dozen roses and the bill for the course."

A biker with shoulder-length auburn curls, a leather jacket hooked on his meaty finger, and studded leather pants tight as a lizard's skin strode past us into the men's room. On the back of his T-shirt was a message: "If you can read this, the bitch fell off."

Margot followed his passage meditatively. "I'll bet that guy's lawyer is ready to suck gas." She gazed at the door to the men's room. "Do you think they fell in?" She walked over and pounded on the door. Almost immediately, Jason emerged. He looked grey. The events of the day were taking their toll, but Margot didn't cut him any slack.

"Next time you have to go to the john, take me with you," she said. "I have five brothers. If I see anything I haven't seen before, I'll throw a hat over it." She grabbed his arm and, high heels clicking on the marble floor, steered him towards the lobby.

Sean appeared next. When he spotted me, his face lit up. "I saw you in court," he said. "Ginny went back to check on Chloe – can I buy you lunch?"

"Sure," I said. "But it should be my treat. We were very grateful for your help driving Zack after the party."

"But Zack wasn't grateful enough to see me as partner material." There was an edge in Sean's voice, but his crooked grin was still engaging. "What the hell. Let's have lunch."

When Ed came through the door of the men's room, Sean was clearly taken aback. "I didn't see you in there."

"Stalls," Ed said.

I looked between them. "Do you two know each other?"

"Ginny introduced us at the party," Sean said. "It's nice to see you again, Ed."

"Sean's going to join us for lunch," I said.

"On second thought, I'd better pass," Sean said, patting his trial bag. "I should go back to the office and run over a few things."

"I understand," I said. "There'll be other times."

"I hope so," Sean said. "See you later, Ed."

"Sooner rather than later," Ed said. "We'll be in court this afternoon too."

"It will be worth your while," Sean said, then he strode out the door without looking back.

Ed watched him thoughtfully. "They play rough, don't they?" he said.

"Who?"

"Lawyers like Sean," Ed said.

"The stakes are high: people's futures."

"I guess you're right," Ed said, smoothing his cotton shirt. "Let's fortify ourselves against what's to come."

When we stepped out of the courthouse, it was easy to forget the sad mess of mismanaged lives we'd left behind. The sun was bright, the sky was silky blue, and a breeze was stirring the branches of the trees across the street in Victoria Park. Ed took a long slow breath and exhaled contentedly. "The air at this time of year is so delicious, I could eat it with a spoon," he said.

I pointed across the street. "If you want something more substantial, the vendors are out. Care to dine al fresco?"

"It would be my pleasure. Are you finding this whole Monaghan-Brodnitz battle as heartbreaking as I am?"

I nodded. "The things we do to our kids."

"And to one another," Ed said. He shook off the sadness. "Let's get a move on. Bratwurst at its peak is a dish to savour, but it's quick to wizen."

We avoided the subject of the trial during lunch. It was good just to talk about summer plans and feel the sunshine on our faces. When he'd finished his brat on a bun, Ed wiped his mouth on the paper napkin and turned to me. "Are you up for another?"

"I took extra sauerkraut," I said. "One is my limit."

"Indulgence is a land without limits," Ed said. "Tennessee Williams had it right: 'Nobody gets out of this life alive.'"

"True enough," I said. Five minutes later, brats on buns in hand, we made our way back to the courthouse.

Sean was at the lawyers' table shuffling papers, and Ginny was reading a computer printout that she held up when she saw us. It was an article titled "Self Injury – From a Teen Perspective."

"Did you learn anything?" I asked.

Ginny's lips tightened. "Just that there's a lot to learn."

"How is Chloe?" Ed said.

"Fine, I guess." Ginny folded the printout carefully and dropped it in her bag. "I stopped by the girls' school on the pretext that they'd forgotten their lunches. They, predictably, were furious at me." Her voice was heavy with discouragement. "Even when I make an effort, I do the wrong thing."

Ed reached out a plump hand and patted her arm, but he was wise enough to stay silent. I looked over at the lawyer's table where Margot sat. It was empty. So was Jason's seat in the first row.

Ginny followed the direction of my gaze. "Shouldn't they be here by now?"

For the next ten minutes that question, spoken or unspoken, was on the mind of everyone in the courtroom. Madam Justice Gorges was a stickler for punctuality. The door through which she would enter cracked open every minute or so. At first, there was whispering; then people fell silent, waiting. The hush was electric with anticipation, like the hush in a theatre when an actor has failed to make an entrance.

Just as people began surreptitiously to check their BlackBerrys, Margot swept in, grabbed her barrister's robe from the back of her chair, shrugged it on, and sat down. Her face was flushed, and she closed her eyes and breathed deeply, steeling herself. Jason followed her slowly. He collapsed into his seat and stared straight ahead. Ginny strained towards him, whispering his name, but he ignored her.

Almost immediately, the door from the judge's chambers opened. When the court clerk entered and declared court in session, we spectators rose and Madam Justice Gorges entered. Her face revealed nothing. Margot sprang to her feet. I could see that her hands were clenched into fists. She was fuming.

Madam Justice Gorges was cool. "Thank you for joining us, Ms. Wright. I assume you have some thoughts regarding the custody assessment."

Margot's intake of breath was audible. "Madam Justice, if I may address the court, I have consulted with my client over the break and he has advised me that he no longer wishes to pursue custody and access issues at this time."

For a beat, there was silence, then the whispers began. Madam Justice Gorges looked fierce and the whispers stopped. But Ginny was beyond admonishment. She turned to me, her face uncomprehending. "'At this time'? Does that mean he's going to try again?"

"I don't think so," I said. "Ask Sean, but I think this is over."

Ginny turned towards her ex-husband. "Why?" she asked. Jason Brodnitz stared fixedly at his counsel's back.

Madam Justice Gorges had the husky rasp of a woman who enjoyed a good smoke and a shot of bourbon. "Mr. Brodnitz," she said. "Is your lawyer correct? Is her statement an accurate reflection of your intentions?"

Jason nodded.

"The court clerk will require a verbal response," Madam Justice Gorges said coldly.

Jason Brodnitz stood. "Yes, my lawyer is expressing my wishes."

Now it was Susan Gorges's turn for fury. "Mr. Brodnitz, the court takes custody and access matters very seriously. Our resources of time and money are limited, but we have expended both in our attempt to arrive at a fair and equitable decision that would serve your daughters' well being. Now, at the eleventh hour, having wasted our time and our money, you decide that you don't want to play." The judge's eyes drilled into Margot. "You're an experienced barrister. A rigorous examination of your client before he brought this matter before the courts would have unearthed his ambivalence. You could have advised him accordingly and saved this court the time and expense of a frivolous suit. That said, if Mr. Brodnitz no longer wishes to pursue custody and access issues at this time, the court must honour his decision."

Margot knew when to suck it up. "Thank you, Madam Justice," she said. She lowered her head slightly. "I apologize to the court for the inconvenience."

Susan Gorges then turned her attention to Sean. "Mr. Barton, does your client consent to the withdrawal of Mr. Brodntiz's claim?"

Sean rose. He was unruffled. He swivelled to look at Ginny, then turned back to the judge. "There was no way we could have anticipated this, Madam Justice. May I consult with my client?"

"Of course. I understand this sudden reversal must have come as a shock."

Sean came over to Ginny. "Do you consent to Mr. Brodntiz's withdrawal of his claim to pursue custody and access issues at this time?" His voice was loud, clearly intended to be heard publicly.

Ginny's voice was low and urgent. "I don't consent to anything, Sean. I don't want this surfacing whenever Jason decides the time is convenient."

"That won't happen," Sean said. Then he smiled. "Trust me. This is over."

Ginny nodded, then looked past Sean to the court clerk. "I consent," she said.

Susan Gorges directed her gaze at Sean. "Can you assure this court that you've done your job and your client understands exactly what it is she's consenting to?

"Yes, Your Honour. I've done my job. Ms. Monaghan is fully aware of the implications of her decision." And he added, "She is also fully aware of the gravity of her decision. No one wants to further waste the time and resources of this court."

"That's reassuring," Susan Gorges said. "Court will now adjourn so the parties may formalize a consent judgment. We'll meet in the conference room on the main floor. I assume Ms. Wright and Mr. Barton know the location."

The court clerk said. "All rise."

Madam Justice Gorges disappeared through the door at the back of the courtroom, and the room erupted. The media pressed towards Ginny. Sean stopped them. "We have nothing to say at this time. Nothing." He turned to his client. "Ginny, this won't take long. I've already started on the consent form."

Ginny rose. Her face was tentative, like that of an accident victim who can't quite believe she's escaped without injury. She reached out her hands to Sean. "I don't know how to thank you," she said.

"It was a good win," he said, smiling.

Ginny turned to Ed and me. "It's over. Wow! This changes everything." She scanned the area around us to make sure that she could speak privately. "Time to kick-start the campaign again."

The juices were flowing. Ginny cocked her head and gave me an impish smile. "You disapprove," she said. "If I were a man, would you be disapproving?"

"Yes," I said. "But I'd be offering my hand. Congratulations, Ginny."

"Thanks," she said absently. Her mind was already occupied with the next move. "We only have two weeks, so we'll have to move fast. We should have a strategy meeting tonight – I'll have somebody call you about the time and place, Joanne."

I touched her arm. "Ginny, I know I promised not to offer advice, but I think you should spend the evening with the twins – no politics. Your daughters are going to need you to help them understand what happened here today."

Ginny slapped her forehead with her palm. "I'm an idiot."

"There's a lot coming at you at once."

"And my job is to handle it," Ginny said furiously. "Well, no more amateur mistakes." She squared her shoulders and headed towards the side exit where Sean was waiting. Then the two of them disappeared.

"People are full of surprises, aren't they?" Ed said. "Jason didn't strike me as a man who would make that kind of sacrifice."

"You think he withdrew because of Chloe?"

"Without a doubt." Ed said. "When I was in the stall in the men's room, Sean and Jason were quarrelling. They kept their voices down, but I heard one of them – it must have been Jason – say, 'If that got out, it would destroy their lives.'"

"I guess Sean decided he had to go for broke." I said.

Ed's face was grim. "He wouldn't have played that card without Ginny's consent."

"She must have known Jason would protect the girls."

"So she called his bluff," Ed said. "Well, good for Ginny. But the next time you see her, tell her she lost my vote."

Willie was waiting just inside the door when I got home. I bent down to give him a nuzzle. "Where's our big, sparkly, star-spangled top banana?" I whispered, and Willie roared towards the office we'd added to the back of the house. Pantera was, as always, lying across the threshold, protecting his master. Taylor's cats were, in the weird way of cats, flopped over Pantera's back, asleep. I stepped over them and went to kiss my husband. He was in jeans, an open-necked brown shirt, and an ancient blue sweatshirt.

"I take it court is adjourned," I said.

Zack ran his hand over his head wearily. "I won my case." He pointed to a worn and eyeless Care Bear on the couch by the window. "Francesca gave me our friend over there as a thank-you present."

"She's happy with the outcome, then."

"She's relieved," Zack said. "I don't think Francesca has been happy in a very long time." He stroked his jaw. "Anyway, it's over."

"Sean's case is over too," I said.

"Whoa," Zack said. "That's a surprise. Susan Gorges must be taking the chief justice's admonition to speed things through the courts seriously."

"The case never got to the judge," I said. "Jason decided not to go for custody."

Zack's eyes widened. "What happened?"

"Well, I gather the issue was resolved in the men's room."

"Issues often are," Zack said. "God, I'll bet Margot was pissed."

"She was," I said. "And judging from her demeanour in court this afternoon, I don't think she knew what was coming."

"Margo doesn't often let herself get broadsided."

"I guess today just wasn't her day. Actually, I probably know more about what happened than Margot does. Ed Mariani was in the men's room when Sean and Jason Brodnitz had it out. Ed says Jason backed down because he didn't want his daughter Chloe's personal life brought up in court."

"That doesn't mesh with what I've heard about Brodnitz, but I guess even selfish pricks can love their kids." The corners of Zack's mouth twitched. "Boy, I'll bet Susan Gorges tore a strip off Margot: 'A responsible barrister would have examined a client rigorously, exposing any ambivalence before this court's time and money was wasted,' et cetera, et cetera."

I laughed. "That's just about word for word."

"I've appeared before Madam Justice Gorges more times than I care to remember," Zack said. "Margot has my sympathy."

"So you're over the time Margot threw tacks in front of your chair?"

Zack chortled. "She told you that? Not her finest hour – or mine, to be fair. But it was nothing personal. Just lawyers butting horns – you know, like elks."

"Female elk don't have horns."

"Margot has strap-ons," Zack shook his head. "I usually have a pretty good feel for these things. I can't believe the Monaghan-Brodnitz case just went away."

"It didn't just 'go away,'" I said. "Chloe Brodnitz used the blade of a box cutter on herself last night."

The fun went out of Zack's face. "Was she trying to kill herself?"

"No. According to Ginny, Chloe was careful not to cut anything that would affect her game. The school has a charity basketball game coming up, and Chloe didn't want to jeopardize her performance."

"So she was letting the world know she needed help."

"That's what the ER doctor thought."

Zack shook his head. "Poor kid."

"Yes, especially because the other kids look at her and see a golden girl who just glides through life. Gracie Falconer thinks Chloe and Emma are robots: talented, no freckles, no weight problems, no self-doubts."

"Does anybody ever get out of high school unscathed?"

"I take it that's a rhetorical question."

Zack grinned. "Yep. Anyway, it's always good to know what's going on. I'll wait a couple of days before I approach Margot."

"What are you going to approach her about?"

"Becoming a partner at Falconer Shreve. She's a terrific lawyer, and your warnings that I have to cut down my case-load are beginning to seep in. I want to be around to grope you in our golden years."

"I want that too," I said. "I'll try to ignore the fact that Margot's a gorgeous blonde with a great body."

"There's nothing wrong with your body," Zack said. He drew me close. "What are you doing for the next half-hour?"

"Not a thing," I said. "And we have longer than half an hour. After school, Taylor's going to get her hair cut."

For me, getting ready for sex meant kicking off my shoes, taking off my clothes, brushing my teeth, and sliding into bed. Nothing physical was simple for Zack, and I had learned to stay away when he was forcing his body through movements that were both painful and, in his eyes, demeaning. That afternoon, I lingered outside, carrying the geraniums Ed had brought into a spot where they'd get the afternoon sun, and casting a critical eye on a juniper that had not wintered well. When I decided that Zack had had enough time to get ready, I went back in the house. There was a complication. The doorbell was ringing, shrill and insistent, and the dogs were barking. I peeked out the window and called to my husband. "Better lay low," I said. "It's Margot, and I don't think she's going away."

Margot didn't wait to be invited in. When I opened the front door, she pushed past, planted herself firmly in the centre of the entrance hall, and cast an accusing eye about her. "All right. Where the hell is he? And don't tell me he's not here. I can see his car."

"I'll get him," I said. "Margot, it's a gorgeous day, why don't you wait for Zack out on the deck?"

Saskatchewan girl that she was, Margot took off her stilettos and padded down the hall in her bare feet. It was an endearing courtesy, and I found myself warming to her. I took her onto the deck to the round wooden table we used for family dinners. "Make yourself comfortable," I said.

"Tell Zack I'm going to kill him," she said.

"I'll pass that along."

Sensing big doings, the dogs followed me back into the house. Zack was pulling on his jeans when I got into our bedroom. "It's Margot," I said. "She wants me to tell you she's going to kill you." I looked at him more closely. "Incidentally, do you realize you're not wearing any underwear?"

Zack glanced down. "Shit. Jo, it'll take me more time to get undressed and dressed again than it will take to hear Margot out. Her storms are intense, but they pass quickly." He pulled up his zipper and snapped the top button. "Besides, going commando will make me feel tougher."

"Shall I make myself scarce?"

"God, no. I'm going to need all the help I can get."

When Zack and I went out to the yard, I left Willie and Pantera in the house. Neither of them handled conflict well, and from the moment Margot spotted Zack and sprang out of her chair, she was ready for battle.

"What the hell happened to my case, Zack? And don't play innocent. There's no way Little Boy Blue could have pulled that off without some grown-up advice."

Zack was sanguine. "If Sean got advice, he didn't get it from me. He handled this on his own."

Margot eyed Zack suspiciously. "You really didn't know?"

He met her gaze. "I really didn't know. Why didn't you ask your client?"

She slumped into her chair. "I did. He's not talking. This doesn't make sense, Zack. Jason was ready to go the distance this morning. Then he and your little protege waltzed into the boys' room together and my client emerged a changed man."

"Love at first sight?" Zack said.

"You've become a romantic," Margot said acidly. "And it's clouding your judgment. My client didn't fall in love with Sean, but something sure as hell happened. I did every-thing but bang my forehead on the pavement to get Jason to change his mind or at least explain, but no deal. When we went back into court, I had to tell Madam Justice Leather Lungs that we were withdrawing, so of course she minced me up into tiny pieces. Meanwhile my client's standing beside me with this hangdog expression, like someone kneed him in the 'nads. All in all, it's been a lousy day." She gazed at the garden with longing. "God, this is nice. Am I ever going to live in a big house like you, loverboy?"

Zack and I exchanged glances.

"Why don't you stay awhile, Margot?" Zack said. "Have a drink. Relax."

She eyed him suspiciously. "In our family, we have a saying: don't take the bait – it has a hook in it. What do you want, Zack?"

"You. The firm needs another senior trial lawyer, and you're our first choice."

Margot sat down again, but she positioned herself on the edge of her chair, ready to spring. She narrowed her eyes to slits. "Are you suffering from some deadly disease?"

"I want to spend more time with my wife," Zack said.

"Fuck that," Margot said. "But as an opening gambit, it's not bad. That said, I'm happy where I am. I like being on my own. I don't want you breathing down my neck."

"I wouldn't be breathing down your neck," Zack said. "I'd be at home breathing down Joanne's neck."

"Until a serious client showed up, then you'd be down at the office faster than a speeding bullet. I know you, Zack. You have to be Numero Uno. You'd never let anyone else handle a really big case."

"I'd let you handle a big case because I respect your work and I trust you. Contrary to what you may believe, I'm not an egomaniac. I take on tough cases because clients deserve the best representation our firm can give them."

Margot chortled. "And that's you."

"Until you join the firm, yes."

"You think I'm as good as you are."

"I think you will be."

"Bullshit."

Zack held out his hands, palms up. "The offer's on the table."

Margot gazed at our yard and house with undisguised lust. "I'll have to look at the books, of course," Margot said. "If Falconer Shreve is tanking, I'm not bailing you out. In any event, I'll want a limited liability partnership, and I want a draw from the profits – a substantial draw."

"Why don't I get the drinks while you two negotiate," I said. "Margot?"

"Gin and tonic, please, but light on the gin. I don't want loverboy to charm me out of what is rightfully mine."

I turned to Zack "Loverboy?"

"Heavy on the gin," he said. "Numb myself against defeat. And thank you, Ms. Shreve. I'll take care of dinner."

"Does he really cook?" Margot asked.

"He orders in," I said. "But he does it well."

Pantera made a break for the yard as soon as I opened the door. Every second away from Zack was agony to him. Willie, loyal and dumb as ever, stayed with me. The phone was ringing. I picked up and heard Sean Barton, sounding surprisingly vulnerable. "Joanne, it's Sean. I wanted to thank you for coming to the custody hearing. You brought us luck."

"You must be delighted at how the case worked out."

"Delighted and relieved," he said. "For a while there, I didn't think it would go our way."

"Well, it did, and that's cause for celebration."

"And hope," Sean's voice was tentative. "Have you talked to Zack about what happened in court today?"

"Of course. He was really pleased."

"That's a good sign, isn't it?" Sean didn't wait for an answer. "So is he around?"

I glanced out the window. Margo was sitting on the grass

rubbing Pantera's belly, and Zack was watching them, looking like the cat that swallowed the canary.

"He's busy at the moment. Could he call you back?"

"Absolutely. I'll be here at the office for the next couple of hours. After that, he has my cell number. Any time is good."

I took out the tray with the drinks. Margot pushed herself to her feet, wiped her hands on her skirt, and reached for her glass. There was mud on her skirt and a smear of dog drool on her jacket.

I groaned. "Margot, your suit."

She shrugged. "That's why God gave us dry cleaners, and I miss having a dog. Until I moved to Saskatoon to go to university, there wasn't a day in my life when I didn't have a dog. My dad farmed, so there were always yard dogs. Whenever there was a runt in a litter, my dad would say, 'Well, we'll have to find a little bullet for that one.' So of course, I'd pitch a fit until I got the puppy." She beamed at the memory. "Every dog I ever owned was named Bullet. Dogs on farms never live long – giving them all the same name made life easier."

Margot's childhood had been a happy one, and as she talked about her twelve-year-old niece, Larissa, it struck me that A.E. Milne was wrong when he said we can't retrace happy footsteps. Like her aunt, Larissa was growing up in duck-hunting country, and as Margot described teaching her how to clean ducks so she could charge rich hunters top dollar to deal with the mess of blood and feathers their expensive rifles brought down from the autumn skies, her eyes shone.

After Margot's sleek BMW disappeared down Albert Street, Zack was smug. "I would call that a good afternoon's work," he said.

"It'll be handy having a partner who knows how to clean ducks," I agreed.

Zack snaked his arm around my waist. "Duck hunters," he said happily. "Another client base to tap."

"I hate to puncture your balloon," I said. "But Sean called while Margot was here. I think he's hoping his win today might change the partnership picture."

Zack frowned. "Why would it? Sean caught a break today. It happens. Margot's client turned out to be a more decent human being than our client. If a first-year law student had been representing Ginny Monaghan, the outcome would have been the same."

"Is Sean really no better than a first-year law student?"

Zack shook his head. "That wasn't fair. Actually, Sean's pretty good. Otherwise, we would have let him go long ago. He's just not partnership material."

"Why not?"

"Truthfully? Because Sean doesn't understand that the law is about human problems. At the centre of every case, there's a real human being in trouble. The law is there to help them get justice. Sean doesn't care about that; he just sees the law as a means to an end."

"Money?"

"No. I've never heard Sean even mention money. It's something else."

"What?"

"I don't know. I just know human beings aren't part of the equation."

Taylor and I hadn't talked about how she was getting her hair cut. Except for a brief flirtation with hair products when she was in Grade Six, she had always worn her dark hair long. Braided, ponytailed, or brushed loose, it had been one of her glories, but when she bounced through the front door that afternoon, it was clear she had decided it was time to move along.

The new haircut was boy short, with just a wisp or two around her face – *très mignon*, as the French would say. The gamine look transformed her face: her brown, long-lashed eyes seemed even larger; her cheekbones, more defined; her generous mouth, broader; her pretty neck, longer. The marriage of Taylor's birth parents had been a disaster, but they had given Taylor a deep and enviable genetic pool from which to draw, and she'd been lucky. She'd inherited her mother's talent but not her wildness, and even with the fierce mood changes of adolescence roiling inside her, Taylor had Stuart Lachlan's steadiness. She also had his dark hair and delicate colouring, a combination that somehow softened her mother's dramatic features. In every way that mattered, Taylor had always been a lovely girl, but suddenly I saw the physical beauty of the woman she would become, and I knew Zack saw it too. We exchanged a quick glance.

"Well," Zack said.

Taylor's face crumpled. "You hate it. I know it's . . . extreme, but I thought . . . well, never mind what I thought."

Zack clapped his hands together. "It's a knockout," he said. "Your mother and I are just a little overwhelmed at how terrific you look." He wheeled towards the door. "Hey, where's that camera Blake and Gracie gave me for my birthday? I'll take a picture and you can see for yourself."

I walked over and put my hands on my daughter's shoulders. "It's a great haircut, Taylor, and you look sensational. You are sensational." I felt my throat tighten. "I'll get the camera. It's in Zack's office."

The grey, eyeless Care Bear Francesca had given Zack to celebrate her freedom was still on the couch. I stared at it for a moment, then went to the bookshelf, took down the camera, and walked up the hall, grateful beyond measure for a life filled with incandescent moments.

CHAPTER

5

Except for the comics and a quick glance at the front page to see if there were trials of note, Zack never read any of our morning papers. Whoever made it to the porch first brought the papers in, but after that Zack left them for me to read or recycle as I saw fit. That morning, there was a change in our pattern. When I came in from my run with the dogs, Zack held out the *Globe and Mail*. "Some nice coverage of Ginny in here," he said.

I took the paper, poured myself coffee, and read. The front-page coverage of Ginny was positive: a large and flattering photo of her with the twins as they came out of court and the headline, minister of family wins daughters. I read the article. The account of the custody dispute was factual, but the slant was positive: no hint of Ginny's sexual adventures, and Jason Brodnitz's decision to withdraw his case hinted at indiscretions he did not wish made public. The article concluded with Ginny's response to a reporter who asked how she planned to spend the evening. "With my daughters," Ginny said. "They'll have questions and we'll have to help one another find answers."

I put the paper back on the table and measured out the dogs' food. "That article couldn't have been more glowing if Ginny had written it herself," I said.

"Nope," Zack agreed, "and the other two are even better."

I sat down opposite him. "So, a good news day."

Zack shook his head. The *Leader-Post* was folded in his hand. "Cristal Avilia made the front page too."

I took the paper and turned it to the lower fold. The picture of Cristal was smaller than the one of Ginny, but it was large enough for me to see what she looked like. I don't know what I'd expected, but she was a surprise. The woman in the picture was fine-boned, with dark hair swept back to reveal a high forehead and dreamy eyes. She looked liked the kind of young woman I'd see at the opening reception of a small gallery or a performance art piece.

"Well," I said.

"Well what?" Zack said.

"She isn't what I expected. She looks like a girl out of a locket – very sweet and innocent."

"I guess that's why her billing rate was the same as mine," Zack said dryly.

"How many clients did she have?"

"I don't know. She told me once she kept it to three clients a day, and her bookings were two hours minimum. Plus, she warned me against counting on a weekend date because she was often away with clients from Friday to Sunday."

"At $500 an hour," I said, "Cristal must have earned serious money. Why would she blackmail Ned for $10,000? That would be small potatoes for her."

"Good question," Zack said. "And I guess now we'll never know the answer. There are a lot of things we'll never know."

I looked at the photo again. Unexpectedly, I felt my throat tighten. "And a lot of things Cristal will never know," I said. "When I was thirty-four, I had two children and no idea at all of who I was or what I wanted out of life."

Zack winced. "Jo, I already feel like a shit about this. If hauling my ass over a mountain of broken glass would make you feel better, I'd do it, but this is just making us both miserable. Cristal doesn't have anything to do with the life we have now."

"I know," I said. "But she isn't going to go away." I poured us both coffee, folded the paper so I wouldn't have to see Cristal's photo, and turned to another front-page story about the impact Jason's withdrawal of the custody suit would have on Ginny's political fortunes and on those of her party. Despite everything, it was absorbing reading.

For much of my adult life I had been involved in electoral politics: first as the candidate's wife, later as an activist, finally as an academic. I had managed campaigns, cooked turkeys, knocked on doors, hosted coffee parties, and sat in drafty halls enduring endless windy speeches. I'd hated almost every minute of it. I knew people who came alive with campaigns. They were addicted to the adrenalin rush of picking up the paper every morning and looking at poll numbers; they relished the gossip and thrived on trying to guess the shifting whims of the electorate. I found the process frightening and exhausting, but because I believed in what our party was doing, I stayed in. In mid-life, I came up for air, took a hard look at the party my family and I'd given our lives to, decided either it had changed or I had, and I walked away.

Now, I was back in – at least as a spectator. That morning as I left for the strategy meeting Ginny's campaign manager had called, I automatically assessed her chances in the upcoming election. I knew Ginny's federal riding, Palliser, intimately. It took in the southwest corner of Regina and the territory extending to and including Moose Jaw. It was a prosperous area and politically volatile, seesawing back and forth between the parties of the right and the left with the outcome often determined by fewer than a hundred votes. Until news of her ugly marital difficulties surfaced, Ginny had seemed unbeatable, but the jokes and innuendo had taken their toll. Despite the fact that she'd worked her constituency hard and delivered on her promises, the party's internal polling on the night before the hearing opened showed Ginny trailing the candidate for my old party. Jason's abrupt change of heart about custody of his daughters would stop the hemorrhage of votes from her campaign, but as I pushed the security buzzer in the lobby of her condo, I knew that the meeting ahead would be dominated by one question: was Ginny's career salvageable?

Ginny herself met me at the door. She was wearing running shorts and a tank top, and her hair was damp with perspiration. "Perfect timing," she said. "I got in my run and I'm just about to hit the shower. Have you seen the papers?"

"I have."

"Then you know that I used your line about staying home with the kids last night because that's where I belonged. My campaign manager said it made him want to blow chunks, but he thought it was effective."

"That's a start," I said. "I don't imagine that he's thrilled to have me here this morning."

"Ignore him," Ginny said. "But an old friend of yours is coming, and he is thrilled that you'll be here."

"Who's the friend?"

"Keith Harris. When he called from the airport to get my address, I told him about our agreement. I thought if he had concerns, we should deal with them up front, but he was delighted. How do you two know each other?"

"Remember that line about politics making strange bedfellows?" I said.

"I've heard it two or three hundred times," Ginny said dryly.

"Sorry," I said. "Anyway, Mieka was married to Keith's nephew, and Keith and I were on a political panel together for a couple of years."

Ginny cocked her head. "I had a feeling there was more to it than that."

"There was," I said.

Ginny raised an eyebrow. "That must have been interesting."

"It was," I said. "For a while."

A young man in khakis, a black T-shirt, and a Blue Jays ball cap came out of the kitchen. He had a newspaper in one hand and a half-eaten Crispy Crunch bar in the other.

"Milo, this is Joanne Shreve," Ginny said. "She's going to be with us till E-Day. Joanne, my campaign manager, Milo O'Brien."

Milo's smile was not pleasant. "So you're the Trojan horse."

Ginny's voice was wintry. "Back off, Milo. Joanne's here at my invitation."

"You've already screwed up once, Ginny," he said. "And it may cost us this election."

Ginny shot him a look that would have curdled milk, but it bounced off her manager. "Are you sure we can trust her?" he said.

"I'm standing right here, Milo," I said. "Why don't you ask me?"

He turned his eyes on me. They were a startlingly bright blue. "All right, Joanne Kilbourn-Shreve, can we trust you?"

I met his gaze. "Yes," I said.

Ginny laughed. "There's your answer, Milo. I'm going to shower. You and Joanne get acquainted."

Milo crammed the rest of his Crispy Crunch bar in his mouth and headed down the hall. I followed him into the kitchen. The room was bright and attractive, but like the rest of the condo it had the unused quality of a show home. It even smelled new. Milo went to the kitchen table, pulled out a chair with the elaborate courtesy of a waiter in an over-priced restaurant, and gestured to me. "Madam?" Then he pulled another Crispy Crunch bar from his pocket, peeled back the wrapper, took a bite, sat down, and began talking on his cellphone.

Somewhere in the apartment a phone began ringing. It stopped and then began again. Milo didn't move. I took out a notepad and pen and began making notes. Milo narrowed his eyes at me and kept on talking. In fifteen minutes, Ginny was back. She was dressed in a pullover and slacks and talking into a portable phone. She nestled the phone between her ear and her shoulder, took a bran muffin from a paper bag on the kitchen table, and continued fielding questions from her caller.

Left to my own devices, I studied Milo. He had a wild kinetic energy that kept him constantly in motion: drum-ming on the table with his fingertips, tapping his foot, rolling the wrapper from his Crispy Crunch into a ball, and tossing it towards the wastebasket. All the while, he was wheedling, cajoling, cursing, and threatening the luckless souls on the other end of his cell. The purpose of his endless stream of calls was no mystery. The party had written Ginny off and moved her workers to other, more winnable ridings. Milo was giving it his best shot, but I knew from experience that once the workers had been moved, it was almost impos-sible to get them back. If Milo hadn't been such a putz, my heart would have gone out to him.

When the buzzer rang from the lobby, Ginny was in the middle of yet another interview. She gave me a beseeching look, and I walked over, pressed the entry pad, and went to the hall to wait.

Keith Harris was older, thinner, and more drawn than he had been the last time I saw him. With his laptop case slung over his shoulder and his suit-bag hooked to his forefinger, he looked like a traveller at the end of a long and unsuccessful business trip, but as always, he was gallant. He stepped inside, dropped his luggage, and held out his arms. "May I kiss the bride?"

"No longer a bride," I said. "Zack and I have been married a year and a half, but I'm still me, and I'd welcome a kiss."

"Good," he said. The kiss was warm but not passionate: a kiss between loving friends. When it ended, Keith stepped back and looked at me. "Marriage obviously agrees with you."

"It does," I said. "We're very happy. And you?"

Keith shrugged. "Getting by."

Milo came out into the hall, pocketed his Crispy Crunch, and shook Keith's hand. "God, am I glad to see you," he said. "Did they arrange any accommodation?"

"No. This trip was a last-minute decision."

Milo's young face creased with anxiety. "But you are staying?"

"As long as I'm needed," Keith said.

"Thank God. I'll call about a hotel room. Smoking, right?"

Keith sighed. "Nope, I've quit yet again. Doctor's orders."

Milo had no interest in other people's doctors. "Okay, nonsmoking," he said. "Keith, we've gotta pull this out. If Ginny wins, we win it all. But we need people."

"Then we'll get them," Keith said evenly.

Milo's nod was solemn, but halfway down the hall, he did a little side kick of happiness.

I turned to Keith. "Looks like he's glad you're here," I said. "By the way, is Milo certifiable?"

Keith chuckled. "Everybody in this business is. But he gets the job done, and as you know, a political campaign is not exactly Plato's symposium."

As if to underscore the point, when Keith and I walked into the kitchen, Ginny had her head in the refrigerator. She was still responding to interviewer's questions and still trying to put together her breakfast. When she heard Keith's voice, she turned, waved, then reached in and extracted a litre of milk. She answered a question about her sex life, opened the milk, sniffed, made a face, checked the best-before date, and poured the milk down the sink. Milo watched the action and gallantly offered Ginny the rest of his Crispy Crunch. By my count, it was his third since I arrived.

Keith poured himself coffee and sat down at the table. "Okay, the fun's over," he said. "Milo, where are we?"

"No longer beached on shit creek," Milo said. "The custody thing helped big-time." He chomped his bar. "Two problems: time and bodies. E-Day is fourteen days away and the only volunteers we've got left can't leave home without their Depends or their nitro – sorry, Keith."

Keith made a faint gesture of dismissal, and Milo barrelled on. "Anyway, we need a media blitz, but the ads Ginny's got now are shit – worse yet, they're generic shit. Ginny's gotta go for specificity. If she's gonna win Palliser, she needs to get our core group of Christian family-values wackos to the polls and she needs to appeal to the spoiled brats with the renovated houses in Old Lakeview and the Crescents. That means the campaign needs bodies and it needs new ads, and that means money quick and on the table. Again, and for the record, I think we can win this thing, but we have to move fast."

Keith handed him a list of names and numbers. "I drew this up on the way out. Call and tell them to be on the next plane."

Milo glanced at the list. "Half of these people are from Ontario."

"From safe seats in Ontario."

"It's going to cost serious money to get them out here."

"Elections are about serious money."

"True enough," Milo said. "I'll find me a little corner and start dialing. What about the media buys?"

"Get what you need. We'll cover it."

Ginny ended her call, flicked off her phone, and joined us.

"So, how's it going, kiddo?" Keith asked, and I could hear the affection in his voice.

Ginny went over and planted a kiss on his cheek. "Better now that you're here," she said. The moment passed quickly. She straightened up and went to the chair opposite him. "Jason's withdrawal seems to have shifted the winds. When the custody question hit court, there was a sense that where there was smoke, there was fire. For the last few weeks the smoke's been hovering over me, but now, Jason's the one under suspicion." She picked up the muffin she'd buttered ten minutes earlier and took a bite. "There's speculation that my ex has a few nasty skeletons in his closet," she said carefully.

Keith cocked his head. "Does he?"

An odd expression flickered across Ginny's face. "Everybody does," she said tightly. "But when it came to the girls, Jason was always on the side of the angels."

"No use letting that get out," Keith said. "We did some polling last night, Ginny. Character is still an issue for you."

Ginny looked at her muffin with distaste. "This tastes like gerbil droppings. So how do I deal with the fact that the good people of Palliser think there have been too many men in my bed since Jason and I split up?"

Keith turned to me. "Any thoughts?"

I raised my hand in a halt gesture. "Uh-uh," I said. "I'm here as an observer."

"If you weren't an observer, how would you handle it?" Keith asked.

"I'd get Ginny on Jack Quinlan's radio program. Everybody listens to it, and he's sympathetic to your side. He'll let

Ginny deal with the character issue head-on, but he won't kill her with it. Apart from that, put her into as many soft situations as you can: arrange for photos of her at daycares, old folks' homes, women's shelters. Show that she has a heart and remind people that she has a record supporting programs for women and kids and seniors. Also have her spend as much time as possible with her daughters between now and E-Day." I extended my hand, palm up to Keith. "Now, give me a loonie for anything I suggested that you didn't think of."

Keith handed me a loonie. "There wasn't anything, but it's always fun listening to your ideas." He turned to Ginny. "Why don't you call Quinlan yourself? Tell him you want his show to be your first live interview since the custody was resolved."

"Jack does his show from Saskatoon," Ginny said. "If I'm going to be on today, it'll have to be a phone in."

"Uh-uh," I said. "Quinlan likes face to face. Ginny, tell him you'll fly up there this morning."

Ginny picked up her cell, called Information, punched in the numbers, and began talking. When she was done, she rang off. "The producer's delighted," she said. "So we'll take the next flight up, and go live in the second hour." It took her a minute to realize Em and Chloe had come into the room. She smiled at her daughters. "God, I'd almost forgotten you were here," she said.

The twins were identical, but I knew instinctively that the one who stepped forward and spoke was Em. "Probably best if you don't say that too often till the election's over," she said. The girls exchanged a private smile. They were poised young women. The twin who'd spoken first performed the introductions. "I'm Emma Brodnitz," she said. "And this is my sister, Chloe."

Keith nodded at them. "We met the last time I was here. I went to one of your basketball games. Let's see," he

said, pointing to Emma. "You're the shooting guard," and
he pointed to Chloe, "You are the point guard."

The girls exchanged glances. "You've got it backwards,"
they said in unison.

"Guess it's lucky I'm not the one running for office,"
Keith said. "This is Joanne . . . do you go by Shreve?"

"Depends on the situation," I said. "But Joanne is fine." I
shifted in my chair to face the girls. "My daughter Taylor is
going to Luther next year, so we've been watching the Lions
with interest. You had a great season."

"Did you get to a game?" Emma asked.

"No. But I promise I'll be a regular next year."

"Come tonight. It's a charity game for Ranch Ehrlo," she
said. "Bring your daughter. We're playing Sheldon. They're
solid, so it should be a good game."

"Sounds like fun," I said.

"Luther gym. Seven o'clock." It was the first time Chloe
had spoken. "Get there early if you don't want to climb up to
the top of the bleachers."

"How would you feel about your mother coming?" Keith
asked.

Emma's tone was derisive. "Why not? It'll be a great
photo op."

Ginny ignored the slight. She walked over to her daughters and draped an arm around each of them. The three
women – all rangy and athletic – made an appealing triptych.
"Want me to ask Milo to make a run to the Great Canadian
Bagel before school? Our choices here seem to be mouldy
muffins and outdated milk."

"Thanks, but Chloe and I have a secret stash," Em
said. She opened the freezer compartment and pulled out
a plastic sack of bagels. "Whole wheat and multi-grain.
Want one?"

"A multi-grain," Ginny said. "Thanks."

Em offered the bag around. "Anybody else?" As the girls toasted their bagels and poured juice, the meeting continued. I took notes. When the girls were through eating, they excused themselves.

"You don't have to leave," Ginny said. "You're not in our way."

Emma's expression was too cynical for a girl her age. "Sure we are," she said. Then she and Chloe vanished.

Quinlan Live was broadcast province-wide between 8:30 a.m. and 12:30 p.m. and rebroadcast at night. The tag for the show was, "Stop banging on your steering wheel. Call Jack." Judging by the ratings, a lot of people did. For many years running, Jack Quinlan had been voted one of the most influential people in Saskatchewan, and for that reason and many others, it made good sense to announce Ginny's political re-entry on his show.

We had twenty minutes to catch the plane for the forty-five-minute flight to Saskatoon. I called Zack on the way to the airport.

"Hey, my lucky day," he said. "A minute later and I would have been in court with my cell turned off."

"I'm glad I caught you. I'm going to Saskatoon this morning. Ginny's going to be on the Jack Quinlan show, and the campaign people have decided she'll be more effective if she's with him in studio. Anyway, I'm tagging along."

"But you'll be back tonight, won't you?"

"I'll be back by lunchtime. We're flying."

"Whoa. Are you okay with that?"

"No, but I should see Ginny's performance first-hand."

Zack knew I hated flying. "I wish I could be there, so you'd have a hand to grip."

"So do I," I said. "Promise me my martini tonight will be extra dry."

"You've got it," he said.

When we boarded the shuttle to Saskatoon, I felt the familiar clutch of panic. Keith looked at me closely. "Anything I can do to help?"

"Take my mind off the fact that I'm sitting on an airplane," I said. "Tell me what's been going on in your life."

"Lately I've been paying for a lifetime of mistreating my body. Too many cigarettes. Too much booze. Too many late nights. Too much stress. Too much fast food. I've been spending a lot of time with my cardiologist."

"But everything's okay now?"

Keith shrugged. "I don't want to waste our time alone together talking about my medical history. Tell me about Mieka and the girls. How's the move to Regina working out?"

"Fine. They're living in my old house, and it's nice to watch another generation of kids growing up there. Of course, we love having them close. Mieka's doing well. It took a while for her to figure out what she wanted to do. She thought about going back to school, but academics were never really her thing. She didn't want to go back to catering because she hated being away from the girls, so she came up with a business plan that seems to be working."

"So what's the business?"

"It's called UpSlideDown. Mieka took the money from her catering business, bought an old hardware store over on 13th Avenue, and redesigned it as a combination giant play area and coffee shop. The kids play, the parents sip coffee and chat, and everybody's happy – especially Mieka because she gets to earn a very tidy income and spend time with the girls."

"Good for her. And Taylor is still Taylor?"

"Taylor is magnificent," I said. "We'll have to get you over to the house so you can see for yourself."

"I'd like that," Keith said. "It's good to know the Kilbourn women are thriving."

"We are. And our men are doing well too. Angus is being vastly overpaid for a summer job with a law firm in Saskatoon, and Peter's walk-in clinic is making as much money as walk-in clinics in the inner city make, but he's content. How does Greg like Montreal?"

"He's coping. Sometimes that's all you can do."

"I wish he were closer," I said.

"It's not easy being an ex-husband, especially when you still love your ex-wife. Greg thought a clean break was best." Keith cocked his head so he could read my expression. "You don't agree."

"No," I said. "But nobody asked me."

"Or me," Keith said. "Now, before we hit the big city, can you think of any questions that will poleaxe Ginny?"

"Quinlan's good at cutting off questioners who make you want to dig out their eyeballs with a spoon," I said, "but there are some legitimate concerns about Ginny's priorities, and he'll let them through. Ginny's sex life is her own business, but the stories are out there. Even Taylor's heard the jokes."

Keith's headshake was almost imperceptible. "Ginny's been in public life long enough to be prepared for those. For anything she might not have considered."

"There's something about Jason that Ginny knows and isn't telling," I said.

"I sensed that too," Keith said. "Any idea what the mystery is?"

"No. But this is Saskatchewan – there are only a million people in the entire province."

"So you think somebody else will know the secret."

"I do," I said. "And I'll bet they're ready to tell."

Over the years, I'd been on Jack Quinlan's show a dozen times. The first time I'd been promoting a book I'd written about Andy Boychuk, a man who had been our province's last best hope until he was murdered. Later, I'd been on air as an academic from the left whose views on the politics of culture, race, and land claims lit up the phone lines. Until lately, the studio for *Quinlan Live* had been so small and congested with old scripts, memorabilia, stained coffee cups, and junk that the host had to stand on his chair to see into the control room. But stellar ratings for private radio bring their own reward. The building that housed the new studio was charmless and functional, but the setting on the bank of the Saskatchewan River was prime.

Our timing was split second. We arrived at the top of the hour while the news was being read. Jack Quinlan came out to the reception area, greeted Ginny, and jumped back in mock surprise when he saw me.

"I'm here as an observer," I said.

"Well, come in and observe," he said. In the studio, he pointed Ginny to her seat, and offered me a stool next to his. "If you get bored, you can look out at the river. The view from here is spectacular." He handed Ginny her headphones, picked up his own, and they were on the air.

Every phone-in show has its regulars: some have an opinion on every issue; some have a passionate opinion on one issue and feel compelled to share that opinion regardless of the topic under discussion. Quinlan's audience was, on the whole, politically astute, but his regulars were predictable. As a caller from Elbow wound up for his well-worn joke about how Saskatchewan's refusal to accept daylight saving time meant our province would forever be consigned to the

Dark Ages, my eyes drifted to Jack Quinlan's computer screen. I had time to read the message twice before he noticed the direction of my gaze and minimized the window. "GINNY MONAGHAN DESERVES TO WIN. WHEN THE TIME IS RIGHT, I'LL GO PUBLIC WITH THE TRUTH ABOUT HER EX-HUSBAND."

Jack glanced at me quickly, then went to the next caller. She was hostile. The next three callers were men – also hostile. It wasn't Ginny's morning. She was handling the enmity, but I could hear the tension in her voice. The fifth caller was a young woman from Regina who sounded as if she were reading from a script. She praised Ginny's accomplishments as an MP, then dropped the bombshell. "Your accomplishment is even more remarkable," the young woman said, "when one considers that while you were working for the people of this country, your ex-husband was living off the money he took from prostitutes in this city."

The caller was cut off, but the damage was done. Ginny sat bolt upright and glared at Jack. He raised his palms to indicate helplessness and cut to a commercial. Ginny ripped off her earphones and turned to Jack. "Why didn't you stop that girl?"

"I thought she was a plant from your party," Jack said. "You'd had four rough calls. The girl was obviously reading. I figured she'd pitch you a soft question, and you could knock it out of the park while you caught your breath."

"We have a family," Ginny said. She was visibly upset, but it struck me that she didn't seem surprised.

"We're back," Jack said. Ginny picked up her earphones and took the next call. From that point on it was smooth sailing, with more supportive than hostile callers. When the hour was over, Jack thanked Ginny for taking the time to come on his show, and Ginny responded with a gracious statement about how it was always a pleasure to have a chance to talk to the people of Saskatchewan.

Jack walked us out. At the elevator, he and Ginny shook hands. "You should know this isn't the first time someone's been in touch with that gossip about Jason," Jack said. "I don't expect you to tell me whether the rumour's true, but you should know that it's making the rounds."

Ginny nodded acknowledgement. The elevator doors opened, and she stepped in, leaving the pertinent question unasked. Keith wasn't so reticent. "So," he said. "Is the dirt about Jason helping us?"

Jack stared at him coldly. "It explains why Ginny might have been seeking consolation elsewhere," he said. "Is that what you need to win?"

"We use what we get," Keith said, extending his hand.

"I guess Santa came early for you this year," Jack said. He turned and walked back into his studio, leaving Keith's hand outstretched and unshaken.

News about the enticing rumour passed along by Jack Quinlan's mystery caller moved fast. By the time we got on the plane, Keith had made some calls of his own, and the pulse beating in his temple suggested his excitement. The reports were good. Ginny's seat was back in the undecided column, and that meant there was the possibility of forming a government.

Ginny and Keith huddled together, conferring in whispers on the flight back to Regina. I sat next to a woman whose son had been in grade school with Angus, and we caught up on each other's news. Time passed quickly, and I was surprised when the plane touched down.

Keith and Ginny dropped me off at my house. Ginny was spending the afternoon canvassing, and I wanted to clean up and have a sandwich and a nap before I joined her. I checked the mail and found the usual mix of bills and ads. There was also an unaddressed padded envelope containing a DVD.

That, too, was no surprise. NationTV had been taping since the candidate left the courthouse triumphant, and I knew they would have great footage of Ginny Agonistes, the combatant who wouldn't quit.

I walked into the house, left a message on Zack's machine telling him I'd survived two flights, and went out to the yard to throw a ball around for the dogs until I'd come down from all the tensions of the morning. It didn't take long before the dogs collapsed in the sunshine, and I went inside to make myself a sandwich and watch the DVD.

I was so mentally prepared for shots of Ginny on the steps of the courthouse that it took me a moment to understand what I was watching. The quality of the picture was sharp, but the camera's eye was static, so the effect was like watching a scene through a security camera. A woman, very slender with dark hair cut in a sleek bob, was sitting cross-legged on a bed, stroking a cat. I recognized her immediately. It was Cristal Avilia. She was wearing a T-shirt, and her legs were bare. She stood, walked out of camera range, and when she returned, she wasn't alone. Zack was with her. He was wearing a robe.

He handed her an envelope. She placed it, unopened, on an armoire and moved in front of him; then she took her fingers and began stroking herself. She began to moan and took her fingers and held them up to his lips. "Taste it," she said.

He took her fingers in his mouth. "That always works," he said. He began to stroke her, and she thrust herself at his hand, whimpering.

As Zack told me the night he explained his relationship with Cristal, from that point on, it was all business. He wheeled his chair next to the bed, pivoted his body onto the sheets, and they had sex. I couldn't move. I watched until it was over, and Cristal slid out of bed. She was naked, she walked off camera, in a few minutes she came back, still naked, with washcloths and a towel. Zack cleaned himself, and she left the room as he dressed and moved back into his chair. When he was ready to leave, he wheeled towards the door without saying goodbye.

"You never look at me, you know." There was bitterness in Cristal's voice; there was also longing.

"We both know why I'm here," he said. When he was gone, she threw the towel he'd been using against the door. "Bastard," she said. Then the screen went black.

I hit eject. What was on the disc was not a surprise. Zack had told me that he'd bought sex from Cristal Avilia. But knowing it and watching it were two different matters. I put the disc into the pocket of the folder that contained my notes about "Women in Politics." I called Ginny's cell and told her I couldn't make the canvass this afternoon, but I'd meet her at Luther for the basketball game after supper.

Then I made myself a sandwich that I didn't remember eating, went outside, and started breaking up the soil in the patch beside the house where we'd decided to plant tomatoes. The bed hadn't been worked before, and as I dug, the sun pressed down on my back like a hand. By the time I'd prepared the soil and given it a soak, I was sweaty, stiff, and thirsty, but I felt better. When I went back inside to shower, the phone was ringing. It was Zack.

"Jesus, I was starting to worry," he said. "Your cell must be turned off, and I've called home about a dozen times. Everything okay?"

"I was out digging that bed where we're going to put the tomatoes," I said.

"You sure you're okay? You don't sound like yourself?"

"I don't feel like myself," I said. "Somebody left a DVD in our mailbox. It was of you with Cristal Avilia."

There was silence on the other end of the line. "And you watched it."

"Yes. Not the smartest move I ever made."

"I'm coming home," he said.

"You don't have to."

"I know, but I want to."

I went to the little greenhouse Zack had had built for my birthday and began carrying out the tomato plants we'd been growing. They were thriving. I heard his car come up, but I didn't go out to greet him. In a few minutes, he came up behind me and touched my arm. "So where do we start with this?"

"I don't know," I said.

He reached out to me, but I moved away. He wheeled his chair close to the plants. "How do you know when they're ready for the big move outdoors?" he said.

"You kind of ease them into it," I said. "I'll take them back inside tonight. When they're ready and we can trust the weather, I'll plant them. I used to help my father do this when I was a kid."

"You never told me that. In fact, you've never told me much about your father at all."

"I didn't see him much," I said. "He was a doctor, and doctors are busy people. But he liked to grow cherry tomatoes from seed. And he let me help him."

"So that's why you wanted to do this."

"I guess. My father didn't spend much time at home, but during tomato season, he'd always leave a little dish of these on the kitchen counter, and they'd be there when I woke up. It always made me feel good imagining him out there in the dark picking the tomatoes, thinking about me."

Zack took my hand. "Jo, what can I do to fix this?"

"Make it go away," I said.

"I can't," he said.

"Then I guess we just have to keep on keeping on," I said.

CHAPTER

6

That afternoon, Zack and I followed the adage that the best thing to do when confronted with a problem is to sleep on it. We took a nap, and when I awoke with his body warm against mine, and the branches of the honeysuckle outside our window tracing shadows on the bedroom ceiling, I knew we had to do whatever it took to hold on to our life together. As if he'd read my mind, Zack reached for my hand. "We can't blow this," he said.

I laced my fingers through his. "We did take those vows."

"It's your call about where we go from here," Zack said.

"Let's just get on with it," I said. And so we did. We dressed and went into the kitchen. Zack made tea; I took a pan of lasagna from the freezer and put it in the oven for dinner, then like other busy couples, we sat down at the table and checked our messages.

Mine were predictable: a call from Mieka reminding me that the next day was the first anniversary of UpSlideDown and that I'd promised to have lunch there with her and the girls. The rest of my messages were from Ginny's campaign: two from Keith asking advice about media buys; one from

Milo O'Brien, whose staccato intensity as he summoned me to a breakfast rally the next day at the Pile O' Bones Club made his invitation sound like a threat; and one from Ginny telling me she was going to the Luther game early to watch the twins warm up and she'd save seats for us.

I wrote down what I needed to remember and poured the tea. When I handed Zack his cup, he was still checking messages, and I was smug. "Beat you," I said. "My life is more manageable than yours."

He exhaled wearily. "You don't know the half of it, Ms. Shreve. I have a message from the pal who referred me to Cristal. It turns out he'd recommended her to other guys, all lawyers, and all of them had very personal DVDs hand-delivered to their family mailboxes today."

"Without explanation."

"Right," Zack said. "No explanations, no demands, no nothing. Just seven DVDs of married men doing what they shouldn't have been doing with Cristal Avilia." He rubbed his head. "You know, until now, I thought I had a pretty good idea of how that disc ended up in our mailbox."

"You never said anything."

"I wanted to make sure I was right. Jo, I thought Debbie Haczkewicz put it there."

"Debbie Haczkewicz? Come on, Zack, she's a police officer. Why would she risk her job to hand you evidence?"

"Because it wasn't evidence. It was just something that happened to be in Cristal's condo. Debbie knows I didn't kill Cristal, and she knows I am married. She is also aware that Denise Kaiswatum opens and logs every piece of mail that arrives at Falconer Shreve and that much of the time I work at home. When you told me about the disc, I assumed that Debbie slipped it in our mailbox and didn't have a chance to call and tell me it was there."

"Why would Debbie try to protect you?"

He sipped his tea. "Because she thinks she owes me. Her son, Leo, was in an accident three years ago. He flipped his motorcycle on the Ring Road and broke his back. He's a paraplegic. Nineteen. Not easy to be that young and know that you're going to be stuck in a wheelchair for the rest of your life. But, like the rest of us, Leo didn't have a choice. The doctors patched him up and packed him off to Wascana Rehab so he could 'adapt to an altered lifestyle.'"

"And Leo didn't want to adapt?"

"He wanted to die. I remember the feeling." Zack's lips were tight. "That's when Debbie called and asked me to visit him."

"What happened?"

"I introduced myself, and Leo took a swing at me. Strong kid," Zack said admiringly.

"Did you swing back?"

"God, no. I remembered my own days in rehab. Our most potent weapon was our catheter. Disconnect one of those, aim it, and –"

I put up my hand. "I get the picture."

Zack smiled at the memory. "Anyway, I let Leo flail away and rant about how unfair it was that he had to spend the rest of his fucking life in a fucking wheelchair. And when he was finished, I told him I'd be back the next day and I wheeled off in my fucking wheelchair."

I shook my head. "How come you never told me this?"

"The kid deserved his privacy, and when I met him, he was not at his best. Leo was a tough case. I must have gone there every day for three solid weeks before he finally cracked."

"You won him over with your charm," I said.

Zack shook his head. "No, I bought him off with a T-shirt I got on the Internet. On the front there was a cartoon of a guy in a wheelchair saying, 'I'm only in this for the parking.'"

"And the cartoon got through to Leo?"

"Something did. He stopped yelling, and we started talking. He turned out to be a really nice kid. We still keep in touch."

"So where's Leo now?"

"At U of S, majoring in English, which, as Leo points out, is a lame subject anyway, so what the hell?"

I took Zack's hand. "We're laughing again," I said.

"Yep, and we can freeze the frame right here if you want. I can tell you more uproarious stories about my adventures in rehab, and we can declare the subject of Cristal off limits."

"Except it's always better to know than not to know," I said. "So let's have it. I'm assuming the fact that the DVDs went to other people besides you rules out Debbie Haczkewicz as the source."

"Absolutely," Zack said. "So we're back to square one."

"Square one times seven," I said.

"With a couple of significant differences." Zack ticked off the points on his fingers. "My relationship with Cristal had been over for two years when she died, and you knew that I'd been with her."

"And the men who called this morning had wives who were still living in blissful ignorance," I said.

Zack lowered his eyes. "Right. And, of course, these guys are terrified that now that the genie is out of the bottle, they'll lose their families."

"Maybe they should have thought of that sooner."

Zack pushed his chair back. "Jo, all of Cristal's clients, me included, took a stupid risk, but what we should have done is no longer an issue. We have to deal with the stuff that's hitting the fan now. And I need to know where it's coming from."

"Talk to the other men," I said.

"That's not a problem for you?"

I shook my head.

"I'd like to keep this whole thing as quiet as possible. Would it be all right if we met here tonight?"

"Of course," I said. "But, Zack, I'm assuming these are people I know."

"Some of them are," he said, "and if it's going to be awkward for you, say the word."

"It's going to be awkward for everybody," I said. "It might be wise to make sure Taylor and I have already left for the game when your guests arrive and that they're gone by the time we get back."

"Got it," Zack said. "To be fair, Jo, most of these people are decent. They've done something foolish and they've jeopardized things that should not have been jeopardized, but they're not beyond the pale. Try to hang on to that."

"You think I'm being judgmental."

Zack's dark eyes met mine. "I think none of us knows what goes on in other people's bedrooms."

As soon as Taylor and I arrived at Luther, she spotted Blake Falconer's Mercedes in the parking lot. "Hey, there's Gracie's dad's car. Okay if I go in and find her?"

"Uh-uh," I said. "Gracie's probably with her team, warming up. And there are going to be a lot of people at this game. In that new hoodie, you're going to look like every other Luther student in the gym."

Taylor patted the emblematic lion on her shirt. "I want to fit in."

"Wherever you are, you fit in," I said.

Arms outstretched, Taylor did a 360-degree twirl, taking in the campus. "Isn't this just the greatest?" she said.

It was a green and gold evening in May. The sun was moving down in the sky and as its light hit the jets of water from the lawn sprinklers, it shattered into prisms, small rainbows blooming in the rich grass. The air was silky and filled with the sounds of spring: birdsong, young voices, and the rustle of new leaves in the wind.

I put my arm around my daughter's waist and squeezed. "You bet," I said. "This is the greatest."

We didn't need directions to the gym. It was half an hour till game time, but this game was being played for a charity and the halls were already choked with donors and students, most wearing the Luther black and gold, but many wearing the red and yellow of their rivals, the Spartans. Rowdy, animated, and flushed with excitement, the kids moved towards the gymnasium, where the hormones boiling inside them could erupt as soon as the whistle blew. The donors, many of them wearing smart scarves in the colours of their alma mater, were carried along by the crowd and by the hope that, when the whistle blew, their own hormones would kick in.

I didn't have any trouble spotting Ginny. She was sitting in the front row of the bleachers, wearing jeans, a sweatshirt, and a black ball cap. More than a few people glanced her way, but Ginny's focus was her daughters, who were doing layups with the rest of their team. I sat down beside her. "Quite a crowd," I said.

"Ranch Ehrlo's a good cause," she replied, but her eyes stayed on her girls. When their coach whistled the team off the court, Ginny turned to me. "I'm glad you're here. You, too, Taylor."

"Thanks for keeping seats for us," Taylor said. "I hate sitting way up at the top."

"Me too," Ginny said. "That's why I always made sure I was in the game."

I laughed. "How did the door-knocking go this afternoon?"

"Not bad. No one threw stones at me and no one called me a slut. Getting custody of the girls is helping."

"Good career move?" I said.

Ginny made a moue of mock disgust. "You're so cynical, Joanne."

We both laughed. "So what's next?" I asked. "Milo called about the breakfast rally."

"Bring yogurt," she said. "I have to choke down all that grease, but there's no reason you should."

"This isn't my first breakfast rally," I said. "I know to bring yogurt."

"Good. Hey, Keith tells me he's bounced a couple of ideas off you, and you're brilliant."

"Keith overestimates my contribution," I said. "They're his ideas. I just confirm that they're brilliant."

"Well, whatever you're doing, thanks. This campaign is a mess. We need all the help we can get. Speaking of help, I really appreciate Mieka letting us shoot a couple of TV spots at her business."

"You're taping at UpSlideDown? How did that happen?"

"Keith arranged it. He said it would be perfect. It's in the constituency, and those yummy mummies and their toddlers will help people forget my libidinous hijinks."

"And Mieka was all right with it?"

Ginny's smile was puckish. "My libidinous hijinks?"

I laughed. "The TV spots. She's not exactly right wing."

"I might be conservative, Jo, but I'm not a dinosaur. And the TV shoot was Mieka's idea."

We were interrupted by a man who wanted Ginny's autograph, then by a woman who asked Ginny if it was true she supported same-sex marriage. When Ginny said she did, the woman called her an abomination and huffed off. "I believe I just lost a vote," Ginny said mildly.

I was reading the history of Ranch Ehrlo in the souvenir program, trying not to listen to Ginny defend her stance on

Canada's role in Afghanistan to a very angry young man, when I saw Blake Falconer. He was still wearing a suit and tie, but he looked unkempt. His eyes were red and swollen and his face was haggard. I went over and tapped him on the shoulder.

"Hi there," I said.

For a moment, it seemed he couldn't quite place me. "Sorry," he said. "I wandered off there for a bit."

"Are you okay?"

He tried a smile. "Bad day. But Gracie's playing, so here I am."

"Why don't you sit with us?" I said. "Ginny saved a place for Zack, but he has a meeting."

Blake nodded. "I'm aware of the meeting."

"Did you get a DVD?"

"No. My relationship with Cristal was . . . different." His voice broke. "Jesus, the hits just keep on coming, don't they?" He took out a handkerchief and blew his nose.

"When was the last time you got some sleep?" I asked.

"I don't know," he said.

I touched his arm. "Go home and go to bed," I said. "I can bring Gracie by after the game."

"Thanks, but she always looks for me in the stands."

He sat beside me, head down, staring at the gleaming wood of the gym floor. Only when the teams were announced, did he raise his eyes. Gracie flushed and freckled, her explosion of red curls tamed into a ponytail, swept the stands with her eyes, found her dad, gave him the thumbs-up, and ran into place. The Brodnitz twins, sleek in the Luther black and gold, had already found their places, and they were bouncing lightly on their toes, impatient to start.

When the whistle blew, the stands erupted. At first it seemed the teams were evenly matched. Close to the half, the score was 32-26 for Luther. The fans leapt to their feet and stayed there despite the rising temperature. Taylor knew nothing about basketball, but, her face shining with excitement, she was on her feet cheering or groaning whenever everyone else wearing the black and gold cheered and groaned. Only Blake and Ginny seemed immune to the contact high. Blake watched through unseeing eyes, his face frozen in a half-smile. The noise in the gym was ear-splitting, but Ginny observed the action with professional concentration. She didn't cheer for her daughters: her connection to their game was deeper than that. When either of them took possession of the ball, Ginny would stretch her own strong wide hands, willing them to play their best.

And after the half, their best was sensational. The coach might have been unwise in praising the Brodnitz twins so fulsomely to their teammates, but she hadn't been inaccurate. The other young women on the team played with enthusiasm and skill; some, including Gracie Falconer, showed flashes of real ability, but Emma and Chloe Brodnitz were brilliant.

Strong, quick, and tenacious, the twins generated their own force field: creating plays, leaping, shooting, scoring. Their game had nothing to do with chalkboards and strategies, and everything to do with body wisdom. They didn't react. They seemed to know what was going to happen next, and when it happened, the twins were already there. Luther won: 72-48. The Brodnitz twins had been responsible for fifty of those points. As the opposing teams shook hands, Ginny permitted herself a small smile. During the obligatory team hug, Chloe and Emma remained distant, and they moved away from the celebration quickly. Em glanced in our direction, saw her mother, and she and Chloe ran over to our front-row bench.

Ginny treated her daughters as peers. "Nice game," she

said. "A couple of plays that I imagine you'd like to reassess but, on the whole, great job."

Chloe gazed at the crowd. "Is Dad here?"

"I don't think so," Ginny said.

Em narrowed her eyes at her sister. "Get used to it. The case is over." Then she turned to her mother. "You can come back to the locker room if you want. A couple of the girls said they'd like to meet you."

Ginny stood up. "My pleasure." She turned to me. "See you at the breakfast?"

"I'll be there," I said. "Em and Chloe, it was a thrill watching you tonight."

"Thank you. It was nice of you to come," they said in unison.

Gracie, a girl as generous as she was gregarious, finally broke from her teammates and came running over to us. Damp with perspiration, she was still making connections. "Taylor, there are some girls you absolutely have to meet. I know you'll absolutely love them, and they'll absolutely love you."

Taylor looked at me beseechingly. "Is it okay?"

"Absolutely," I said.

Gracie rolled her eyes. "I overuse that word, don't I?"

"Maybe," I said. "But you're so absolutely great, nobody cares. Now, I think your father and I should get out of here. This room is a steam bath. We'll meet you outside."

Gracie groaned and threw her arms around her father. "Dad, I didn't even say hello to you. I am such a loser."

Blake buried his face in his daughter's crinkly red hair. "You're not a loser," he said. "You're the best thing that ever happened to me."

The sorrow in Blake's voice was palpable. Gracie stepped back and gave her father a searching look. "Are you all right?"

"I'm fine," he said. "Joanne and I will meet you out front. It really is a steam bath in here."

Reluctant to have the evening end, students from both Sheldon and Luther were lingering in the halls, and progress was slow. When Blake and I finally made it out of the brightly lit school into the gentle half-light of gloaming, I took a deep breath. "Feel that coolness," I said. "I've always loved this time of day."

"For a lot of years now, I've hated it," Blake said. "When the sun goes down, there are no more distractions – it's time to face reality."

"Is reality that bad?" I said.

"Tomorrow's Cristal's funeral," he said. "It doesn't get any worse than that."

The sprinklers had been turned off, and as we walked the ground was cool and spongy beneath our feet.

"Did she mean that much to you?" I asked.

"She saved me," he said flatly. "And if I hadn't been such a coward I could have saved her."

The relationship among the partners and families of Falconer Shreve was particularly intimate. We lived within blocks of one another in the city, we all owned cottages on the same bay at the lake, and the daughters of three of us were close friends.

In the year in which they articled, the members of the Winners' Circle went their separate ways. Delia Wainberg went to the Supreme Court; Blake, Kevin, and Chris Altieri were scooped up by big-name law firms outside the province; Zack went to a small firm in Regina where he got tons of court time, very little supervision, and wasn't the token guy in the wheelchair. All five of them had lucrative employment offers when their articling year was over. The money was tempting, but none of the members of the Winners' Circle gave a moment's consideration to anything other than practising law together.

There had been discussion about the order in which their names would appear on the office door and letterhead. Sensibly they headed off the problem of wounded egos by consigning the decision to fate. Delia Wainberg was a runner, so the members of the Winners' Circle threw their names into one of her cross-trainers and the boy who delivered the pizza did the honours. No one complained. They moved into an office above a company that made dentures, painted the name Falconer Shreve Altieri Wainberg and Hynd on the door, and looked forward to a glowing future.

After twenty-five years, the glow had dimmed. Zack and Delia Wainberg were still true believers, dedicated to the law as it was practised by Falconer Shreve. Chris Altieri was dead, and after two years, his suicide was still a raw wound in the hearts of those who loved him. Kevin Hynd, having found the practice of law soul-scouring, left the firm for five years while he searched for answers; Chris's death brought Kevin back to the firm, but he was a changed man whose New Age beliefs did not always sit well with his old partners. And Blake Falconer, the lucky guy whose name had been picked first from Delia Wainberg's cross-trainer, had turned out to be grimly fated for tragedy.

I met Blake Falconer at the beginning of the last summer of his marriage. Despite the fact that even he had lost count of the number of times his wife had been unfaithful in their fifteen years together, Blake's passion for Lily was still painfully intense. During the two months when the Falconer marriage ran out its last dark moments, I saw Blake almost every day, and I was struck by the gulf between his public and private lives. Professionally, he was a successful lawyer with a golden touch for real estate and development; privately, he was a driven man trying desperately to hold on to a woman determined to destroy herself. Ultimately, the demons that had driven Lily throughout her life claimed her. Until that night on the tranquil campus of Luther College, I hadn't realized they had almost claimed Blake as well.

After we found a bench where we could sit while we waited for our daughters, Blake fell silent. I was relieved. I'd heard enough about Cristal to last me for a long while, but it turned out Blake was just gathering his thoughts. Very quickly, he made it clear he needed to talk.

"If it hadn't been for Cristal, I think I might have killed Lily," he said. "The first time I went to Cristal's condo, I was so filled with rage that I could barely function. I'd never been with a prostitute, but I was crazy. Lily had taken off with somebody else – again. This time I saw her actually get into the truck with the man. He was the guy who delivered bottled water to our firm. Of course, Lily, as office manager, had chosen the company. It was called Pure.

"The man's name was Steve and he was nineteen years old – a bodybuilder and a real smartass. Before that day, when Lily wandered, I'd always been able to force myself into some sort of perspective. I'd think about Gracie and my partners and my friends and my career. But when I saw Lily get into the truck with that cretin . . . something snapped. I knew I couldn't take it any more: the humiliation, the rage, the wreckage of everything we were supposed to be to each other. I had never been unfaithful to Lily – not once – but when I thought of her spreading those beautiful legs of hers for that animal . . ." He swallowed hard. "I wanted her to know how it felt."

"So you went to a prostitute."

Blake nodded. "Cristal came highly recommended. She was safe, and she was discreet. She also turned to be my salvation.

Everybody knew about Lily, of course, but I never talked to anyone about our marriage – not even Zack, and he's the one I'm closest to. But from the moment I met Cristal, I knew I could tell her everything, and she would understand." As he talked, Blake had kept his head down; now he turned and looked into my face. "Cristal made me understand why Lily was so determined to destroy our life together."

"And what Cristal told you made sense?"

"Given Lily's past, it did. Cristal said she understood women like Lily because she was like that herself. She said Lily didn't believe she was worthy of a good life, and so she did everything she could to make sure that she got the kind of life she deserved."

I remembered how often and how harshly I'd judged Lily. My throat tightened. "Blake, I'm so sorry."

"You couldn't have done anything. Lily was determined to destroy us, and she did. At least now I understand why she did it."

I looked across the lawn. Gracie and Taylor, in their matching Luther hoodies, were running towards us. "Here come the girls."

"Time to shape up." He squared his shoulders and tried a smile. "Convincing?"

"You're in luck," I said. "It's dark."

He gave me a quick glance. "Jo, Zack should know this. I don't want him thinking Cristal was just another whore."

"I'll tell him," I said.

Gracie barrelled into her father. "Everybody says if it weren't for the Miraculous Brodnitz Twins, I could have been the game all-star."

Blake held his daughter's shoulders. "Life is full of Brodnitz twins," he said. "But there are rewards for the rest of us too. How about we go to the Milky Way and get some ice cream?" He glanced at me. "Joanne?"

"Why not?" I said. "But I'll buy. We'll have to take something for Zack, and he is not a cheap date."

When we got home, there were two empty liquor bottles by the kitchen door, destined for the recycle, and Zack was putting drink glasses into the dishwasher.

"Looks like you had yourself quite a party," I said.

"Nobody had any fun," he said. He spotted the sundae Taylor was carrying. "Is that for me?"

Taylor handed it to him. "Yes, because you missed the game, but the ice cream's melting, so you'd better eat it fast."

"That will be no problem at all," he said. "Thank you, ladies."

"I'm going to have a shower," Taylor said. "It was super hot in the gym, but it was a great game, wasn't it, Jo?"

"It was," I said. "Why don't you tell Zack about it?"

Taylor grinned. "Like I know a single thing about basketball. Luther won, and I had a blast. That's it!" She kissed us goodnight and vanished.

"Hard to believe that's the girl who made me understand the significance of Monet's windows," Zack said, spooning ice cream and butterscotch sauce.

"How did the meeting go?" I asked.

"If the intent was to figure out what the hell's going on, it was a waste of good Scotch. But you'll be relieved to hear that our Glenfiddich smoothed the way to some serious male bonding. My group of seven has decided to stick together."

"Like the seven dwarfs," I said.

Zack dug into the chocolate ripple. "Are you pissed off?"

"No. Just bemused."

"If it's any consolation, these guys are sweating bullets. They're all guilty as hell when it comes to fidelity to their marriage vows, but they all swear they had nothing to do with Cristal's death. That said, they're savvy enough to know that sooner or later the police investigation will turn up their names."

"You're all lawyers," I said. "Someone must have floated the idea of going to the police before the police came to you."

"Actually, everybody here tonight was a defence lawyer and that means they know how to play the odds. Somebody sent them DVDs of their private activities, which is weird but also legal because there was no threat and no attempt to extort. In short, there is no crime. So the consensus was that the potential loss outweighed the potential gain."

"So everyone was cool."

"No. They're going through hell, waiting for the other shoe to drop."

"And the other shoe would be. . . ?"

"Blackmail – like Cristal tried with Ned."

"But Cristal's dead."

"And the DVDs still arrived in our mailboxes. That's why people are so scared. With blackmail, it's always a plus to know the blackmailer. That's how you reach some mutually acceptable accord. Obviously, these men knew Cristal intimately. But because she's dead, we don't know who's calling the shots. I never thought I'd say this, but in a way Ned Osler was lucky. He knew exactly who and what he was dealing with."

"Did he? Zack, did it never strike you as curious that, out of all of her clients, Cristal chose to blackmail the one who treated her well – the one who brought her books and believed she was, like Henry James's character Isabel Archer, too good for this world?"

He nodded. "It crossed my mind, but then Cristal was dead, and there were all these other problems, so I guess I just shoved that one aside. Jo, the truth is, there's a lot I can't figure out about this. I listened to those guys tonight, and usually when I hear the stories, I get a feel for what's happening, but not with this one. I'm flummoxed, Ms. Shreve." He picked up one of Taylor's black and gold pom-poms and twirled it. "But at least Luther won."

"And while Luther was winning, Blake was disintegrating," I said. "After the game, Gracie took Taylor around to introduce her to some of her friends, and Blake and I talked. He's in terrible shape, Zack. He blames himself for not saving Cristal."

Zack smacked the pom-pom against his hand. "Shit. Talk about a train wreck you can see coming. Cristal was Lily all over again, you know."

"I know," I said. "Blake knows too, but that's not making the loss any easier. He says Cristal was the only one he could really talk to about Lily."

"Jesus, Jo, how dumb can he be? Doesn't he understand that Cristal's schtick was being whatever the man wanted her to be? That's why she was able to charge $500 an hour. Remember me telling you that when I saw the tape of Cristal with Ned, I couldn't believe it was the same woman I'd been with? Well, that was true right across the board. Every guy here tonight talked about what Cristal had been like with him. You wouldn't have known they were talking about the same woman. She changed her act for every customer. The first night I was with her, she poured me a drink and asked me in that little girl voice of hers what my fantasy was."

"What did you tell her?"

"I said my fantasy was to be able to get it up. She said, 'So you're not paying for games, just expertise.' I agreed, and I got what I paid for. Just the way every guy here tonight got what he paid for. These were commercial transactions – nothing more."

"Blake doesn't see it that way. I think he loved her, Zack."

Zack drew his hand across his eyes. "You know I don't think I can deal with that tonight. I'm exhausted, Ms. Shreve."

"Me too," I said. "Boy, it wouldn't take many days like this one to make a dozen, would it?"

Zack put his arm around me. "Nope, but at least you and I are headed for the same bed."

"And it's going to stay that way," I said.

CHAPTER

7

The next morning when the dogs and I went for our run, fog hung over the lake and a light rain was falling. Puddles of water were spreading on the grass, so we stayed on the concrete. Willie and Pantera revelled in mud, but I didn't, and after months of power struggles and the intervention of a dog trainer, I had established myself as the alpha or, at least, as the one who held the leashes. Running in what my grandmother called "the Scottish mist" was always a joy to me. The familiar world was suddenly a place of Brigadoon mystery, and while heather on the hill was in short supply in Wascana Park so were bridges of doom. In my view it was a saw-off. And that day as the dogs and I made our way along the rain-slicked walkway beside the Broad Street Bridge, there was another reward. On the sandy shoreline on the south side of the bridge, a pair of American avocets was foraging in the shallow water with their elegant upturned bills.

The southern part of our province was a favourite breeding place of the avocet, but this pair was the first I'd seen this year. I wasn't a knowledgeable birder, but I'd always been attracted to quirky pieces of information and avocets provided a romantic one: after mating, the pair crossed their slender bills and walked away together. I was still smiling at that image when the dogs and I started home.

Zack was in the kitchen finishing his coffee and dressed for work in one of his beautiful silk suits. "You look like the cover of *GQ*," I said.

He smiled. "Thank you. You look like you could use a kiss and a shower."

"Maybe, not in that order," I said. "I'm sweaty."

"I thought I detected a powerful pheromonal waft." Zack held out his arms. "Come on, you can't let your body send out signals like that and not let me at least cop a feel."

I kissed him. "Now you're the one sending out signals," I said.

Zack looked at his watch. "Damn, and I haven't got time to follow through. I've got a meeting in half an hour. I picked up a new case last night."

"One of your bad boys?"

"No, a case that one of my bad boys was supposed to be handling. He's in-house counsel to Peyben, the company that's developing that new housing tract out by the airport. Peyben is being sued by a clairvoyant who claims she had a vision that the land would be developed and she passed along her vision to one of their executives."

"And now the clairvoyant wants some of the lolly," I said. "How come the Peyben lawyer's handing this off to you?"

Zack raised an eyebrow. "Because he's obsessed with the Cristal Avilia case, and he's afraid that if he met with the psychic, she'd be able to read his mind."

"Oh what tangled webs we weave," I said.

Zack chortled. "If only you knew. I'd better get a move on, but I'll see you at UpSlideDown for lunch."

"You're coming? That's a nice surprise."

"Maddy phoned last night and asked me herself."

"Get there early," I said. "Ginny's filming a campaign spot. So there'll be cameras and lights and people."

"Everything's coming up roses for Ginny?"

"The polls say yes."

"I heard a bit of her interview on *Quinlan Live*. It seemed to be going well."

"You didn't hear the whole thing," I said. "At one point a young woman called in. She was reading from a script."

"A script?"

"It happens," I said. "Talk-show producers get to know the voices of campaign workers, so sometimes they keep them off air. That's when organizers turn to novices to spread the good word."

"Using a script."

"Novices get off message."

"And this caller got off message."

"I don't think she did," I said. "I think she read exactly what she'd been given to read. The script was literate, and it started innocently enough. The girl commended Ginny for her good work in the past; then she said Ginny's contribution was particularly praiseworthy because while she was working for her country, her ex-husband was living off the money he took from prostitutes in Regina."

Zack's eyes widened. "Did the caller mention any names?"

"No. Do you think she was referring to Cristal Avilia?"

"These days it seems that all roads lead to Cristal, but I guess she wasn't the only sex-trade worker servicing rich clients."

Zack's words were blunt, matter of fact, and his lack of emotion infuriated me. I slammed down my mug, spilling coffee on the table. "Why is that, Zack? Do guys just finish at work for the day, close down their computers, buy an hour of love, then go home to the wife and kids?"

Zack picked up a napkin and mopped my coffee. "It's more

complicated than that," he said. "Can we talk about it later?"

"Sure," I said. "And by then, I may have some insights for you. Later on this morning I'm meeting a woman who ran an escort service."

"Why ever would you do that?" Zack was very still and his voice was almost a whisper. I'd seen him use that technique in court. It had a way of making witnesses feel small, foolish, and exposed. It didn't work on me.

"Jill thinks the Cristal Avilia case is going to be big news," I said.

"And she wants you to get involved."

"We thought it would be useful if I acquired a little knowledge."

"You're making a mistake, Joanne."

"Well, I won't be the first one to do that, will I?"

Zack looked at me hard. "No, you won't. So, do you want to take another shot at me, or can I go to work?"

I picked up a towel and started wiping off the sweat. "Go to work," I said. "There's not a lot to hold you here."

He winced. "Jesus, Jo. Let's not start the day this way. Can we just let this go – at least for a while?"

For a beat we just looked at each other. The shadows under his eyes were pronounced. I knew he wasn't sleeping well. "Okay," I said. "We'll start again. I saw something neat on my run this morning. The American avocets are back."

"The ones who do that crossed-bills thing? Where were they?"

"Down on that little beach by the Broad Street Bridge."

"Want to go over tonight and have a look?"

"If the rain keeps up, it might be tough to get down there in the chair."

"I'll manage," Zack said.

"You always do," I said. I picked up our dishes and took them to the sink.

"So who's the woman you're seeing?"

"Her name is Vera Wang."

"Well, you're in good hands."

"You know her?"

He nodded.

"Did you use her services, too?"

"Nope," Zack said. "She used mine. Vera kept what we, in our archaic legal way, call a common bawdy house. Section 210 of the Criminal Code has a problem with her line of work. I'm a lawyer, Joanne. From time to time, people who run afoul of the law come to me." With that, he started to wheel out of the room. "I'm not always the bad guy. Cut me a little slack."

Ginny's breakfast was being held at the Pile O' Bones Club; the name was a romantic allusion to our city's past, but the club itself was a utilitarian concrete structure that, ugly as it was, had been constructed within Palliser riding, and that was all that mattered. When I got into my Volvo to drive to the event, I tuned in Jack Quinlan's show. There'd been new polling the night before. Nationwide, the election was still too close to call and of Saskatchewan's fourteen federal ridings, nine were considered in play. Palliser was one of them. The topic for the morning was predictable: what do you think the outcome will be on Monday? I recognized the voice of the first caller. Malcolm had been a staunch supporter of my old party for years. He was knowledgeable and wildly partisan. Our former premier used to say that if our party had nominated Judas Iscariot and the opposition had nominated Jesus Christ, Malcolm would have voted for Judas. That morning, Malcolm was ruminating on Ginny's changing fortunes. He was surprisingly even-handed, saying he felt the personal attacks on her had been boorish and unfair, but expressing surprise that the polls had turned so dramatically because of the outcome of the custody suit. Malcolm's view was that, whatever she did in her personal life, Ginny had a political record that thoughtful voters should peruse, and when they saw what Ginny was politically, they would reject her for the right reasons. At first, it seemed the next caller's comments grew out of Malcolm's. She argued with enviably perfect diction that while the Honourable Ms. Monaghan's personal life should not be an issue, the excesses of Jason Brodnitz – "a well-known denizen of the city's red light district" – should concern decent citizens of every political stripe. Quinlan warned against slandering and took the next call. By that time, I was at the Pile O' Bones Club.

The parking lot was filled, and so were the parking spaces on the streets adjacent to the club. I had to drive three blocks to find a parking space. Ginny's campaign was clearly moving in the right direction. In my lifetime, I had probably attended a hundred breakfast rallies. They were easy to plan because the menu was as invariable as the program. The faithful chowed down on watery scrambled eggs, greasy bacon, and cool, limp toast while a local MLA with a reputation as a wit warmed them up. Then a colleague of the candidate introduced her, the candidate took centre stage and wowed the crowd, and after party supporters had handed over their money and promised to get out to vote on E-Day, they were free to leave.

When I walked into the Pile O' Bones Club, Keith Harris was right inside the door. I checked out the room. "Another good sign," I said. "You had to open the concertina wall – that means you've got at least two hundred and fifty people."

Keith smiled. "Three hundred and twenty, and counting," he said. "And the most important one just arrived."

"Smooth talker," I said.

"I have to do something to make up for the food," Keith said. He pointed to the steam table. "You know the drill," he said. "Fill a plate, and listen to your arteries scream for mercy." He smiled. "I guess a septuple bypass would indicate that my arteries have already spoken. "

Even after a night's sleep and a fresh shave, Keith's colour was not good. I reached into my bag, pulled out the container of yogurt, and handed it to him. "Eat this," I said. "I've had a run, and I've got a long day ahead. I can use a manly breakfast."

I filled a plate and we found the table at the back where the professionals always sat. Milo O'Brien was already there, stabbing at his BlackBerry and eating his Crispy Crunch. He gave us an absent wave, but he made no attempt to join us.

Our timing couldn't have been worse. I had just forked my first bite of sausage when the warm-up man, the local MLA, ran onstage. His blond toupee looked thatched, like a roof in a fairy tale, and his stories were cringe-inducingly blue. After a joke about the number of political bones that had been present in Ginny's body, Keith made a moue of disgust. "How did this idiot get elected?"

"The Liberals and the NDP split the vote, and he slithered up the middle."

"How did he get nominated?"

"In the land of the blind, the one-eyed man is king."

"The bar for political candidacy does seem to have been lowered," Keith said equitably. He looked at me. "Is that why you stopped being involved with your party?"

"Partly. And partly I just got tired of sounding old – harkening back to the days when political discourse was civil and people had principles. The new gotcha politics makes me sick."

"Is that why you were so open to Ginny?"

I nodded. "I thought there was an excessive licking of chops when the details of her private life became public."

"But it's more than just principle," Keith said. "You like Ginny, don't you?"

"I do."

His smile was sly. "So are you going to vote for her?"

"Now that would be a huge step. As one of Jack Quinlan's callers said today, a vote should be decided on where a candidate stands on the issues, not on personality."

"Ginny's not that far from you on most issues, and you know the argument there: better to elect someone who can be in the government tent arguing for you than to vote for someone who'll be a voice in the wilderness for the next four years."

"So you think you're going to form government again?"

"Probably with a minority, but yes, I think we'll pull it off. We've got our political base. If we can get them to the polls, then convince enough Canadians we're not as crazy as our political base, we've got it nailed." Keith glanced up at the stage. "Looks like Buddy Hackett's finished. Can I get you some more coffee before the main event?"

"My turn to buy," I said. I stood and picked up our cups. Then I heard a familiar voice coming through the PA system. I looked at the stage, then back at Keith. "What's Sean Barton doing up there?"

"He appears to be introducing Ginny," Keith said.

"When did he join your campaign?"

"Last night. Another sign that we're going to win. When smart young lawyers sign on this close to E-Day, you suspect the breaks are coming your way." Keith's gaze was appraising. "I take it this will be news to your husband."

"News, but not a surprise. Sean hasn't been happy at Falconer Shreve lately, so he may be looking in another direction."

"If he's looking in our direction, I'd appreciate knowing if he comes with baggage."

"No, I don't think he does. He's smart and he's charming. Zack just thinks he doesn't have the right feeling for the law. He says Sean is less concerned about people than he is about moving the pieces around so he can win."

Keith raised an eyebrow. "If Sean wants a career in Ottawa, that won't be a liability."

I looked across the room at Ginny, surrounded by well-wishers pushing one another to get closer. I thought of the actress Elizabeth Taylor's wry observation: "There's no deodorant like success." Seemingly, the peccadilloes that had so alarmed Ginny's political base just days ago had become insignificant. "Keith, if Ginny wins Palliser again, what's next for her?"

"She goes after the leadership."

"Character will no longer be an issue?"

"It can be handled," Keith said. "People's memories are short, and Ginny does have custody of her daughters."

"And you'd support her?"

Keith nodded. "It's time for a woman prime minister – not just somebody dropped into the shark tank to finish out a term but a person who can really lead the country. Ginny has a vision of what Canada can be that's genuinely compelling. All this talk about her private life has obscured it, but she's smart and she's thoughtful. Most importantly, with those girls by her side, she'd be a dynamite candidate."

"So if Ginny wins Monday night, Tuesday morning you start sharpening the knives and go after the current tenant of 24 Sussex Drive."

Keith nodded. "That's the way it works," he said.

I picked up our empty cups. "I forgot to get our refill. I'll buy you fresh and better at Mieka's."

"I'll hold you to that," Keith said, and we sat back and listened to Sean do a masterful job of being grateful, humble, and excited about introducing Ginny, and Ginny do an equally masterful job of being grateful, humble, and excited about the challenge of winning the election and serving Palliser again. Neither Keith nor I responded to the financial appeal. Keith was already a maxed-out donor, and, as a woman who'd spent her adult life working for the party that opposed Keith's, I would have had a Dr. Strangelove moment if I'd attempted to contribute a single loonie to the Conservative Party.

The room cleared out quickly, but Keith wanted to talk to Ginny, so I stayed behind at our table. I was reading through Ginny's new campaign brochure, when I spotted Francesca Pope at the bottom of the stairs to the stage. Ginny and Sean were still at the podium, chatting with supporters, and Francesca was staring at Ginny with an intensity that I found unsettling.

I walked across the room to Milo. "Get Ginny out of here," I said.

"What's going on?"

"Probably nothing," I said. "But I'm spooked. That woman over there has a history of mental problems. Her name is Francesca Pope, and something about Ginny sets her off. During the custody suit, she saw Ginny in the lobby of the courthouse and she started yelling at her."

Milo licked a dab of chocolate off his finger. "Thanks for the heads-up," he said. "I guess even Trojan horses have their uses." He moved past Francesca quickly, took the stairs two at a time, whispered something in Ginny's ear, and steered her towards the exit at the back of the stage. As always these days, Sean was close behind. Francesca scanned the room, using her hand as a visor. Finally, her eyes rested on me and she came over.

"I remember you," she said. "You're my lawyer's wife."

"Joanne Shreve," I said.

She adjusted the straps of her backpack. "It's hard to do the right thing when everybody thinks you're crazy," she said. Then without elaborating, she covered her hair with a plastic grocery bag and walked through the doors into the rain.

Ed Mariani had arranged for me to have my meeting with Vera Wang in the garden of the home he shared with his partner, Barry. Ed met me at the door, took my umbrella, and hustled me inside. "God, has there ever been a spring this wet? It may be time for the prudent to build an ark. Anyway, dishing among the daffodils is definitely out. Too bad too, I was longing to peer out my kitchen window and watch you and Vera speak tête-à-tête in the gazebo."

"You could hide behind that shoji screen in the living room."

Ed patted his girth. "I'd crash through it like an elephant. I'm just going to have to trust you to share every delicious detail."

"Ed, how do you think I should approach Vera? I don't want her to feel that I'm using her."

"But you are using her. She understands that. She's using you too."

"For what?"

Ed slipped my jacket onto a hanger. "Like all of us, Vera wants to be respected, and she wants to be valued. Her occupation has pretty much put her beyond the pale. She's sixty-seven – not old, but certainly at an age where a person wants to set the record straight."

"What is the record?"

Ed's smile was enigmatic. "I'll let her tell you." He peered out his living-room window. "You won't have to wait long. The lady is on her way."

I gazed past him. "Is that her with the stunning umbrella?"

"It is, and I'm glad you'll have a chance to watch her make her entrance," Ed said. "Vera has learned the secret of the royal family: the more slowly you move, the more people pay attention."

Indeed, there was something regal about the way in which Vera moved up the suburban street. Although the rain had stopped, the wind was shaking drops from the new leaves and Vera kept her umbrella raised against them. She was dressed, head to toe, in the softest grey, but her umbrella was flamboyant – huge red poppies in a sea of green.

When Ed opened the door, she shook the rain from the umbrella's canopy and the poppies danced. Ed took her umbrella and looked at the handle admiringly. "Solid hickory," he said. "Very nice."

Vera's smile was satisfied. "I always told my clients, you get what you pay for."

"Oh, good," Ed said. "We're not going to waste time on pleasantries. Right down to business."

"Time is money," Vera said evenly.

When Ed introduced us, she held out her hand to me. She was wearing gloves of the softest kid, and she took charge of the interview immediately. "I know you have questions, Joanne, but Ed has promised us a cup of his excellent cappuccino, and I've been looking forward to it."

"I've set you up in the breakfast nook, so you can look out at the daffodils while you chat," Ed said. "Follow me."

Vera was one of those rare beings who feels no compunction to make small talk in a social situation. As she gazed at the garden, I fixed my eyes on her. She was a small, softly contoured woman who'd made no attempt to compromise the natural process of aging. Her grey hair curled gently away from her face. Her skin was exquisite, but there were lines around her eyes and at the corners of her lips, and her chin and neck were no longer taut. She was clearly comfortable with her appearance, but her reputation was apparently another matter.

Ed presented our cappuccinos with a flourish. "Among his many talents, my Barry is a skilled barista," Ed said. "He has taught me how to pour the milk in a pattern on the espresso. As you can see, I'm a beginner: all I can do are swirls and hearts. Barry, of course, can pour out the entire *Last Supper*."

"That is impressive," I said.

Vera laughed. "Can Barry pour out Mary Magdalene?"

"I'll ask him," Ed said. "Now if you ladies will excuse me."

"Of course," Vera said. "It's time Joanne and I got started."

From the moment she began, it was obvious this wasn't the first time Vera had told her story, but she explained her success with a matter-of-fact narrative skill that was mesmerizing.

"Like most women, I came to prostitution from necessity. I was in an arranged marriage. He was abusive, and I had to get out. I had no money, and the only thing I had to sell was myself. My husband was a busy man, I had many hours on my own, and I used them profitably. When I had enough money, I left Vancouver and moved here to make a new start. My father was a merchant, and I understood business. I examined mainstream possibilities and I didn't like what I saw: buying a corner store, working fifteen hour days, seven days a week, keeping kids from stealing candy, their older brothers from robbing me, and their parents from running up bills they would never pay. I would live over the store, and when I died no one would even know my last name. It did not appeal. Prostitution was a more congenial option. I bought a house, sought out girls, paid off the right people, and set up business. I ran a clean house – only a liar promises no disease, no drugs, no insanity, but I monitored my girls closely and I culled the ones who didn't fit. I knew that men come to whores for something more than sex."

"What do they come for?"

She picked up her spoon and swirled the milk on her cappuccino, blurring the hearts.

"Joanne, do you know how many men use the services of a prostitute in their lifetime?"

"I have no idea."

"Neither do I," Vera said. "But each of those men would have his own reasons."

"Did you know Cristal Avilia?" I said.

Vera gave the foam on her spoon a catlike flick of the tongue. "I'd seen her, of course, but I knew her only by reputation. In our small circle, she was a legend."

"Because she was so good?"

Vera's eyes narrowed. "Why are you interested in Cristal, Joanne? Is it just that her life ended so dramatically?"

"Not just that," I said. "A member of my family was involved with her."

Vera nodded. "I understand. Well, she was good – superlative. I had a little mantra for my girls to repeat before a date: 'Listen – really listen – to the man. Learn what it is he really wants – beyond the orgasm. Give him what he dreams of, and he'll come back.' From what I heard, Cristal lived that mantra." Vera picked up her porcelain cup with her gloved hands. "She lasted fourteen years in our business – that's phenomenal. Most girls don't make it past two."

"Did you ever see her with a man?"

Vera's laugh was curiously girlish. "Of course. Being with a man was Cristal's business, Joanne. I often saw her with men – at dinner, in a hotel lobby, getting into a taxi."

"Any man in particular?"

"She had many repeat customers."

"And you knew them."

"Some of them."

"But you're not going to name them."

"That's right. I'm not."

"Did she have a boyfriend?"

Vera raised an eyebrow. "A pimp? Yes, I'd heard rumours about a man in her life. He didn't sound pleasant, but they seldom are."

"Did you hear a name?"

"No, and this time I'm not being discreet. I truly never heard a name, but I did hear that their relationship was an ugly one."

"Ugly enough that he might have killed her?"

"Unlikely," Vera said. "Cristal was, after all, his little money-making machine, but I guess even a little money-making machine can drive her owner to murder."

"My God. The world can be a terrible place."

Vera's look was pitying. "Are you just discovering that, Joanne?"

When I arrived at UpSlideDown, the newest recruit to the campaign greeted me. Sean's crooked smile charmed me as it always did, and the sight of a forest of tiny bright umbrellas in the vestibule finished the job. UpSlideDown was a welcome, noisy reminder that life can be good.

"All's well," Sean said. "Ginny's chatting up the parents and Mieka's already signed the release to let your granddaughters appear in the spot. We have not had a single parent turn down our request to let their child appear in an ad with Ginny. I believe this campaign is starting to go very, very well." He frowned. "You look a little down. Bad morning?"

"I've had better," I said. "But this is nice."

Sean gestured towards a vastly pregnant woman with two sons under the age of five. The boys spied the umbrella stand, chose their weapons, and started duelling. We watched as the mum removed the umbrellas from her sons' hands and bent towards them. "Enough," she said. "Got it, Sawyer?" Sawyer gave her an angelic smile. "Got it, Finn?" Finn's chuckle was deep, charming, and utterly noncommittal.

"I'd better get her to sign the waiver fast," Sean said. "Keith's around here somewhere. Since I told him you were coming, he's been eyeing the door."

"I'll find him," I said. "Good luck with the pretty mum."

Sean approached her and held out the release form. "This is just to let you know that your boys might be photographed as part of a political spot for Ginny Monaghan. If you're uncomfortable with the situation, UpSlideDown will give you a voucher for three hours free playtime another day."

The young woman patted her belly. "It's raining. I'm pregnant. I seem to have given birth to Satan's spawn. I don't care who they're photographed with. I just want to sit down, sip chamomile tea, and listen to Nora Jones on my iPod."

"Sign here," Sean said. "It's nice to meet a fellow Nora Jones fan."

The woman scrawled her name and headed off after her boys, who had already scaled the walls of a play-castle and interrupted the tea party of two young girls with tiaras and attitude.

As soon as she spotted me, Ginny came over. "I seem to have lost Mieka," she said. "And I need to freshen up. Is there a bathroom I can use?"

"There is," I said. "But the adult female bathroom is a single. You'll wait forever. The children's bathrooms, on the other hand, offer endless possibilities if you're prepared to squat and wash up at a teeny-tiny sink."

Ginny shrugged. "Any port in a storm. Hey, your old pal is over there waiting for you."

Keith was seated at a little red table with my grand-daughters. Madeleine was wearing jeans and a shirt that read, "Girl Power." Lena was still wearing her new ladybug raincoat and rainhat. I knew without asking that she had simply refused to take them off, and Mieka was waiting her out. I also knew that Mieka would wait a long time to see that raincoat come off. Lena was a determined child. Keith and the girls were building something elaborate and myste-rious out of Lego, and they were so content that I stopped for a moment just to watch them.

The girls were five and three and their personalities were beginning to declare themselves. They were their own people, but there were recognizable family traits: Madeleine, fair-haired and hazel-eyed, was, like Mieka and me, earth-bound and pragmatic; Lena, dark-eyed and mercurial, was like my late husband, Ian. As I watched Keith, I wondered whether he was seeing traits in the girls that connected them to the Harris family.

He looked up and smiled. "There's a fourth chair at this table," he said.

"We're building a corral for the horses," Lena said.

"Where are the horses?" I said.

"We have to build them," Madeleine said.

"Fair enough," I said. "If you tell me the pieces you need, I'll hand them to you, but Lego is not my forte."

"What's a forte?" Lena asked.

"Something you're good at," Madeleine said. "Like your forte is running and climbing and doing the monkey bars."

Lena nodded happily. "I am good at the monkey bars."

Mieka appeared with a tray of juice boxes. "Madeleine is too modest to point out that her forte is reading. Keith, your older grandniece is already reading chapter books."

"I'm impressed," Keith said. "With both the monkey bars and the chapter books. They're great kids, Mieka."

"I have lots of help," my daughter said. "Of course, I also have Zack to deal with. Mum, do you know what he sent the girls this morning?"

"Let me tell," Lena said, her dark eyes growing large. "A bunch of candy."

"The idea is it's like a bouquet of flowers," Madeleine said. "Except instead of flowers it's all lollipops. It's really pretty. Of course, Lena wanted to eat it."

I put my arm around Madeleine's shoulder. "And you want to keep it the way it is forever."

Madeleine put a last piece of Lego on her corral. "Not forever," she said. "Just for a long time."

Lena was facing the door. Suddenly, she leapt up with such force she almost knocked the little table flying. "Here's Zack."

Madeleine was off too.

Keith watched as the girls reached out to my husband. "I wish I'd thought to bring a candy bouquet," he said, and his tone was wistful.

Mieka grimaced. "Well, I don't. One overindulgent male in their lives is enough."

"Still, it would be nice to get the kind of greeting Zack's getting."

"The girls spend a lot of time with Zack and Mum. Why don't you come over to the house tomorrow night for supper? Get to know the kids better."

"I'd like that," Keith said.

At that moment, Zack joined us, and as always when he came into a group, the dynamic changed. He was the least egotistical of men, but his charm was potent.

"It's the candy man," I said.

"Don't be dismissive. It took me an hour on the Internet to chase that thing down."

"My hero." I said. I went over and kissed him.

He drew me close. "Thanks for the kiss," he said. "Everything okay now?"

"It will be," I said.

"Good," he said. He extended his hand to Keith. "Zack Shreve," he said. "And, of course, I recognize you. It's good to finally meet you."

Mieka turned to me. "Mum, I could use a little help with crowd control while Ginny's people set up their cameras. Why don't we let these two get acquainted?"

It was pleasant to be in a room bright with the colours of a crayon box, listening to the sounds of kids laughing while the rain pounded down outside. Mieka served sandwiches and juice and cookies; the shoot went well. Even Milo O'Brien seemed to relax. When I walked by he had a piece of broccoli in his hand.

"Is that what I think it is?" I said.

He laughed. "You know, it's not half bad."

The questions from the young mothers and a few fathers were centred naturally enough on family, and Ginny talked consistently about family values in a way that made that hackneyed shibboleth of the right sound like something other than a code for exclusion of all but the few. I had never really listened to her before, and she was impressive. I was beginning to see Keith's point. Whenever I glanced their way, Keith and Zack seemed to be enjoying each other's company. As Sean said, all was well.

I was picking up empty sandwich plates when my husband beckoned me over. "Keith, I know this is rude, but there's something I have to talk to Jo about."

"Not a problem," Keith said. "I should go and check in with Ginny anyway. I enjoyed our talk."

"So did I. Come over to the house for a drink before you leave town. We can continue our discussion about the Jays' amazing ability to self-destruct."

Keith smiled. "A topic with infinite possibilities. I'll be there."

I sat in the chair Keith had vacated. "So what's up?"

Zack leaned close and lowered his voice. "Blake just called. He wanted to let me know that, against my advice, he's going to Cristal's funeral."

I closed my eyes. "I am so tired of Cristal Avilia."

"Well, she's incinerated and in an urn at the funeral home, so I can't see her posing a threat for much longer."

"Now you're angry," I said.

"You bet I am. Cristal's dead. You and I are alive – seemingly to fight another day. But this is neither the time nor the place for us to duke it out. I just wanted you to know that I'm going to the funeral with Blake."

"Why? Blake's an adult. He doesn't need a chaperone. If he wants to be there, he should be there."

"Jo, we should probably try to keep our voices down. People are staring at us. I wouldn't give a shit except this is Mieka's party and I don't want to wreck it. And, to answer your question, Blake should not be at the funeral. There'll be cops there. They still haven't found Cristal's killer, and they entertain the not wholly unfounded belief that murderers go to the funerals of their victims."

"Blake was in love with Cristal," I said. "He wouldn't have killed her."

"People kill people they love every day of the year, Jo. Blake doesn't have an alibi. The police haven't nosed around, because they have no reason to connect him with Cristal, but if he shows up, they'll start wondering why. And Blake is in no shape to deal with a cop who decides to come down hard on him."

"So you're going to go to the funeral with him."

"Right. If I'm there, the focus will shift. Debbie knows I had a connection to Cristal, and she knows I didn't kill her. Blake could just be there as my friend."

"That's not good enough," I said.

"You're probably right, but I'm out of options. I'm also a little tired, so unless you pull a Margot and throw tacks under my wheelchair, I'm out of here."

I stood up. "I'll come with you," I said.

"Suit yourself," Zack said. "The funeral is at Speers at two."

"Half an hour."

"Plenty of time. I guarantee parking won't be a problem. I don't imagine many of Cristal's intimates will want to run the gauntlet."

"I guess funerals aren't part of their fantasies," I said.

Zack looked at me hard. Then he turned his wheelchair and began his careful passage through the kids and the blocks, past the pink plastic castle and the fort with the drawbridge till he came to the door that opened out into the real world.

CHAPTER

8

Zack had arranged to drive to the funeral with Blake, so I went alone. As my husband had predicted, parking wasn't a problem, but I chose a place two blocks away because I needed a walk to cool down.

There were no mourners in sight, and when I opened the door to Speers, six people in the solemn garb of funeral-home employees leapt to attention. Obeying a choreography as perfectly executed as the movements in a kabuki dance, one of the employees took my umbrella, a second led me to the memorial book where a third opened a page, still blank, and handed me a pen. When I had written my name, a young man with a crewcut so short that his scalp peeked pinkly through, placed two fingers under my elbow, waited as another employee handed me a funeral program, then guided me past the gleaming empty pews to a seat in the second row behind the only other mourner in the room.

If I'd been quick, I would have said that my husband, who would be joining me, was in a wheelchair and that we'd be more comfortable sitting at the back, but the tensions of the morning had beaten me down. I sat where I was told to sit.

When I murmured my thanks to the usher, the young woman ahead of me turned to stare.

Surprisingly, she giggled. "I might as well sit next to you, right? Or maybe you could sit next to me?" Her eyes took in the empty room. "I thought there'd be more people." She looked back at me. "So will you? Sit with me, I mean? I'm Mandy Avilia – Cristal's sister."

I moved to the place beside her. At first I couldn't detect a family resemblance. Cristal had been slight, doll-like, and ethereal. This young woman was unabashedly carnal. Her sleeveless black dress was cut low to showcase the peachy skin of her arms, throat, and breasts. Her shoulder-length hair was dark and springy with life, and her mouth was wide and sensual.

"Were you a friend of my sister's?" she asked.

I thought of Blake. "A friend of a friend," I said.

"Well, that's nice," Mandy said. She held the funeral program in front of me. "Do you like the picture I chose?" she asked. "When Cristal was little, the photographer in our town had a beautiful baby contest. Cristal won. The prize was a picture on her birthday every year till she turned sixteen." Mandy gulped. "After she turned sixteen, Cristal still got her picture taken every year for her birthday. That's the last one. I just love it."

It was a professional photograph, soft-focused and romantic – the kind of portrait a girl might give to her lover or use to announce her engagement. Cristal's hair was blonder and longer than it had been in the DVD with Zack. She'd grown out her bangs and added a soft wave that framed her heart-shaped face. A swath of ivory chiffon was draped around her bare shoulders. Her lips were slightly parted, but she wasn't smiling. There was a private sadness about her. Underneath were the words *Portrait of A Lady*.

Out of nowhere I remembered the stillness and grace of Ned Osler's apartment at the Balfour – how the fire had burned low as he and I talked. That was how Ned saw Cristal, that chameleon woman who could become any man's fantasy.

"She was beautiful, wasn't she?" Mandy said.

"Yes," I agreed.

"That day when the man from the lawn service found her, she was holding a book called *Portrait of a Lady*. The police say the murderer must have put the book in her hands. Why would anybody do that?"

"I don't know."

Mandy turned her eyes to me. "There is so much I don't understand. I loved my sister, but I never really knew her. I never knew what it was she wanted. When I saw the book, I thought maybe that was it."

"To be a lady."

Images of Cristal thrusting her body against Zack's crowded my mind, and I turned away from Mandy's large and trusting eyes.

There was a murmur of voices at the back of the room, and I saw Zack and Blake. Zack beckoned to me.

"The man in the wheelchair is my husband," I said. "I should go back and sit with him."

"There's plenty of room in the aisle right beside me," Mandy said. "I don't want to sit alone." That seemed to end the discussion.

I went back and bent close to my husband. "That's Cristal's sister. There's no one to sit with her."

Zack muttered an expletive under his breath, but he turned his wheelchair and came up the centre aisle. Blake followed. They positioned themselves so they were on either side of Mandy and me. The portrait of Cristal was on a table beside an urn whose purpose was unmistakable. A spray of purple cattleya orchids drifted between the portrait and the urn. When he took in the arrangement, Blake flinched, but he remained composed.

Zack leaned towards Mandy. "I'm Zack Shreve. I'm a lawyer. Your sister paid me to represent a homeless woman who'd run into some legal difficulties. It was an act of real kindness."

Mandy's eyes welled. "Cristal was a good person."

Blake held out his hand to Mandy. "She helped a lot of people."

Mandy looked around. "Then why aren't more people here?"

"I don't know," Blake said.

The funeral director who had led me to my seat came and reminded Mandy gently that it was two o'clock – time to begin the service.

"Could we wait five minutes?" she asked. "There might be other people."

She was right, there were other people – four of them. The first two – an imposing woman in grey and a younger man with a powerful body that appeared to strain the seams of his black suit – arrived together. When I caught Zack's attention, he mouthed the word cops. Francesca Pope required no identification. Her appearance at Cristal's funeral seemed inevitable. Like a persistent and troubling image in a Fellini film, Francesca seemed destined to appear and reappear until her role in the drama became clear. The final mourner was a surprise to everyone but Mandy. Just as the first lugubrious notes of "Amazing Grace" filled the chapel, Margot Wright joined the party. She came straight to the front and took Mandy's hands in hers.

The tears streamed down Mandy's face, but she was beaming. "I knew if you could possibly make it, you'd be here," she said.

Margot's own eyes were welling. "Hey, Cristal was a Wadena girl, and Wadena girls stick together, right?"

Margot pulled a pocket pack of tissues from her bag. She took one and handed the pack to Mandy. Beside me, my husband was, for once, speechless.

The service was generic and mercifully short. The minister, who introduced himself as "the Reverend Kevin," had an overbite and a gentle manner. When he offered the standard apology for "not having had the privilege to know Cristal in life," Zack and I exchanged glances. The Reverend Kevin didn't dwell on the specifics of Cristal's life. He talked about the mystery of human existence – a topic with which no one could take issue – then he led us through the Twenty-third Psalm and the Lord's Prayer. The service concluded with the children's hymn "Jesus Loves Me."

When the service was over, Francesca and the police vanished, Zack and Blake and I shook hands with Mandy Avilia, and Margot offered to take Mandy out for a drink. We walked outside together, then we went our separate ways. Blake went back to the office, and Zack and I got into my car to go home. As soon as we were inside the car, I exploded.

"Why weren't there more people there?" I said.

Zack's jaw was set. He was trying to control his anger. "Jesus, Jo, you're not twelve years old. You know the answer to that." He lowered his voice. "You're not going to like this, but I've seen the DVDs that were sent to Cristal's clients. She gave each of those men something they weren't getting anywhere else."

"Sex?"

"Intimacy. I know you think Cristal's clients were self-indulgent pricks, but if you'd been at our house the other day, you might have a different opinion. Those men lost something precious, and they were grieving."

"Privately," I snapped. "Away from the prying eyes of their wives and children. Did it occur to any of them to do the hard work of finding intimacy in a real relationship? You know, the kind where you don't pay to get your own way, where you ask the woman about her needs?"

"Let's get out of here," Zack said.

Dinner that night was a tense affair. After we'd cleared the table, and Taylor went to her room to do homework, Zack turned to me. "Do you want to go over and see the avocets?"

"It'll be too muddy for your chair," I said.

"Fuck it. If I get stuck, I get stuck. You can leave me there."

I felt my throat close. "I'll never leave you, Zack."

He pulled his wheelchair closer to me. "Then why are we sitting here making each other miserable? Jo, we're not kids. If there were an actuary here, do you know what she would say?"

"No."

"She'd say, 'Look at the numbers – they'll give you an idea of how much time you have left together. Go and see the fucking avocets.'"

And so we put on our jackets and drove to the south side of the Broad Street Bridge. The slope that led down to the sandy shoreline was slick, and Zack needed help with his chair, but we made it. We found a spot where we could sit and watch the avocets and the willets and the sandpipers without intruding in their world. The heart of the city was five minutes away, but that cool, misty evening, the only noises we heard came from waves slapping against the sand and shorebirds going about the business of their lives.

For the first time since Cristal Avilia's murder, we were

at peace, and when Zack reached out and took my hand, I felt something broken in me slide back into place.

"It would be nice to stay here forever, wouldn't it?" he said. "No phones. No problems. No fights."

"Just us and the birds." I said. I smiled at him. "You'd miss your martinis."

"You'd miss the kids," he said. "Actually, there's a lot we'd miss. I think we're going to have to face it, Ms. Shreve – becoming the bird people by the Broad Street Bridge may not be in our future."

"We'll have to figure something else out," I said. I moved closer to him. "Do you remember what the dean said at our wedding?"

Zack nodded. "I remember everything about that day, Joanne. I remember everything about all our days. James said that marriage is a leap of faith, but we'd make it if we remembered to hold on to each other and never let go."

I raised our linked hands. "I guess we just have to keep holding on."

"That's no problem for me." Zack gazed at the sky. "It's getting dark. Time to call in the dogs, piss on the fire, and saddle up."

I looked at the muddy slope we had to climb, pushed myself to my feet, and took the handles of Zack's chair. "Okay," I said. "Let's go home."

In the next week, Zack and I slipped gratefully back into our old and comfortable ways. We stopped using words as percussive instruments with which we could set each other vibrating, and the silences between us were no longer heavy with things unsaid. Life went on.

The campaign moved into warp speed, and for Ginny the signs were good. Experienced politicians don't need a

psephologist to know how an election is going. If the candidate is dogged by a persistent cold; if the campaign literature
arrives from the printers late and with a typo stating the candidate has given his life to pubic service; if the bus breaks
down; if the heavens open up on the one scheduled outdoor
event; if the crowds dwindle; if the media's attention
wanders; and if the staffers are snarling at one another, a
campaign manager knows without checking Decima or Ekos
that the candidate is tanking.

I had worked in campaigns like that. I knew what it was
like to wake up in the morning with my stomach in knots
because there was no way to stop the grim downward spiral
of loss. That's where Ginny's campaign had been the night of
Zack's birthday, but after Jason Brodnitz withdrew from the
custody battle, the public's assessment of Ginny underwent
a tectonic shift, and Ginny knew it. I could see it in the way
she strode up front walks to knock on the doors of her con-
stituents. She was sniffing victory. As we criss-crossed
Palliser, the riding that I knew better than any, visiting the
cafés with the chrome tables filled with farmers in John
Deere caps who met every morning to discuss what needed
discussing, and showing up at all-candidates meetings with
attendance swollen by Ginny's sudden possibilities, the
campaign became fun.

One sweet May day, after ordering Monaghan Maple-
Walnut at the Moose Jaw ice-cream shop where the propri-
etor had labelled an ice cream with each candidate's name
and tallied votes on the basis of how much of each ice cream
sold, Keith and I sat outside on a bench, and he talked about
his next big push.

He had decided to look past this election towards the big
leadership challenge – the one that would rout the social
conservatives and return his party to the principles Keith
espoused. He wasn't looking for a squeaker in Palliser; he

was looking for a big win that would turn the party around.

In the days after she gained custody of her daughters, everything broke Ginny's way. Momentum – "the big Mo," as politicos and sports announcers call it – was with her. Media stories became soft focus, crowds swelled, and senior party people, scrutinizing her anew, liked what they saw: a smart, affable, seemingly tireless candidate. When, at Sean Barton's urging, Ginny's daughters agreed to campaign with their mother, Keith shook his head. "I don't know what dark magic Sean used, but having the twins out there with Ginny is the best thing that could have happened for us."

Indeed, the sight of these three powerfully built women with the identical engaging smiles silenced the cynics. Suddenly, family values, the two most semantically loaded words in modern politics, was Ginny's issue, and the Monaghan campaign milked it. Three days before Mother's Day, Sean arranged for a friend on the local paper to photo- graph Ginny and the twins bicycling in Wascana Park. The chokecherries were flowering, and the three women were positioned against a tree that had exploded in blossoms. It was the best of photo ops for the ad-fat Mother's Day edition of the paper, and sister papers owned by the same chain in big markets picked it up. But Ginny's campaign was more than just pretty pictures. She ended all her speeches with the same sentence; "We are the real party of the people." The message was simple, positive, and utterly meaningless, but it was catching on, and the pundits had noticed.

One of our national newspapers published a story under the headline "nothing but blue skies for ginny monaghan," and indeed the consensus seemed to be that it was smooth sailing all the way for Ginny. Those of us closer to the centre of the campaign knew better. Francesca Pope's appearances at Ginny's events became almost hallucinatory, like the troubling presence of a mysterious figure in a dream. More significantly, something was terribly wrong between Ginny and her ex-husband.

Ginny, who had seemed so indifferent to custody, suddenly was demanding full custody, and her demands had nothing to do with politics. She seemed genuinely concerned about allowing Jason to see the girls without a third person present. I heard her on the phone with him one night. "I'm getting these anonymous phone calls about you, Jason. They're frightening. They say you're a pimp. We both know what we know, but this is new, and it's ugly. We've got to talk." Seemingly they never did. Ginny watched the girls carefully, and whenever they saw their father, no matter how busy her schedule, she went along.

When I told Zack about the conversation I'd overheard, his reaction surprised me. "You know the woman at the centre of this is going to be Cristal."

"Isn't that a bit of a leap?"

"I don't think so. According to Debbie Haczkewicz, the cops are getting nowhere trying to identify Cristal's boyfriend. This guy was a genius at covering his tracks. They've talked to everybody – including Cristal's sister – all they've got is that Cristal's boyfriend was a mystery man who had to protect his reputation at all costs."

"Vera Wang told me the relationship Cristal had with her pimp was a troubled one."

Zack raised an eyebrow. "Those relationships are never made in heaven. And Jason Brodnitz would have solid reasons for keeping the relationship with Cristal secret."

"Both professional and personal reasons," I said. "Until a year ago, he was a pillar of the community. He must have wanted to get back his reputation."

"And he wanted his daughters," Zack said. "Being exposed as a pimp would put the kibosh on both those dreams."

I thought of Jason's abrupt change of heart after he encountered Sean in the men's room of the courthouse. "Zack, would Sean have known that Jason was involved with prostitution?"

"Ginny was his client. If she was aware of the situation, she should have told him."

The image of Jason watching with dead eyes as his counsel announced that he no longer wished to pursue custody flashed through my mind. "Zack, when Jason came back into court that day, he was in shock. If there was some secret between Ginny and him, it wasn't that."

Zack shrugged. "It's possible the truth came to light after the hearing started – some kind soul might have dropped Ginny an anonymous note."

"Regina's a gossipy town," I said. "You must have heard rumours about Jason."

"Actually, in the last year I heard a lot, but they weren't about Jason's love life, they were about his business."

"And what were people saying?"

"Pretty much that he was a guy to avoid. When he was working for Tatryn-Mulholland, he was hot stuff – a stockbroker with the Midas touch. He decided he was good enough to go it alone."

"And it didn't work out?"

"Nope. As soon as he was on his own, Jason lost his magic. He also lost a hell of a lot of money for his customers."

"I hate stories like that. I've chosen mid-risk investments all my life, and I always get a cold feeling in the pit of my stomach when the quarterly report arrives in the mail."

"I'm glad you weren't watching our investments the first couple of months we were married. Luckily for us both, Ms. Shreve, I had a stock fraud client who gave me some solid advice about what to hold on to and what to sell. You and I are in good shape."

"But Jason isn't? His finances came up a couple of times during the custody suit, but Margot gave the court the impression he'd turned a corner."

Zack frowned. "That surprises me, because I don't know anybody who would have trusted Jason to handle their spare change. Of course, it's entirely possible Margot was blowing smoke. I've done that myself when I got broadsided during a trial."

"Margot's your partner now. You could ask her."

"Good idea." Zack picked up his cell and hit speed-dial. "Hey, it's me. I've got some questions, and don't get pissed off and start telling me it's none of my business, because I think it may be. How much did you charge Jason Brodnitz?" Zack whistled when he heard Margot's answer. "You don't come cheap. Has he paid you? Good. Now, Joanne tells me that during the custody dispute, you implied that Jason's business reverses were over." He listened. "Fair enough. The truth is always open to interpretation, and if he paid your bill up front, no worries. One more question. Is Brodnitz named as a beneficiary in Cristal's will? Really? That is weird. Anyway, easily solved. Just go online with the Law Society and ask the firm that handled the will to get in touch with you."

He held the phone away from his ear. "Yeah, yeah, yeah. But for all your expertise, you haven't found the will, have you? So keep at it. If Brodnitz was Cristal Avilia's boyfriend, we may have an interesting situation on our hands."

The Friday before Mother's Day, Zack flew up north with a client who was the CEO of a mining resources company. Their meeting was in La Ronge, and the client took pleasure in flying his own plane and doing some serious sightseeing en route. I spent the day trying not to think of my husband suspended over one of the heart-stoppingly immense lakes that make the north so beautiful and so deadly. At three-thirty, I left Ginny campaigning in a seniors' home and picked Taylor up at school. We were going shopping.

Taylor surprised me by suggesting we start at Value Village. "Sometimes they have neat stuff," she said. "And I don't want to be like everybody else. I guess I'm kind of like my mother." Her dark eyes scrutinized my face, watching for a reaction. I sensed there was something more she wanted to say, so I waited. "Did it matter to my mother that she was beautiful?" she said finally.

I shook my head. "No. The only thing that ever mattered to your mother was the art she made." It was the truth, but that didn't make the statement any less thoughtless.

Taylor didn't let it pass. "And me," Taylor said. "I mattered to my mother."

"Yes, you did. Very much."

"Because I had talent."

"She loved you," I said. "Your talent was just something else that connected you to her."

Taylor's look was assessing. "I guess some day I'll figure out whether that's true."

I put my arm around her. "In the meantime, we might as well check out the bargains."

The shopping gods were with us that afternoon. Value Village offered up a genuine treasure – a white cotton jersey T-shirt with cap sleeves and printed with Andy Warhol's acerbic observation "Everyone will be famous for fifteen minutes" in black and pink. The moment Taylor put it on, she knew what she needed to complete the look: fitted black cotton pants, pink Capezio ballet flats, and a black cardigan. We continued shopping, stopped for a bowl of soup at the Creek Bistro, then went home. While Taylor changed, I let out the dogs and tried Zack's cell, but he was out of range. I'd just started to riffle through the mail when Taylor came in wearing her new outfit. She looked like a very young Audrey Hepburn.

"So what do you think?" she said.

"I think for a girl who used to go to birthday parties in frilly dresses, pyjama bottoms, and odd socks, you've developed a definite fashion sense."

"Did you really let me go out wearing my pyjama bottoms?"

"Sure. You were happy. That was all that mattered."

Taylor lowered her head and stared at her pink Capezios. "Jo, what would have happened to me if you hadn't taken me?"

"Where did that come from?"

"Lately I've been thinking about it a lot. You know, just kind of wondering . . ."

"Well, my guess is that some amazingly lucky family would have adopted you, and you would have been fine." I touched her cheek. "But, Taylor, I wouldn't have been fine."

Her voice was small. "You wouldn't have known."

"I would have known," I said.

"You have the other kids."

"But I wouldn't have had you, and I cannot imagine my life – any of our lives – without you."

Her lips were tight. "I can't imagine not having you either."

"Then let's let it go for the time being," I said. "But if you want to talk, I'm here."

Taylor swiped her eyes with the back of her hand. I reached across her desk and took a tissue from the box and handed it to her.

"Thanks," she said. She blew her nose ferociously.

"Angus says you're always there whether we want you there or not."

"Angus is right," I said. "Now, we both have homework, but as soon as we get that out of the way, let's make some popcorn and watch an episode of *Battlestar Galactica*."

"Sweet," Taylor said. "Can I ask Isobel to come over? She is so into Tahmoh Penikett."

"As opposed to you," I said.

Taylor dimpled. "I'm not as fanatic as Isobel. She sleeps with his picture under her pillow."

When Taylor went off to call Isobel, I picked up the mail again. At first glance, it seemed like the usual: two magazines, a brochure encouraging us to holiday in Prince Edward Island, a tax receipt from a charity, and a bill from our water-softener company. But at the bottom of the pile there was a surprise – a peach greeting card envelope addressed to Joanne Shreve. The hand was unfamiliar, and there was no stamp. Neither fact set off any alarms. Zack liked surprises, and he always said I was a hard woman to spoil. There'd been another mystery envelope in the mailbox at Christmas. That one had contained the key to Chris Altieri's cottage – the one closest to ours at Lawyers' Bay. Zack had bought his partners' shares of the cottage so that our grown children would have a place to stay when they visited. I smiled at the memory and opened the flap.

The envelope held three condoms and the bulletin from Cristal Avilia's funeral. Across the picture of Cristal someone had scrawled a message in pink ink: "Is your husband missing her? I'll help him forget." There was a telephone number. I scanned the room to make certain Taylor hadn't come in, then I picked up the phone and dialed. My hands were shaking, but I was tired of being jerked around.

When a woman picked up, I pressed on. "This is Joanne Shreve," I said. "I got your card. Who are you?"

The woman on the other end of the line sounded young and stoned. "My name's Bree," she said. "Are you mad at me?"

"Not yet," I said. "But I want to get to the bottom of this."

"It will cost you," she said.

"How much?"

"Is fifty dollars too much?" she said.

I exhaled. "No. Fifty dollars is fine. Where do you want to meet?"

"Nighthawks?"

"I'll be there in fifteen minutes," I said. "And, Bree, you'd better be there too."

As I freshened my makeup, my resolve began to weaken, but Bree was expecting me. There was no turning back. Taylor's bedroom door was open. She was at her desk, with Bruce and Benny at her feet.

I went over to her. "I have an errand," I said. "I'll be back in an hour. If I'm going to be longer, I'll call."

She nodded and kept working. "Isobel's coming over in a few minutes to do homework with me."

I leaned over to check her math exercise book. The pages before me were scrubbed thin with erasures. I rubbed her shoulder. "Taylor, do you need a tutor?"

She bent to her task again. "Uh-uh," she said. "I just need a brain."

I would have bet a cup of joe that the owner of Nighthawks on Broad Street hadn't named his establishment after Edward Hopper's signature painting of three customers seeking refuge from the loneliness of the night in a big city diner. Sealed off from the world by the diner's expanse of glass, sealed off from one another by their own impenetrable isolation, the three customers in Hopper's picture are a poignant reminder that, in the small hours, we are all alone. The people who haunted Nighthawks didn't need Hopper's painting to remind them of that. They knew they were alone every night when they inserted the key into the lock of their cheerless room and every morning when they hit the sidewalk and passersby averted their eyes at the sight of them.

When I stopped to withdraw cash from a bank on Broad Street, it occurred to me that I hadn't asked Bree how I could identify her, but she made it easy. She was sitting at a table by the window, and when I came in, she jumped up and waved as if we were old friends. She was an anorexic with patchy white-blonde hair and she was definitely high on something other than life. Her long fingers never stopped fluttering and her pale feral eyes darted as she talked. "I'm having pie," she said as I took the chair opposite hers. "They have really good saskatoon berry pie here. Do you want some? I can order it for you. I know the manager."

I settled back in my chair. "I'm a big fan of saskatoons," I said. "But I don't want to take too much of your time."

"My time is your time," she said. She slipped her hand under the table. It took me a moment to realize she was waiting to be paid.

Over drinks at a rival firm's holiday party, Zack had articulated his rule of thumb: "Pay an informer four times what they ask for and they're yours." I knew I needed Bree on my side, so I opened my wallet and took out four fifties.

When she saw the bills, Bree's pale eyes took on a hectic glitter. Her white halter top hadn't been constructed with room for a deposit, and her studded shorts were skin-tight, but she knew how to handle her finances. She scooped up the money, and either out of habit or hope of more, when she stood to slide the money into her back pocket, she thrust her pelvis at me.

"Now tell me exactly how you came to send out those cards," I said.

Bree's pie arrived and she took a spoon and began digging into it, moving the pieces around. "I have this page on MySpace – do you know what that is?"

I nodded.

"On my page, I say I do odd jobs for money. Most of the jobs I get are sex-related. I don't care. At least it's not boring." She forked a piece of pastry loaded with saska-toons and licked the berries. Several of them fell on her halter top. She swept at them, smearing them on the shiny material covering her small breasts. "Turning people on gives me a rush," she explained. "But that's not why you handed me all that money. You want information, so here it is. What happened was I got a hit a few days ago from someone who said they would pay me big for doing a prac-tical joke. I wrote back saying my life was a practical joke, and this person said everybody's life was a joke, and if I sent them my home address, everything I needed would be sent to me."

"You sent a stranger your home address?" I said.

"Why not?" Bree said. "Strangers come to my home all the time." She stared at her nails meditatively. "My French manicure looks like shit. Anyway, the package was deliv-ered. Everything was there – the condoms, the pictures, the envelopes, the addresses of the people I had to deliver to – and there was a note telling me what I had to write on the girl's picture."

"You delivered the envelopes by hand?" I said.

"By taxi," she said. "It was easy. I had the addresses, so I just had the taxi take me from house to house. Boy, that dead girl must have had some client list – those houses were all mega expensive."

"Was I the only one who called you?"

"So far."

"How much did the person give you for the deliveries?" I asked.

"Five hundred, but I had to pay for the taxi out of it."

"Didn't all this strike you as a little weird?" I asked.

"No. Weird is the guy who comes to my place every Sunday afternoon and asks me to peel a hard-boiled egg and stick an old-fashioned pen into it while he jacks off." She was starting to twitch. Clearly, money burned a hole in her pocket. "Anything else you need to know? I've got to motor."

"You haven't eaten your pie." I said.

She looked at me with her glittering eyes. "The fun was in knowing that I could," she said.

I touched her arm. "Bree, did the person who hired you tell you his name?"

She arranged her features in an approximation of thoughtfulness. "Maybe yes. Maybe no," she said.

I slid another fifty-dollar bill across the chrome table. "That's all I have," I said.

"The person's name was Jason. It was written on the instructions," she added helpfully.

My heart was pounding, but I tried to stay cool. I reached into my bag, removed one of my university business cards, and wrote my cell number on the back. "You can get in touch with me at that number if you hear from the person who hired you."

"I'll give you my number too," Bree said.

"I already have it. Remember, I called you?"

"Then I'll give you my MySpace address." She took a piece of paper from her pocket, borrowed my pen, and laboriously wrote out the url.

Isobel was playing with the cats and Zack was helping Taylor with her math when I got home. He held out his arms, and I was grateful to fold into them. "I'm so glad you're here," I said.

"Me too," he said. "Where've you been?"

"Downtown on an errand," I said. "We can talk about it later. How's the math going?"

"Better," Taylor said. "Zack showed me how to figure out square roots and cube roots. So I'm ready for *Battlestar Galactica*."

"I could use a little escape myself," Zack said. "It's been a while since I studied pre-algebra."

"Why don't you put in the DVD, and the girls and I will get the drinks and popcorn."

"Can we watch 'Scattered'?" Taylor asked.

Zack scowled. "Isn't that the one where Kara and Helo try to find a way to bring the *Arrow of Apollo* back to the fleet?"

Isobel stuffed her homework into her backpack. "Yes. How come you know?"

"Because we've watched that episode four times," Zack said. "Why don't we watch another one?"

Taylor rolled her eyes. "Because 'Scattered' is the episode with all the dreamy close-ups of Tahmoh Penikett."

It had been a long day for both of us, but that night as we got ready for bed, Zack was buoyant. His meeting had gone well, and his client had flown low over the big lakes so Zack could see the islands. He'd taken dozens of pictures, and he was eager to share.

After I'd looked through them, I handed his camera back. "It really is spectacular country."

"Gary says he'll fly us up there any time you say the word."

"Is Gary aware of the fact that I spent every spare moment today praying that you'd come back to earth?"

"And here I am," Zack said. He lifted himself from his chair into bed. When he was settled, he patted the place beside him. "Come and tell me about your day."

"The good part was that Taylor found the perfect outfit for the Farewell."

His eyes bored into me. "And the bad part . . . ?"

"The bad part was an adventure in bizarro world," I said.

Zack winced when I handed him the peach envelope that had been dropped in our mailbox. But he listened without comment as I described my encounter with Bree. When I was finished he said. "Pretty stupid of Jason to give Bree his name, wasn't it?"

"That's what I thought," I said.

"Do you think someone's setting Brodnitz up?"

"I don't know," I said. "He could have just slipped. We'll have to wait until we hear from Bree again."

Zack sighed. "It won't be long. Whoever hired her has found a trustworthy courier."

"So you think there'll be more messages."

"Sure. And I'll bet if I turned my cell on right now, we'd discover that you weren't the only one who got a Mother's Day card."

"Zack, this isn't about money, is it?"

"No," he said. "I think it's about something a lot uglier than money." He reached over and turned out the light. "Jo, why did you go downtown tonight?"

"Because Taylor could easily have been in the room when I opened that envelope. I don't want this filth touching her life. I want this over, Zack, and I'm going to do what I have to do to make it stop."

CHAPTER

9

Zack met the seven dwarves at his office on Saturday morning. As he'd predicted, they had all received envelopes in their mailbox the day before, and they were all eager to talk. Four of the wives had opened the cards, but the men were all trial lawyers, skilled at turning the cube of reality, and they had convinced the women in their lives that the cards were some kind of sick joke. When Zack told them what I'd learned at Nighthawks, they agreed to a man that a meeting was in order.

I had my own meeting. As soon as Zack left, I called Vera Wang. Our conversation got off to a rocky start when I announced myself as Joanne Shreve.

"I'm sorry," she said. "I don't know anyone by that name."

"We met at Ed Mariani's last week," I said.

"Ed introduced you as Joanne Kilbourn."

"Kilbourn was my name before I remarried. I still use it professionally."

"Is your husband Zachary Shreve?"

"Yes."

There was a pause. "That must be interesting," she said finally.

"It is," I said. "Do you have a few minutes to talk?"

"I was just going off in search of black pansies," she said. "But that can wait."

"Dutch Growers has some," I said. "I was planning to go out there after I talked to you. I'd be happy to pick up a flat of pansies and drop them by your house."

"Good. I can answer your questions then," she said.

"I'll be there within an hour," I said. "As you pointed out in our previous meeting, time is money."

Vera met me out front and led me through a side gate into her backyard. It took my breath away. Her street was resolutely suburban – with well-kept split-level homes and landscaping that was mature, pleasing, and unexceptional – but her yard was a work of art. The elements of rock, water, trees, and flowers had been arranged with an eye to proportion and variety, and the result was an intimate space that conveyed a sense of balance and harmony. We walked slowly around the garden, with Vera pointing out the shape of a particular tree, the way in which the reflecting pool had been positioned to catch the sunrise, and the pattern of the stones on the footpath. As she had been at Ed's, she was dressed in the softest of greys, and again she was wearing gloves. She never removed them. We had tea by the koi pond, and as soon as she'd poured, Vera got down to business.

"How can I help you?" she asked.

I gazed at her garden. "This is a place of such beauty," I said. "It feels wrong to bring ugliness here."

Vera bent to watch her koi. "Ugliness paid for this beauty, Joanne. What's your question?"

"What do you know about Jason Brodnitz?"

"Two things," she said. "He was into rough sex, and after his career dealing with legitimate clients failed, he approached a number of high-end call girls about acting as their investment counsellor."

"What kind of man is he?" I asked.

"He's weak," Vera said. "Apparently, the need for rough sex didn't come from his childhood the way most of these behaviours do. It came to him late."

"After his marriage failed."

Vera smiled. "You are a romantic. Actually, it was after his business failed. I'd retired by then, but, of course, one stays in touch."

"Was he a client of Cristal's?"

"He couldn't have afforded her. At least not at the beginning. Cristal's rates were high and she insisted on a minimum two-hour booking. She wasn't a girl who gave blow jobs in an alley."

"Would Jason Brodnitz have used women who were – "

"Affordable? Of course. When the need is great, any whore will do." Vera shifted her chair so she could watch the progress of her koi. "Joanne, unless a girl gets off on entrapment and panic, she doesn't do s&m. If a man needs it, he has to go cheap or go young."

My stomach lurched. "How young?"

"As young as he has to."

"And Jason . . . ?"

"From what I hear, he went young."

I thought I was going to vomit, but I hung on. "So Jason got these young sex workers to invest through him."

"Joanne, workers that young don't have anything to invest. Their money goes for drugs, and if there's any left over it goes to support the habits of those nearest and dearest to them. They live day to day." Vera's tone was faintly condescending. I was proving to be a dull pupil.

"So who did Jason invest for?"

"People like Cristal. I said he couldn't afford her. I didn't say he didn't know her. From what I heard, he was a frequent visitor and she recommended him to other women. Development in the warehouse district was still in its early stages. Jason was encouraging sex workers to buy into the neighbourhood. And from what I hear, they're doing well."

"Is it possible he became more than just an investment adviser to Cristal?"

"You mean her boyfriend? I suppose anything's possible."

"I have another question," I said. "Do you know a girl named Bree? She has a website where she lists herself as a person who does 'odd jobs.'"

"The name's no help. Those girls change their names frequently. Most often, they name themselves after their favourite soap opera characters. So what kind of odd jobs does Bree perform?"

"Sexual," I said. "Fetishes. She told me she has a client who brings a hard-boiled egg to her room every Sunday and has her peel the egg and inject it with an old-fashioned fountain pen while he masturbates."

Vera's face was impassive. "If Bree has those kind of dates, she's at the bottom of the tank. It's strange, but the girls who worked for me didn't like fetishes. Fucking in all its permutations and combinations didn't trouble them, but satisfying those odd little quirks made them uneasy. Of course, I never forced any of my girls to do anything they found repugnant."

"I don't think Bree has anyone to protect her from those kinds of clients."

"She works alone? That can be a mistake, but if she's into drugs, the dangers won't matter to her. If you want to know about Bree's world, check out some of the cruder porn sites. Look at the eyes of the girls performing. They don't even know where they are."

I stood. "You've been very helpful," I said.

"Yet, you're clearly unsettled."

"Sometimes I think I'm a very naive fifty-six-year-old."

Vera laughed softly. "There's something to be said for holding on to one's illusions. Thank you for the black pansies, Joanne. I hope we'll meet again."

When I got home, I took my own bedding plants outside. It wasn't long before Zack wheeled onto the deck to watch as I arranged the little pots of sweet potato vines and purple and blue pansies in a planter.

"That's going to be pretty," he said.

"Not as pretty as Vera Wang's garden."

"When were you at Vera's house?"

"This morning. I called her after you left, and she invited me over."

He raised his eyebrows. "You'll notice I'm not saying anything."

"I've noticed." I took out the pots and started digging. "Is Vera a reliable source?"

"Very."

I began planting the pansies in clusters of purple and blue. As I worked, Zack knocked the individual plants loose from their pots with his palm and handed them to me. When I'd finished with the pansies, I sat back on my heels and checked the effect. "What do you think?"

"Looks great," he said.

I reached into the planter to pat down the soil around a plant that looked vulnerable. "Zack, those rumours that have been circulating about Jason are true."

"He's a pimp?"

"I don't know, but he is handling investments for women who work as escorts."

Zack whistled. "No wonder he backed down on the custody thing. A man whose income comes from sex workers isn't exactly a candidate for father of the year."

"Vera says Jason's into rough sex with young girls."

Zack rubbed the back of his neck. "What a prince. You know, I try not to judge, but people who hurt kids make me crazy."

"There's a lot about this that makes me crazy," I said.

"So where do we go from here?"

"To the ornamental sweet potatoes," I said.

Zack grinned, loosened the first small sweet potato vine, and handed it to me. I placed it so its bright leaves would trail over the planter's rim.

"Zack, when you represented Vera, what was the charge?"

"Attempted murder."

"And the victim was . . . ?"

"A john. It was an outcall in a hotel, and the date was going badly. The girl managed to alert Vera, but by the time she arrived, the girl was just about dead. Anyway, Vera beat this guy senseless with nunchuks, then she dialed 911 and left."

"And you got her off."

"It wasn't easy, but I was able to show that Vera had sustained a trauma earlier in her life that put her actions that night into context."

"What was the trauma?"

"When Vera's husband found out she was leaving, he knocked her out, bound her hands and feet in rags, poured lighter fuel on the rags, and set them on fire. She managed to get her hands loose and she pounded out the flames on her feet, so she could run. Both her hands and her feet are pretty well fried."

"Hence the gloves and the slow movement." I said.

Zack nodded. "Hence the gloves and the slow movement." He held out another sweet potato plant. "Do you
want this or have you had enough?"

"I've had enough," I said. "But I can't stop now."

Mieka's Mother's Day present to me was a gathering of our
family for a swim and dinner at her house. She had been
offered a Sunday-afternoon catering job that was too lucrative to turn down, so we were celebrating on Saturday.
Angus had sent his regrets, saying he couldn't get away from
work, so I was surprised when I walked into Mieka's yard
and my younger son was there, setting tables.

I held out my arms to him. "I thought you couldn't make
it."

"Zack called and set me straight about a few things."

"Such as the fact that your mother might want to see you
on Mother's Day?"

Angus's smile was sheepish. "That and a few other
things – like becoming a lawyer doesn't mean becoming an
asshole. Mum, I really am sorry. I seem to be turning into a
major-league idiot."

"Is the summer job not working out?"

"No. It's fine. Better than fine. The people at Matheson
Calder treat me really well. I don't have a lot to do, but the
projects I have are really interesting. And I like everybody at
the office. Some of the juniors have a softball league and
they invited me to join. It's a great job. Zack says they want
me to be happy so I'll article with their firm."

"What does Zack think about that?"

"He says I'll go to Matheson Calder over his dead body.
He wants me to work with him."

"Two big law firms vying for you," I said. "You must be
doing something right."

"Not where it counts," Angus said. "Leah broke up with me."

My heart fell. "We love Leah. I was so sure you two would end up together."

"That's what I thought. But Leah says since I started law school, all I ever talk about is law and myself. She says she's tired of both of us being focused on me, and she's met somebody else."

"She can't have been involved with this other man for long. When she was here for Zack's party, you two seemed fine."

"She didn't want to wreck Zack's birthday. She told me about the other guy when we were driving back to Saskatoon."

"Is the new man somebody she met in medical school?"

Angus's headshake was vehement. "No. Leah said she won't make the same mistake twice."

"Meaning?"

"Meaning she's not getting involved with a guy who's totally into his career. Leah's new boyfriend is a hair stylist – *her* hair stylist. That's how they met. Apparently, he's Mr. Empathy. He 'really listens' to her."

"Mr. Empathy may be carrying a lesson for you," I said.

"Am I that bad?"

"You're not bad at all, but it wouldn't hurt if *you* actually listened once in a while."

Angus dropped his head. "That's what Zack says."

"Then it must be true," I said. "Come on, let's get a beer and meet the new woman in Peter's life. You can test out your new listening skills."

"I've already met her," Angus said. "Her name is Dacia, and she's like a female Peter, except really pretty in kind of a round way."

"What does that mean?"

Angus swooped his hands through the air in a volup-
tuous silhouette. "She's curvy and very alternative. Nice
hair – black and long and wavy – Birkenstocks, peasant
shirt, rumpled shorts. She works in a cheese shop, and she
showed Maddy and Lena how to make a whistle out of a
blade of grass."

"Sounds promising," I said.

"Pete thinks so. At least one of your kids is lucky in love."

I put my arm around him. "You've been lucky in love
your whole life. Everybody in this family loves you, and
Leah certainly did. My guess is that if you sat down with her
and told her you realized you'd been –"

"An asshole?"

"I was going to say self-absorbed, but you're closer to the
situation than I am. Anyway, you and Leah invested a lot in
each other. I bet that if you promise to shape up, she'll give
you another try."

"What if she tells me to take a hike?"

"Tell her you understand. Pretend you're Mr. Empathy."

We both laughed. "Come on," I said. "Why don't you give
your sister a hand with the burgers while I say hello to the
woman who can make grass whistle."

Dacia Lehrer was sitting on the grass with Madeleine and
Lena. They were making up a story together that, judging by
the giggle level, was absolutely hilarious.

When she saw Angus and me, Dacia sprang to her feet.
"You're Peter's mum. He just went into the house to get us
a cold drink. Storytelling is thirsty work."

"I'll bet," I said. "You must be Dacia – the first Dacia I've
ever known."

"And probably the last," she said cheerfully. "Not many
parents give their kids the name the Romans used for south-
east Europe."

"Your parents must be history buffs."

She laughed, showing the whitest teeth I've ever seen. "They're everything buffs. My dad says they're autodidacts; my mum says they're just old hippies."

"Nothing wrong with that," I said. "So are you having fun?"

"I am. These young women and I have been telling one another stories, and it's my turn now."

"May I join you?"

"Please do."

For the next fifteen minutes Dacia told a fantastic tale about the friendship between an English sparrow and a peacock. Her voice was mesmerizing: musical, full, and expressive. The girls were enthralled.

"You're a great storyteller," I said when she finished.

Dacia leaned close. "I can juggle too."

"Really?"

"Really," she said. "But I didn't bring my devil-sticks to the party. Have to give you some reason to invite me back."

There have been many Mother's Days when I awoke to breakfast in bed. Once, when Angus was in charge, the menu was blue Kool-Aid and Sugar Pops. This Mother's Day I woke up to a large and luminous abstract propped against the wall at the foot of our bed. I had spotted the painting, titled *Firebrand*, at a gallery in Saskatoon, and I knew it was the kind of painting I wanted to see first thing every morning. There was a beginning-of-the-world intensity about the way the artist, Scott Plear, used colour that made my spirits soar, but Zack had been noncommittal, and I'd assumed the work hadn't evoked the same passion in him that it had in me. I'd been wrong.

"You have no idea how hard it's been for me to wait till today to bring this home," Zack said. "I wanted to see

Firebrand in this room, and I wanted to watch your face when you realized we owned it."

"I didn't think you were paying attention when we were at the gallery."

"When it comes to you, I always pay attention," Zack said. "Are you in the mood for a little quid pro quo?"

"It's a big painting," I said.

Zack checked his watch. "By my calculations we have at least five hours till church."

It was a morning filled with uncomplicated happiness. Taylor, who had been in on the purchase of the Scott Plear, had painted a companion abstract in blues, silvers, and greys that was the perfect complement for the Plear with its fluid reds, orange, and saffron. Abstracts were new turf for Taylor, and she was critical until she saw the pieces side by side. "They're right for each other," she said simply, and so they were.

While we were having breakfast the phone rang. It was Milo O'Brien. His telephone manner was less than impeccable. "You go to church, right."

"Right," I said.

"Which one?"

"St. Paul's Cathedral," I said. "It's not in the constituency, Milo."

"So which church is? Sunday morning is pretty much a dead loss for campaigning, so I figured Ginny and the twins might as well attend a service somewhere."

"Lakeview United is within walking distance of their condo. If you alert your pal at the *Leader-Post*, you might even get a photo of Ginny and the girls in their Sunday best strolling down the avenue."

"I'll make that call. See ya."

"See ya," I said.

When we picked up Maddy and Lena for church, they

were wearing their Easter hats and clutching pictures of the dogs they had drawn for our refrigerator. The dean's sermon, on the complex relationship between mothers and children, was thoughtful, and after the service, reasoning that we are all children of mothers, he stood outside with a basket of gerberas and presented each of us with a flower. In the car going home, Taylor, Maddy, and Lena made a bouquet of our daisies and planned our afternoon together. There were a number of possibilities: the science centre had a new Lego exhibit, there was a children's festival in Victoria Park, and there were three playgrounds within walking distance of our house. One possibility they didn't consider was starting our afternoon with a visit from the police, but as it turned out, that was what happened.

I hadn't met Inspector Debbie Haczkewicz until that day. She'd been at Cristal's funeral, but she'd left before we could be introduced. She was a tall, powerfully built woman with assessing eyes and a gentle manner. She and Zack greeted each other warmly if warily, and he introduced me. When I unlocked the door, the dogs came bounding. I bent to stroke their fur and set their minds at ease. "The girls and I will put the dogs outside and start lunch," I said. "Give me a shout if you'd like coffee or something cold to drink."

Inspector Haczkewicz's voice was even. "Actually, Mrs. Shreve, you're the one I've come to see."

I felt my heart lurch. "It's not about someone in my family, is it?"

"No," she said. "No, this isn't a family matter."

"Then what?"

Debbie Haczkewicz's eyes drifted towards Taylor and my granddaughters. "Maybe we should talk privately."

I turned to my daughter. "Taylor, could you get the girls a sandwich?"

"Sure," she said, but she looked worried. I put my arm around her. "It's okay," I said. "Inspector Haczkewicz just needs information about a case she's working on."

When the girls left, Zack led Debbie into the living room, and I followed.

"What's this about, Deb?" he said.

Debbie Haczkewicz didn't answer him. She turned her eyes on me. "Mrs. Shreve, are you comfortable having your husband present at this interview?"

"Of course," I said. "Why don't we sit down?"

The inspector and I sat on the couch and Zack wheeled up close.

Debbie Haczkewicz plowed right in. "What's your connection with Bree Steig, Mrs. Shreve?"

I glanced at Zack. His nod in response was barely perceptible, but I knew it indicated I should answer what I was asked.

I turned to face the inspector. "Yesterday, when my daughter and I came back from shopping around six o'clock, there was what appeared to be a Mother's Day card in the mailbox. The envelope was peach, and it was addressed to me. There was no stamp, and I didn't recognize the handwriting, but Zack likes surprises, so I assumed it was a gift."

"But it wasn't," the inspector said.

"No,"

"I'll get the envelope," Zack said. His eyes met mine. "Tell Debbie what she needs to know." I picked up his cue: I was to divulge only what I had to. When I saw the set of Inspector Haczkewicz's jaw, I knew that she'd picked up the warning too.

She pulled a notepad from her jacket pocket. "Whenever you're ready, Mrs. Shreve."

"It starts with Cristal Avilia," I said. "I'm aware of the

connection between Zack and her, inspector. The relationship was over before we were married, but he did tell me
about it, and he told me about the blackmail attempt."

"When did he tell you all this?"

"Just after you called on the night Cristal Avilia was
murdered."

"Go on."

"A few days after Cristal's death, a DVD appeared in our
mailbox. It was in a small padded mailing envelope. There
was no name on it, but I assumed it was for me. I've been
covering Ginny Monaghan's campaign for a program I'm
pitching to NationTV, and they often send along footage they
think I'll find helpful. Most often, they send it electronically,
but not always. Anyway, I put the DVD in our machine. It
was of Zack with Cristal. They were having sex."

Debbie Haczkewicz's head flew up. "I thought that disc
had been destroyed."

"Apparently not," I said.

Zack came back in and offered the envelope to the inspector. She pulled a pair of white cotton gloves from her bag. "I
assume when they dust this in the lab, they'll find prints
from both of you."

I nodded.

"Zack, your prints are on file, but we'll need yours,
Mrs. Shreve."

"I'll stop by this afternoon," I said.

"Thank you." Debbie Haczkewicz opened the envelope
flap, pulled out the contents, noted them in her book, and
replaced them. "What did you do when you saw what was
in this, Mrs. Shreve?"

"I was sick – not literally – just angry and frightened. You
met our daughter in the hall, inspector. She could easily
have been in the room when I opened the envelope. It was
an unsettling thought. I'd already had a few sleepless nights

wondering how Zack and I could have explained the DVD to Taylor if somehow she'd happened to see it. Anyway, I was furious, and I wanted these invasions of our home to stop. I picked up the phone, called the number on the funeral program, and Bree answered. We arranged to meet at Nighthawks. We talked for a few minutes. I paid for the information she gave me. She was obviously high, so she didn't have much to tell me that was useful. Just that she hadn't met the person who asked her to deliver the envelope." I shifted my eyes to Zack, and when he blinked slowly, I knew not to volunteer the information about Jason. "Anyway, I wrote my cell number on my business card and left it with Bree. She wanted to reciprocate, so she wrote her address on a slip of paper. And that's the end of the story."

"Not quite," Debbie Haczkewicz said, and her face was touched with sorrow. Apparently, what she was about to say never got easier. "Bree Steig was attacked last night. She was on foot. Her assailant grabbed her, pulled her down an alley, and beat her."

"Is she dead?"

"She's in a coma. The doctors don't know whether she'll recover."

I felt myself go cold. Zack came over and took my hand. Debbie Haczkewicz's eyes were steely. "Your business card was in Bree's pocket, Mrs. Shreve, and she still had her cellphone. The records suggest she called you ten times last night."

I turned to Zack. "I turned my cellphone off before we went to Mieka's," I said. "I never thought to turn it on again."

"Do you have your phone with you?" Debbie Haczkewicz asked.

I reached into my bag, pulled it out, and handed it to her.

"Ten text messages," she said.

Zack leaned forward. "Deb, you're free to read them. Joanne has nothing to hide."

Debbie's face grew grimmer as she read the messages. When she was through, she handed the phone to me. "Bree was trying to get in touch with you. Do you have any idea why?"

"No," I said. "None." The messages were garbled. It was obvious Bree had gone straight from Nighthawks to her dealer. She was incoherent but obsessive. She had two preoccupations: the pie at Nighthawks and the possibility that the slip of paper she'd given me contained a telephone number she needed.

"Do you still have the slip of paper?" Debbie Haczkewicz asked.

"It'll be in my purse," I fetched the purse. Bree's MySpace address was on one side. On the other was a telephone number. I passed the paper to Debbie Haczkewicz; she wrote down the number and handed the paper back to me. "Could you call that number please?" she said.

I picked up my cell and dialed. The person who answered was Jason Brodnitz.

CHAPTER

10

By the end of the next day, Zack had settled Peyben's case with Evangeline, the clairvoyant, and Bree had taken a turn for the better.

Zack phoned me from the office after his lunch with Evangeline. He was riding high; he was also a little drunk. "Hey, Ms. Shreve, I just got offered a job – house counsel for Peyben – salary in the high six figures, bonuses, stock options, use of the company jet. You can quit working and become the lovely piece of fluff on my arm."

"Gee, that just sounds like so much fun," I said. "I take it you settled Peyben's case out of court."

"I did. Evangeline and I went to Peyben's private dining room. I ordered a bottle of Pouilly-Fuissé and asked her to tell me her great dream of life. She revealed that her dream was to spend a summer on the beach, watching boats bob on the Adriatic, drinking fine wine, and perfecting her tan. We had another glass of wine, and I confided that, although I wasn't a clairvoyant, I could foresee two distinct futures for her. In one, she accepted Peyben's generous offer and was in Belgrade soaking up the rays before Canada Day; in the other she grew old, hanging around gloomy courtrooms watching the kind of lawyers she could afford being eviscerated by lawyers like me. We ate our meal, finished our wine, ordered another bottle, and Evangeline accepted Peyben's cheque before our mousse au chocolat arrived.

"Two bottles of wine. Want me to come and get you?"

"Nah, I have to hang around here for a while. Francesca called. She needs to see me, so Norine has managed to squeeze her in later this afternoon."

"Tonight's Ginny's debate, so we're eating early. Okay with you?"

"Everything's okay with me," he said grandly. "One more piece of information: Jason Brodnitz has wisely secured the services of my new partner."

"To deal with the fact that his phone number was in Bree Steig's purse?"

"Among other things," Zack said. "Incidentally, I called Debbie this morning to check on Bree. They're keeping her in an induced coma, so her brain can heal."

"That's good news," I said.

"Yep. Incidentally, how old do you think Bree is?"

"Hard to tell," I said. "Late twenties, early thirties?"

"Seventeen," Zack said. "Gotta go, kiddo."

"The corporate jet awaits?"

"Actually, I have to take a leak."

"I'll pick you up at four-thirty."

"I don't need to be picked up."

"I think you do," I said. "We pieces of fluff have to protect our investment."

The debate among Ginny Monaghan and her opponents was being held in the gym of St. Pius School. When I arrived, citizens were not yet storming the doors to witness democracy in action, but Francesca Pope was there, sitting in the front row of empty chairs, her backpack of bears on the chair beside her, her hands folded primly in her lap. She evinced no surprise when she saw me; she simply stood up, slid her arms through her backpack straps, and walked over.

"Tell Zack I'm sorry I didn't come to his office today," she said. "I tried, but the lights inside were too bright." She raised her hand to her eyes, shading them from the memory. "I waited outdoors until I saw someone I recognized. His name is Blake Falconer. Zack introduced us. He's Zack's partner, so I thought it would be all right if I gave it to him."

"Gave what to him?" I asked.

"The journal I had for Zack."

"Is it yours?"

"No," she said. "It was Cristal Avilia's."

Apparently that ended our conversation. Francesca walked over to a table where someone had set out coffee, juice, and plates of cookies. She pocketed some cookies, poured herself coffee, then went back to her place and left me to my thoughts.

I wasn't alone for long. The NDP candidate, a former student of mine named Evan Shattuck, came over to say hello. He was twenty-six years old, and he'd been the sacrificial lamb nominated when Ginny was riding high. When her fortunes fell, his rose, and for a brief and shining moment, there had been talk that he would take the seat. Now the wheel of fortune had taken another spin, and Evan was on the bottom again. As he held out his hand to me, he didn't seem particularly disheartened.

"Having fun?" I said.

His smile was rueful. "I was having more fun a couple of weeks ago," he said. "But what the hey. This is my first time out."

"The game's not over," I said.

Evan made a face. "Sure it is, but I'm still going to give it my best shot."

"That's the spirit," I said.

When Keith Harris came over, I introduced them. Evan was clearly overwhelmed. "I know this sounds stupid," he said. "But even though, in my opinion, you're on the wrong side politically, you've been a hero of mine since I was a kid."

Keith shook his hand. "That means a lot," he said. "It's good for the process when people like you agree to run. So are you glad you're doing it?"

Evan's eyes were shining. "Are you kidding? Every day I learn something new and every day I meet a lot of great people. It's a blast. Look, it really was an honour meeting you, but I'd better go shake some hands."

After Evan was out of earshot, I turned to Keith. "Makes it harder when you like the other guy, doesn't it?"

"It does," Keith agreed. "But never lose sight of the fact that he *is* the other guy."

Evan was head and shoulders above Ginny's other two opponents. He was smart and he'd done his homework. In truth, he'd overdone his homework. His answers would have earned him top marks in a seminar, but they were too long and too detailed for a debate, and the moderator was repeatedly forced to cut him off. As well, either out of nervousness or the belief that a debate was a discussion among four people running for the same office, Evan focused on the other candidates, and the audience repaid him by growing restive during his answers. He was a much better candidate than he appeared to be that night, and I found myself longing for the chance to sit down with him the next morning, go over the debate tapes, and talk about ways he could improve his performance.

Ginny didn't need my help. She was thoroughly professional, and she was having the time of her life. Her answers were crisp, clever, and often funny. The audience loved her, and she loved them back.

"She's having a good night," I said to Keith.

Keith sighed. "It scares me when a campaign is going this well. I know it's only a matter of time till the dragon crawls out of his lair and tears us apart."

When I got home, Zack was already in bed with his laptop on his lap and his trial bag on the nightstand beside him.

"How did it go?" he said.

"Ginny was brilliant. I think Keith's right. If she can win big in Palliser, there'll be no stopping her."

"You look excited."

"Contact high from the crowd," I said. "Politics can be a lot of fun."

"There's something we need to talk about," Zack said.

"That sounds ominous."

"It's not good."

I sat on the bed and kicked off my shoes. "It would be nice to have one evening that didn't end on a shitty note."

"Your call – we can talk in the morning."

"No. Let's get it over with. Better to know now than be awake all night wondering."

Zack reached into his trial bag, pulled out a journal, and handed it to me. On the cover there was a tranquil picture of a dark-haired young girl in a silk dress sitting under a tree with her dog. There was a cat on her lap, and one on the branch above her. The girl was reading.

"That belonged to Cristal," Zack said.

"So Blake got it to you," I said.

Zack's forehead creased in surprise. "How did you know about that?"

"Francesca Pope was at St. Pius tonight. She told me she couldn't keep her appointment with you today because the light in your building was too bright. She waited outside until she saw someone she recognized." I started to undress. "Poor Blake. Of all the people Francesca could have given it to."

Zack's face was grim. "No doubt about it. Blake has all the luck. And of course, he read the journal before he handed it over to me. He's devastated, but to be fair, Cristal's account of her life is pretty devastating."

"Let me finish getting ready for bed, and I'll take a look," I said. When I had my pyjamas on, I sat beside Zack on the bed and opened the journal. The handwriting was precise, but so tiny I couldn't read it without my glasses. I hooked Zack's off his nose. "Can I borrow these?" I said.

"Be my guest," Zack said. "But stay close. This is ugly reading."

Writing in fragments, connecting her thoughts with dashes, Cristal had recorded a life of sadistic abuse with breathtaking immediacy. Nothing distanced the reader from her narrative. Every sentence was raw with pain. As I read, I could hear Cristal's small, breathy voice, and I could feel her panic.

The journal opened with the phrase *bad day*. It was a fitting epigraph for what was to follow.

Bad day – told 3 I can't deal with it any more. I'll do the rest – even the ones who want me to pretend I'm their little girls, but no more hoods and no more gags – in the night my heart pounds – I'm dying because I can't get out – choking to death – it happens – girls die. 3 says I have to trust him – our love is about absolute trust. He knows what's best – letting a date gag me and tie a hood over my head shows 3 that I love him – knowing I'll do whatever he wants is the way I prove my love. 3 says he never hurts my body – sometimes I think that would be easier – the worst is when he won't speak to me or touch me – even when I'm on my hands and knees in front of him, begging him like a dog – and he ignores me until I agree to submit.

April 7 – This is hell – 3 says I have to tell N I can't see him any more – that he disgusts me. N doesn't disgust me – he makes me feel valuable. He gave me a book – *Portrait of a Lady* – he says I'm like Isabel. To become a lady, she had to learn to live with sadness and disappointment, and N says that's what I have to do too. He says I've earned the right to be happy.

This afternoon I forgot to turn off the camera when N and I were talking. When 3 was reviewing the tapes he heard N tell me I have to get out. It's never been this bad – he spit on me and then he walked out – anything's better than this.

I looked up. My voice was shaking "Zack, I can't read any more of this."

"Just read April 13," Zack said. "That explains why Ned was the client singled out for blackmail."

I turned the pages of tiny handwriting. There were references to encounters with other men, but always the number three was there dominating, manipulating, wounding. Finally, I came to the notation.

April 13 – 3 made me write to N – tell him I'll put the pictures of us on the Internet unless he pays me off. 3 says N has to learn that a whore is a whore is a whore is a whore.

April 14 – N is dead – shot himself – my fault, my fault, 3 says. He's right. Could my 3 be 666? Evil – Evil.

I handed Zack the journal. "That day you took her the cheque, Cristal asked if you believed in evil. She was starting to see the truth, wasn't she? She was beginning to realize 3 was a monster. Ned died because 3 had to show Cristal that she was nothing – just a whore who needed to be taught a lesson."

Zack tented his fingers. "I guess the next question is who is 3? The current wisdom seems to be that it's Jason Brodnitz."

"I can't believe that," I said. "Ginny Monaghan was married to Jason. He was a husband and a father."

"Sociopaths don't have horns, Jo. I've defended some. They blend in. That's how they get away with the things they do."

"But if Jason is such a ruthless manipulator, why would Ginny shield him?"

Zack shrugged. "Maybe she didn't want her daughters to know their father was a monster. Maybe she was safeguarding her reputation. Living with a sadist isn't exactly evidence of sound judgment."

"Zack, none of this makes sense. Cristal wasn't a stupid woman. Why would she let herself be abused like that?"

"According to Blake, Cristal thought that's what she deserved."

"No wonder Blake was devastated."

"Devastated and furious. I've never known Blake to lose control. He's always been able to keep it together – even when Lily was putting him through all that shit. But tonight if Jason Brodnitz – or whoever 3 is – had walked through that door, Blake would have ripped him apart."

"More misery," I said. I took my husband's hand. "I want us out of this," I said. "It's like that old story of the tar baby – every time we touch this Cristal Avilia mess, we get in deeper. Let's walk away. Tomorrow morning call Debbie Haczkewicz and tell her you'll bring the journal down to headquarters. Then get a hold of Blake and suggest he go out to the lake for a few days – get some rest – figure things out."

Zack didn't hesitate. "Okay. I've had enough too." He reached over and turned off the light. "Tomorrow will be better," he said.

"It had better be," I said, and even I was surprised at the anger in my voice.

The next morning when the dogs and I stepped outside for our run, the air was mild and sweet, and the sun was shining. Its beams were weak and watery, but they were persistent. The grass, after so much rain, was dazzlingly green, and the flower bed closest to the deck was shining with daffodils. The prospect of having breakfast outside was seductive.

When I got back, Zack was on the front porch taking the morning papers out of the mailbox. Pantera leapt towards his master and tore the leash from my hand. Even for a mastiff, Pantera was big and there'd been more than one occasion when he'd knocked Zack's chair over. Zack never minded. "I'm just grateful he's on my side," he'd say. This morning we were lucky. Pantera was enthusiastic but restrained.

"The daffodils are putting on a show," I said. "Do you want to have breakfast on the deck?"

"Sure. Everything's ready to go. The porridge and coffee are made, but you might want to stay inside. That hyper kid who's running Ginny's campaign called."

"Milo."

"Right – the one who mainlines candy bars. Ginny's going to be on *Canada This Morning*."

"Good for her," I said. "But I opt for daffodils and no newspapers. Let's just eat our porridge and let the universe unfold without us for a while."

It wasn't that simple. While Zack was making calls on his

cell, I got a call of my own. It was Keith saying that the interviewer on *Canada This Morning* had sandbagged Ginny with a question about whether her campaign had fuelled the rumours circulating about Jason's unsavoury business alliances. There'd been some troubling follow-up questions, and Keith wanted me to watch when the show was broadcast in our time zone. He thought Ginny had handled the situation, but he wanted my opinion about whether she needed to make a statement.

When Zack got off the phone, his expression was grim. "According to Debbie Haczkewicz, Cristal kept a journal from the time she left home. There are dozens of her diaries in a personal storage unit on the north side. The journal I have was the last one, and Debbie's chomping at the bit to discover how it happened to fall into my hands. She's sending someone over."

"No breakfast on the deck?" I said.

"Not today, my love. And there's another shovel of shit on the pile. I can't find Blake. His housekeeper, Rose, says he didn't come home last night, and he's not answering his cell."

I poured more milk into the porridge, turned up the heat under it, and began stirring. "So we've got Ginny, Blake, and Bree Steig to worry about."

"I don't think there's much you or anybody can do to turn Bree's life around."

"I wasn't thinking about rehabilitation; I was thinking about police protection outside her room at the hospital. Zack, I don't believe for a minute that the attack on Bree was random."

"You think I should call Debbie?"

"I do."

Zack hit the speed-dial. When he rang off, he looked satisfied. "There'll be a uniformed officer outside Bree's room in twenty minutes."

"Good start," I said. "Now let's see how Ginny makes out. After breakfast you can start trying Blake again."

When the porridge was ready, I called Taylor for breakfast and Zack and I headed to the family room. She had just joined us with her bowl and her juice when the interview with Ginny started. "How come we're eating in here?" she said.

"I want to hear what Ginny has to say."

Taylor spooned on brown sugar, reached for the pitcher, and flooded her porridge with cream. "Is she going to win?"

"I think so, but there's many a slip between the cup and the lip."

"I don't get it," Taylor said.

"It means life is full of surprises."

As the interview segment opened, there was no reason to suspect things would go badly. The establishing shots of Ginny and her daughters attending church on Mother's Day were a portrait of family devotion, and as the host turned towards Ginny, his mouth curled in a practised smile. He didn't look dangerous.

"Our guest this morning is the Honourable Ginny Monaghan, minister of Canadian heritage and the status of women. Welcome, Ms. Monaghan."

"Thank you, Troy, I'm pleased to be here." In a lemon suit that revealed her powerful athlete's legs, Ginny looked like a woman who could run the country, but she had looked like a winner before. That promise had evaporated in a miasma of whispers and scabrous jokes and as Troy Selwyn framed his question, Ginny was alert.

"This has to be a good day for you," he said. "As far as your party's concerned, the big picture's still in doubt, but there's no doubt about your future. The polls show you're headed for victory in Palliser, and you're already being talked about as your party's next leader."

Ginny's voice was cool. "Troy, I'm sure you're aware that kind of talk is premature. Until the ballots are counted, nothing is certain. As for the leadership, we have a leader, and I support him."

It was a careful response that left the door open. Ginny knew that sound bites have the power to draw blood as well as attention, but this one was toothless. It was also ambiguous. Those steadfast in their allegiance to the prime minister would remember Ginny had reiterated her support for him; those hungering for new leadership would remember that Ginny's statement of support had not been effusive.

"Still, even you must be surprised at the turn of events in Palliser," Troy Selwyn said pleasantly. "Two weeks ago, most political observers had written you off. You were sitting in a courtroom fighting for custody of your daughters, and the accusations about your personal life were, to say the least, damaging."

"My daughters are now safely under my roof," Ginny said, but her eyes were wary.

"So they are," Troy said. "But your twins are with you because your ex-husband suddenly withdrew his suit for custody. You're a powerful political figure, Ms. Monaghan. Were pressures brought to bear upon Mr. Brodnitz? Was he intimidated?"

"He came to his senses. We both did." The camera, hoping for a flash of fear or anger, zoomed in, but Ginny didn't crack. Eyes on the camera, voice strong, she explained. "We were finally able to get over our anger and focus on our children. We reached the kind of agreement Canadians reach every day. We decided jointly that the interests of our girls would be best served if Jason withdrew his demand for custody and the twins lived with me."

"You must be aware of the rumours that have circulated about your husband."

"Rumours circulate about all political spouses and ex-spouses."

"Are you aware of the rumour that the stories about your husband's activities originated in your campaign?"

Ginny looked genuinely surprised. "No. I hadn't heard that one. The stories about Mr. Brodnitz were out there from the beginning. I didn't dignify them with a response then and I won't now." If she'd stopped there, Ginny would have been home free, but in politics, it's the human moment that makes the difference – the flash of temper, the eyes welling with tears. Ginny's discipline held, but her voice was ice. "Whatever else he is, Jason Brodnitz is my children's father. I owe it to them to protect his reputation."

"Are you aware that Jason Brodnitz has called a news conference for this afternoon to discuss these rumours?"

"No I wasn't aware of that."

"What do you think of it?"

Ginny smiled through tightened lips. "I think it's ill advised." The camera lingered on Ginny's face, but she had nothing more to say, and so Troy Selwyn thanked her and wrapped up the interview.

Zack clicked the remote and the screen went blank. Taylor frowned. "What was that all about?"

Zack turned his chair to face her. "Do kids still play Truth or Dare?"

"Little kids do," Taylor said.

"Well, I think we just saw the beginning of a pretty high-stakes game of Truth or Dare." He wheeled towards the door. "Now I'd better get a shower. I'm going to be late for work."

I called Keith. "What did you think?" he asked.

"Zack says Jason's started a game of Truth or Dare."

"That's what I think too. I'm just not sure why. I know Jason's reputation has taken a beating, but that wasn't

Ginny's doing. All this crap about the rumours originating in our campaign."

"Did they?" I asked.

There was a pause. "Good question," he said finally. "I'll find out. Yelling foul before I knew for sure there'd been a foul would be a pretty elementary mistake."

"You've got a few things on your mind," I said.

"Thanks, but there's never an excuse for stupidity."

"How's Ginny doing?"

"She's furious. She's got a bunch of interviews lined up for this morning. They were supposed to be the first steps down the yellow brick road to the leadership, but now she has to deal with Jason's press conference."

"Has she talked to him?"

"He's not taking calls," Keith said. "As soon as Ginny's through with her interviews, she's going to go to Jason's and see if she can work something out – maybe some kind of joint statement about the heat of the moment and cooperating. Anyway, I've changed my plane ticket. I'll hang around Regina until this is worked out. It shouldn't take long."

I'd just got out of the shower and into my jeans and shirt when the police cruiser pulled up outside. Zack greeted the officers at the door with the journal and a smile. "Here you are, and I'll need a receipt."

One of the officers was female, and both were very young. The male officer scribbled a receipt and handed it to Zack. "We have a few questions."

"Shoot."

"You are Zachary Shreve?"

"I am."

"And this journal belonged to the deceased Cristal Avilia?"

"It did."

"How did it come into your possession?"

Zack gave them his shark smile. "Can't answer that. Lawyer-client privilege."

"Who's your client?"

Zack's smile grew wider. "Come on – you know better than that."

"Did you read this journal?"

"Yes."

"Did anyone else?"

Zack smiled and remained silent.

The officers may have been rookies, but they knew enough not to waste time on an immovable object. They gave Zack his receipt, thanked him for his cooperation, nodded in my direction, and left.

A minute later Blake Falconer pulled into our driveway. I opened the door for him. Blake's shirt was fresh, his tie smartly knotted, and his slacks had a knife-edge press, but he looked haggard and spent.

"What were the police doing here?" he said.

"Taking possession of Cristal's journal," Zack said.

Blake winced. "Well, that was the right thing."

"Where the hell have you been?" Zack said.

"Here and there."

"You're going to have to do better than that," Zack's tone was scathing.

"Can I at least sit down?" Blake said. Without waiting for an answer, he walked into the living room and sank into the armchair by the fireplace.

"I'll leave you two to talk," I said.

"Don't," Blake tried a smile. "Zack's always easier to deal with when you're around."

I sat in the other armchair. Zack wheeled close to Blake. "Okay. Where exactly is 'here and there'?"

"After I read Cristal's journal, I drove around for a couple of hours." Blake's eyes met mine. "Did you read it?"

I nodded.

"Then you know that Cristal lived in hell for the last month of her life."

I nodded.

"Jason Brodnitz is a fiend," Blake said. "What he did to her was sick . . . inhuman."

Zack's voice was soft. "No one knows for certain that Jason Brodnitz was Cristal's boyfriend."

"I know," Blake said.

Zack's head shot up. "Cristal told you Jason Brodnitz was her pimp?"

"Not in so many words, but I knew Brodnitz was managing her finances. A few months ago, Cristal asked me to review her real estate portfolio. I'd handled the original purchases and she wanted to liquidate her assets. I refused. Her holdings were all in the warehouse district and prices were skyrocketing. I advised her to hold on. A few days later she called me back. She thanked me, and said she'd found someone who she trusted to protect her interests."

"And she told you the person she found was Jason Brodnitz?" I said.

"Yes," Blake said. "But I didn't tell her what I should have told her: that Jason was a terrible choice, had a lousy track record, and was living off his wife. I didn't say anything. I was afraid that if I did, I'd lose her." Blake turned to Zack. "I know, I know – exactly the same mistake I made with Lily." His voice broke. "Same result too. I lost them both."

"Blake, you look exhausted," I said. "Why don't you get some rest? You and Zack can talk about all this later."

"No," he said. "Because I may have screwed up, and Zack should know. When I read Cristal's journal and saw how that sick bastard Brodnitz had manipulated her, I went to his house. He wasn't there. I pounded on the doors and on the windows, but he never came. Then I got in my car and waited for him. Apparently, I fell asleep. When I woke up, there was a car parked in front of his house – I guess it was his. I stood on the lawn and screamed his name for about twenty minutes. Then, suddenly, it was as if I could see myself – this raging beast. I thought about Gracie, growing up without either parent. I went back to my car, drove to the office, showered, changed, and came over here."

"Did anybody see you?" Zack asked.

"You mean last night?"

Zack nodded.

"I'm sure they did. I was hardly rational. I'm surprised no one called the cops."

"You were lucky."

"I know." He held his hand out to Zack. "Lucky in a lot of ways. Thanks. I'd better check in at home now. Let them know I'm all right."

Zack looked at him curiously. "Are you sure you are?"

Blake stood. "I'm sure. The worst is over."

Zack and I went to the door together to watch Blake drive off. "Well, that was a hell of a way to start the day," Zack said.

"But you heard the man. The worst is over, and you know what I'm going to do?"

"What?"

"I'm going shopping."

"Retail therapy? That's not like you."

"I'm going to food shop. How do you feel about going up to the lake tonight, just the two of us?"

"What about Taylor?"

"She can stay with Mieka. Taylor loves being with Maddy and Lena, and I thought I'd sweeten the pot with Mieka by offering to take the granddaughters up to the lake with us this weekend."

"Give Mieka a chance to invite Sean over for a candlelight dinner?"

"No. I think that fizzled. I haven't heard anything about Sean in a while. Mieka seems to have decided that she and the girls are doing fine on their own."

"Well, that solves a problem for me."

"What to do about Sean?"

Zack nodded. "Actually, Sean may have solved the problem himself. I'm pretty certain he's going to work for Ginny. If Mieka's heart won't be broken, it'll be a win-win situation all around. Good for Sean, good for Ginny, and good for Falconer Shreve. Disgruntled associates have a way of poisoning the well. Now, I'd better get going. I'm in court this afternoon, and if I don't want to step on my joint I should go through the files again. There's other stuff, but I guess I can take that to the lake with me."

"No," I said. "You can't."

Zack grinned. "Right you are, ma'am."

That afternoon, all my needs were met on three blocks of 13th Avenue. My first stop was UpSlideDown. There was a birthday party in progress, and it was time for cake. Eight red chairs had been drawn up to two yellow tables and eight mothers were trying to herd eight little boys into place. There was a Bob the Builder cake, Bob the Builder party hats, and Bob the Builder balloons and noisemakers, which were wholly redundant because the noise level was already ear-shattering.

I smiled at my daughter. "Testosterone central," I said.

Mieka looked wistful. "You know how much I love my ladies, but I always thought it would be fun to have a boy too."

"You have time."

"True, but you need either a man or a turkey baster to get things started, and I'm still using my turkey baster for basting turkeys."

"Funny girl. What happened with Sean?"

"Nothing. Apparently a lot of women get a crush on their divorce lawyers. You're feeling vulnerable and all of a sudden you've got somebody who's on your side and taking care of all your problems."

"And that's all it was? Just a crush?"

"I wanted more. I guess Sean didn't. Mum, I really am fine with this."

"So if Sean were to take a job with Ginny and move to Ottawa, you wouldn't be heartbroken."

My daughter picked up a noisemaker and blew. The sound it produced was somewhere between a wheeze and a death rattle. Mieka grimaced. "Unlike this noisemaker, I will survive," she said. "Now, pushy mama, I've got a Bob the Builder cake to dole out. Do you want to give me a hand with the drinks?"

"Sure," I got the juice boxes from the fridge and put one at each place. Mieka brought the cake with the candles blazing and the mothers sang, "Happy Birthday."

I put my arm around her. "Have I told you how proud I am of you?"

"About a thousand times," she said. "But, hey, shut up some more."

"Listen, I have a favour to ask. Could Taylor stay overnight at your place tonight?"

"That's no favour. Taylor plays hide and seek with the girls for hours, and she helps with baths."

"I thought in return, Zack and I could take the girls to the lake for the weekend."

Mieka's eyes widened. "Now that's a favour." She smiled impishly. "Gives me a chance to try out a new turkey baster."

After I left Mieka's I went to Pacific Fish, a shop that, despite its name, had the best pickerel and northern pike south of Lac La Ronge; then to Bernard Callebaut for our favourite dark chocolates; and finally to the Cheese Shop where, Dacia had assured me, I could get the Boursin au Poivre Zack loved. The Cheese Shop had only been open since the beginning of May and this was my first visit.

Dacia was with a customer, so I had a chance to look around. On the counter by the cash register was a simple glass vase of gerbera daisies: white, yellow, and flaming orange. The mingled smells of a world of cheeses were heavenly. Dacia was wearing white overalls and an orange shirt, and her pretty hair was tied back with an orange and white striped kerchief. Her skin was olive and already tanned – she looked very Mediterranean and, as Angus said, very lovely in a round way. When her customer left, she came over. "My spies tell me you're on the lookout for some Boursin au Poivre," she said in her lyrical storyteller's voice.

"Your spies are right," I said. "It's Zack's favourite."

"And your favourite is Gorgonzola," she said. "Here, have a taste."

"Keep paying those spies," I said. "That is superb."

"There's more where that came from," she said. "We have an Oka that is the best I've sampled."

"Bring it on," I said. As we tasted and talked, Dacia told me what to look for in various cheeses.

"How did you get so knowledgeable?" I said.

"My grandmother had a cheese shop in Saskatoon. I grew up working there. She decided it was time to expand, so she bought this shop for me when I graduated from university."

"What's your degree in?"

"Comparative religion. My grandmother thought I'd need a way to support myself while I found truth."

"Very sensible."

"My grandmother's a very sensible woman. Speaking of family, Peter and I had dinner with my parents last night."

"How did that go?"

"Peter was a hit. He's a great listener, which is lucky because both my parents are great talkers. And you'll be relieved to hear that his name is numerologically sound. My last boyfriend's name was Walter Johnson, and my parents were always trying to get him to change his name to Volter Ivanovski – more positive vowels. My parents take it very seriously. For me it's just a party trick – something fun to do when you meet somebody new."

"So the name Jason Brodnitz would be . . ."

Dacia did some quick figuring. "He would be a six."

"So much for that theory," I said.

"What theory?" Dacia asked.

"Zack's working on a case in which someone is identified by a number. I had a hunch about the numerology thing, but it didn't work out."

I paid for my purchases, invited Dacia to join us at the lake for the July long weekend, and went out to my car. Once again, I'd left my cell on the dash. It was ringing – Zack's ring tone. I picked up. "God, I'm glad to get you," he said. "Where've you been?"

"Buying you Boursin au Poivre. Zack, is something wrong? You sound a little . . . tense."

Zack's laugh was short. "I'm more than a little tense, Jo. Jason Brodnitz is dead. Ginny called me. She's at Jason's house. She went there to talk to him and found him with a knife in his chest."

CHAPTER

11

Suddenly the sunshine I had welcomed in the first hours of the day seemed too bright and too harshly revealing. I thought of Jason Brodnitz, the broken, defeated man I had seen in court on the day he withdrew his suit for custody of his girls; then I thought of 3, the sadistic monster in Cristal Avilia's journal. Two lives running their parallel courses: one public, one hidden – both now ended. All the secrets would be unpacked. The agony that lay ahead for Ginny and her girls was unimaginable.

"Are you going to represent Ginny?" I asked.

"Looks that way," Zack said. "And I've got a call in to Sean. Ginny trusts him, and he's familiar with Brodnitz's background."

"This is all so terrible," I said.

"Agreed," Zack said. "But there's work to be done. I'm going to be holed with my client and the cops for a while. Could you call Keith and let him know what's happened? And, Jo, I'd be grateful if you'd track down Blake and tell him to get away for a few days till the dust settles."

Leopold Crescent, the tree-lined street of handsome old houses where Jason Brodnitz lived and died, was in our neighbourhood. Getting from here to there in a city the size of Regina is seldom a logistical problem, but it can be an emotional one. Often the shortest distance between two points is a straight line that leads past the house of an ex-husband, an ex-friend, or an ex-lover. That day every route between my parking space in front of the Cheese Shop and my house took me past streets that were arteries to the Brodnitz house. I calculated the odds, drove straight down 13th Avenue to Albert Street, and made it home without running into a police barrier.

As soon as I walked in the door, I called Keith. There was no way to break the news of Jason Brodnitz's murder gently, and when Keith heard he sounded stricken. But he was an experienced politician, accustomed to assessing disaster and moving on. He hadn't known Jason Brodnitz except as an impediment to Ginny's future, so he didn't waste any energy on crocodile tears. His analysis of the situation was cogent: the faster Ginny was cleared of suspicion, the better, and the lawyer he wanted to do the job was Zack.

"She needs the best, and that's your husband," Keith said. "I'd ask him myself, but if the request comes from you, he'll do it."

"No request necessary," I said. "Zack's already signed on."

"One less hurdle to jump," Keith said. "I don't want Sean Barton handling this."

"Don't do your victory lap yet," I said. "Zack told me he needs Sean's help on the case."

"That's okay, as long as . . ." Keith stopped himself. "Forget it. Zack knows what he's doing." He sighed. "Life is never easy, is it?"

"Nope. That's why the Scots gave us Glenfiddich."

When Keith laughed, he sounded like himself, and I felt

better. After I talked to Blake Falconer, I felt worse. His reaction to Jason Brodnitz's murder was unnerving. He didn't
seem surprised. "People like that deserve to die," he said,
and his voice was toneless. When I didn't respond, he ended
the silence. "Is there anything else?" He didn't question
Zack's decision that he should leave town. He agreed and
said he'd be in touch. As I dropped my cell in my bag, I felt
a jab of dread. Like Miss Clavel in Lena's favourite *Madeline*
bedtime story, I knew that something was not right.

The morning papers were still on the kitchen table. I
flipped through them. The picture of Ginny and her daughters coming out of church had made the front page of all
three. It was a clean sweep.

Until that moment I had been baffled by Jason Brodnitz's
decision to call a press conference to clear his name. He was
not naive. If he was the man Cristal Avilia referred to as 3,
Jason would know that media scrutiny would, in the end,
expose him. But more than once, Zack had pointed out the
obvious to me: if human beings were always guided by
reason, there'd be no work for lawyers.

When human beings are choked with resentment, overcome by anguish, or filled with rage, passion trumps reason.
As I looked at the morning papers with their images of
Ginny in possession of everything Jason must have longed
for – public affirmation, a brilliant career, the love of his
daughters – I understood why Jason had called the press conference. If he were destroyed, his family would not be spared.
It was an ugly thought, and I felt the need to banish it. For
me, the solution was to swim laps until the tension disappeared from my body and my mind was clear. I changed
into my suit and headed for our pool. Jill Oziowy's phone
call caught me just as I was about to dive in.

As always when she was working a story, Jill's adrenalin
was pumping. "This Ginny Monaghan thing is going to be

big," she said, "and you've spent the last three weeks with her. You're in the right place at the right time. Any chance you'd be willing to go once more into the breach for NationTV? On air would be great, but you can do background. We'll take what we can get."

"Definitely not on air," I said. "And I'll have to think about the other. I may just be too close to this one. Zack's representing Ginny Monaghan."

"How about trading a little information?"

"We can give it a try," I said. "You go first."

"Well, at the moment, we're playing connect the dots with the Cristal Avilia case and this one."

I was shocked that someone from outside had linked the cases so quickly. "What makes you think there's a connection?" I said.

There was an edge of exasperation in Jill's voice. "Oh come on, Jo. All during the campaign there were rumours about Jason Brodnitz being involved with hookers. Cristal Avilia was a hooker. And now they're both dead."

"So somebody who doesn't like hookers and johns killed them both?"

"Or somebody who was married to a john got pissed off at him for associating with prostitutes and risking her career and reputation. Look at the facts: Jason announces a press conference where, tittle-tattle has it, he's going to identify Ginny's campaign as the source of the rumours besmirching his good name. But before he gets a chance to tell his side of the story, he's murdered, and guess who finds the body? Ginny. And guess who removes the knife sticking into Jason's chest?"

Now it was my turn to be exasperated. "Come on. Do you honestly think someone as disciplined as Ginny Monaghan is going to jeopardize her future because her ex-husband is on the prowl?"

Jill was measured. "I don't know because I don't know Ginny Monaghan. You tell me."

"She didn't do it," I said. "I've heard Ginny talk about her training as an athlete. Reading a situation and staying in control is second nature to her."

"So, are you sporting a *Monaghan for PM* button?"

"Not yet," I said.

"Got anything more?"

"Nope."

"That's a fair start. Keep working on the Avilia-Brodnitz murders."

"I thought I was working on a program about women in politics."

"Ginny Monaghan's a woman in politics," Jill said. "Boy, talk about a role model. Ginny's ex-husband threatens to derail her career, so his girlfriend gets pushed off a balcony and he gets a kitchen knife in the heart. Who says women aren't as tough as men?"

I rang off, dove into the pool, and started doing laps. On days as sunny and warm as this one, I often longed for my old outdoor pool, sometimes so much that I went over to Mieka's and swam there. Today I was happy to be cut off from the world – safe in my house. I was still swimming when Zack came home. "Want some company?" he said.

"I'd love some," I said.

In a few minutes, he was back, wearing trunks. He lowered himself onto the steps that led into the pool, eased in, and sighed with pleasure. "God, this feels good," he said. "And necessary. I had fucking leg spasms this morning."

"Because we haven't been doing this enough," I said.

"There's a lot of things we haven't been doing enough," Zack said. We swam in companionable silence. After half an hour, Zack said. "Time to go. I've got to stop by the office before I go to court."

"What about lunch?"

"I'll grab something." He moved towards the stairs and started pushing himself out of the pool. I climbed out too. Zack frowned. "Hey, you don't have to stop. Stay in. Take it easy."

"I want to watch you towel off."

He grinned. "That means I get to watch too."

We showered and then went to our room to dress. "Jill called this morning," I said. "NationTV wants me to do something on Ginny Monaghan."

Zack shook his head. "Could you give this one a pass?"

"I already have," I said. "I told Jill that you're representing Ginny. She understands the problem. We did, however, agree to some selective information sharing."

Zack raised an eyebrow. "Did you get anything good?"

"The media are working on the link between Jason's murder and Cristal Avilia's."

Zack stopped drying his head. "And?"

"Jill floated a scenario that Ginny killed them both because she was angry about his association with a hooker."

Zack snorted. "Jeez, the stuff that's out there, eh? Well, here's some info that's not for sharing. When I got to the Brodnitz house, Ginny wasn't alone with the deceased. Margot was with her."

I poured some lotion into my hand and rubbed it on Zack's back. There were some worrying abrasions there – pressure sores – too much time in the chair and not enough time taking care of skin. I didn't say anything, but when Zack flinched the first time I touched a raw spot, I went into his bathroom for the Polysporin and dabbed some on the abrasions. "So, what was Margot doing there?" I said.

"Hovering," Zack said. "When it comes to her clients, Margot's part mother hen, part pit bull."

"That's an interesting image," I said.

"Accurate too," Zack said. "Margot's a good person to have on your side. She's protective and she doesn't back away from a fight. According to Margot, the first she'd heard about Jason's news conference was on *Canada This Morning*. Of course, Margot being Margot called him and told him not to do anything till he'd talked to her."

"So Margot talked to Jason today," I said.

"Don't I wish? He didn't answer his phone. Margot left a voice mail. At that point, as far as she was concerned, Jason was just an ex-client who was about to do something stupid. She wanted to talk to him, but he wasn't at the top of her list. She had appointments with clients who were racking up billable hours. His news conference wasn't until mid-afternoon. She thought she had plenty of time."

"But she didn't."

"No. She tried calling him a couple more times, then she assumed he just wasn't answering his phone, so she went to his house."

I took a pair of silk briefs from Zack's dresser and handed them to him. "And Ginny was there. It must have been quite a scene to walk in on."

"It's one I won't forget for a while." Zack shuddered. "There was so much blood. Ginny was soaked. By the time we were finished with Debbie and her gang, someone had notified the press, and they got some peachy shots of Ginny coming out of her ex-husband's house covered in blood."

"She's not under arrest?"

"No. The police can't do anything until they collect the evidence. If they think Ginny's concealing something, they'll keep an eye on her."

"So what's next?"

"Ginny's going to call me after she's talked to the twins."

"Those poor girls."

"Losing a father when you're that young has to be rough."

"I wonder how Em and Chloe will remember him."

Zack shrugged. "Time will tell. Right now the priority is to get their mother out from under this." He pulled on his socks – cashmere, winter and summer, because his circulation was so poor. "Ginny wants you there when she and I get together. I said I'd ask, but nobody's going to blame you for taking a bye on this one."

I screwed the lid back on the Polysporin. "Lately, my attempts to put my head in the sand haven't met with much success. I might as well do what I can."

We finished dressing in silence, weighed down by the thought of what lay ahead. Zack chose a lime green and hot pink tie that I especially liked. He was knotting it when the phone rang. He answered and mouthed Ginny's name.

"We'll be there in ten minutes," he said. "Joanne's coming too." He paused, listening. "I'll tell her." He rang off. "Ginny's grateful. Time to move along, Ms. Shreve."

"I know," I said. I thought of the leg spasms, the abrasions on his back, and the weariness in his voice. "Zack, let's still go to the lake tonight. I've already done the shopping. Mieka's looking forward to having Taylor. And this case will be here when you get back."

He looked at me hard. "That is so tempting."

"Give into temptation," I said. "After the meeting at Ginny's we can swing by the house, pick up the dogs, and have the barbecue smoking and the martinis poured by six."

"Sold," he said. "I love the lake before the people come. It's nice to be safe from human mischief."

"People do complicate things," I said.

෨ ෧

We took Zack's car to Ginny's – a mistake as it turned out because a shiny new Jaguar with a vanity plate AMICUS is more noticeable than a Volvo station wagon of indeterminate age with a licence plate that says nothing. There were media vans parked in front of Ginny's condo. Zack pulled into a parking spot well away from them. "What the hell do they think they're going to see?"

"Us," I said. "Lucky you wore your pretty tie."

"Thanks," he said. "Jo, how do you think Ginny should handle this publicly? It's not just a question of optics; her behaviour could have ramifications down the line."

"Legal ramifications?"

"Yes. If this comes to trial – which I hope to God it doesn't – Ginny's behaviour in the next few hours could be significant."

"You can't expect her to perform, Zack. She must still be in shock. Whatever her feelings were about Jason, seeing him like that must have been a nightmare."

"Ginny's strong – she'll do what she has to do."

"Then have her issue a brief statement expressing her shock and sorrow and asking that the media respect her children's right to privacy at this sad time."

Zack grunted. "You really think the media are going to buy into that?"

"Reporters have kids of their own. They should know when to draw the line."

"How about the voters? What do you think Jason's death does to Ginny's election chances?"

"It finishes them," I said simply. "Ginny may not have been charged, but the suspicion that she had something to do with his murder is there. And purely pragmatically, she needs to be campaigning, but the moment she steps out in public, she's fair game – the press can ask her whatever they want."

"So she just holes up in her condo until this blows over?"

"It beats the alternative." I pointed at the media vans. "Those vans are going to be a permanent fixture till the police figure out what happened to Jason."

"Any suggestions? Deb isn't going to let Ginny leave the jurisdiction."

"Lawyers' Bay is near Regina. It's a gated community, and we have a guest house sitting there empty."

Zack smiled approvingly. "Good plan, Ms. Shreve." He glared at the media. "Time to face the ravening hoards." He opened his door and reached into the backseat for his chair. The TV people were on him like the proverbial ticks on a dog. Zack unfolded his chair and gave them his barracuda smile. "How about backing off until I get into my chair? And, incidentally, the answer is 'no comment.'"

The bravest of the group stood his ground. "We haven't asked anything yet," he said.

"Whatever you ask, that's the answer." Zack slid into its seat and wheeled towards the condo. I stayed right behind him.

There were six of us at the meeting: Ginny, Keith, Margot, Sean Barton, Zack, and me. Ginny was sitting cross-legged on the window seat. Framed by a wash of blue sky, her open-necked white shirt crisp, Ginny could have been an ad for the benefits of condo living, but her face was pale and her eyes unfocused. We exchanged muted greetings, then Zack moved close enough to Ginny to take her hand. He always connected physically with his clients. It was, he said, his way of telegraphing to a judge or jury that his clients were human beings in whom he believed.

"How are you doing?" he asked.

"Okay. Telling the kids was rough."

"How are they doing?"

"I'm glad they have each other."

"Joanne has an idea that should help," Zack said. He glanced at me.

"I thought you and the girls might like to get away for a few days," I said.

Ginny's eyes moved to Zack. "Will the police let me do that?"

"I'll talk to the inspector in charge of the case and see. I think I can get her to agree. The cottage we own is just forty-five minutes from the city, so if the police have questions you can be at headquarters in an hour. I think as a good faith gesture, you should stay in town till tomorrow night. By then the first rush of questions will be over. That'll also give you a chance to issue a short statement expressing your shock and sadness about Jason's death and asking the media to respect your daughters' right to privacy at this sad time."

Ginny nodded. "I should also make certain everyone knows I'm still in the race."

"Good point," Keith said. "But we have to make sure we get the balance of regret and determination right in your statement. Incidentally, Jo's right about getting out of town. If you're here, you'll be getting ugly questions, and every story will link your name with Jason's."

Ginny's laugh was grim. "Ginny Monaghan, ex-wife of murdered businessman Jason Brodnitz, dropped in on a daycare centre today."

"You've got it." Keith said. "Let's get the statement out, then talk about how we can handle the campaign without Ginny."

Crafting a short statement that conveyed both sorrow and grit proved daunting, and as everyone worked on the wording, my mind drifted to the day my own father died, and I felt an almost palpable connection to Ginny's daughters, sequestered somewhere in the condo. Finally, I got up and walked over to Ginny. "Would it be all right if I talked to the girls? I thought I could mention the cottage."

Ginny nodded. "Actually, I'd appreciate that. I don't know quite what to do there. I think they're in Em's room – down the hall, second door on the left."

When I knocked, both twins came to the door. They'd been crying, but they were poised. "Were you looking for the bathroom?" one of the twins said.

"Actually, I was looking for you. Could we talk for a minute?"

"Sure. Come on in."

The room had the usual teenage clutter, plus an impressive array of home-gym equipment: a treadmill, a stationary bike, a step bench, and an assortment of free weights. "If you can find a place to sit, sit," one of the twins said.

I narrowed my eyes. "I'm sorry. I really can't tell you two apart. You're . . . ?"

"Chloe," she said.

I cleared off a corner of the bed and told them about the cottage. As they listened, some of the misery drained from their faces. "That would solve one of our problems," Em said, snaking her arm around her sister's waist. "It's hard to know what you're supposed to do when your father dies."

"I remember that," I said. "Sitting in my room while my mother was downstairs talking to people."

"How old were you?"

"Sixteen. My father died an hour before my sweet sixteen birthday party was supposed to start. My mother made me promise not to tell the guests because she'd gone to a great deal of trouble arranging things, and she didn't want the party ruined."

Chloe's jaw dropped. "She must have been a witch."

"She was," I said.

"So what did you do?" Em said.

"I went to the party. It was being held at a place called the

Granite Club in Toronto – very classy. I told my best friend, Sally, what had happened. She knew one of the boys who worked in the bar, and she got him to give us a bottle of cherry brandy and a package of Rothmans. We went outside and drank the brandy and smoked the cigarettes until I threw up on my dress. Then we went to my sweet sixteen."

Chloe's eyes were huge. "Your mother must have been furious."

"She didn't talk to me for a month."

The corners of Em's mouth twitched into a smile. "But it was worth it, eh?"

I nodded. "It was worth it."

"So what did your dad do for a living?" Em asked. Her tone was casual, but as she waited for my answer, she was intent.

"He was a doctor."

"Nothing to be ashamed of," she said. "Not like us."

"You have nothing to be ashamed of," I said.

"Right," Chloe said. "We're the incredible Brodnitz twins. Too bad our father was a pimp."

"Let it go," her sister said. "He's dead."

"But we're not," Chloe said, and she ran from the room.

Em's eyes flashed with anger. "There are times when I hate both my parents." She inhaled deeply, then exhaled. "Coach would say that's a waste of my energy."

"Coach would be right. Em, is there anything I can do to help?"

"Yes," she said wearily. "Wait three minutes and go knock on Chloe's door. She didn't thank you for the cottage, and if she doesn't do the right thing, she beats herself up for days."

Chloe's room was immaculate; so were her manners as she apologized for losing her temper and for neglecting to thank me for offering their family the cottage. As I walked back to the meeting, I knew that being Chloe Brodnitz had never been easy, but it was about to become a lot harder.

By the time I returned to the meeting, the statement had been drafted and the focus had shifted to tasks.

Keith spoke first. "Six days to E-Day, and Ginny, unless there's a miracle, I don't think you're going to be able to campaign. My thought is that we establish a group, the Friends of Ginny Monaghan – high-profile, well-respected people who will go into the community and act as your surrogates. What do you think?"

Ginny's smile was wan. "Looks good on paper, Keith. Let me know if there's a stampede when you ask for volunteers to risk their reputation for an alleged sexaholic who may have murdered her ex-husband, the pimp."

Keith didn't flinch. "Well, you're looking at volunteer number one," he said. "As for the rest, you underestimate your power, kiddo."

Ginny bit her lip. "Thanks," she said. "I should have known . . ."

Margot had been quiet during the discussion. Now she was ready to contribute. "Well, before there's an Oprah moment here, I'm appointing myself the Friend of Jason Brodnitz."

Zack looked at her curiously. "That's a new wrinkle. Not many lawyers continue working for a client after he's dead."

"I do," Margot said sharply. "Jason may have been a lot of things, but he wasn't a pimp. I've dealt with those guys and they always made the hair on the back of my neck stand on end. I never got that with him." Margot turned to Ginny. "I know this may seem as if I'm not on your side, but I am. I have a sense that when I find out the truth about him, I'm going to find out who would have a reason to want him dead."

Zack shot his new partner a hard look. "You're wasting your time, Margot. The police are digging into every aspect of Brodnitz's life even as we speak."

"I have my own sources," Margot said.

"Who?"

"Mandy Avilia and my sister, Laurie. One of them will know who Cristal's boyfriend was, and I'm putting my money on the boyfriend as our bad guy."

"I'll come along," Sean said. "I'm working with Zack on this. I may pick up something useful."

Margot caught my eye. It was just a flicker, but I knew she didn't want Sean along.

"Round-trip it's a five-hour drive, Sean," I said. "Zack won't be able to spare you for that long. I'll go with Margot. I met Mandy Avilia at Cristal's funeral. We didn't have a chance to talk that day, and I have some questions of my own."

"So, it's settled then," Margot said briskly. She stood and smoothed her skirt. And with that we went our separate ways.

Zack and Sean stayed behind to discuss the case with Ginny, but Keith, Margot, and I left together. When the elevator doors closed, Keith chuckled. "That was a pretty smooth manoeuvre you two pulled off. I don't think Sean knew what hit him."

"I disagree," I said. "Sean doesn't miss much."

"I don't like that boy a bit," Margot said. "You've done your good deed, Joanne. The prospect of a day with Sean did not set my girlish heart a-flutter, but you don't have to come to Wadena."

"I know," I said. "But I'm tired of sitting around, waiting for the other shoe to drop. I want this to be over, Margot. Let's go to Wadena and find out what we can."

Margot looked at me approvingly. "You know, I think you and I are going to get along just fine. I'll pick you up tomorrow at nine."

Our cottage was in an area called Lawyers' Bay. The spot had been named in the 1940s with a sneer by locals nettled by the fact that Henry Hynd, a Regina lawyer, had snapped up the horseshoe of land fringing the prettiest bay on the lake. Henry and his wife, Winifred, were long-range thinkers. They planned a big family, and their dream was that their children would grow, marry, build cottages of their own on Lawyers' Bay, where Henry and Winifred (who was called Freddy by friend and foe alike) would watch them swim and grow during the hot months of summer.

But life has a way of scuttling plans. When the Hynds' first child, a son, was born, Freddy almost died. Lawyers' Bay remained undeveloped until their son, Henry Junior, also a lawyer, married Harriet and they produced a single child, Kevin. Our cottages had come about because Kevin Hynd, in his first year at law school, found a family in four students in his first-year class. After Kevin and his friends graduated and became successful law partners, they built the cottages that Henry and Freddy Hynd had dreamed of.

By the time Zack and I married, Henry Senior and Freddy had gone to their respective rewards, and Henry Junior and Harriet were living in cozy proximity in an assisted-living home in Regina. The families occupying the lake homes that dotted Lawyers' Bay bore little resemblance to the senior Hynds' dream of happy families in cottages with squeaky doors, sandy floors, and guest books with wooden covers, of memories that focused on good times and good coffee.

Kevin never married; Blake Falconer's marriage ended in tragedy; Chris Altieri committed suicide; Delia Wainberg married a man who graduated bottom of their class at law school and never practised law but found joy in raising their daughter and in creating life-sized woodcarvings of animals and people. And there was Zack, who, when we met, had been the most successful and solitary of them all. He had built his cottage at the urging of his partners. He hired a housekeeper, bought a big, expensive boat; then, except for the three long weekends of summer, he forgot about the place. That changed when we got together.

From the beginning I loved the cottage. The architect had understood the importance of light, and there were enough windows and skylights to please even me. Because of Zack's wheelchair, all the rooms were large and all the doorways wide. Zack had handed the interior designer a blank cheque and told him to do whatever he thought would work. The decision had been wise.

The designer had chosen the coolest of monochromes for the walls; sleekly unobtrusive furniture for the public rooms, and abstract art throughout the house that was pleasing but not challenging. Only the concert-sized Steinway and the collection of moths mounted in shadow boxes were of Zack's choosing.

When Zack and I married, he told me to make whatever changes I wanted to. I didn't change a thing. The large uncluttered spaces were great for a family that included a man in a wheelchair, a daughter still at home who had many friends, two granddaughters, two big dogs, and two cats. I liked the spare decor and the hardwood floors. My favourite room was the sunroom that overlooked the lake. The designer had found a partners' table at a country auction – a massive piece with twelve matching chairs. It was ornate, out of fashion, and, for that reason, dirt cheap.

That late afternoon, Zack and I had our pickerel there, so we could watch the sun blaze its shining path on the lake and keep an eye on Pantera and Willie.

After Pantera ripped down the hill, did a face plant into the sand, shook his square head, lumbered into the lake, and began swimming, Zack turned to me. "The dogs love it here."

"No leashes," I said. "I love it too. Same reason."

"Any time you want to move out here, say the word."

"Four more years," I said. "After Taylor finishes high school."

"Fair enough," Zack said. "So what are you going to do out here?"

"Nothing," I said.

"I'm going to get an office in town," Zack said. "No partners, no clients, just my name on the door. Pantera and I aren't like you and Willie. We need a destination."

After we ate, we went down to the lake. It was chilly, and I went back up to the cottage to get our jackets. When I glanced out the window, Zack was sitting on the dock with Pantera. They were at peace, and I wondered how long it would be before they were at peace again.

I walked down to the dock and handed Zack his jacket. "Penny for your thoughts," I said.

"Just trying to sort out the tangle. There's always a loose end that starts unravelling it all. I'm just trying to figure out where it is."

"Maybe Margot and I will find it in Wadena."

Zack leaned back in his chair. "I wouldn't be surprised. One lousy choice and an entire life changes."

"Are you talking about what happened to you?" I said.

"No," Zack said. "No complaints here. No one has had a better life than me."

"Don't use the past tense," I said. "You and I are just hitting our stride."

We sat in silence as the path of light on the lake grew wider and finally disappeared. The sky grew dark. Usually, this was the signal for other cottagers to turn on their lights, but that night there was no one there but us. There was a tang of skunk in the air and, except for the slap of the waves on the shore, the world was quiet. Finally, Zack sighed. "Time to go to bed, Ms. Shreve. We've got a long day tomorrow."

"I know," I said. "But we still have tonight."

CHAPTER

12

It didn't take long for the harmony that had enveloped us to disappear. As I drove back to the city the next morning, Zack thumbed his BlackBerry and muttered an expletive. "I guess it was just a matter of time," he said.

"Till what?"

"Till the cops got hold of Cristal's client list. And someone made the job easy for them – sent it to them electronically. The police have been quick to request the men whose names appear on the list to honour them with their presence."

"Including you?"

"Including me."

"Any idea who supplied the police with the list?"

"According to the e-mail address, it was Bree Steig. Comatose, under twenty-four-hour watch, but apparently still able to use her Hotmail account."

"Someone knew her password."

"Right. Debbie Haczkewicz must be pulling her hair out. Almost two weeks since Cristal was killed – no arrest and the number-one suspect just got murdered. Now, some public-spirited citizen sends Debbie the names of thirty-two of our city's best and brightest, with the suggestion that one of them had a very good reason for killing both Cristal and Jason."

"It would be interesting to know who sent the e-mail."

"Interesting but not easy. Trying to discover the user of a Hotmail account is right up there with counting the number of angels that can dance on the head of a pin. Interviewing all the men on that list is going to take time and personnel, and that gives us our silver lining."

"How so?"

"Because it'll take some of the heat off Ginny. It's hard to imagine circumstances under which she would have found Cristal's client list and sent it to the police."

"It's not hard at all," I said. "If Jason had the list, Ginny could have picked it up the morning he died. I don't believe that's what *did* happen, but it could have. I wouldn't count on the police easing up on Ginny quite yet."

"I didn't need to hear that."

"Well, while I'm on a roll – we haven't talked about Blake."

Zack's jaw tightened. "What about him?"

"When I told him Jason Brodnitz was dead, Blake said 'People like that deserve to die.'"

"Well, thank God he's out of town, eh? You say stuff like that to the cops, they start asking questions."

"There were many men in Cristal's life," I said. "Some of them might have felt that way about Jason too."

"Especially if he was trying to shake them down. Jo, there were names on that list that surprised even me. The one thing they share is they're all guys who aren't used to being fucked over."

We drove past fields tender with the green of new growth. "So what's next?"

"First thing I have to do is tell the seven dwarfs to find legal representation. I also have to tell my partner that.

Ginny is my client, and looking out for Blake would be a conflict of interest."

"You're ready to cut Blake loose for Ginny?"

"I have to, but I've known Blake for almost thirty years. He didn't kill anybody."

"You think Ginny might have?"

Zack didn't answer, and when he didn't answer, I knew better than to ask. I changed the subject. "Do you think I'm spinning my wheels trying to find out about Cristal's life?"

"Honestly, I don't know. By this time, the cops will have done their job. I've had my run-ins with the force over the years, but they're competent and they're honest."

"They could have overlooked something," I said. "Cristal had a private life. She and 3 must have gone out for dinner or taken a walk or rented a video. Surely, someone saw them together."

Zack was silent. "I wonder," he said finally.

"You wonder what?"

"I wonder if Cristal paid my bill because Francesca saw something. They live in the same neighbourhood – in fact, Francesca's favourite haunt is that warehouse next to Cristal's condo. But Francesca's terrified of cops – she'd never let one get close enough to ask questions."

"She'd let you get close enough," I said. "And she trusts you."

"That's because I like her," Zack said. "I'll see if I can carve out some time this morning and take a spin through the warehouse district." He grinned. "I love it when the pieces start to come together."

Zack's BlackBerry rang. He checked the number. "Margot," he said. "Probably anxious to hit the road and wondering what I've done with you." He picked up. "Falconer Shreve Wainberg Hynd and Wright." He grinned. "I thought you'd like that, and, no, your name can't be first on the list. So what's up?" He listened for a moment. "Joanne's at the wheel. We should be home in ten minutes, but she obeys speed limits, so make it fifteen. Why don't you meet us at the house?"

Zack punched in another number.

"Now who?" I said.

"Norine," he said. "I might as well get caught up on what's happening at the office. Hey, it's handy having a driver."

"Then let's hire one," I said. "Then we can both be boors."

"Sorry, Ms. Shreve. Sometimes I forget your socialist roots. Hey, Norine, what's going on there?" He listened. "It's eight forty-five. How can the day be this fucked up already? Don't try to answer, that was just rhetoric. Get Sean to call his investigators. I want them to find out everything they can about the men in Cristal Avilia's life. I'm sending a list of the names. And, Norine, can you clear an hour for me sometime today? I've got to find Francesca Pope. Good. And no calls forwarded except from Blake."

Margot's black BMW was already in our driveway. When we pulled up, she leapt out.

"Ready to hit the road?" she said.

"Don't rush off," Zack said. "Come in and I'll make us coffee."

Margot raised an eyebrow. "You make coffee?"

"It's not exactly verifying the string theory," Zack said. "Just grind the beans, put the filter in the cone, measure the coffee into the filter, and pour the boiling water."

"I'm impressed," Margot said. "And you passed your bar exams too."

We took our coffee outside. When I let out Taylor's cats, they streaked to the one patch of sun on the back deck and took possession.

"We're in for a warm day," I said. "Those cats have an uncanny ability to predict weather."

Margot moved her chair so she could pat Pantera while we talked. "I had a phone call last night," she said. "Mandy Avilia has something very important she wants to talk to me about. Probably a new shade of nail polish they just got in at Cut 'n' Curl, but she's a sweet girl, and she is Cristal's sister. Sisters tell each other things."

"If Cristal told her sister that Jason was her boyfriend, would you tell me?" Zack asked.

"Sure. I play by the rules, but it ain't gonna happen." Margot touched the lovely flame-coloured scarf she was wearing. "I'll bet you this scarf against that tie you're wearing that Jason wasn't 3."

"What would you do with my tie?"

"Wear it."

"You're on." Zack said. "Full disclosure – we're hiring a firm of investigators to find out everything they can about the men in Cristal Avilia's life."

"Joanne and I will find out more in an afternoon than they will in a month."

Zack cocked his head. "The people of Wadena don't like strangers?"

"Wadenans are the friendliest people on the prairie," Margot said. She went over and fingered Zack's tie. "You just have to know the right questions to ask."

Wadena is two hours northeast of Regina. The drive is a pleasant one through gently rolling farmland and poetically quivering aspens, and Margot and I were both determined to enjoy our time together. Our topics of conversation were inconsequential: a new restaurant that had opened in town, some delicious gossip about a mutual acquaintance, summer plans. It wasn't until we came to the sign welcoming us to Wadena that we talked about Cristal Avilia.

"I still can't believe she's dead, you know," Margot said.

"Were you close?"

"No. She was six years younger than me and that's a lot when you're in school. But Cristal was in my sister Laurie's class, so she was around the house."

"What was she like?"

"Pretty, smart, quiet, not the girl you would have expected to end up living the life she did. There were girls who were more likely candidates, the ones they called the town bicycles because every boy had a ride on them, but Cristal wasn't like that. She seemed focused, and – this is going to sound so high school – she was *nice.*"

"Do you have any idea why her life got off track?"

"No. I'm sure if you walked up and down Main Street – which, incidentally in Wadena is called Main Street – you would get fifteen hundred theories, but I've been a lawyer too long to waste time on root causes. Something happened, and Cristal gets a shitty life and an early death. That's really all that matters."

"Not to Zack. He's convinced he needs to know what happened, at least in the time between the beginning of the shitty life and the end."

"If anybody will know that, it'll be my sister. That's why we should see her before we see Mandy. I left Wadena twenty-two years ago. When I came home, I heard things about Cristal, but I didn't pay much attention. I was busy, going to school, building a practice, having fun." Margot slowed and pointed to a small brick building covered in painted daisies. "That's the Cut 'n' Curl, where Mandy works. Anyway, my focus was not Wadena. My sister's was. She'll remember."

Laurie and her husband and kids lived in a pale blue split-level house opposite the high school. There was a station wagon in the carport and an impressive number of sturdy plastic vehicles for kids on the asphalt driveway. Two boys about ten were throwing a football on the front lawn. When they spotted Margot's car, they came running. She jumped out and opened her arms. When she put them both in a hammerlock, the boys didn't protest. With the boys trapped under her arms, she introduced them. "The squinty-eyed one who looks like Roadrunner is Roger," she said. "The one who looks like the bad guy in a Quentin Tarantino movie is Sam. Men, this is Joanne Kilbourn. You may have seen her on television."

The boys smiled politely; it was clear that whatever kind of television I was a part of wasn't appointment TV for them. "Nice to meet you," Sam said, and Roger nodded agreement.

"Nice to meet you too." I said.

"Did we miss lunch?" Margot asked.

"Nope," the boys said. "If you let us go, we'll tell Mum you're here."

Margot released the boys, and they ran for the house. "How do you feel about Kraft Dinner?" she said.

"It's been a while," I said. "But it's a taste worth revisiting."

Margot raised a perfectly arched brow. "Or experiencing for the first time," she said. "I believe KD now comes in yet another distinctive flavour."

There were six boxes on the counter. Sam identified them as Creamy Cheddar, Three Cheese, Spirals, White Cheddar, Tomato, and Normal. Congenitally risk-averse, I chose Normal. When the boys started the water boiling, their mother and the two other children came in from the backyard. Margot performed the introductions. "This is my sister, Laurie and" – she held out her arms – "our big guy, Jack, and the baby in the family, Cass." Margot's sister wasn't as blonde or as buff as Margot, but she had the same

cornflower blue eyes and the same husky alto voice. She was
holding a squirming towhead wearing a Dora the Explorer
shirt and a diaper. Jack, without prompting, sauntered over
to his aunt and hugged her. I remembered my boys at fourteen and thought Auntie Margot must be more than an occa-
sional visitor.

The big kids served up the KD while Laurie spooned lunch
into Cass, who turned out to be a determined and enthusiastic eater. The boys talked across us. Kraft might have
developed new permutations of cheese and noodles, but the
conversation that ping-ponged across the lunch table was
the same talk I remembered from lunch hours at our house
when my kids were young: a pungent mix of bad jokes,
sibling torment, and classroom gossip. After the boys left for
school, Margot and I cleaned up and made tea while Laurie
put Cass down for a nap.

We took our tea into the living room where we could see
the high-school kids straggling out of the parking lot into
school.

"Is that the school you and Margot went to?" I asked.

Laurie leaned towards the window. "That's the one. But
you didn't drive all the way to Wadena to hear about the
time Steve kissed me under the blue whale in the gym."

Margot frowned "I don't remember any blue whale in the
gym."

Laurie shot her sister a pitying look. "That's because your
class didn't choose The Great Sea of Life as the theme for its
grad dance. But the topic is Cristal. Of course, she's been
Topic A ever since she died. Everybody remembers her, but
nobody really knew her."

"She was a pretty girl," I said. "She must have had boyfriends."

"Not really. I was just trying to remember who she went
with to the grad dance. I think it was another leftover, you

know, somebody who's still alone after all the popular kids have paired off. But I don't remember Cristal having a serious boyfriend till she left here."

Margot leaned forward. "You never told me you knew about a serious boyfriend."

"It's because I didn't remember till I was in Crawford's shopping for underwear for Jack this morning." Laurie rubbed absent-mindedly at a spot of dried egg yolk on her jeans "They had these really cute Spiderman boxers, and I'd put two pair in my cart when I remembered that Jack is fourteen now, so I put them back and got the same kind of tighty whiteys I buy Steve."

Margot glanced at me. "My sister's narratives are not linear," she said dryly.

"I'm approaching the point," Laurie said. She turned to me. "When I got pregnant with Jack, Steve and I had one of those hurry-up weddings, and this being Wadena, Cut 'n' Curl was abuzz. Oh, I had a bridal shower and a baby shower, even if they were a little too close together, but there were some disapproving glances. The only person who seemed really happy for me was Cristal."

Margot punched her sister on the arm. "I was happy for you."

"Okay," Laurie said, "I should have said the only person outside the family. Now who's derailing the narrative? My point was that the December I was pregnant with Jack, I ran into Cristal on Main Street when she came home from university."

"Cristal went to university?" I said.

Laurie bit her lip. "I told you she was smart. Anyway, she hugged me, and it wasn't one of those fake girly hugs. It was sincere. She said, 'I hear you're getting married. Me too – same reason.' Then she asked me when I was due – it was a couple of weeks before she was due, so we shared a hormonal moment. I remember us standing in front of the office of the Wadena News blubbering, then wiping our eyes. And Cristal leaned close to me and asked me if I loved Steve.

"Of course, I said yes. Then she said she loved the man she was marrying too. She said – and I remember this – 'If I couldn't have him, I wouldn't want to live.' She asked me if I felt that way about Steve. Of course, I said I did, but that wasn't the truth. Don't get me wrong. I love Steve. He's a good husband and he's a big part of my life, but I've never felt I wouldn't have a life without him."

Cass started to cry in the other room, and Laurie stood up to go to her.

"Wait," I said. "What happened to Cristal's baby?"

"I have no idea," Laurie said. "The next time I saw Cristal, I had Jack with me. She didn't even look at him and she didn't say a word about the time we talked at Christmas. I remember trying to check her left hand without seeming to. There was no wedding ring. I assumed the man she couldn't live without decided that he preferred to live without a wife and a baby."

We didn't stay long after Laurie came back with Cass. We still had to talk to Mandy, and Margot had a late appointment with a client in Regina.

Mandy Avilia's house was on the street next to the golf course. It was a nicely kept bungalow with a picture window, a double carport, and two concrete-resin deer grazing on the lawn. When we pulled up outside, Margot took her BlackBerry from her purse.

"What did lawyers do before there were BlackBerrys?" I said.

Margot cocked her head. "I can't speak for the profession, but I, personally, was on my cellphone all the time, checking my voice mail and hectoring my assistant to see if I had any messages." She scrolled down the items in her in-box and whistled. "Now this is why we have our little office in a pocket."

"Something useful?"

"Very. Mandy didn't know where her sister's will was. So I went on-line to the Law Society and asked if anyone had a will for Cristal Avilia. No news till today. Guess which firm did Cristal's legal work?"

"Falconer Shreve?"

"Bingo. I'm going to call my new partner and see if he can get me the file." After Margot talked to Zack, she handed the BlackBerry to me.

"How's it going?" he said.

"Fine," I said. "I'll tell you when we get back. Anything happening there?"

"I have a new client – a doctor who's suing another doctor for malpractice. We don't get many of those. And Cristal's client list has ended up on the Internet, so the shit is hitting the fan."

"Busy morning," I said.

"I'm not through. Pantera ate the remote."

"That's the third remote he's eaten. What did you do?"

"Ordered another one."

I laughed. "Never a harsh word for that dog."

"Nope. Love my dogs, love my kids, love my woman."

"I'll call you when we're close to the city."

"Why don't you bring Margot in for a drink? I'll have Norine courier the Avilia file here – save Margot a trip downtown."

"And if you're lucky, she'll open the file in front of you, and you'll know what's going on."

"You know my methods, Ms. Shreve."

"I do indeed."

Mandy led us into the living room. Like the rest of the
house it was spotless except for the dining-room table that
was covered with everything a dedicated scrapbooker would
need. "Come, see," she said. "You'll be interested in this,
Margot, and Mrs. Shreve – "

"Joanne," I corrected.

She dimpled. "Joanne, you might think it's fun too. Do
either of you scrapbook?"

Margot and I both shook our heads.

"Well, I do, and I love it." Her face looked hollowed. Her
sister's death had hit her hard, but she was still full of spikey
energy. "Sometimes I get so interested in what I'm doing, I
forget to eat. Anyway, I'm really proud of the scrapbook I'm
working on now. Do you want to see it?" When we said yes,
she took us both by the hand and drew us towards the table.
"Did you know that this year will be the twenty-fifth
anniversary of Cut 'n' Curl?"

Margot was pensive. "I guess that's about right. Rhondelle
gave me my first dye job there. My mother just about killed
her – and me."

"If you can find a picture, I'll make a page for you. We're
having a surprise party for Rhondelle at George's Steak
House on the long weekend. I'm going to present her with
this scrapbook." Mandy picked up a page from the table. A
photo was already glued into place in the upper left quadrant
of the page. "That's Cristal getting a spiral perm for grad."
The photo was of a very young Cristal, draped in a plastic
cape, half her hair wound around medieval-looking rods,
looking nervously into the beauty shop mirror as a gener-
ously proportioned redhead wound another strand of her hair
around yet another rod.

Mandy picked up another picture, one of Cristal in her

prom gown. Rhondelle had triumphed. Cristal's hair was an explosion of curls. "Remember what Rhondelle used to call this style?" Mandy said.

Margot chortled. "Jacked-up-to-Jesus hair."

"I was going to write that on the page," Mandy said. "'Cristal with her Jacked-up-to-Jesus hair,' but I was afraid it was sacrilegious."

Margot touched the photograph of Cristal gently. "Put that on the page," she said. "It's not sacrilegious. It's just Rhondelle being Rhondelle."

"Well, if you're sure," Mandy said.

"I'm sure," Margot said. "Look, Mandy, I'm sorry. We can't stay very long, but I wanted you to know where things stand with Cristal's estate. I've just discovered the name of the law firm that drew up the will. I should have some information for you tonight."

Mandy bit her lip. "I really appreciate this. I don't have a clue how these things work."

"Well, I do, but I don't know how to cut hair, so we're even." Margot said.

Mandy looked down at the photo of her sister. "If Cristal's boyfriend gets involved, I won't have to deal with him, will I?"

Margot stiffened, suddenly alert. "I didn't know Cristal had a boyfriend."

"Oh yes. Those other men – that was just her business. He was the one she loved."

"Do you know his name?" I asked.

"She never told me. He didn't want anybody to know who he was."

"Was he married?" Margot said.

Mandy looked miserable – trapped. "I don't know. All I know is she said she loved him, but she was afraid of him" –

suddenly, the old bounce was back – "and you should never be afraid of the man who's supposed to love you."

"Did you and Cristal talk about this?" I asked.

Mandy placed the scrapbook page back on the table, positioned the photograph of Cristal on her prom night, then laid a paper frame carefully over it. The frame was the same shade of foam-green as Cristal's dress. "The frames just came in the mail today," Mandy said. "I was afraid the colour wouldn't be right."

"It's a perfect match," I said.

Margot swept her hand across her eyes. "Goddammit," she said. "Mandy, this is important. Did Cristal never tell you her boyfriend's name?"

"She said if it got out they were together, it would hurt him professionally."

"And that didn't worry her?" Margot's hands were at her sides, balled into fists.

"It worried me," Mandy said simply. "And I must have asked her a million times to tell me his name. She'd never tell me. She'd just laugh and say he was her perfect three."

I felt my nerves twang. "And that meant something to you?" I said.

Mandy's brown eyes were guileless. "Sure. It was a game the girls at our school played. It's been around forever." She looked at Margot. "You must remember."

Margot nodded. "The girl subtracts the number of letters in the name of the boy she likes from the number of letters in her name. The difference is supposed to be the number of kids they'll have when they get married."

"And Cristal wanted three children," I said.

Mandy shot me a grateful look. "That's right," she said. "Cristal always wanted three kids: two girls and a boy. I guess when her life turned out the way it did, she had something done so she wouldn't get pregnant."

Margot sat down in the chair opposite Mandy and leaned forward with her chin cupped in her hands. "Do you have any idea why your sister ended up the way she did?"

"As a prostitute? You can say the word. Cristal knew what she was, but she wouldn't talk about how it happened. I think it was because of her boyfriend."

"He made her do it?" I said.

"I don't know for sure. All I know is that the last time I talked to her, Cristal said she did everything he wanted, but it was never enough."

Margot couldn't seem to get out of the house quickly enough. She embraced Mandy and told her she'd call her that night, then she sprinted to the car. I barely had my seat belt buckled before she backed her BMW out of the driveway and hit the road. We didn't get far. As soon as we were on the outskirts of town, Margot drove onto the lot in front of an Esso gas station.

"Is there a problem with the car?" I said.

"No, there's a problem with me. I knew if I didn't get out of there, I was going to spontaneously combust. Why would any woman let a man do that to her life? What was the matter with Cristal? God damn it to hell. What was going on in her head?" Margot banged her fists against the steering wheel until the tears came. Then she blew her nose, checked her lipstick, and turned to me. "I'm okay now."

"Are you okay enough to do a little elementary math?"

Margot narrowed her eyes. "Shoot."

"There are thirteen letters in Jason Brodnitz's name and there are thirteen letters in Cristal Avilia's name. Thirteen minus thirteen is zero."

"Jason's not Cristal's perfect three."

"Apparently not."

☙ ❧

I called Zack when we were on the outskirts of the city. "We'll be home in ten minutes," I said. "You can open the Bombay Sapphire."

"Hallelujah."

I closed my cell. "The martinis will be waiting," I said. "Are you going to claim Zack's tie?"

"On the basis of a game Cristal played with her boyfriends' names? I may be a cockeyed optimist, but I'm not stupid. I have to tighten my case before I take Zack's tie." She gave me a sidelong grin. "But I will take immense pleasure in drinking his martini."

When Margot turned onto our street, Sean Barton's blue Camry Hybrid was in our driveway.

"Company?" Margot said.

"Sean Barton."

"As ever, eager to serve," Margot said tightly. "Joanne, I'll come in to get my file, but I'm going to take a rain check on that drink."

"You don't like Sean."

She shrugged. "I'll learn to get along with him. I just don't want to start today."

Zack and Sean were in the office. They both had their laptops open, and the dogs were with them.

I went over and kissed Zack. "Good day?"

"Profitable," Zack said.

Sean stood and offered Margot his chair, but she refused with a smile, then bent and put her arms around Pantera's neck. "How are you doing, big boy? That remote you ate giving you any problems?"

"So far so good," Zack said. "I called Peter, and he said to let it pass."

"Oldest vet joke in the book," I said.

"But good advice," Margot said, scooping up the sealed

envelope that contained her client's file and dropping it in her briefcase.

Zack raised an eyebrow. "Am I ever going to know what's in there?"

"After my client does," she said. "That's the way it works, remember?"

Zack chuckled and looked between Margot and me. "Exactly what I need in my life, another ethical guide."

Margot met his gaze. "An ex-boyfriend of mine said men get the women they deserve."

Sean was smooth. "Then the men of Falconer Shreve are lucky. I understand that you're joining us."

"I am," Margot said.

"That's good news for me," Sean said. "It appears I have a lot to learn."

"We all do," Margot said. "That's why they call it 'practising law.' I'll call you later, Zack."

Zack and I saw the two of them out and watched as they drove off.

"Alone at last," Zack said. "How was your day?"

"More questions than answers," I said. "Let's save the talk till later." I moved behind him and started rubbing his shoulders. "Your neck is tight," I said. "You need a swim."

"A martini works quicker."

"But the effect doesn't last. Swim first, then a drink."

"You're tough."

"But I'm fun. Come on, let's get our suits on."

We'd just started our swim when Taylor came in from school. "Anything you need me to do?"

"Sure," I said. "You can make dinner."

Zack came over and grabbed the edge of the pool. "I'll take care of dinner," he said. "Where do you want to go?"

Taylor was quick off the mark. "The Chimney," she said. "I am so in the mood for liver."

"Fine with me," I said. "There are days when only organ meat will do."

"That's settled then," Zack said. "Want to put on your suit and join us, Taylor? Your mother is counting my laps. You can distract her."

"You always tell me to do what Jo says. Besides, I really, really want to get back to this painting I'm working on." She gave him her winsome smile. "If it turns out, you can have it for your office."

Zack groaned and pushed away from the pool's edge. "We pay for our pleasures in this world," he said. Then he began moving his powerful arms and propelling his body through the water. Unprompted, he did ten extra laps, but he beamed when I said it was time to towel off.

We took our drinks outside. When Zack took his first sip, he closed his eyes with pleasure. "That was worth waiting for."

"Deferred gratification," I said. "So any new developments in the case?"

"Nothing good. Ginny came over this morning. Her position is not enviable. She had a motive. She had the opportunity and, of course, the fact that she pulled the knife out of Jason's chest and contaminated the crime scene doesn't endear her to the cops. Plus her prints are all over the place, so it's a real mess."

"Any luck finding Francesca?"

"Nope. I'm batting zero for two." He took another sip. "And the cops found $50,000 cash in Jason Brodnitz's house."

My heart sank. "So Jason is 3."

"Yep. It appears that you're the new owner of Margot's red scarf."

"I wish I wasn't."

"Me too. I'm not looking forward to telling Ginny. When she came over this morning, she was hopeful. She knows she's in deep, but she believes in the system, and she's really looking forward to being at the lake. She thought that while they were there, she and the girls could come up with some way to honour Jason."

"And now they're going to have to deal with this. Zack, this is going to be tough on Margot too. After our day in Wadena, we were both certain Jason wasn't the man in Cristal's life."

"Mandy Avilia knew something?"

"In retrospect, I guess she didn't. Mandy told us about a game Cristal played: she'd subtract the number of letters in her boyfriends' names from the number of letters in her name. The remainder was supposed to be the number of children they'd have together. Cristal wanted three children."

"So 'three' was her ideal."

"Yes, and Jason Brodnitz, like Cristal, had thirteen letters in his name. Margot thought that was a good sign. But I guess the discovery of $50,000 cash in Jason's house trumps his coming up zero in Cristal's name game."

"It's not unheard of for evidence to be planted," said Zack. "You and I both thought there was something fishy about the fact that Bree Steig was carrying around a piece of paper with Jason's phone number written on it."

"There's a difference between a number on a paper and $50,000. That's a pretty substantial investment."

"Not if you want to frame somebody."

"You really don't believe Jason was the man in Cristal's life, do you?"

Zack shook his head. "I didn't know the guy at all, but sometimes you have to go with a gut feeling. I think Brodnitz had a lousy couple of years. I think his ego had been bashed around and I think he made investments for prostitutes because no 'respectable' clients would come within a hundred feet of him. I think it's even possible he was laundering money, but I don't think he was that sadistic creep Cristal was involved with."

"Neither do I," I said. "So we're back to finding out who that sadistic creep really was. She never said anything to you about her past?"

"We didn't trade life stories. I was with Cristal for one reason and we both knew the reason." Zack put down his drink. "Now you have that 'how-did-I-end-up-married-to-this-prick?' look on your face."

"That's a lot to read into one expression," I said. "I don't think you're a prick. I just think it's an odd world where a man and woman can do something as intimate as make love and not know anything about each other."

"Cristal and I didn't make love, we had sex. That's a whole different thing."

"She was more than just a body, Zack. Today when we were in Wadena, I caught a glimpse of the woman Cristal was. If we're going to untangle this mess, I think we have to go back to the beginning."

"Which is . . . ?"

"The man Cristal fell in love with in university."

"I didn't know Cristal went to university."

"Well, she did, and she got pregnant in her first year. Margot's sister, Laurie, was pregnant at the same time. Laurie told me that when she and Cristal talked about their lovers and the babies they were carrying, Cristal just glowed."

"So what happened?"

"Laurie didn't know. Cristal came back to Wadena when the semester was over without a baby and without a wedding ring."

"But if the guy Cristal was with in university moved along, he wouldn't be connected with her life here in Regina."

"He would if he came with her. Zack, Mandy told us that her sister had only ever loved one man. She also said that Cristal did everything her lover told her to do, but it was never enough, and at the end she realized that and decided to get out."

"And so he killed her, and if we find the boyfriend, my client will be off the hook." Zack rubbed the bridge of his nose – a sure sign of weariness with him. "God, I wish it were that easy. Maybe it will be. The cops have the same information we have. Right now, their computers will be smoking. Debbie Haczkewicz won't be satisfied until she knows everything about the men on that list."

"The boyfriend's name wouldn't be on that list."

"I know, but in my experience, if you throw enough rocks in the water eventually the bottom feeders come up to see what's happening."

CHAPTER

13

The first rock to hit the water was Cristal's will. When Margot called to fill him in, Zack picked up a pen and paper and scribbled a heading. Thirty seconds later, he laid down his pen and just listened. He heard what he needed to hear, rang off, and turned to me. "So, do you want to know about Cristal's will?"

"Is it ethical to tell me?"

"Sure. One of the two beneficiaries already knows, and the other one's decided to make herself scarce. Anyway, it's just a matter of timing. After the will is probated it's registered on the Queen's Bench file and anybody can see it."

"Any surprises?"

"Enough. The will is dated two days before Cristal died. Blake did all the legal work. Cristal left $25,000 to Francesca Pope."

"That doesn't sound as if she was paying Francesca off to stay silent."

"I agree," Zack said. "It sounds as if Cristal was genuinely concerned about Francesca's welfare. Apart from that bequest, everything was left to Mandy. Someone named Rhondelle

Bakker is the executor. Does that name mean anything to you?"

"Rhondelle owns the hair salon where Mandy works."

"Let's hope Rhondelle has a good grasp of property prices in Regina. Cristal left some significant real estate. Blake appended the pertinent information. Mandy Avilia now owns Cristal's condo and another two in the same building that Cristal sublet."

"Those places cost three-quarters of a million dollars."

"They do indeed."

"According to Margot, when it came to real estate, Cristal didn't make many missteps." He rubbed the back of his neck. "And that raises a very large question."

"Why was Cristal involved with a man who terrified her when she had all that money?"

"According to Cristal's journal, 3 said it was a way of proving her love for him."

"You think this creep got off on terrifying Cristal?"

I bit my lip. "That's exactly what I think."

"So this prince among men is a power junkie."

"Among other things. And Cristal spent the last fourteen years of her life trying to please him, but there was always another hoop for her to jump through."

"Except at the end, she decided to stop playing. If Blake drafted her will two days before her death, he might know what was going on in her mind. Deciding who gets what in your will is a big step – clients have a way of justifying it to their lawyers."

"Do you want me to call Blake?"

"Would you? It's time my partner came home, and it's best if I can truthfully say I haven't known Blake's where-abouts for the last few days."

I found the number of Blake's hotel in my address book and tapped it in. He answered on the first ring.

"It's Joanne," I said.

"Has something happened?"

"A lot. Zack thinks it's time you came back to Regina. Are you up for that?"

Blake was silent for a beat, but when he answered, he sounded like the old Blake – open and hopeful. "I think I'm on top of it, but it's weird, Jo. There are whole stretches of time I don't remember."

"For example?"

He laughed softly. "For example, I don't remember getting to this hotel, and I couldn't tell you how long I've been here. Remember when you were a kid just getting over the flu? That's what I feel like. It's hard to figure out what really happened and what was just the fever."

"But the fever has burned itself out."

He laughed softly. "Yes," he said. "I think it finally has. Tell Zack I'll be on the next plane home. I'll come to your place straight from the airport."

"It'll be good to have you back, Blake."

"It'll be good to be back."

I rang off and turned to my husband. "He'll be here tonight," I said.

Zack nodded. "Thanks, Ms. Shreve. I'm sorry to put you in the middle of this. You can have my onions at dinner."

"You'd never give up your onions."

"Wrong. I'm indebted to you, and I honour my debts." He picked up his BlackBerry. "Just let me make one quick call. I want to see what Sean's investigators have turned up about Jason's business dealings."

"What are you looking for?"

"I don't know. What I'm hoping for is an innocuous explanation for that $50,000 the cops found at Brodnitz's house."

"You want Margot to win your tie?"

"Small price to pay for giving back Ginny's daughters a father they don't have to be ashamed of."

Zack wheeled over and took my hand. "We've had enough for one day. Let's get Taylor and eat some liver."

The Chimney was a family restaurant in the strip mall next to Ginny's condo, so it shouldn't have come as a surprise to see Ginny standing at the cash register where customers wait for their takeout. She was wearing running shorts and a T-shirt, and her hair was slicked back. She looked pale and weary, but when she saw us, her smile was genuine.

"Friendly faces," she said. "A welcome sight. I never realized waiting for a pizza could be so gruelling. Everybody who comes in gives me the eye."

"The Chimney does deliver," I said.

Ginny sighed. "You know, that possibility never crossed my mind. Our condo's so close – we always just run in. I guess I'm not thinking very clearly." She slumped. "The phone never stops ringing. And the media people seem to be taking turns leaning on the buzzer downstairs."

I squeezed Taylor's shoulder. "Why don't you go ahead and see if you can score Zack's favourite table?"

Taylor turned to Ginny. "He likes to sit near the fireplace even if it's thirty-eight degrees outside." Her face grew serious. "I'm sorry about all your trouble," she said.

"Thanks," Ginny said. "I appreciate that."

We watched Taylor move through the dining room. When she claimed the table by the fireplace, she pumped the air in triumph.

"She's a nice girl," Ginny said.

"She is," I said. "How are your girls holding up?"

"Not well," Ginny said. "Chloe's started cutting again. When I saw the blood on her stomach this afternoon, I wanted to scream. The whammies just keep on coming. I've got all these basketball clichés wired into my brain – usually, they do the trick, but 'don't give an inch until the final buzzer sounds' seems to have lost its power. I'm used to the hits, but the girls aren't. Two weeks ago they were the Incredible Brodnitz Twins. Now they're just freaks. They've heard the same locker room talks I've heard: 'How you respond to the challenges of the second half will determine what you become after the game – whether you're a winner or a loser.' But Em and Chloe aren't getting a chance to regroup. Everything reminds them of what's happened."

Her voice was ragged. Zack wheeled closer. "Debbie Haczkewicz hasn't got back to me yet about letting you go to the lake. Let me try her again." He pulled out his BlackBerry and hit speed-dial.

It was clear at the outset that Debbie was turning down Zack's request, but then he pulled out all the stops. When he mentioned that Chloe was reacting to the pressure by cutting herself, Debbie relented. She was, after all, a parent as well as a cop. Zack ended the call and gave Ginny the thumbs-up sign. "You can take off for the lake whenever you want."

Ginny exhaled. "That is such a relief. The girls and I need to get some sleep so we can figure out where we go from here." She turned to me. "I really can't thank you enough."

"We're glad we're able to help." I took out a business card, wrote out the combination to the gate on the back, and gave Ginny my key to the guest cottage. "See you tomorrow night," I said.

As we went into the dining room, I touched Zack's shoulder. "You didn't tell Ginny about the money the police found in Jason's house."

"That's right," he said. "I didn't." With that, we joined

Taylor, ordered our liver and a bottle of Shiraz, and sat back as our daughter filled us in on her plans for the Farewell, the challenges of working on unstretched canvas, and a boy she'd met at the 13th Avenue Coffee House who had the most amazing hair.

Ready or not, life was moving on.

Blake's taxi pulled up just as I came back from giving the dogs a run. I waited until he'd paid the driver. When Blake came up and took Pantera's leash, I waited for the big mastiff to freeze. He was a rescue dog with a troubled history, and his reactions to strangers were unpredictable. But he just collapsed in a heap at Blake's feet and gazed up, waiting for the next instruction.

"I'm impressed," I said. "Pantera's loyalties are pretty well reserved for Zack."

Blake rubbed Pantera's ear. "He and I know each other from the office." He jerked Pantera's leash. "Okay, big guy, time to talk to your master."

Zack was in his office. When he saw Blake, he held out his arms. "Welcome home," he said.

As they talked, I was struck again by the closeness between the two men. After a lifetime of friendship, they had a kind of shorthand that allowed them to get to the point economically and effectively.

Zack began. "So how come you didn't tell Margot that you drew up Cristal Avilia's will? She found out Falconer Shreve had the will when one of our summer students responded to her notice on the Law Society website."

Blake had taken the chair facing Zack. He looked down at his hands. "I wasn't thinking clearly."

Zack sighed. "Fair enough. Had there been a will before this one?"

"Yes. I never saw it. Cristal said she had a will, but she wanted to make some major changes, so she thought it was best just to start over."

"Did she elaborate?"

Blake nodded. "She said she and her boyfriend had split up and she didn't want him listed as a beneficiary. I was relieved to hear she'd left him."

"So she'd talked to you about him?"

"Only once. It was last month. She called me." Blake smiled sadly. "The one and only time the woman I loved called me for a date. She was distraught. They'd had a fight and it turned ugly."

"Was he abusive?" I asked.

Blake shook his head. "Not physically, but I had a feeling that was only because he'd found more effective means of keeping Cristal in line. And, of course, he didn't want to leave marks that would get clients asking questions. In the last few days, I've been able to see things more clearly. You know, I really think the only kindness that animal ever showed her was to kill her."

Zack's voice was steely. "Don't share that insight with the cops, eh?"

"I won't." He stood. "I'd better get home – spend a little time with Gracie."

"Where did you tell her you'd been?" I said.

"Business trip," Blake said. "Gracie's used to that, and as long as Rose is there, helping her with her homework and making bannock, Gracie's fine." He smiled. "And so am I. From the day we brought Gracie home from the hospital, Rose has been there – the one consistent presence in our lives."

"Joanne and I are going to the lake this weekend," Zack said. "But you and I can talk more tomorrow before we leave. One thing you should know: I'm representing Ginny Monaghan."

"So if I've left any bloody footprints, I shouldn't count on you to explain them."

Zack met his gaze. "That's right."

It had been a full day, and we decided to make an early night of it. Zack was already in bed reading when the doorbell rang.

There was no one there, but when I stepped out to investigate, I saw that Francesca Pope's backpack with its cargo of Care Bears had been dropped inside the big planter on our porch. As soon as I picked up the backpack, Francesca came out of the shadows, her face streaked with tears. The night was warm, but Francesca, as always, was bundled in layers of clothing, protecting her against the demons outside and the demons within. When I called to her, she began to run. Her bicycle was lying on the front lawn. She righted it, jumped on, and rode off. I watched until she disappeared from sight, then I took the backpack inside. The bears smelled of mould and mildew, and the backpack itself was wet and muddy. I'd soaked the soil in the planter that afternoon to ready it for the Martha Washingtons. Inside the door, we kept a wicker laundry hamper with towels for the dogs. I dropped the backpack inside and carried the basket to Zack.

He removed his glasses when he saw me. "What's going on?"

I came to the side of the bed and showed him the laundry basket. "Francesca left this on our doorstep," I said. "Actually, she dropped the backpack in the planter; the laundry basket is ours."

"Moses in the bulrushes."

"In the mud," I said. "I was planning to transplant the Martha Washingtons there tomorrow."

Zack took the basket, looked down at the bears, and shook his head. "Leaving those here must have been agony for Francesca."

"It was," I said. "She was crying. I tried to talk to her, but she got on her bike and rode off."

"So, we don't know why she left the bears with us." Zack frowned, reached into the outer flap of the backpack, removed a paper, and read the two words that were printed on it. "'At risk,'" he said. He peered over his glasses at me. "That's the phrase they use in family court to identify children who aren't safe in their home situation."

"Francesca feels threatened," I said.

"If she's abandoned her bears, she must be at the breaking point. If it were anybody else, I'd call the cops and get them to check into it, but Francesca's terrified of the police."

"So we do nothing," I said.

"Well, there's nothing we can do tonight. Tomorrow, I'll swing by some of Francesca's haunts and see if I can find out what's going on."

I picked up the laundry hamper and carried the bears into the mudroom. The smell of mildew was heavy, and I opened the window to let in some fresh air. It was a moonless night, and as I flicked off the light, the room was plunged into darkness. I started up the hall, then, driven by an impulse that I'd given into many times in my years as a parent, I retraced my steps and opened the door a crack to let the light in.

I had planned to spend the next morning shopping and packing for the lake, but life intervened. Jill Oziowy called from Toronto to see how I was coming with the Ginny

Monaghan project. When she said there were rumours that Ginny and her daughters had gone underground, I didn't enlighten her, but I was more forthcoming when Keith Harris called. He was brisk, but his concern was palpable. "Jo, I've been trying Ginny's cell all morning – no answer. Do you have any idea where she is?"

"I'm sorry," I said. "Somebody should have let you know. Ginny and the twins are at our cottage. She and the girls were running on empty, so Zack suggested they take off for the weekend."

"Smart move. Normally, Ginny has amazing equanimity. She says it's just a question of reading the situation and responding, but this has her reeling."

"With cause," I said. "She's taken a lot of hits lately."

"And the knockout punch is on its way," Keith said.

"Have you heard something?"

Keith didn't answer. Finally he said, "Look, is there any possibility you could get away for lunch? I could use an hour staring at a human being who isn't about to burst into flames."

I laughed. "Why don't you come over here? I have a bottle of Glenfiddich. It's a proven flame-retardant, and by the time you arrive, the sun will be over the yard arm somewhere."

"Consider me an emergency case," Keith said. "Your address please."

Twenty minutes later, Keith was at the front door. He was freshly shaved, but he had an unhealthy pallor, and as he removed his jacket, he sighed as if even that small effort tired him.

"Why don't you come into the kitchen with me while I get the Glenfiddich," I said.

"I'll gladly sit in your kitchen," he said, "but I'll just have a glass of soda. Single malt is on my forbidden list."

"An old friend of Zack's used to say that at the end we all lose everything. It's up to us to decide the order in which we lose things."

The spark came back into Keith's eyes. "In that case, I'll have three fingers of Glenfiddich – might as well be hung for a sheep as a lamb."

"I didn't mean to be the bad angel," I said.

"You weren't," Keith said. "I just realized that one of the last things I want to lose is the chance to have a drink with you."

Keith sat on the loveseat that looked out on the bird feeder as I poured the drinks. "I've always been partial to kitchens," he said. "Mine's all chrome – it's about as welcoming as a surgical unit – doesn't matter since I don't spend any time there. The couch is a nice touch."

"It was Maddy and Lena's idea. When I'm cooking, they like to curl up there and give me a blow-by-blow account of what's happening in the world of birds and bugs."

I handed Keith his glass and sat down beside him. A soggy robin flew towards the crabapple tree where it was building its nest. "So how's the campaign going?"

"Federally, we'll probably squeak through with a minority. But Ginny's going to lose Palliser."

"Are you sure?"

Keith swirled the Scotch in his glass. "Not a doubt. You can overcome a lot in a campaign, but not the suspicion that your candidate is a murderer. The people campaigning for Ginny are getting doors slammed in their faces – and they're the lucky ones. The unlucky ones get to listen to a litany of Ginny's sins."

"I'm sorry, Keith. I know you thought Ginny was the one who could bring your party back to its roots."

"She was. She still is. She's smart, she's progressive, and

she's pragmatic. She's got that roaming ambition politicians have to have, and she's cool. She has a way of suggesting to voters that they need her more than she needs them – just the right mix for an electorate that's long on irony and short on information." Keith sipped his Scotch. "The perfect candidate, but it's not going to happen." He sighed. "God, it's good to talk. Everyone around Ginny's campaign is so despondent, I find myself in the role of cheerleader."

I smiled. "Not a good fit for a man with your disposition. Where's Crispy Crunch boy in all this?"

"Trying to put the genie back in the bottle. Milo is a true believer, and as you know in politics, true believers always get their hearts broken. Looking on the bright side, Milo's lucky it happened sooner in his career than later."

"Do you regret what you've done with your life?"

Keith sipped his drink. "Too late now for regrets, and I've had a lot of fun, especially in the last couple of weeks."

"Fun for me too," I said.

"Think you might get back into politics?"

I took his glass to the sink. "No, I like my life the way it is. I've had enough glimpses of the dark side of politics to remind me of why I left." I filled two bowls with gazpacho, pulled a baguette out of the oven, and fetched a plate of cheeses from the counter.

Keith's eyes widened. "I just called twenty minutes ago. How did you manage to conjure this up?"

"I rerouted some of the gazpacho that's headed for the lake. River Heights bakery is two minutes away by car, and Peter's new girlfriend, Dacia, works in a cheese shop."

Keith smeared some Gorgonzola on a heel of baguette and bit in. "You know, I'd forgotten eating can be a pleasure."

"Life's full of pleasures," I said. "Every so often you just have to turn a blind eye to the rest of reality."

"Not so easy these days. Jo, I hate to louse up a great lunch, but what's Zack doing to get Ginny out from under all this?"

"He's ruled out trying to prove that Ginny couldn't have killed Jason. She had motive and opportunity, and she was the one who called 911. So he's focusing on exploring other possibilities."

"Any star candidates?"

"Sean Barton's looking into Jason Brodnitz's business dealings. It looks like Jason was involved with Cristal Avilia."

There was a pause. "Then I owe Sean an apology," Keith said. "I tore a strip off him for fuelling that particular rumour during the campaign. But if it wasn't a rumour . . ."

"It's not that simple," I said. "The rumour was that Jason was involved with the business of prostitution. So far, it looks as if he was just acting as a kind of broker for Cristal's real estate dealings."

Keith's laugh was short and humourless. "Of course, our boy Sean was smart enough not to lie. All he ever said was that Jason Brodnitz had financial dealings with prostitutes. He didn't correct the media when they inferred that Jason was a pimp."

"You don't like Sean, do you?"

"You don't think I'm being fair?"

"Putting a potentially damaging statement out there and leaving it open for interpretation is an old political trick," I said. "You've done it in the heat of a campaign. So have I."

Keith sighed. "I'll give Sean a call. Incidentally, what's his status with Falconer Shreve these days? Things were a little iffy there for a while, weren't they?"

"More than iffy. Sean was disappointed when he wasn't named partner. Zack thought he'd leave, especially when the firm brought in another trial lawyer. But apparently Sean's decided to stick around, and so far it's smooth sailing."

"Just to satisfy my curiosity, why wasn't Sean named a partner?"

"Zack thought he cared more for the game than for the people in the game."

"That was exactly my take on the way Sean approaches politics."

"Maybe he just has to grow up."

"Still the same old Jo. Everybody's perfectible."

"Still the same old Keith," I said. "There are three decent people in the world: thee, me, and some other guy whose name I can't remember."

Keith laughed. "I'm just jealous because Sean is young and smart and studly and I'm none of the above."

"You're two of the above," I said. "Now stop feeling sorry for yourself and eat your gazpacho."

For the next hour we reminisced about the old days. It was pleasant talk and Keith seemed reluctant to leave. "I'd better be getting back to what we still refer to as headquarters, although with no candidate and no campaign, I'm not exactly certain what we're all doing there." He took out a cigarette, looked at it longingly, and placed it beside his plate. "Jo, when do you think I should tell Ginny that it's over."

"I imagine she already knows," I said. "Give her the weekend. We're all going to the lake. Why don't you come up on Sunday? You can visit with Maddy and Lena, and then when the moment's right, you can talk to Ginny."

He shrugged. "Who knows? There may be good news by then."

I laughed. "Political people are the last adults on earth who believe in miracles. Let me get you one of our maps." When I came back from Zack's office with the sheet of directions to our cottage, Keith had moved from the kitchen table and was standing at the back door looking out at the garden. His cigarette, still unlit, was between his fingers.

"How long has it been since you had one of those?" I said.

He looked at his watch. "An hour and a half."

"Do you want it?"

He sighed. "There are a lot of things I want," he said. "This is just the only one that I have any chance of getting."

"In that case, why don't we go outside and have a cigarette together."

Keith grinned. "You too?"

"It's been more than twenty years, and I'll probably throw up, but it's the least I can do for a friend."

CHAPTER

14

When we drove through the gates at Lawyers' Bay that night, Ginny and her daughters were shooting hoops on the court that Blake had built for Gracie. As soon as they spotted us, they stopped their game and came over to help us unload the cars. The three women had obviously been playing hard; their faces were pink with exertion and damp with perspiration, but they no longer looked like accident victims, and when Chloe took the other end of a laundry hamper heavy with groceries, I was grateful for her help and for the chance to chat.

"How's it going?" I said.

"Not bad," she said. She gave me a sidelong glance. "I've been thinking about that story you told Em and me about hurling on your dress at your birthday party."

I smiled at her. "It's a memorable story," I said.

She stopped walking and looked at me. "It was the same as me cutting, wasn't it? You know, a way of saying, 'Hey, does anybody actually realize that I'm in here, going crazy?'"

"It took a while, but I did finally figure that out."

Chloe's eyes were like her mother's, grey and probing. "That's because you didn't have the benefit of professional help."

"So how do you feel about the cutting?"

"Now you sound more like my therapist than the girl who puked on her dress."

"Sorry," I said.

"It's okay. It's a fair question." She levelled her gaze at me. "So when you're under pressure, do you still drink cherry brandy till you blow chunks?"

"No," I said "It doesn't seem to help."

Chloe shifted the hamper. "Well, there's your answer," she said.

As soon as the cars were unloaded, Ginny and the twins went back to the court and resumed shooting hoops. They were still there when, as on dozens of other evenings after we'd arrived at the lake, we took our granddaughters for a run along the shore to get out the kinks before we sat down to dinner.

The basketball court was deserted by the time we got back and slipped into the grooves of our familiar routine. We ate at the partners' table so we could watch the birds on the lake; then Zack and Taylor cleaned up and I gave the kids a bath and readied them for bed. Zack was always the hands-down choice to read bedtime stories. Years in the courtroom had taught him how to draw in an audience and keep them with him as he wove a narrative. Like countless juries before them, the girls thrilled to his booming bass, as Taylor and I accepted our fate and walked the dogs.

That Friday night, as we passed her cottage on our way home, Ginny waved us over.

"Can I interest you in a drink?" she asked.

"Not me, thanks," Taylor said. "Jo and I made up this book list, and she says that, starting this weekend, I have to read fifty pages a day, so I'll be ready for high school in the fall."

"What are you reading?"

"It's called *A Complicated Kindness*. My friend Isobel says it's good, but I haven't even started it yet."

"Better get on it, then. Joanne, can you stay?"

"Are you sure you want company?"

Ginny nodded "I'm sure. Can I get you anything?"

"I'm fine."

"So am I," Ginny said. "Or at least moving in that direction." We watched as Taylor and Pantera walked towards our cottage. "A girl and her dog," Ginny said. "It's a nice reminder that life doesn't always have to be complicated." She stretched out in a Muskoka chair and motioned to the one beside her. "I know I should call Keith or Milo, but truthfully, I don't want to deal with what they're going to tell me."

"There's no rush. Keith's coming out for dinner on Sunday. You can talk to him then."

"Is this visit your idea or his?"

"Both," I said.

"You two were a kick together. That was such a great campaign."

"Past tense?" I said.

"Past tense," she replied. "Joanne, I know I'm going to lose Palliser."

"Sounds as if you've come to terms with it."

"I don't have an alternative," Ginny said. "Vince Lombardi may have believed that winning is the only thing, but even kids know that every time somebody wins, somebody else loses."

"Have you thought about what you want to do next?"

"Well, until this mess is cleared up, I can't do anything. Even then, I imagine it'll be a long time before the corporate headhunters come knocking at my door. Financially,

I'm in good shape. Maybe I'll just coach the twins and see what happens."

"You're amazing," I said.

Her smile was sardonic. "I'm faking it," she said.

Willie, curled up by my feet, began to moan. The awareness that Pantera had headed home without him was dawning. I picked up his leash. "Ginny, if you want to talk, we're around, but I'm not going to press it."

"I appreciate that," Ginny said.

When I got back to the cottage, Taylor was sprawled on the living-room couch engrossed in Miriam Toews's novel. The little girls were in bed asleep, and Zack was in his chair beside their bed reading *Charlotte's Web*.

I touched his shoulder. "You do realize the kids are down for the count," I said.

He raised an eyebrow. "That's why I'm not reading aloud. I wanted to know how the book ends."

"You're not going to like it," I said.

"Does Wilbur die?"

"No."

"Not Charlotte!"

"Zack, the lifespan of a spider is about a year. But Charlotte does have her magnum opus."

He narrowed his eyes. "Which is?"

I kissed his head. "Finish the book."

We spotted Ginny and her girls often over the weekend: running on the beach, playing tennis, kayaking. We waved at one another and shouted greetings, but we went our separate ways. They were obviously relishing the chance to be alone and, as someone who has experienced that need many times in my own life, I understood.

Besides, we were busy. Zack and the little girls barrelled through to the end of *Charlotte's Web*. He and I were both relieved that Madeleine and Lena, unlike their grandfather, showed no signs of being scarred forever by Charlotte's passing and were comforted by the fact that Charlotte completed her magnum opus before she died. Taylor, too, had been gripped by literature. She had never been a reader, but *A Complicated Kindness* captured her interest and made me hopeful that she might get more than a mercy pass in Grade Nine English.

Not all our pleasures were literary. Our front lawn ended in a sandy hill that ran straight to the lake, and on Saturday morning Maddy and Lena embarked on an ambitious project of digging and dam building that occupied us all for much of the weekend. The plan was to create a stream bed that would allow them to dump water at the top of the hill and watch while it made its way to the lake. There were many impediments in their way, not the least of which was the unassailable truth that sand swallows water, but the girls were determined. They dug and piled up dirt, shoring the sides of their waterway with twigs and stones as they worked. After half an hour, I set aside the biography of Matisse I was reading and got down on the sand to help. Zack, who normally hated being out of his chair, slipped onto the ground and dug along with us. We burrowed patiently down the slope. When it was time for lunch, Zack waved off my offer of assistance, hauled himself back up the hill, and, dirty but triumphant, got back into his chair.

That afternoon, Taylor and I took the girls for a canoe ride, then returned to the sand project. The next day, after a run with the dogs, an intense reading session, and lunch, we were back on the hill. When Ginny and her daughters came by to check our progress, the sun was hitting the sandy slope, and the air was warm and inviting. Emma and Chloe looked at the hill with narrowed eyes. "Looks like you could use some help," Emma said.

Lena wiped her nose with the back of her hand. "Do you know how to dig?"

"Sure," Emma said.

Taylor handed each of the twins a trowel and they all walked down to the excavation site. I turned to Ginny. "Do you want to dig, or do you want to sit under that aspen and watch the kids slave away?"

Ginny's face brightened. "They're young. Let's watch. As you may have noticed, the girls and I have decided that the way to get through this is to keep moving."

"Whatever you're doing seems to be working. You look great."

"Great is probably stretching it, but I do feel better. It's been so good being with Em and Chloe. They're remarkable." Her smile was rueful. "They're also twenty-five years younger than I am, and I wouldn't mind an hour under a tree doing nothing."

When Zack joined us, Ginny and I were talking about daughters. "You two look content," he said. "How's it going, Ginny?"

"Better, thanks."

"And the twins?"

"We're all doing fine, but I have a feeling you're about to burst my bubble."

Zack's voice was gentle. "Nope. Just going to pass along some information you need to have. We've had a team of investigators going through Jason's business dealings, and Sean, Margot Wright, and my partner Blake are spending the weekend examining their findings. Sean just called with a kind of preliminary report. Ginny, there's no doubt that Jason was brokering real estate deals for sex-trade workers."

Ginny swallowed hard. "But he wasn't a pimp."

"He was living off money he received from prostitutes.

Some people might find it hard to make the distinction."

"Does Sean think he was killed because of his association with those women?"

"He thinks it's a possibility, but there's something else. In the weeks before Cristal Avilia's death, she and Jason were in constant touch. Cristal had sizable real estate holdings. She went to my partner Blake and asked him to put them on the market. Blake refused. He said real estate prices in the warehouse area were going to skyrocket, and that Cristal should wait."

"So she went to Jason instead," Ginny said.

"Apparently. Luckily for Cristal's heir, these things take time. But Jason did manage to sell two of the condominiums that Cristal owned in another building. The deposits were both paid in cash. The police found $50,000 in cash in Jason's house. The problem is that the rest of the money is missing. It's a large amount. Sean thinks it's possible that Jason murdered Cristal for the cash."

"And then someone associated with one of those women killed him."

"Yes." Zack took a breath. "Ginny, I know this is ugly, but there is a silver lining. The police will have the same information we have. I don't think you're a serious suspect any more."

Ginny rubbed her temples. "Tell everybody how grateful I am, especially Sean. He never gives up. He's a terrific lawyer, Zack. Your firm is lucky to have him."

"I take it you and Sean have talked about his future."

"Yes. I'd offered him a job with me before everything blew up, but he's very loyal to you. He says Falconer Shreve is where he wants to be."

"And that's where he's going to be. After we talked this afternoon, I offered him a junior partnership and he accepted."

"I'm happy for him," Ginny said, and her voice was fervent. "He deserves the best."

Keith Harris arrived just as the girls finished digging the last metre of their waterway. He had time to throw off his jacket and lift a ceremonial shovel of sand before the Brodnitz twins and Taylor scooped buckets of water out of the lake, carried them up the slope, and Maddy and Lena tipped the first bucket. As the water made its way down the system of culverts and dams, we held our collective breath; when, finally, it emptied into the lake, our cry of joy was spontaneous. Beside me, Chloe and Em gave each other a high-five. They were the mirror image of each other, and when Chloe's face crumpled, Em's did too.

"For a moment I almost forgot," Em said. "But it's all still there, isn't it?"

Chloe draped her arm around her sister's shoulder, and they turned and walked towards the cottage: two handsome young women caught in the web of private grief.

As we watched my granddaughters tip bucket after bucket into the waterway, then run down the hill to watch the water arrive in the lake, Ginny decided a communal accomplishment demanded a communal celebration. As her thank you for the weekend, she offered to take us all out to dinner. Given our range of age and moods, there was only one choice: Magoo's, a diner across the lake where for $10, a hearty eater could plow through homemade cheeseburgers, greasy onion rings, homemade slaw with a vinegar kick, and milkshakes so thick they had to be eaten with a spoon. After dinner, patrons could drop quarters in a jukebox and burn off the calories on an old wooden dance floor. Chief among its many draws was that Magoo's could be reached by boat, and so by five-thirty, we were all down at the dock, donning life jackets and taking our places. Keith, who wanted to get to know his grandnieces, went with Zack, Maddy, Lena, and me; Taylor, who wanted to get to know the Brodnitz twins, went with them and their mother, who was driving Blake Falconer's Chris-Craft.

Musically, Magoo's was heavy on nostalgia, and as the motors were cut and we glided towards the dock, the plangent notes of Rick Nelson's "Garden Party" filled the air. It was an evening for an anthem to the truth that you can't please everyone, so you might as well please yourself, and as Ginny steered her boat expertly into the slip beside ours, she was humming along.

That night exists for me in sharp-edged memories: Keith's gruff delight as Maddy and Lena took his hands and pulled him onto the dance floor where they all rocked to Buddy Holly until our food orders arrived; my husband putting a quarter in the jukebox, pushing the button beside the Beach Boys' "God Only Knows," and never taking his eyes off my face until the song ended; Ginny and her daughters, all three ponytailed and in jeans and sweatshirts, bending over their plates and eating with the stoic determination of athletes who know that, no matter what, bodies must be fuelled; Taylor flushing with pleasure when a boy she remembered from the summer before came over and asked her to dance.

The emotional shoals were everywhere. Jason's brutal death and uncertainty about what was next were fresh in the minds of every adult at the table, but Maddy and Lena's delight in every detail of the evening was infectious and the sweet optimism of the music was tonic. The sun was setting as we drove back across the lake, but none of us wanted the evening to end. Taylor and the Brodnitz girls went over to their cottage, and after Zack and I tucked the granddaughters

in, we brought out the brandy and snifters and sat on the deck
with Keith and Ginny until the sun fell beneath the horizon
and the first firefly appeared.

The next morning was not as chaotic as our leave-takings
from the lake often were when the girls had school. It
was the May long weekend, so we dawdled over breakfast,
took the dogs for a long walk, then paid a last visit to the
miraculous waterway. The long-term weather forecast was
for continuous rain, an ominous prospect for a structure
made of sand, but neither Zack nor I mentioned that to
Maddy and Lena. Ginny and her daughters came over to help
us load the cars, and walked to the gate to wave us off.
Despite everything, we'd enjoyed one another's company,
and when I told Ginny they could go back to the guest cabin
after E-Day and stay as long as they wanted to, I meant it.
    Taylor rode back with Zack. He was anxious to talk to
Blake, and Taylor was keen to talk to Gracie. I dropped off the
dogs, then drove to UpSlideDown. There were at least a
dozen kids on the outside play structures and a dozen
mothers at Crayola-coloured wooden tables, sipping coffee
and watching their children. It was quiet inside, but the smell
of brewing coffee and fresh baking was welcoming. When
Mieka came out of the kitchen, Maddy and Lena ran to her.
    Mieka knelt and held out her arms to the girls. "Did you
ladies have a good weekend?"
    "Really good," Maddy said. "We dug up a hill, went for
three boat rides, and ate onion rings and milkshakes."
    "Sounds like a full schedule," Mieka said.
    Lena wandered off towards the castle. "Charlotte died,"
she said over her shoulder.
    "I'm sorry to hear that," Mieka said. She turned to me.
"Were they good?"

"They're always good," I said. "So how was your weekend?"

Mieka frowned. "Perplexing. Sean called and invited me to dinner."

"That sounds promising. So what happened?"

"In a word – nothing," Mieka said. There was a dust-up between two small boys who had divergent ideas about who got to go down the curvy green slide first. Mieka scanned the situation until the mothers of the adversaries separated them, then she turned back to me.

"I can't believe I'm telling you this, but I have to talk to somebody. It started out to be one of those enchanted evenings, and I was beginning to rethink my theory that Sean was just a post-divorce crush. He brought me a bouquet of white tulips, some truly great champagne, and a box of truffles – 'for afterwards,' he said. We ate out on the deck, we watched the sunset, then we went into the house, fell onto the couch, and made out like people who were more than just friends. Everything was moving in the right direction and then it wasn't. I've reconstructed this a few thousand times since Friday night: all I can think of is that everything went off track when we went up to my room and Sean saw that picture of the girls on my night table."

"Did he say anything?"

"Yes. He said, 'I can't do this.' Then he straightened his clothing, apologized, mumbled that he hoped we could still be friends, and beat a hasty retreat."

"Do you think he felt guilty because of the girls?"

Mieka rolled her eyes. "This is the twenty-first century, Mum. People don't feel guilty. I think maybe he just didn't want to get involved with a woman who has children."

"Well, it's his loss," I said "Are you okay?"

"My pride's a little dented. I'm ticked that I spent all that money on new underwear, but I'll survive." She wiped the surface of an already-shining tabletop. "Mum, the ladies and I have a very good life. I don't need a prince charming, even if he is a really good kisser and has the sexiest smile besides Val Kilmer's."

Election day dawned chilly and drizzly. Spring was with-holding her favours, and those who took politics seriously were not surprised. No matter what the weather on E-Day, it was bad news. Sunshine and tree-riffling breezes sent voters to golf courses and picnic grounds; rainstorms kept them parked in front of their TVs; blizzards brought road closures. It was a universally acknowledged political truth: one way or another, the weather would screw you.

There was another truth: no matter when the writ was dropped, E-Day was always the longest day of the year. Suddenly, the campaign was whittled down to now or never. The time for strategizing was over; people had either made up their minds where to put their X or had decided to close their eyes, hold their nose, and let fate guide their hand. All the professionals could do was control their own voter turn-out. That meant scrutineers in every polling station striking off names of party members as they voted, and runners who took the marked sheets to safe houses where other workers called to harangue supporters who hadn't voted. Busy work, but at least it was work.

The candidates weren't so lucky. Since the night they were nominated, the candidates had been putting in sixteen-hour days, in which every block of time was accounted for. Now they had nothing to do but be photographed before they stepped into the polling booth to vote for themselves, then go home to sweat it out.

Ginny's polling station was at Lakeview, Taylor's school,

and Zack and I had already dropped Taylor off and voted when Ginny came in with Keith, Milo, and her daughters. The Friends of Ginny Monaghan were nowhere in sight. A week ago, people had been elbowing one another to get close to the woman who had a good shot at becoming the party's new leader, but there's truth in the axiom that, in politics, a week is a lifetime. Ginny had been in the game long enough to know that even when it's over, you have to look as if you believe it's not. She and her girls were dressed for victory: Ginny in a smart pantsuit in her party's new eco-friendly team colours of teal and cloud white, and the twins in long skirts and shirts with button-down collars.

The girls came over to us as their mother disappeared behind the cardboard shield intended to keep her vote private.

"Good to see you," Zack said. "You're doing the right thing. Stay in their faces. Make them know you're there."

Em looked at him with interest. "Same as in basketball."

"Same as in a courtroom. Same as in everything. Don't let your opponents dominate the game."

"We've adopted a new family motto," Em said. "It was in that old song we heard at Magoo's. Remember: 'You can't please everyone, so you've got to please yourself'?"

"Words to live by. So are you going back to the lake when this is over?"

"Our school is cool with us staying away till next week." Em swallowed hard. "My dad was cremated today. That's a weird thought." She squared her shoulders and pasted on a smile as Ginny emerged from the polling booth, handed her folded ballot to the returning officer, and then, smile broader than ever, faced the photographers.

"It's worse for her," Chloe said thoughtfully. "She's lost everything."

I looked at the two fresh-faced young women. "No, she hasn't," I said.

When Ginny came over to us, I could see the tension in the set of her jaw. "So did I get your vote?" she asked.

"I always vote for our clients," Zack said.

Ginny cocked her head at me. "And you, Joanne?" Her slate-grey eyes were measuring. "Were you prepared to throw away your vote?"

"I didn't throw it away," I said. "But I did vote for you. You were the best candidate."

"Past tense," Ginny said. "But thanks anyway. So, are you doing a stint for NationTV tonight?"

"I am. From the times the polls close here till we know who forms the next government."

Ginny laughed. "Well, better you than me." She turned to her daughters. "Let's rent some movies and get you guys settled in back at the condo. I've got a day of visiting polling stations and a concession speech ahead, but if it's all right with the Shreves, we can go back to the lake tonight."

"It's fine with the Shreves," I said. "Stay as long as you want."

The rain was coming down in sheets when Zack and I left the school. I opened our umbrella and held it over him. "I'll walk you to your car," I said. "And then I think I'll just go home. I was planning to drive to Moose Jaw and trail after Ginny on her last day as a candidate, but that overpass near Belleplaine scares me when it's raining."

"Then stay put," Zack said. "You've got a long evening, and you've been working hard. Take the day off and do your homework."

"You always tell me exactly what I want to hear," I said.

"That's because I'm not stupid," Zack said, then the two of us raced through the rain towards his car and whatever future election day would bring.

As soon as I got home I went to our room to change into my

jeans. *Firebrand* and *Abstract #1* were still propped against the wall at the bottom of the bed. I picked up the phone, called Ed Mariani, told him that we had two new paintings, and asked for his help in deciding where to place them. When he heard the pieces were by Scott Plear and Taylor, Ed was enthusiastic. "I'll be over in twenty minutes," he said. "I've got a class at twelve-thirty, but that should give us time enough."

Ed arrived carrying his tool-case and wearing a bright yellow slicker. As I took them from him in the front hall, water dripped onto the hardwood. Ed kicked off his shoes and scurried to the kitchen in search of a mop. "Sorry, Jo. Barry had that thing specially made because he worries that some driver might not spot me in the rain and plow into me, even though I'm not exactly a slip of a thing like him. I say, 'Get over yourself, Mary,' but Barry still makes me wear that football field of tarpaulin every time a drop descends from the heavens."

I hung the slicker on the hall tree and slid one of the dogs' towels under it to catch the drips. "Zack makes me carry my cellphone when I run Willie and Pantera," I said, "in case I slip. I guess we should be grateful we're loved."

"I am grateful," Ed said. "As the poet says, when we love, we give hostages to fortune." He rubbed his hands together. "Enough of this. Take me to your prizes. I'm an ardent admirer of Plear. In my opinion, he's one of the great contemporary colour field painters, and as for Taylor, well, Barry and I are very proud of our collection of her early works."

"You were smart to get in on the ground floor," I said. "This is Taylor's first abstract. I think we're all going to be glad we can say we knew her when."

"That good?" Ed said.

"Come see for yourself."

Ed followed me down the hall into the bedroom. When I flicked on the overhead lights, the large flat areas of colour on the two paintings roared to life. Ed was one of life's great celebrators, and when it came to praise, he didn't stint.

"Talk about a feast for the eyes," he said as he approached *Firebrand*. "Plear layers those reds, golds, and oranges as if he's laying on the colours for the dawn of the world. And the textures . . . If I touched that paint, I wouldn't be surprised if it came off on my fingertip." He leaned closer to Taylor's piece. "Her silvers and blues are sublime and that little wash of black at the top of the canvas – genius. How did she know?"

"Instinct?" I said. "I guess that's what makes Plear and Taylor the ones who paint and you and me the ones who are grateful, and I am grateful. Those pieces are perfect together."

"That's because they belong together," Ed said. "The colours, the technique. Taylor was working off what Plear had done."

"She worried about being derivative," I said. "But she needed to learn."

"And she did," Ed said. "They'll be spectacular side by side. You've got that huge wall. *Firebrand* is vertical and – what does Taylor call her painting?"

"*Abstract #1*," I said.

"Delicious," Ed said. "And *Abstract #1* is horizontal. This is going to be such fun. Now let the humble craftsman do his part."

In fifteen minutes the paintings were hung. "Satisfied?" Ed said.

"Completely," I said. "The last few days have been rough, and there's such joy in those paintings."

Ed's attention had been drawn by a framed illumination over Zack's dresser. He read the words. "'The lyf so short, the craft so long to lerne.'" Ed raised an eyebrow. "I wouldn't have guessed Zack was a Chaucer man."

"It was a gift from an old lawyer friend who obviously believed Zack had a few things to learn. He treasures it."

"As well he might," Ed said. He turned back to Taylor's painting. "Let's raise a figurative glass to your daughter. May she have all the time she needs to perfect her skill."

"That's a nice thought," I said. I flicked off the light and started back up the hall, with Ed and the dogs padding after me.

"So, are we going to be raising any glasses tonight when the election results are in?" Ed asked.

"Depends who you voted for."

"I voted for Ginny," Ed said.

"That surprises me," I said. "I thought you'd written her off."

"I had," Ed said. "But only because I thought Jason had withdrawn his custody suit to protect his daughters. Then it turned out the only one he was protecting was himself. His business dealings with prostitutes don't exactly bolster his reputation as a solid citizen."

"So you believe the rumours."

"I know they're true," Ed said. "Saturday night, Barry and I had drinks with our friend David, the one who has a condo in the same building as the murdered woman. He says Jason Brodnitz was a frequent visitor."

"Not a customer?"

"Not unless Jason needed satisfaction several times a day," Ed said. "Now I'd better be on my way."

I helped Ed on with his slicker. He checked his reflection in the hall mirror and shuddered. "God, I look like a giant Smartie."

CHAPTER

15

In a TV studio on election night, the real pitched battle is not between political parties: it's between television's need for scripted precision and the stretches of blank time when nothing happens except the counting of votes of citizens who live in five and a half different time zones. That year, NationTV's strategy for goosing the interest level during these wastelands was an innovation the network called "The Pulse." On election night, the atrium of the shining glass building would be open to the general public whose reward for staring at large screens filled with an endless procession of politicos would be the opportunity to offer on-air comments when nothing better was going on. When I arrived at five o'clock, the joint was already jumping. I picked my way over the cables snaking across the atrium floor and entered the doors that led away from the public space into the working studios and the makeup room.

Like a six-year-old awaiting an unwelcome haircut, Keith Harris was poised on a stool, staring glumly at his mirrored reflection while a bored young woman tucked a towel into his collar to keep makeup off his shirt. I positioned myself on the couch behind him so we could see each other in the mirror.

"I didn't know you were part of tonight's festivities," I said.

"I'm a last-minute substitution," Keith said. "The officially sanctioned spokesperson for the party is sleeping off a massive bender."

"How's it going?" I said.

"Our turnout in the Maritimes is heavy – good news for us this time out – because our party has actually treated the Maritimes decently. Quebec is Quebec. We can't count on much there. Voters in the 905 belt around Toronto are trooping out, and the clowns we have masterminding our campaign are convinced this gives us cause for celebration. They're wrong. There are more tract houses than century homes in the 905 area these days. Besides, living in a century house is no longer a guarantee that you vote the way grandpa did. Too soon to tell abut the 416 vote, but there's no reason to think we'll do well. Torontonians think our rhetoric is stale, and they don't get the social conservatism. That puts them in step with many other Canadians. If Ginny were leader, it would be a different story, but as it stands, we will not do well in the Greater Toronto Area."

"You really think Ginny could have brought in the GTA vote?"

"I do," Keith said. "But it's a moot point, isn't it?"

The young woman with the pancake makeup was working magic. Keith's pallor was gone; he looked as if he'd just come back from two weeks in the sun. "Stop talking, please," the young woman said. She patted under his eyes, dusted his shining pate with powder, ran a comb through what was left of his hair, and whipped off the towel. "You're done," she said.

Keith smiled at her pleasantly. "You have no idea how right you are," he said.

The young woman motioned me into the chair, and within minutes the crow's feet around my eyes were barely discernible, my cheeks glowed with health, and my lipline was smooth. Miracles all around.

"Want to go out in the atrium and take the pulse of the people?" I said.

Keith shook his head. "Nah. Let's sit in the green room and eat NationTV's Cheezies."

The evening began slowly, as election nights always do for Western Canadians. Until the polls closed in Saskatchewan and Alberta, our role was to watch and wait. But during the watching and waiting, some intriguing patterns were developing. As Keith had predicted, his party was doing well in the Maritimes, and Quebec, as usual, was carving out her own destiny. A heavy vote in the 905 was usually good news for the Tories, but tonight significant numbers of voters were apparently shifting to the middle. The Tories weren't losing seats, but their margins of victory were razor-thin. People in the area surrounding Toronto were voting like the Torontonians many of them had been until they moved to the burgeoning towns that ringed the city.

By the time the Saskatchewan and Albertan results started coming in, the three national networks were declaring that Canada was headed for a minority government and that the party controlling the government would be decided in the West. Alberta would be in the Tory column, but Saskatchewan and British Columbia were question marks. It was a night for caffeine and chewed fingernails, but there'd be no chewed fingernails in Palliser. By early evening, it was clear that Ginny Monaghan had lost the riding to the NDP's sacrificial lamb, Evan Shattuck.

Ginny didn't prolong the agony. When word came that she had arrived at the Pile O' Bones Club and was about to concede defeat, the network producer signalled me over. The network was picking up Ginny's speech live and wanted commentary.

As always, one picture was worth a thousand words. Tonight, there was no need to pull back the divider between the two banquet halls. Milo had done his best to cluster Ginny's supporters in front of the cameras, but defeat has a way of thinning a crowd.

Keith and I were seated side by side watching the monitor, and as Ginny came to the podium flanked by her slender, long-limbed daughters, his breath was ragged. I shot him a worried glance, but we were both wearing lapel mikes, so his only reassurance was a companionable wink before we both turned back to the monitor.

Ginny's speech was short and gracious. She thanked all her opponents on a hard-fought race, congratulated Evan on his victory, and then launched into her remarks.

"Winston Churchill once said that the Chinese ideogram for 'crisis' is made up of two characters: one means 'danger,' the other 'opportunity.' When the final votes are counted, there's a strong possibility that Canada will have a minority government and we will not head that government. The danger for our party is all too apparent. This crisis could bring out the worst in us. We could waste the next months in recriminations, accusations, and back-biting. That's one option. But as Churchill reminds us, there's another response to crisis. We can see this crisis as an opportunity – a chance to rebuild, to reach out to all Canadians: people of colour, people who are white, gays, lesbians, bisexuals, straights, Muslims, Jews, Christians, Buddhists, agnostics, atheists, those who are pro-choice as well as those who are pro-life. We can say to all Canadians, 'We are the real party of the people.' And we can mean it. Thank you for allowing me to represent you all these years."

The applause at the end of Ginny's speech was perfunctory. The red light on the camera in front of Keith and me
came on. In my earphone, a disembodied voice said, "So,
Joanne, is this the end for Ginny Monaghan?"

"No," I said. "That was a thoughtful speech – people will
remember it."

"You don't believe her husband's murder has put an end
to her political career?"

"No," I said. "Jason Brodnitz's death was a tragedy.
Tragedies happen. Obviously, Ginny's first priority now is
her family. But when she's ready to make plans, there'll be
many options open to her."

"Including politics?"

"Including politics," I said.

"You think the electorate will forgive her?"

"There's nothing for them to forgive." I said.

The next question was directed at Keith. It was a rework-
ing of the question about Ginny's future, and Keith's answer
was articulate and incisive.

When the red light went off, I gave him the thumbs-up.
"Nice answer," I said.

"Remember what Eugene McCarthy said about politics?"

"Eugene McCarthy said a lot of things about politics."

Keith nodded. "True enough," he said, "but I've always
had a particular fondness for this observation. McCarthy
said 'Politics is like coaching football. You have to be smart
enough to know how the game is played and dumb enough
to think it's important.'"

"And you're fond of that quote because . . . ?"

Keith's laugh was short. "After all these wasted years, I'm
still dumb enough to think it's important."

For the next hour, Keith and I sat on the set, waiting. He
made some phone calls and took some phone calls – notably

one from Ginny. Before he rang off, he said. "Well, if I don't see you before I leave, take care of yourself. I'll be in touch." Then he turned to me and said, "Ginny and the girls are going back to the lake. She'll call you in the morning."

"Sounds like you're not going to be around much longer either," I said.

"I've got my ticket for the three-fifteen flight tomorrow afternoon."

"That was sudden."

"Not really. My job here is done. I wasn't successful, but there's nothing I can do to change the results. Besides, there's a big meeting tomorrow night in Ottawa."

"Are you going to be in trouble?"

"No. You were right about Brodnitz's death. Tragedies happen. Besides, what are they going to do, fire me?"

"You don't seem very worried."

"I'm not."

When it finally became clear that the answer to the election would come in Alberta and British Columbia, the network producer thanked us and waved us off.

"The party's over," I said. "Let's get out of here."

"We're still wearing pancake makeup."

"Everyone will assume we're people who matter."

"We are people who matter," Keith said.

He took my arm and we ran through the rain to my car. Keith was breathing heavily by the time we got there.

"So where to?" I said. "We could go back to our place for a drink, or would you rather get back to your hotel?"

"Let's just sit here for a moment and enjoy the peace," Keith said.

"Fine with me," I said. "Give us a chance to talk."

"About what?"

"About what's next for you. Ginny's speech was stirring, but we both know the knives are already out for your leader.

In the next couple of weeks, the boys and girls who want to replace him are going to be knocking on your door."

"I won't be answering," Keith said. "This was my last campaign, Jo."

"Finally going to let the big guys buy you off with a Senate seat?"

Keith took out a pack of Rothmans and placed one, unlit, between his lips. "Even the Senate beats what's ahead for me. I'm dying, Jo. I only have a couple of months left. The other carotid artery is almost blocked. I've decided against surgery – the outcome is uncertain, and what happens after the surgery is hell. My cardiologist, who happens to be an old poker buddy, said if he was in my spot, he'd just enjoy the time he had left."

I took his hand and we watched the raindrops slide down the windshield. "I'm so sorry," I said finally.

"Don't be," he said. "I've had a good life, and I don't have many regrets. I've missed some chances, notably with you, but even that worked out for the best. You and Zack appear to have caught the brass ring."

"We did," I said. "And I wouldn't have had the confidence even to reach for it if it hadn't been for you."

"How so?"

"You were the first man in my life who didn't make me feel I was a disappointment."

"Did Ian make you feel that?"

"He didn't mean to, no more than my father did or Alex did, but they all had a way of making me aware of my short-comings." I rubbed Keith's hand. "Somehow you managed to convince me that I was worth being with. And I hung on to that when I met Zack."

"Well, that's something, isn't it?" he said.

"It was for me."

By the time we pulled up on the street beside the hotel, the rain had stopped. When Keith got out of the car, I did too. He looked at me questioningly. "I'm going to walk you to the front door," I said.

The steps leading to the lobby were brightly lit and a doorman was waiting to spring to attention if a guest approached. Halfway up the block, I stopped. Keith stopped too. We moved towards each other and embraced. Our kiss was deep and lingering – a farewell kiss, sweet with un-expressed words and deeply felt emotions. "That was nice," Keith said.

"It was," I said. "I'll drive you to the airport tomorrow."

"That would be nice too," Keith said.

I touched his cheek. "I'm going to miss you so much," I said. Then I turned, walked back to my car, and drove home, weeping, to my husband.

Zack was in our bedroom watching the election results when I came in. He beamed when he saw me. "Hey, you were terrific, but you weren't on air enough."

"Did you call the network to complain?" I said.

"Better than that – I phoned in a bomb threat."

"That's my boy," I said.

"Can I get you anything?"

"No, thanks. It's been a long night." I started undressing. As I took off my dress, Zack saw that I was wearing a black slip that he particularly liked. He wheeled close to me and rubbed my arm. "What is it about you in that slip?"

"I don't know," I said. "But as soon as I realized the effect it had on you, I ordered two more exactly like it."

Zack gave me a searching look. "Let's call it a night, Ms. Shreve."

"Want me to leave on the slip?"

"You bet."

I went into my bathroom, creamed off the pancake makeup, brushed my teeth, and tried a smile. It wasn't convincing. I got into bed and moved close to Zack. "So what's wrong?" he asked.

"Keith's dying," I said.

Zack flinched. "Jesus. How long does he have?"

"A couple of months. Apparently, he could have surgery, but even his cardiologist says it's not worth the agony."

Zack kissed my hair. "I'm sorry, Jo. Really. Keith seems like a good guy."

"He is," I said. "And I'm grateful to him. He taught me a lot."

Zack's grip tightened. "Then I'm in his debt."

"So am I," I said. "Let's make the most of it."

When I turned on the radio the next morning, it was clear that much, including which party would govern us, remained undecided. There would be many, many recounts. For days, the air would be filled with talk of uncertainty and chaos. Hand-wringing economists would muse about financial repercussions, and earnest academics like me would fret over the long-term implications of political uncertainty. Once again, we were on the brink. But as the dogs and I started along the levee beside the creek, I knew that nothing essential had changed. The creek still flowed, the ducklings still swam behind their mothers, the birds still sang. My morning would unfold as all my mornings did – in a secure world with people I loved. Then I thought of Keith, waking up alone in a hotel room, catching his flight back to Ottawa and the chrome kitchen where he never had a meal, missing this glorious day, missing so much, and my throat tightened.

Zack was on the front porch taking the morning papers out of the mailbox when we got back. "The porridge and the coffee are ready, but you had a couple of calls you might want to return before we eat: Mieka called – everything's fine, but she needs a favour – and Jill Oziowy called – nothing's fine and she needs a favour."

"Give me five minutes," I said.

Zack undid the dogs' leashes and looped them over the hook by the door. "How does Jill function with that level of anxiety?" he said.

"She works in network television. I think her level of anxiety is a requirement."

I went into the kitchen, poured myself a mug of coffee, and dialed Mieka's number. "How's everything in your kingdom?" I asked.

"So far, so good," Mieka said. "Madeleine found that hideous rapper hat that I hid at the back of her closet, so she's happy. Lena invented a new kind of cinnamon toast, so she's happy, and Sean invited me out for dinner at the Creek Bistro Friday night, so I'm happy."

"I thought cinnamon toast had already been invented," I said.

"Ah, but Lena used chili powder instead of cinnamon. She also used about a cup of organic brown sugar."

"Sounds tasty," I said. "And you're giving Sean a second chance?"

"Why not? I like him, and he asked very nicely. He said this would be a dinner between friends to celebrate his junior partnership. Mum, he's so excited. He just worships Zack."

"Don't we all? So you'd like us to stay with the girls Friday night?"

"If you can. Sean's picking me up at seven."

"We'll be there," I said.

Jill must have read my number on call display because she started in before I even said hello. "Okay, here's the pitch. My boss wants Ginny Monaghan as the lead segment on this week's Here and Now. Problem is Ginny's not talking to the media. Can you get her to talk to us?"

"I won't even try," I said. "Ginny's a friend, and she's been through enough."

"She's also an adult," Jill said testily. "Why don't you let her decide for herself?"

"I'll call her and give her your number. She can take it from there."

"Tell her that I'm a terrific person and that we're not planning to exploit her."

"I'll tell her that you're a terrific person," I said.

There was a long silence. "Or used to be," Jill said. "Did I sound like a maniac just now?"

"You sounded like somebody who's headed straight for the top at NationTV."

"That bad?"

"That bad," I said. "Jill, why don't you quit? You don't need the money. You hate your new boss. Bryn's in university. The world's your oyster."

"I'm allergic to oysters," she said. "By the way, your proposal for another instalment of Issues for Dummies has been green-lighted. How soon can you get something to me on your 'Women in Politics' piece? We have a listening with marketing Friday afternoon."

"I take it that a listening is what we used to call a meeting."

"You take it correctly." Jill said. "So how soon can I have something to pitch?"

"Friday noon," I said. "And it's not going to be great. There's been a lot going on."

"Give that lady a cigar. Guess why you got green-lighted? We've got some dynamite footage of Ginny."

"That's what I figured."

"But you're okay with using Ginny because it's your project?"

"No, I'm okay with using material about Ginny because she understood from the outset this program was going to be about how women in politics were treated differently from men."

"Strike two," Jill said.

"Actually, that was strike three," I said. "When I called, you didn't even bother to say hello."

"So, are you counting me out?"

"Never," I said. "Jill, remember what you used to say to servers who gave us lousy service in a restaurant?"

"'Why don't you try to find a job you actually enjoy?'"

"It's still good advice," I said. "I'll have the story on Ginny to you by Friday noon."

Zack and I had our breakfast on the deck alone. Taylor was on the decorating committee for the Farewell, and they were meeting that morning to scope out the gym. When I carried the breakfast tray out, the papers were stacked neatly by my plate. "Let's ignore the news." I said.

Zack reached over, took the three newspapers in hand, and dropped them on Taylor's empty chair. "What news?" he said.

He chortled when I told him about Lena's cinnamon toast but frowned when I mentioned the babysitting Friday night. "I'm in Saskatoon," he said. "I've got that dinner for Morton Lamb, the judge who's retiring from the bench at least ten years too late. I thought I told you."

"You did," I said. "I forgot. Anyway, it's not a problem. I'm fine with the girls on my own."

"I'm not fine," Zack said. "I'd rather be with you and the kids than listening to poor old Mort bleat on about back in the day."

"It's only one night," I said. "If you get back early enough Saturday morning, we can go to the lake."

Zack poured us coffee. "I'll get back early enough."

"Hey, guess who Mieka's going out with Friday night?"

"Jack the Ripper."

"Sean."

"I thought that was off."

"This is just a friendly dinner to celebrate Sean's junior partnership."

Zack sipped his coffee. "I'm glad that didn't end on a sour note. Delia and I were talking the other day about trying to get some of the fun back into Falconer Shreve."

"You could start a bowling team. Join a league."

Zack raised an eyebrow. "A bowling team of lawyers? Now that's a scary thought. Wouldn't you feel guilty putting me in a situation where Margot could aim a fourteen-pound bowling ball at me?"

"Not if I could watch," I said. I poured cream on my porridge. "So how does your day look?"

"Not bad. I'm in court this morning, then I'm going to meet with my client, the gynecologist, who is suing her gynecologist over a tubal ligation that ended up with my client giving birth to the nastiest baby I've ever seen. I have three-quarters of an hour to scare the shit out of the fifteen-year-old son of the president of Peyben because his dad thinks the kid is headed for serious trouble and he'd rather pay up front than foot the bill when the kid is tried as an adult. After that, I'm going to try again to find Francesca Pope, then come home and work on my speech honouring Morty Lamb."

"Zack, do you think you should get the police to look for Francesca? She brought those bears over last Thursday. It's been five days."

"Too long," Zack agreed. "But the cops are the last resort. Francesca's terrified of authority figures. If I can't find her myself, I'll get the investigators Sean hired to look for her. They must have women working for them."

"Francesca doesn't like men?"

"She's easier with women."

"But she reacted so badly to Ginny."

"Guess Francesca just doesn't like Ginny," Zack said. "Oh, one other tidbit: Debbie Haczkewicz called when you were on the phone."

"Have the police come up with something?"

"Not that they're telling me. Debbie was pretty tight-lipped, but she didn't press me at all about Ginny so I have a feeling the cops may be closing in on someone."

"But you don't know who?"

"Don't know and don't care, as long as it's not my client. And more good news: the reason Debbie called was to tell me Bree Steig is back in the land of the living. She doesn't remember anything about the circumstances of the beating. That's not unusual with head injuries. In a way, it's a blessing. Anyway, Bree's going to be all right."

"Can she have visitors?"

"I'm sure Debbie will put you on the list. Do you want to talk to Bree?"

"I just thought I'd take her some flowers."

"You're probably the first person who ever has."

"That's why I'm going to take them," I said.

Zack pushed the dish of cashews towards me. "Have a fistful, on the house. One good deed deserves another. So what else do you have on the agenda today?"

"I'm going to persuade Keith to have lunch with me before I drive him to the airport, and I'm going to call your new junior partner and ask him to talk to me about his impressions of Ginny's campaign. He might have something I can throw into the mix."

"And you might find out if his intentions towards Mieka are honourable."

"That too," I said.

I spent a couple of hours in my office having a go at the first draft of my proposal, then I stopped by a florist on 13th Avenue. I chose a spring bouquet for Bree and started looking around for a congratulatory bouquet for Margot. I'd settled on an arrangement of stargazer lilies when I remembered Margot telling me that Zack's invariable gift to women he was dumping was a nice note and a hundred bucks' worth of flowers. I paid for Bree's bouquet and walked up the street to a shop called the Embroidery Works. My aim was modest, a T-shirt, but when I walked inside, I knew that this was my lucky day. On a sale rack by the door was a single yellow and maroon satin bowling shirt. I took it to the clerk, told her what I needed embroidered on it, asked her to courier the finished shirt to Margot's office, paid, and left triumphant. I was still aglow with self-congratulation when I put my key in the ignition to drive to Regina General. Some days, I just had all the moves.

Bree had been moved from intensive care to one of the wards, but she was in a private room with the door locked, and the nurse at the station asked for my ID before accompanying me down the hall and letting me in to see her patient.

She was propped up in bed. There was a large bandage across the top of her skull and an intravenous tube was taped to the vein of her left hand. Without makeup and wearing her skimpy blue hospital gown, Bree Steig looked much younger than she had the evening I met her at Nighthawks. She was hard at work on a colouring book opened on the tray in front of her.

Her face brightened when she saw the flowers. "Are those for me?"

"They are," I said.

"Pink and purple, my favourite colours. Can I hold them?"

I moved her tray aside and handed her the vase. She sniffed the flowers and beamed. "I feel like a bride." She giggled. "Bet I don't look like a bride, except maybe the Bride of Frankenstein."

"You look fine," I said, and in truth, she did. The hectic glitter was gone from her pale eyes, and her skin had lost its sallow cast.

She lowered her voice. "I've been eating," she said confidentially.

"So you're feeling better?"

Her eyes scanned the room, then she leaned towards me. "I'm fine. I really am fine. I'm just not telling the doctors and nurses."

"Why not?"

"Because I'm safe here. Could you take my flowers? I'm supposed to finish colouring my picture before lunch."

"So the colouring book is therapy."

"They're worried that I'm not focusing my mind. My mind is exactly the same as it was before I got hit on the head, but I don't want them to know that, so I just keep colouring."

"So you do remember what happened that night?"

"I remember everything." Bree's eyes were sly. "I don't know his name, but I could pick him out."

"Tell the police. They'll arrest the man who attacked you, then you'll be safe."

The scorn in the glance Bree levelled at me would have curdled milk. "Right," she said. "Could I have my table please?"

I slid the table back in front of her, and she picked up a crayon and began colouring in the ball gown of one of the indistinguishable Disney princesses.

"Bree, you can't stay here forever."

She cocked her bandaged head. "Do you have a better plan?"

"No."

"Thanks for the flowers. I think the pink ones are the prettiest. What are they called?"

"Tulips," I said.

"Tulips," she repeated. Then, with the tip of her tongue extended catlike from between her teeth, she returned to her colouring.

Keith and I didn't manage a last lunch. There were many loose ends from Ginny's campaign that needed tying, and in the absence of the candidate, Keith stepped in. I picked him up at Ginny's constituency office, and we barely had time to make it to the airport. On the drive, we talked about Maddy and Lena. I told him about Lena's variation on the theme of cinnamon toast, and he told me that when he was a child, his mother had pencilled faces on each of the family's morning boiled eggs and he missed it still.

"Next time you're here, we'll have you over for breakfast. Lena will do the toast, and I'll draw the face on your egg."

"Next time," Keith said softly, but we both knew.

As I turned towards the airport parking lot, Keith touched my arm. "Don't bother parking. Just pull into the five-minute zone over there. If I'm going to catch my plane, I have to make tracks."

I took his hands in mine. "This is no way to say goodbye."

He brushed my cheek with his lips. "For us, it's the only way."

I popped the trunk, Keith went around to the back of the car, took out his laptop and suit-bag, and headed towards security. He didn't look back.

෴

Sean Barton had agreed to meet me at his office at four o'clock. As I stepped into the elevator and pushed the button for the fifteenth floor, I caught sight of myself in the mirrored walls. What I saw was not encouraging. I'd chewed off my lipstick, my hair needed attention, and the coffee I'd bought at a drive-through after Keith disappeared into the terminal had leaked onto my skirt. When the elevator doors opened onto the hard-polished perfection of the reception area, I felt like a woman who'd arrived at the wrong party. But Denise Kaiswatum had a way of making everyone feel that they were in the right place.

"Sean is anxiously waiting, but if you'd like a moment to freshen up, here's the key to Zack's bathroom."

"Thanks," I said, pocketing the key. "I'll need more than a moment. Could you let Sean know I'm here, and I'll be along?"

"Will do," Denise said. She opened her desk drawer and found a container of instant spot remover and held it out to me. "Interested?"

"Very," I said.

Denise handed me the tube. "Zack's at home, you know."

"I know," I said. "I wish I was there too. It's been a long day."

Sean was sitting on the edge of Denise's desk when I came back. He jumped up and offered his arm. "Can I get you anything before we start, Joanne?"

"I'm fine," I said. "So, are you still in your old office?"

"Nope. Moving on up. Come have a look."

I followed him down the corridor to the office next to Zack's. He opened the door and stood aside so I could get a clear view. It was impressive. The room was probably half the size of Zack's, but a floor-to-ceiling window gave it great natural light, and it had been decorated with surprising inventiveness for a business. The walls and furnishings were in complementary shades of brown and taupe, but the ceiling was a bracing asparagus green.

"What do you think?" Sean said.

"I love it. Who did the decorating?"

"I did," he said.

"That colour on the walls is gorgeous. I've been looking for a brown that shade for our bedroom at the lake. What's it called?"

"Moleskin," Sean grimaced. "Terrible name, I know, but I went through a hundred decorating books till I found exactly what I wanted."

"You were just named partner a few days ago," I said. "How did you find the time?"

"I've always known what I wanted," he said. "It was just a question of waiting until I got it."

"Well, congratulations," I said. "On being patient, on the partnership, and on the decorating. I'm going to send Zack around to take notes."

"Please do," he said. "Right now, just make yourself comfortable." He pointed to a reading chair covered in café au lait leather. "That particular chair is very restful."

"Another time," I said. "If I settled into that, I'd never leave."

I walked over to his desk and pulled out the leather client chair. His framed law school diploma was on the seat. I picked it up. "You don't want to lose this," I said.

Sean coloured and grabbed the diploma from me before I'd had a chance to really notice anything but the date.

"That's nothing to be ashamed of," I said.

"Zack says if you need to have a diploma on your wall proving you've mastered the law, you're in the wrong business." he said tightly.

"You're a partner now. Put whatever you want on your walls. Besides, you know Zack. He doesn't care what you do with your office. All he cares about is that you love the law the way he does."

Sean's eyes met mine. "The only thing I've ever loved is Falconer Shreve," he said. His face was blank; it was clear he had no idea how much he had just revealed. I felt a chill. "Let's talk about Ginny's campaign," I said.

"It was like everything else," he said. "Just a series of trade-offs."

"I thought you believed in Ginny."

"Not really," he said. "But I needed leverage to get what I wanted at Falconer Shreve."

"Ginny was just leverage?"

Sean's baritone was smoothly reassuring. "Everyone is leverage, Joanne. You invest in a person, hoping that the potential return from your investment is great. Sometimes it is, but sometimes people disappoint us. When we realize that our investment is worthless, it's time to move along."

"And that's what happened with you and Ginny?"

"Among others," he said.

I thought of how Sean had suddenly spurned my daughter. "So what do you do when an investment doesn't pay off?" I asked.

"Like any other investor, I cut my losses," he said. "Now, let's talk about the future. I can't tell you how excited I am to be part of the Falconer Shreve family."

CHAPTER

16

Friday morning when I flipped through the business section of our local newspaper and saw Falconer Shreve's announcement that Margot Wright and Sean Barton would be assuming new positions with the firm, I knew Sean would be over the moon at being publicly acknowledged as a member of the Falconer Shreve family. The pictures of Margot and him were equally flattering; more importantly, they were of equal size and side by side. By his own assessment, Sean was a patient man. It was only a matter of time before his name would be added to the letterhead of Falconer Shreve.

When I handed the paper to Zack, opened to this page, he grinned. "Hey, nice picture of the newest members of our bowling team."

"They look promising," I said. "Margot could bowl a perfect game without breaking a sweat or a single one of her fabulous red, red nails, and Sean is certainly single-minded."

Zack raised an eyebrow. "Do I detect a note of criticism?"

"No," I said. "If you're happy with the hires, I'm happy with the hires."

"I'm happy. I know it started as a joke, but Delia's convinced we have to find our soul again. Maybe bowling is a start."

"Well, if it is, I get to be in the team picture," I said. "It was my joke."

"*Palman qui meruit ferat.* Let him bear the palm who has deserved it," Zack said. "But it was neat that Margot picked up on the joke."

"She does look sensational in that bowling shirt," I said.

"We were lucky to get her," Zack said. "And not just because she looks good in a bowling shirt. She's a hell of a good lawyer."

"Were you lucky to get Sean?"

"He'll be fine," Zack said. "He doesn't have the feel for the law Margot does, but I was impressed with the work he did tracking down the sources of Jason Brodnitz's income. I was also impressed that he wasn't afraid to use what he knew to get Brodnitz to back down on the custody case."

"You don't think what Sean did was ruthless?"

"Sean wasn't the one who was living off money he earned from prostitutes. We all have to live with the consequences of our actions." Zack pushed his chair back from the table. "Speaking of, I'd better get a move on or I'll miss my flight."

"I hate being apart overnight," I said. "How come you're always the one who has to speak at these dinners?"

"Because, Ms. Shreve, your husband is the only lawyer in the province who knows when to leave the podium."

We weren't in a rush, so I parked and waited with Zack in the terminal until his flight was called. We had a cup of bad coffee from a kiosk and talked about the weekend ahead. When the announcement came, Zack drained his cup and pitched it in the recycling bin. "What do you think about calling our team the Piranhas?"

"I think it stinks," I said.

Zack reached out and pulled me towards him. "Behind every great man is a woman rolling her eyes, " he said.

I spent the morning at my laptop looking at video clips of Ginny's career. The material was familiar, yet I found myself moved and saddened by the documentation of Ginny's rise and fall. Her career had the kind of arc that television loves: beginning with her promise as an athlete, moving onto her success in business, building to her political wins, her exemplary handling of her cabinet post and the growing belief that she was destined for great things, and then suddenly the climax – when at the moment where everything seems possible, the protagonist self-destructs, leaving nothing behind but the shards of lost possibilities.

At a little before noon, I e-mailed my draft proposal to Jill, then called the massage centre Zack and I used and booked an appointment. In my opinion, I'd earned an afternoon of indulgence. I had a glass of wine with lunch, then I had a nap and a swim and went to my massage. Two hours later, with the life force once again flowing unimpeded through my body, I came home, made a salad for Taylor and myself, and took my Matisse biography outside with a glass of iced tea. The good life.

Ed Mariani called just as Taylor and I were about to leave for Mieka's. "Glad you caught me," I said. "Taylor and I were just on our way out the door."

"Actually, I wanted to talk to Zack," Ed said.

"He's in Saskatoon. He had meetings there all day and he's speaking at a dinner tonight. Do you want his cell number?"

"Thanks," Ed said after he wrote the number down. "Everything okay with you?"

"Couldn't be better," I said. "I spent an entire afternoon following my bliss."

"Well, I won't keep you," Ed said. "Thanks for Zack's number."

"Ed, you sound a little distracted. Is something wrong?"

"Nothing that can't be fixed," he said, and he hung up.

Taylor and the granddaughters and I were sitting on the steps of Dessart Ice Cream Emporium when Zack called. "What are you up to?" he said.

"I'm sitting on the steps of Dessart with the young women in your life. We're all eating double-deckers with sprinkles."

"You're lucky. I'm at a reception with a bunch of other lawyers waiting to get our joints bored off by an evening with Morty Lamb."

"Isn't the expression 'tits bored off'?"

"I was attempting to be inclusive," Zack said. "The last time I used the term tits, you took umbrage."

"You sound a little lubricated."

"Probably more than a little. Some of us got together for drinks before we came here."

"Always a good idea to have a few drinks before you go to a reception where the wine will be flowing."

"I'll slow down."

"That's my boy. Hey, did Ed Mariani get in touch with you?"

"I had my cell off. I'll call him later."

"Ed says it's important."

"Okay, I'll call him now. Hold that. We are being waved into dinner. I'll call him after the prime rib."

"Make sure you eat something."

"I will. And I'll call you when I get back to my room. It won't be late. Morty joined us for drinks, and he's already nodding." Somebody who was demanding Zack's attention was speaking to him. When Zack came back, he sounded wistful. "Tell me again exactly what you're doing."

"Sitting on the steps of Dessart with the girls. The sun is setting behind the cathedral. We're finishing our ice cream, and we all miss you."

"That is precisely what I wanted to hear."

The girls were tucked in, and Taylor and I had just started perusing Mieka's DVDs when Francesca Pope called.

She got right to the point. "Your husband can't be trusted," she said. "I want my bears."

"I can't do anything tonight, Francesca," I said. "I'm not at home. You called my cell."

"I know," she said. "I got the number from your voice mail. When will you be at your house?"

"Probably not till around ten. You can come by then if you like."

"It's not safe for me there." Her voice was thick. "It's not safe for them either. I have to get them out of there."

"I'll bring the bears to you tomorrow morning."

"No! It could be too late by then." Her voice rose with desperation.

"All right," I said. "I'll bring them to you tonight. Where can I meet you?"

"At the side of Acme Store-All. It's right next to the Pendryn."

"Where Cristal Avilia lived."

"And died," she said.

My pulse quickened. "Francesca, how close were you and Cristal?"

"She was my best friend," Francesca said, then the line went dead.

I thought about calling Zack but realized he'd be in the middle of dinner. The news about the nature of Francesca's relationship with Cristal could wait, but Francesca's fear stayed with me as Taylor and I settled in to watch *Atonement*.

Mieka came home just as the credits at the end of the movie were rolling. Taylor and I had polished off a pitcher of iced tea and most of a bowl of popcorn. We'd also gone through a substantial number of tissues, but I would have been hard-pressed to identify exactly for whom I was crying.

When Mieka walked into the family room, I stood up and looked past her for Sean. "Where's the junior partner?" I asked.

Mieka scooped out the last of the popcorn. "Where junior partners go at the end of an evening – back to the office."

"Did you have fun?"

"Yes, we did. Very low key, but it was nice." She kicked off her shoes. "Would you care for a beer while you debrief me?"

"I'd love a beer, but I have to go on an errand."

Mieka glanced at her watch. "It's quarter to ten."

"This is urgent. Do you remember Francesca Pope?"

"The Care Bear lady? Sure. She's pretty memorable."

"She left her bears at our house for safekeeping and she's decided she needs them back."

"So you're going to take them to her at this time of night?"

"I'm going to meet her next to the Pendryn – I'll be back in half an hour."

"Mum, that is not a safe area."

"People pay three-quarters of a million dollars to live in that area, Mieka. How dangerous can it be? Besides, I promised."

"Okay, then. I'll go with you."

Taylor was off in the kitchen, making a phone call, but I still lowered my voice. "Mieka, you know how Taylor is about being in the house alone at night."

"She won't be alone. The girls are here."

"The girls are little kids." I picked up the popcorn bowl. "When I get back, we'll have a beer and I'll fill you in on nightlife in the warehouse district."

"At least promise to keep your car doors locked."

"If the car doors are locked, how will I get the bears out?"

"I thought you were the brains in the family," Mieka said. "Hand Francesca the bears through the window."

I'd forgotten to leave any lights on at home, and as I opened the front door I felt the stab of mindless fear I always experience going into a dark house. Taylor wasn't the only one with anxieties. Reassured by the presence of the dogs, I moved quickly, turning on lights and humming to break the silence. I picked up Francesca's backpack and returned to my car. Then, with the bears beside me on the front seat, I drove down Albert Street to the warehouse district.

Our mayor had dreamed of transforming the northeast core of the city into a place where the rich could live and the hip could play at night. As I turned onto Dewdney Avenue, it seemed that at least part of the mayor's dream for the area had been realized. The magenta lamppost pennants that marked the district were snapping in the breeze and the brightly lit streets were filled with people laughing and talking as they moved between nightclubs, bars, and pool-rooms. I drove past Bushwakker Brewpub, the meeting place of choice for my students and the home of my husband's favourite, the Wakker Burger. Everybody seemed to be having fun, and it occurred to me that Mieka and I might leave Zack with the kids some night and come down and hit a couple of clubs. Maybe it was time my cautious older daughter took a walk on the wild side.

The shift in atmosphere when I crossed Broad Street was sobering. Except for the Pendryn, the developers had not yet reclaimed this part of the district, and I found myself in the dark, lonely world of deserted lumberyards and crumbling buildings. There were streetlights, but no one walked beneath them, and the only sounds I heard came from guard dogs barking.

Acme Store-All and the Pendryn shared a city block. The Pendryn was surrounded by a razor-wire-topped security fence, and the swimming pool and Japanese garden behind the condo were as brightly lit as a prison courtyard. Ed had said that one of the beauties of the Pendryn was the spectacular view it offered of the city. The windows of the individual condominiums were floor to ceiling but, without exception, they were dark. Seemingly, I'd come on a night when there was nobody home.

I chose a parking place that gave me a clear view of the cinder yard beside Acme Store-All. Francesca Pope was nowhere in sight, but her bicycle was propped against the wall. I remembered how frightened she was. She was obviously hiding, waiting for me to show myself. I took a deep breath, picked up the backpack, got out of my car, and clicked the locks on my doors. My cell rang before I'd taken a single step.

Ed Mariani was apologetic. "Jo, I'm know I'm being a pest, but Zack hasn't called back, and there's something he needs to know."

I adjusted the backpack. "He's probably still at that retirement dinner. I imagine that right about now they're on the brandy and cigars. Why don't you leave the message with me? Zack will call me to say goodnight when he gets to his room."

"All right," Ed said. "I may be interfering in something that's none of my business, but do you remember that friend I mentioned who lives at the Pendryn?"

"Of course," I said. "He was the one who told you that Jason Brodnitz was a frequent visitor of Cristal Avilia's."

"Apparently Jason wasn't the only frequent visitor," Ed said. "David called this afternoon. He'd seen the photos of Zack's new partners in the paper, and he recognized Sean Barton. He thought Zack should know that Sean was Cristal Avilia's boyfriend."

I felt a coldness in the pit of my stomach. "Is he sure?"

"Positive. David said Sean was there all the time. I guess there were some terrible fights. David even went up to Cristal's condo once to see if she wanted him to call the police."

I glanced at the darkened windows of the Pendryn. "But of course she didn't," I said.

"No," Ed said. "You know how these things are."

"Ed, I'm going to call Zack now. You were right to pass this along. My God, Mieka had dinner with Sean tonight."

"But she's not with him now."

"No. She's home with her girls." Even to my own ears, my voice sounded strained. I was having trouble absorbing the truth about Sean. "Ed, let me call you back after I talk to Zack."

I speed-dialed Zack's number and got his message immediately. Wherever he was, he'd turned off his cell. I wanted to go home, but I could see the shadow of Francesca's shambling bulk against the wall of Acme Store-All. She was waiting for me. I started along the sidewalk. I added up the letters in Sean's name – there were ten, and there were thirteen letters in Cristal Avilia's name. Thirteen minus ten – three. Sean was Cristal's perfect 3.

I scanned the street. I was still alone, but Francesca's silhouette against the brick wall of the abandoned warehouse was a beacon, a reminder that at the moment there was someone even more frightened than me, so I kept on going.

I heard the familiar baritone before I realized Sean was beside me. "Hey, here you are," he said. "Mieka called me at the office. She was worried about your being down here alone at night. She was right. Anything could happen to a woman alone on this street." He reached over and took the backpack from me. "In a neighbourhood like this, a woman needs her arms free in case of a sudden threat."

"I promised to deliver the bears myself," I said. "May I have them back?"

"Why would you want them?" he said. "They're disgusting."

I tried to grab the backpack, but Sean was too fast for me. He threw it to the sidewalk. Reflexively, I bent to grab it. As my hand closed around the straps, he brought his foot down on my fingers. "Garbage," he said pleasantly. "Not worth dying for."

After that, everything happened very quickly. Francesca sprang out of the shadows, picked up her bears from the sidewalk, and cradled them against her breast. Then she began yelling. The words were the same words she'd shouted in the courthouse lobby, but this time their target was clear. Francesca's eyes scanned Sean's face. "I know who you are," she yelled. "I know who you are, and I saw what you did. You are evil," she said. "Evil. Evil. Evil. I saw what you did. You killed her. You killed Cristal."

Sean raised his arm, and the blade of the knife he was holding flashed in the harsh security lights. He tried to plunge it into Francesca's chest, but the bears protected her. When he raised the knife again, she ran. He watched her disappear down the block, then he laughed to himself. "Nobody will believe a word she says." He turned to me. "You, on the other hand, are a credible witness. But you're in a dangerous neighbourhood, Joanne. Anything can happen here. That's what I told Mieka." He moved closer. "A woman like Francesca is unpredictable. She forgets her meds, she sees a good Samaritan like you as a threat, and she attacks." As he created the scene in his mind, Sean's voice became dreamy, mesmerizing. He put the point of the knife against my chest. I could feel the steel through the thin material of my shirt.

"I'll tell them I was too late," he said. "That Francesca had already killed you by the time I arrived."

I took a step back, but Sean stayed with me and so did the knife. "Zack knows about your relationship with Cristal," I said. "Someone recognized your picture in the paper this morning and told him."

"No," he said, and there was real anguish in his voice.

"If I tell Zack you helped me, he'll defend you," I said. "You know how good he is. He'll make a jury understand how it was for you."

Sean's eyes met mine. "You lying bitch," he said. I felt the knife cut my skin and I watched as it sliced a half-moon over the top of my breast to my armpit. A dark pool of blood spread over my white blouse and then I collapsed on the sidewalk. My cell began ringing – Zack's ring tone: the Beach Boys singing "God Only Knows."

When Angus was born, I hemorrhaged. Ian had left the delivery room to make calls announcing that we had a new son and that mother and child were doing well, then suddenly I wasn't doing well. A nurse placed Angus on a metal table against the wall. He screamed in protest, but no one attended to him. Everyone was clustered around me. A great warmth was spreading beneath me, and I heard my doctor's voice, sharp with tension, saying, "Christ, we're losing her." And then nothing until I woke up in intensive care.

After I fell to the ground outside Acme Store-All, I felt that same warmth spreading over me. This time I knew what was happening. I was being bathed in my own blood. I wondered how long I had left, if I would ever see Zack or my granddaughters or any of my children again. Then suddenly there were people in uniforms around me – police and EMT technicians. A young voice flatly declarative said, "The knife went deep. We're losing her."

There was darkness and then – finally – there was light. It was the sickly light of the intensive care unit and I could see the faces of James, the dean of our cathedral, and Zack. I tried to say something, but my mouth wouldn't form words, and I drifted away again. When I awoke again, Zack was alone. This time when I moved my lips, I was able to articulate a single word: "Hello."

"Hello," Zack said. Reaching through the tubes and wires that measured my vital signs wasn't easy for a man in a wheelchair, but there wasn't much my husband couldn't do. As he touched my hair, he gave me a triumphant grin. "Made it," he said. "You're going to be all right, Ms. Shreve." His fingers stroked my cheek. "Is there anything I can get you?"

"Yes," I said. "A toothbrush." Then, for the only time in our life together, I saw my husband weep.

My recovery was slow and frustrating. Someone once told me that the greatest division of life is the one that exists between the world of the well and the world of the sick. After a lifetime of buoyant good health, I was suddenly on the other side of the chasm. Even after I was released from hospital, I lived in a grey world of doctors' appointments, surgeries, and trips to the rehabilitation centre. Most days it seemed I took one step forward and two steps back. My body had always done what I wanted it to do. It was a gift I had taken for granted, revelling in its strength and its seemingly endless ability to bring me pleasure. Now, it was broken, and I was furious.

Every morning I resolved to remain positive, but whenever I watched Ginny and her daughters running with my dogs, or found myself exhausted after swimming three laps in the pool, or was unable to embrace my husband, I raged.

My family had always seen me as strong and capable.
Now Zack hovered, and my granddaughters were tentative
about proposing games or adventures. Taylor checked on me
constantly. "Just making sure you're still there," she said
once, then fled, horrified at the fear she had revealed.
Whenever Peter and Dacia stopped by, I would see them
laughing as they walked arm and arm up the street, but they
would tamp down their joy as they approached our front
door. I was, after all, an invalid. Even Angus became consid-
erate – phoning every night – just to check in.

The fact that three of the people I most loved felt guilty
for what had happened made matters even worse. Zack was
angry at himself for not calling Ed back, Ed was angry at
himself for not pressing the issue, and Mieka believed
herself directly responsible for Sean's attack on me. The old
playfulness between my daughter and me disappeared. She
became obsessively solicitous, anticipating my every wish
or impulse. She dropped by several times a day with something she thought I might like to eat or read or listen to. It
was all too much.

The morning before Taylor's Farewell, I exploded. It was
hot, I was in pain from my surgery, and the bandages on the
wound made movement awkward. I was alone in the kitchen
making a frittata for lunch when I dropped the bowl of eggs I
was beating. The Pyrex bowl skittered across the floor un-
broken, but the eggs spilled everywhere. The prospect of
getting down on my hands and knees to clean them up with
my useless right arm was too much. "Motherfuck!" I said. "I
am so useless. I can't even make a frittata." The explosion
brought Zack into the kitchen. I glared at him. "What am I
supposed to do with this mess?"

Zack picked up the Pyrex bowl, put it on the counter,
looked at the eggs on the floor then at me. "Why don't you
call the dogs?" he said.

So I did, and at that moment, my real recovery began.

We ordered a feast from the Bamboo Gardens. It was an in-service day at Taylor's school, so she and Gracie Falconer joined us for lunch. We all ate far too much and laughed hard. Even the dogs seemed to relax. That afternoon, we took the granddaughters to the playground, threw pennies into the waterfall at the park, and made wishes.

The question of what I would wear to the Farewell had been vexing me. The only dress that fit over my surgical bandage was sleeveless, and the effect was not pleasant. When we got back from the park, Ginny met us at the front door. She'd been rummaging through her closet for an outfit to wear to a job interview and she'd found a lacy shawl that she thought might be the ticket. It was. The shawl not only covered the bandage but made my very simple shift look almost elegant. Clearly, my luck was changing.

The gymnasium at Lakeview School was overheated and overcrowded, the parents were overdressed, and the kids were overstimulated. The girls giggled; the boys were loud. As Taylor had predicted, all the girls except her were wearing sparkly T-shirts, short ruffly skirts, and sandals with plastic flowers. To a man, the boys wore cargo shorts and open-necked shirts. Everybody had a fresh haircut. Taylor's classmates looked exactly as boys and girls should look leaving Grade Eight, shiny and full of promise.

The formal program was mercifully brief. Following Taylor's orders, Zack and I had voted against a PowerPoint presentation of baby pictures, but we had been out-numbered. Since we didn't have any baby pictures of Taylor, we chose a photo I'd taken the day she came to live with us. She was lying on her stomach on the kitchen floor, drawing an Amazon butterfly, and the electric-blue flash she had sketched with her marker seemed to fly off the page. She was four years old. There was no lame poetry, but the principal's brief speech managed to embrace every cliché about graduation that had ever been uttered. The meal, served in the Resource Room by the Grade Sevens, featured ham, perogies, and cabbage rolls. For dessert there were butter tarts, peanut-butter marshmallow squares, and Nanaimo bars.

No surprises except one. After we'd eaten, the principal announced that Taylor Love would offer the toast to the parents. We all picked up our plastic glasses of ginger ale and Taylor rose to her feet. As she stood gazing over the room, she looked so much like Sally that my eyes stung.

"I've never done anything like this before," she began, "but Ms. Jacobs said that all I have to do is speak from the heart. So that's what I'm going to do, and I hope that what I say is what everyone else in the class would like to say to their parents. Before I start, I want to point out my mum and dad. They're sitting over there: my dad's the one in the wheelchair and my mum's the one with her arm in a sling." Someone laughed nervously. Taylor looked in the laugher's direction. "That's all right. You can laugh. We do." This time the laughter was general. Zack and I exchanged glances and Taylor continued. "Anyway, I just want to say thanks to Mum and Dad for being there whenever I need you and whenever I think I don't but I really do. Thanks for helping me with my homework and teaching me to swim and caring about my art. Thanks for driving me places and waiting for me when I'm not ready. Thanks for always making my friends feel they're welcome in our home. Thanks for always making me feel I'm welcome in our home. I love you very much." She raised her glass. "To my mum and dad. To all the mums and dads."

Zack raised his glass and cleared his throat. "That's the first time she's ever called me Dad," he whispered.

"First time she's ever called me Mum," I said.

"Guess we finally made the grade," Zack said. We touched glasses.

"To Mum and Dad," I said.

"To Mum and Dad," Zack replied.

After that night, there were many good moments. Remembering a scene from an old movie he'd liked, Zack came home one night with a bottle of nail polish and an invitation to join him in the bedroom. There, for the first time but not the last, he painted my toenails. Mieka drove me to Bushwakkers for a Wakker Burger and a brew and by the end of the evening we were back to our old easy ways with each other. Angus called a lot either to talk law with Zack, explain law to me, or keep me *au courant* on life without Leah. She was letting her hair grow, and she was still seeing Mr. Empathy, but Angus was hopeful. The first asparagus appeared in the market and the first strawberries, and when I thought of the bounty the garden of earthly delights would produce before the frost, I felt a piercing joy. Peter and Dacia got a new puppy – another rescue dog. They named him Hugo. Dacia taught Maddy how to juggle.

Sean Barton's trial opened on a bracing October day. Zack watched as I got dressed for court. "Are you determined to do this?"

"I have to see it through," I said.

He moved his chair closer. "Why?"

I reached over and touched the vertical line on his cheek. Since the night Sean attacked me, it had grown deeper. "I don't know," I said. "Maybe I just need to understand."

"Jo, there's nothing to understand. The reasons a supposedly normal person does *A* rather than *B* are a mystery. Trying to figure Sean out is pointless. He's a sociopath. Something in his wiring is twisted."

"Maybe I need to understand that."

Zack's smile was weary. "Well, if it matters to you, it matters to me. I'm going with you."

I tied Taylor's Paul Klee scarf and checked the result in the mirror. "I was counting on that," I said.

I hadn't seen Sean Barton since the night of the attack. As I entered the courthouse and walked under the mosaic of the God of Laws holding aloft the balance of right and wrong, my pulse raced. Zack was beside me, and there were officers of the law and of the court everywhere, but I knew that the forces that drove Sean Barton had nothing to do with the law or even with knowing that right and wrong were opposing ends of a continuum. Sean was *sui generis*, and no system of laws could protect his fellow beings against his hungry amorality.

He had elected to act as his own counsel. He had been disbarred, so as he walked into the courtroom and took his place at the counsel's table, he wasn't wearing the traditional barrister's robes. His street clothes had been carefully chosen – a double-breasted charcoal suit, a slate shirt, and a tightly knotted striped silk tie in shades of eggplant and mauve – penitential but not confessional. His blond hair was freshly barbered, and as he walked past me, he flashed me his disarming crooked smile. Zack's hand tightened on my arm.

Linda Fritz was acting for the Crown. She was a tall, slim redhead. I'd seen her in action, and she was formidable: cool, prepared, and unflappable. Her opening address to the jury was a model of restraint and economy. She summarized the facts of the case and stated that the Crown would prove that Sean Barton had, with forethought and intent to kill, pushed Cristal Avilia from her balcony and stabbed Jason Brodnitz. Linda Fritz then gave a quick précis of the evidence the

Crown would bring forth and identified her witnesses. Then, moving close to the jury box, she finished her opening statement with the assertion that the job of the Crown is simply to see that justice is done.

Without witnesses and without evidence that would exonerate him, Sean Barton had nothing but his own story, and in his opening, he cited the metaphor that would inform his defence. He had taken it from Robert Frost's much-anthologized poem, "The Road Not Taken." Sean presented himself as a man who, like Frost's narrator, was confronted with a fork in the road and made a choice that defined his life.

He told his narrative compellingly, casting himself as the protagonist in a tragedy of passion doomed by forces beyond his control. When he met Cristal Avilia, Sean was in law school. She was a first-year student from a small town. They fell in love. They were both broke. After an evening of drinking and watching videos in the apartment of a well-heeled fellow student in the College of Law, Sean took his first wrong turn. One of the movies the group watched was *Indecent Proposal*, a film in which Robert Redford's character offers a desperate young real estate speculator a million dollars to sleep with the realtor's wife. The offer is accepted and a contract is signed.

The student hosting the party had urged Sean and Cristal to stay behind until the others left, then he made them an offer: $1,000 for an hour in bed with Cristal. According to Sean, Cristal's objections that she didn't want to have sex with a stranger were just an act. Sean and Cristal went outside, discussed the proposition, and after a brief fight, she agreed.

The rich young man liked what he paid for and there was a second tryst. The word got out, and Cristal's career was launched. She was twenty years old.

At this point in the opening, Mr. Justice Nathaniel Peters, an affable, heavy-set man, interjected. He was concerned, he said, that Sean was incriminating himself.

Sean gave the judge his disarming smile. "Just do your job," he said "And I'll do mine." At that point, Sean turned to the jury. "Cristal never looked back," he said. I searched the faces of the jury members. They were clearly horrified, but Sean was oblivious.

He went on to describe what he persisted in referring to as their "parallel careers": his in law, Cristal's in prostitution. He was factual and upbeat as he talked about their decision to move from Saskatoon to Regina. His experience at the law firm where he articled had not been a good one, and in his words, "Cristal and I both wanted a fresh start in our careers." He was hired by Falconer Shreve. Cristal, whom Sean praised as "a good money manager," bought a warehouse downtown, had it renovated, and set up shop. Two young people starting out on promising careers.

According to Sean, Cristal liked her work. "She was a real people person," he said. The gasp in the courtroom was audible, but Sean didn't hear it. He was too busy spinning a tale of a life that was, in his telling, just a bowl of cherries until things started going wrong for him professionally. When he sensed that the people who mattered at Falconer Shreve no longer saw him as partnership material, his quarrels with Cristal became more serious. He felt that everything was slipping from his grasp. One of Cristal's clients, an old lawyer who should have known better, started filling Cristal's head with ideas that made her rebellious. She wanted to quit the business. At this point in his narrative, Sean approached the jury box, hands extended in a gesture that begged for empathy. "All of a sudden, it wasn't the two of us against the world. After fourteen years with me, she wanted a different life. I had to get our relationship

back on solid ground. I had to show her who was in charge."
As everyone in the courtroom waited for the sentence that
would loop the noose around Sean's neck, Mr. Justice
Nathaniel Peters uttered his sternest warning against self-
incrimination. Sean ignored him.

As he described the last moments of Cristal's life, Sean's
baritone was seductive. "She was going to leave," he said.
"And I couldn't allow that to happen. She was my soulmate,
and I couldn't be separated from my soul." At that point, he
bowed his head – an actor, waiting for an ovation. The
applause never came.

Finally Sean straightened, squared his shoulders, strode
back to his desk, and set about explaining the death of Jason
Brodnitz.

"The Ginny Monaghan case was make or break for me,"
he said. "Winning that case was my last chance to be taken
seriously at Falconer Shreve." He smiled across at the
Crown prosecutor. "My friend understands that sometimes
we have to tighten a case to make sure we win. I had to do
whatever it took to get Ginny custody of her girls. I'd
learned from inside sources that Brodnitz's professional
rebirth had been financed by sex workers. I used that knowledge to win the Monaghan case."

He walked across to the jury. "By winning the Monaghan
case, I had redeemed myself, but once again there was a fork
in the road. This time I wasn't the one who chose the direction that changed everything. If Jason Brodnitz had accepted
his loss, he'd be alive today, but like Cristal, he pushed and
pushed and pushed and pushed." Sean paused dramatically.
"Once again, I had no alternative but to push back."

As he took the measure of the jury, Sean's head moved
slowly, as if he was memorizing each of their faces. "So
that's it," he said. "I stand before you today because fate led
me down the wrong road. One day my life was full of

promise; the next I met Cristal Avilia. We went to a party. We watched a video. A man made an offer. Cristal accepted, and my life was ruined." He glanced at me. "There was collateral damage. Members of the jury. Judges of the facts. Ask yourselves whether, given the circumstances, you would have acted any differently than I did."

As Sean took his seat, the silence in the courtroom was absolute. Linda Fritz was slow to rise from her desk. Like any good actor, she knew the value of letting an audience absorb the implications of a powerful soliloquy before she moved along. When Linda asked that the boxes containing Cristal's journals be brought in and admitted into evidence, the jurors were riveted. The sheer weight of the evidence was overwhelming. There were 168 journals. On the day she met Sean, Cristal began to record their life together: one journal a month, twelve months a year for fourteen years. The journals provided a dark counterbalance to Sean's sunny account of two young people embarking on successful careers. As Linda read excerpts from the journals, Cristal's obsessive longing for Sean Barton's approval and love, and her pain at his continued manipulation and rejection, sucked the oxygen from the room. When Linda finished reading, there was a sob. Then there was silence. Linda had done her job. She had made certain that Cristal Avilia's voice was heard in the courtroom.

A week later, when Sean finished his closing argument and the case went to the jury, Zack turned to me. "Well, the ship has sailed," he said. "Let me go over to the office and pick up a couple of things, then we can spend the day doing whatever you want to do."

The weather had turned in the week since the trial began. The day was leaden, darkening, and the cold air smelled of dead foliage, long journeys, and winter. The trees in Victoria Park were leafless, stripped to the bare essentials. And

although it was late morning, the lights in the office buildings were blazing.

I hadn't been to Falconer Shreve since the day I'd met Sean
there and he'd shown me his new office. There were changes.
Margot was settled in and there was another new partner.
There were also a half-dozen new associates. When I passed
the office that Sean had lusted after so fervently and planned
for so long, there was a young man behind the glass desk. He
leapt to his feet and came over to be introduced when he
spotted me with Zack. The new associate's name was Rick
Warren. He was short and wiry, with a high forehead and
slicked-back dark hair, and he was charmingly deferential to
the wife of the senior partner. When he noticed that I was
staring past him into his office, Rick stepped aside. "Come
in and have a look around," he said. The room was exactly as
it had been on the day Sean showed it to me. Rick was
watching me carefully, gauging my reaction. "What do you
think?" he said finally.

I took in the asparagus ceiling, the soft brown walls, and
the café au lait reading chair. "It's very handsome," I said.

Rick's eyes met mine. "I haven't changed a thing," he
said. "It's perfect. The minute I walked in here I felt as if I'd
come home."

Unexpectedly, I felt a chill. "Well, congratulations," I said.
"And good luck. I hope you're happy in your work."

"I'm already happy," he said. "I'm part of the Falconer
Shreve family."

Zack and I were out in the garden admiring some persistent chrysanthemums when the phone rang. The jurors
had reached a verdict. We were at the courthouse in ten
minutes. Linda Fritz was entering the courtroom when we
came in. "Quick verdict," Zack said. "What do you think?"

Linda smoothed her barrister's robe. "I think this is always a Xanax moment."

Television would have us believe that when jurors find a defendant guilty, they don't look him in the eye. When the judges of the facts in Sean Barton's case filed into the jury box, each of them stared unsmiling at his face. The foreperson announced the jury's findings without emotion: Sean Terrence Barton had been found guilty of two counts of first degree murder and one of assault causing bodily harm. After the formalities had been observed, Sean was led away.

Francesca Pope had been at the trial every day, and she was waiting for us outside the courtroom.

"Is it over?" she asked Zack.

"It's over," he said. "Nothing to be afraid of now."

Francesca shifted her backpack. "There's always something to be afraid of," she said in her low, thrilling voice. Then she walked away.

Zack came close to me. "How are you doing?"

"I'm okay," I said.

"So what's next?" he said.

I glanced at my watch. "The UpSlideDown Halloween party started fifteen minutes ago. Dacia's juggling. This is her first time working with five balls. Want to see if she can keep them all in the air at once?"

"Sure," Zack said. "I'm a big fan of anybody who can defy gravity."

I called Mieka to tell her we were on our way, and she met us at the door. She was dressed as a genie in swirls of bright silk – a festive costume, but her face was sombre. "One of the parents told me the verdict," she said. I put my arms around my daughter and pulled her close. "May God forgive him," she said.

The room was packed, but Mieka led us to a spot near the space she'd cleared for Dacia's act. Then, hand in hand, Zack and I watched a young woman with shining hair keep five sky-blue balls arcing through the air, while all around us children dressed as kangaroos and tigers and princesses stared open-mouthed at the wonder of it all.

ACKNOWLEDGEMENTS

Thanks to five outstanding women: Dinah Forbes, Bella Pomer, Hildy Wren Bowen, Jan Seibel, and Lara Schmidt. Thanks also to Ted, who, for forty years, has been the man in my life.